The Station Core

A Dungeon Core Epic

Station Cores – Book 1

Jonathan Brooks

Cover Design: Yvonne Less, Art 4 Artists

Acknowledgements

I would like to thank everyone who contributed to this book, which as usual means that I subjected my wife to another round of reading my first draft, complete with errors.

A big shout-out to my alpha reader – **Grant Harrell**. Your feedback has helped to make this book even better!

Many thanks to my beta readers as well – your input helped to fine-tune the story and fix some errors I previously missed:

Richard Griffiths

Matthew Rogers

Kevin Crenshaw-Davis

Table of Contents

Acknowledgements 3

Foreword.. 7

Prologue – Hope 8

Part I – A Whole New World................................ 17

Chapter 1 – And away we go 18

Chapter 2 – Where the heck am I?...................... 25

Chapter 3 – History lesson................................... 35

Chapter 4 – Sciurophobia 45

Chapter 5 – Obtain quests, check!...................... 55

Chapter 6 – The process of shitting a brick 67

Chapter 7 – Bear-ly ready 77

Chapter 8 – Level up!.. 87

Chapter 9 – Roll on down to your hidey-hole 96

Chapter 10 – Trap king... 105

Chapter 11 – Leakage 114

Chapter 12 – *Pop* 124

Chapter 13 – Trap design 2.0............................... 135

Chapter 14 – Epic fail 144

Chapter 15 – Goal-tending 150

Chapter 16 – Puppies! 155

Chapter 17 – Aww...they're almost cute 166

Chapter 18 – The first engagement 175

Chapter 19 – Party up! 185

Chapter 20 – Quick lizards 195

Chapter 21 – You got this 204

Chapter 22 – Bonus! 214

Chapter 23 – Facility fabrication 220

Chapter 24 – Once again into the wild 228

Part II – Natives 236

Chapter 25 – The "Beast War" 237

Chapter 26 – Abilities 245

Chapter 27 – Stupid Picow 254

Part III – Revelations 264

Chapter 28 – Automation 265

Chapter 29 – Bioconversion Laboratory 274

Chapter 30 – Proctans 282

Chapter 31 – Discovery 294

Chapter 32 – Speak now, or forever hold your peace 303

Chapter 33 – Consequences 314

Chapter 34 – The Milton 323

Chapter 35 – Entrepreneurship 333

Chapter 36 – Emergency... 341

Chapter 37 – I'll kill them all!... 351

Chapter 38 – Never split the party 359

Chapter 39 – Underwhelming traps 367

Chapter 40 – See! I told you... 376

Chapter 41 – Mutations.. 383

Epilogue – Rebirth.. 392

Final Stats... 396

Author's Note 397

Books by Jonathan Brooks... 398

Foreword

Thanks for choosing to read The Station Core, book 1 in my Station Cores series!

I wanted this book to be accessible to everyone, not just hardcore stat lovers like me. While reading, you will notice that there are footnotes scattered throughout the story. These are for those who want to dig into all the stat sheets, tables, and other informational tidbits that **enhance** the story – but are not necessary to enjoy it. Even if you don't look at a single one, you are not going to miss out on the story as a whole. They are only there for people like me, who think "the more information, the better," is the way every book should be written. Knowing that everyone doesn't share that same mindset, I wanted to give options to those who either don't like stat sheets or wouldn't miss them if they are not there.

Regardless of how you want to go about reading this book, please enjoy!

Prologue – Hope

"Coming out of trans-dimensional jump now, Captain!" the Promory's pilot announced.

"About time…" the Captain muttered under his breath. He strapped into his chair, just as everyone on the bridge did the same. Although he was expecting some sort of deceleration, it felt more akin to his whole body being forced through a pinhole-sized tunnel that never seemed to end. When they finally arrived, his body sprang back to normal with an awkward and painful wrench.

Praxa looked around from his Captain's chair at his crew comprised of various members of The Collective. On their faces were differing degrees of relief as they realized they made it through the jump with their fleet whole. The trans-dimensional drives were a new technology that was still in the experimental stages and hadn't been fully tested yet. It was developed over the last couple of years as both an escape plan and a way to find allies. He, and those who had come with him, were some of the first to fully utilize the drives – especially at such a long distance. They were able to cut down travel time from years to just minutes by forcing their ships to travel through a parallel dimension. He wasn't sure exactly how it worked; he was just glad that it did.

"Reports from the rest of the fleet report no casualties and no damage to their ships. They are converging on our location now.

Shall I have them engage their stealth shields, sir?" Brolena – one of the Bovene race – was Praxa's Communication Officer, and he looked over at her as she reported to him. Her soft brown eyes looked both excited and apprehensive, which was understandable given their current mission. He gave the order and watched her punch in the command with her daintily-trimmed hooves into the specially-made console. Her hairy ears flicked around the short horns on the top of her head as she listened to communications from the other ships. She raised her hoof up as an affirmative in his direction and he watched as his own console displayed the stealthed fleet falling into formation around his flagship.

"Mid-range sensors detect no hostile defensive stations throughout the system and nothing but some primitive communicative technology in orbit around the planet. The scout ship seemed to be correct – there should be no way for them to detect us," Cromene, his Defense Officer, informed him. Praxa could see that from his readout as well, but he looked at the Porlix in confirmation. Cromene's jowls quivered in either nervousness or anticipation – he could never tell with the pink-skinned, snub-nosed, portly members of his race.

"Very good everybody. Thadlo, you're in charge until I'm back. I'm going to the conference room for a meeting with the ships' captains – I shouldn't be gone long." As he left the room, he watched his second-in-command sit in his vacated chair, his suit circulating water over his body and face. His blue-skinned Aquanix Command Officer was as efficient as his predecessor – his father.

9

Praxa and Thadlo's father, Thendo, had been running starships through the various Collective colonies for years before the attacks. As ship production ramped up in response, the need for new captains meant that Thendo received his own brand-new ship to run. He knew it was in good hands – which is why he asked Thendo to come along on this mission.

As he entered the transportation chamber, he felt a slight resistance as he was transported four decks to the living quarters. Just off the chamber exit, a conference room was located next to the individual crew cabins which he quickly entered and sat in the specially built conference chair. As soon as he sat down, he found himself in a large plain room, surrounded by nine other captains. *I guess I was the last to arrive.*

"Sorry for the wait everybody. Now that we are here, let's go over the plan—" he was interrupted, typically, by Gentif, the captain of the Moufged. His long black-haired face was locked in his typical timid appearance, followed by his unconscious tapping of his hooves together as he stood there. Although they were both Equints, Praxa thought they couldn't be more different. Gentif's demeanor was more like those of the Mouslan, the diminutive and timid people that lived peaceful lives in the grasslands of their homeworld.

"I'm still not sure if we are doing the right thing. My crew and I are expressing major moral objections to this course of action. How is what we are doing any worse than what is being done to us?" Gentif interjected.

Praxa wanted to ignore him, but he had been warring against his own conscience ever since he had learned of their objective. Although he knew they had very little choice, he didn't like it any better than any other member of The Collective. He could see the same concern and objections on the faces of the other captains as well. However, they had come all this way – and braving an experimental drive to get here faster – to go back empty-handed due to moral objections. He needed to make them all see that this was their last chance and that they were different from the warlike and destructive Heliothropes.

"Believe me, I share your concerns. I've been suffering over the morality of this since I first learned of it – but I'm still here. Do I want to do this? No – but I'm still here. We have a duty to save our peoples and this is the last option open to us. This is a last-ditch effort to fight back against the Heliothrope invaders and stop their subjugation and the sacrifices they are using us for. Does our mission make us like them? Quite possibly – but I'm still here.

"Do you know why? Because we all have families back home who are counting on us to push past the ethical quandary we are faced with. I don't want to see my wife, my mother, or my children subjected to the slavery and torture the Heliothropes have brought with them. We can't fight them ourselves because our very nature won't let us. Does the slavery of a few of these 'humans' in our own defense make us bad? Maybe – but I'm still here. And you're still here too – you all know what is at stake. We can't turn back now, we must push on and do that which is anathema to us. It will be hard, but I know I, you, *we* can do it."

After his speech, the room was quiet as the various captains silently considered his words. As he knew he would, Thendo was the first to speak up. "I don't like it, but for my family and my people – I will do this. I'm with you, Captain Praxa."

One after another, the captains in the room agreed to go ahead with the mission until only Gentif was left. Praxa held his breath as he waited to see what he would say. If even one captain was against this, it was possible the others would change their minds. They were already on the fence and a little push might send them over to the other side. With a great sigh, which sounded more like a snort, Gentif agreed with the plan, "I still think there has to be another way – but we are out of time to find it. As much as it pains me to say it, let's do it."

Inwardly, Praxa was conflicted – he was pleased that he was able to convince them all but also sad that he convinced them all. Now they had no choice but to get on with their mission. "Now that we're all in agreement, let's go over what we will be doing. Our scout identified one hundred potential candidates from their greatest military minds and soldiers. Unfortunately, two of those are currently no longer available. We need to discuss other options for who we can get to fill those empty cores.

"As you know, each one we choose must be willing and able to defend themselves and in doing so, defend us from the Heliothropes. Once they are...acquired...their consciousness will be transferred to the Station Cores we have in our cargo bays. Once the Station Cores are installed in their final destinations, their personal memories will be wiped and replaced with unswerving loyalty to The Collective. They will have the ability to construct and develop defensive systems that can put answer to the invasion we have been suffering from.

"These...Earthlings – or so they call themselves – are just the answer we've been looking for. Their ability to experience love, compassion, and kindness is balanced by their ability to wage terrible war on anyone threatening their way of life. They will do what we **cannot** and **will not** do, even to save our own lives – kill the enemy. Our passive defensive systems have proven worthy to defend against other hostile species in the past – but this new enemy doesn't care one whit for our show of force. They have somehow bypassed our defensive planetary shields and taken the fight to the ground, where we have almost no defensive capability.

"But you all know that – it's why we are here. Does anyone have any suggestions for additional candidates? You've seen the scouting reports, so...suggestions?" Praxa looked around the room, hoping that someone had done their homework.

There followed an unproductive discussion, with very few reasonable candidates. One even suggested a schoolteacher, to teach the Heliothropes a lesson on why they should reconsider their current course of action. Praxa realized they were intentionally delaying the inevitable, suggesting these random people in order to stall. He looked at his old CO, who had been silent up to now. As soon as the others realized his focus had changed, they quieted down and waited for Thendo to speak. Although they respected Praxa's authority, Thendo was known more for his intelligent ideas and suggestions.

"I've been thinking about this since I first heard about this mission. It might be a little unconventional and out-of-the-box, but I think I have a solution. Based on the scouting reports, there are many people on this world that play simulations of warfare but are not actually part of the military. These warfare simulations might make them better suited to control a defensive position, since they are used to utilizing defensive and offensive strategies – all without physically doing it themselves. They might be the perfect addition to our Station Core program, but I'll leave it to you to decide," he told the assembled captains.

Now that they had a viable option, the group deferred to Thendo's judgement and approved of the plan. Inwardly relieved, Praxa moved the meeting along and assigned the various targets they had agreed upon to each captain. After that, it was a simple strategy: arrive at the planet in stealth, transport the targets to their holding cells using their molecular teleportation devices, and start the conversion to Station Cores on their way back to home space.

When he got back to the bridge, he took over from Thadlo and moved them into position. This was probably the easiest part of the whole operation, since the primitive people of this world had no way to stop or interfere with their mission. After a very short time – especially in relation to how long they had argued in the conference room – the transportation of their Station Core subjects was complete. Arriving back in formation, they headed out of the system before activating their trans-dimensional drives.

Feeling the blissful expanding of his awareness that signaled the transition to another dimension, Praxa sat back in his chair and thought about the successful mission and what it would mean to all their peoples. He took the lead in this operation because he believed on the potential of these Station Cores; he realized that they were their best hope for salvation. The "Earthlings" they had obtained were already in the process of being converted to their new immortal shells and would be ready to insert into their specific destinations once they arrived. Which, once he looked at the ships' clock, was soon due to these fancy new drives.

"Coming out of trans-dimensional jump, now! We're almost home, Captain!" the pilot announced, with excitement in his voice. Bracing himself for the squeezing pain he had previously experienced, he found that it was actually *worse* when he was expecting it. When it was over, he slumped down in the chair and watched as the rest of the crew did the same.

Suddenly, Cromene sat up and looked at his console. "Incoming Heliothrope ships! Bringing it up on screen!"

Praxa could see the swarm of ships converging on their small fleet on his own console. "Brolena, tell the other ships to jump, NOW! We'll distract them until they're safe." She quickly relayed the orders and Praxa told the pilot, "Defensive maneuvers, let's give them some ti—" He never finished his orders as his ship was impacted by multiple Heliothrope missiles with explosive warheads. Their shields were shredded instantly, and the ship exploded, flinging debris and everything else it contained in all directions in a magnificent display of carnage.

Part I – A Whole New World

Chapter 1 – And away we go

"I don't care where it comes from, Milton, but you need to come up with your portion of the rent in three days. If you had an actual job, I'd feel better about letting you stay here. It's getting really old wondering if you're going to be able to afford rent each month."

Sometimes, Milton thought Terrence was a bit of a douchebag. Even though he knows where Milton gets his money, he always acts this way toward the end of the month. "I'll have the money, don't worry – have I ever let you down?"

"No, you haven't. But that doesn't mean that there couldn't be a first time. I know you're my best bud, but we gotta be real here. How about you work on getting the money earlier in the month, that way I won't be bugging you every day?"

"I'll work on that – now let me through and I'll start working on that rent right now." Terrence took his arm down from where it was blocking the entrance to the apartment and let him past. He saw that Samantha, Terrence's new girlfriend, was sitting on the couch ignoring their whole conversation while she played with her phone. As she brought it up in front of her face and posed, he realized that she was taking selfies and probably posting them online somewhere. Never having taken a selfie, Milton really didn't see what the big deal was – he didn't even own a cell phone. Couldn't afford it – besides, who would call him anyway? He talked to his brother once a week on the apartments' landline and all his friends were either online or living with him.

Entering his room, Milton navigated his way through all the dirty laundry on the floor to his computer. Sure, he was a bit of a slob, but at least he didn't have empty pizza boxes and soda cans everywhere like Terrence usually did in his room. Unlike him, Milton was relatively neat – probably because he didn't eat a lot. Usually, he was too engrossed in playing Crowned Lieges of Destiny to pay attention to something trivial like "eating". This, in turn, made him really skinny – at least compared to a lot of his fellow gamers. Samantha once said he looked "unhealthy", whatever that means.

The one thing he took pride in was keeping his desk neat and organized where his state-of-the-art gaming computer sat. On an all-white desk, he had three 32-inch monitors set up in a concave shape to display as complete a picture of the game as possible. He eventually wanted six monitors set up to have a full 360-degree view of the battlefield – information was power, and the more information he had on the changing states of battle would mean he would have an advantage over those that didn't. Unfortunately, the expense of those monitors was a little out his price-range right now – especially since he still needed to pay rent.

Booting up the computer, Milton put his headset on and waited while CLoD loaded. Soon enough, the screen displayed one of the most thrilling MMORPGs that had come out in the past couple of years. It had everything you would normally see in other

MMORPGs: quests, leveling up, character customization, thousands of skills and abilities, raid bosses, and new endgame content released with frequency. What made it stand out from the others was the guild warfare; it wasn't just about two guilds hacking at each other on a field somewhere. No, it was much more than that – each guild could employ legions of Non-Player Characters to attack and defend locations in real-time battles. And players could participate in the battles as well.

No longer confined to tank-DPS-healer group combinations, the strategy behind these large-scale battles was where you got the chance to show your skills off to the world. There was no set "best formation", you needed to be able to change strategies on-the-fly, taking into consideration your own assets and those of your enemy. Those strongest at this had to have intense concentration, lightning-quick reflexes, and the knowledge of troop and player strength and weaknesses. Only the best-of-the-best were put in position to lead their guild in to battle – and Milton was the best.

That was no idle boast either – the leaderboards spoke for themselves. At 22 years old, he was the Strategy Coordinator for *Ravens*, the top guild in CLoD. They were a guild of elite players that had been playing together for years and will probably continue to do so in the future. If not CLoD, then something else – they all had a love of being the best-of-the-best, no matter what was played. Some of the others tended to let the fame of being on top go to their heads, but Milton liked to think he played it off better than that. He took pride in what he accomplished and enjoyed the challenge of battling against other top players. Whenever he lost – which happened rarely, but it did happen – he saw it as a learning opportunity to fix any mistakes that were made. And he didn't make them again.

Since he spent so much time playing the game, he started using it to pay the bills. Even though they were the top guild – it didn't pay anything. It was more of a pride and boasting thing, but it also helped with his side business by opening doors to potential clients. He *didn't* farm gold – he saw that only being for deadbeat hacks – but he *did* farm hard-to-obtain items for paying clients. His place on the leaderboards lent credence to his trustworthiness and his ability to provide anything for a price.

At first, when his parents stopped sending him money after their divorce, it had been hard to make ends meet. He had taken a job at a local retail store for a couple of weeks, but ultimately got fired because he couldn't keep his focus on what he was supposed to be doing. His mind kept wandering back to a new strategy against a maneuver that beat him the other day – or something similar. After that, job after job payed the bills for a while until he started accumulating a client list in CLoD. Now all he needed to do was take a few well-paying jobs a month and he was set – then he could devote the rest of his time to directing guild battles.

And now it was time to pay rent. Scanning through his in-game messages, Milton found one from an old client that was always prompt with payment – which is what he needed right now. He opened the link to the item he needed to acquire and—what? The

Horn of Dreevus? That would take some time, but he thought he could do it in about two days if he started now. The client was offering more than was needed for rent, so now he'd have some spending money at least. Compiling a quick message, he was about to hit the send button when he felt a strange sensation.

It was almost as if he was becoming lighter while the world around him paused. Something started quickly leaching the color from the computer screen – he thought his computer might be crashing. When he tried to turn his head to see if the other screens showed the same problem, he found that he couldn't move. The colors continued to fade, and he felt less and less whole, as if pieces of him were being taken away without his approval. Eventually, he couldn't even feel the chair he was sitting on and his whole view was white. Unending, all-encompassing, and bland white. He couldn't move, couldn't speak, and sure as heck couldn't feel anything. It felt like he was trapped in that place forever, but in reality, it was more like a couple of seconds.

All at once, the world came crashing back. Milton stumbled and fell as his uncoordinated body collapsed on a cold, unyielding surface. Looking around, he found himself in a small, well-lit room of dull-grey metal, bare walls, and no windows. And he wasn't alone.

He got a little nervous as everyone in the room looked like they came straight from a battlefield. As soon as Milton got to his feet, he had nine weapons aimed straight at his face. He froze and put his hands up in surrender. He was too scared to say anything –

not to mention too confused to think straight – but fortunately, he didn't have to.

"Who are you and why have you brought us here?" The most dangerous man he'd ever seen in his life asked, his rough voice ringing with authority. Not only was he huge – he looked like he could pick Milton up and break him in half with one hand – he was also the only one holding a knife instead of a gun. That normally would make him seem less dangerous, but Milton could sense instinctively that he could still kill him quicker than any of the others with guns. Looking down, he realized that he may have pissed himself a little, but held it together long enough to answer, "I don't know, sir. Please don't kill me, sir!"

Milton had found over the years that it didn't hurt to be respectful, even in tense situations. His father always taught him to treat others as he would want to be treated. It didn't matter if you were talking to a grocery store clerk or a telemarketer – a little respect went a long way. In the first case, they were less likely to 'accidently' overcharge you and in the other case they were more willing to take you off their call list if you politely asked to be removed. This lesson served him well as they relaxed, putting away their weapons after realizing that he didn't pose a threat. Well, all but the scary, dangerous-looking man – *he* still pointed his knife at Milton.

"Why are you different then? We're all from different branches of the military – and not even all from the U.S. You're the odd-man out here – I don't know if you're in charge, but it's too suspicious to ignore. What do you know about all this?" he asked as he waved his knife around, encompassing the entire room. All while looking at Milton with an intense stare – *now I know what a deer looking into headlights feels like*. If he had the answer to his question, he didn't think he would have been able to hold back revealing it.

"Again, sir, I don't know anything. I was playing a game and suddenly I was in this white place and then I found myself here. That's all I know...uh, sir."

He grabbed Milton and slammed him back against the metal wall, his immense strength holding him up in the air by his grimy, retro gaming T-shirt by one hand. His other hand still held his knife, which was currently held against Milton's throat. "Don't give me that shit – TELL ME WHAT'S GOING ON!"

He was saved having to answer when they all heard a loud noise, similar to a semi-trailer releasing its airbrakes. The musclebound military man let Milton go and he slid to the floor, where he stayed, still too frightened to move. "What is—," the man tried to say but collapsed suddenly in a boneless heap. Milton looked around and saw everyone else had collapsed on the floor as well. A moment later he blacked-out, completely oblivious of what was in store for him and all the others.

Chapter 2 – Where the heck am I?

Something jarred Milton awake. He wasn't sure what it was, but as he returned to consciousness he panicked and thought about the Horn of Dreevus. *Did I fall asleep at my computer? That's never happened before – I must have been really tired. I need to start moving and get the Horn, so I can pay rent.* Without opening his eyes, he tried to remove the headset he was wearing only to find out he couldn't move. *What's going on?* As he thought that, he started remembering the weird transportation to someplace else; a strange room with cold metal walls and military personnel, including one scary, knife-wielding maniac.

Did he kill me? Is this what death feels like? His musings were interrupted when he heard something that sounded like a strange birdcall. As he concentrated, he realized that he could hear the sounds of nature all around him: wind rustling through some leaves, high-pitched chittering that most likely came from some small critter, and the faint burbling of a stream nearby. It reminded him a little of the one camping trip that his mom and dad took him on when he was young; he remembered being so proud of himself when he caught a fish – even if his mom made him throw it back.

Even though he couldn't move, he still tried to get his body to do something. It was like everything below his neck was gone – he couldn't feel anything. *I better not be some head in a jar somewhere.*

More angry than scared, he strained to open his eyes, but nothing happened. *I wish I could see something,* he thought – and was overwhelmed as multiple images bombarded his senses. It was as if he suddenly had fifty pairs of eyes open simultaneously, showing him a full 360-degree view of his surroundings. He thought about closing his eyes, but nothing happened – once it was turned on it didn't look like it could be turned off.

He suffered through the information overload, trying to make sense of what he was seeing while trying to maintain his sanity. After a while, he gradually became accustomed to the visual bombardment, allowing him to concentrate on what he was looking at. He was in the middle of a forest clearing, with about fifty feet between him and the closest trees. Speaking of trees, these were some of the largest he had ever seen – and probably the strangest. Instead of the normal green – or various shades of yellow, orange, or red in the fall – the leaves on the trees were bluish in tone, ranging from light blue to an almost dark purple color. The size of the leaves was also strange; unlike most trees he'd seen – which had relatively uniform shapes and sizes – these had both very large fronds and small sequin-sized mini-leaves on the same tree. The contrast was both weird and pleasing to the eye, especially since the colors graduated from darker to lighter toward the top.

He also saw multiple birds flitting from branch to branch, which, fortunately for his already stressed mind, were very similar to birds he had seen before. The only difference was in the coloring, with pinks and oranges being more prevalent than black and brown.

26

On the edge of the clearing, he found the stream that he had heard previously, winding its way through the trees and disappearing from his field of vision after falling down a small drop-off.

I don't think I'm on Earth anymore – at least nowhere I've ever heard of before. If not Earth, where the heck am I? Since he was successful at opening his "eyes", he tried to move some part of his body but found that he was still stuck in place, without even being able to feel anything. He knew he was elevated somehow, since his field of vision was off the ground a bit, so he tried to adjust his "eyes" down to look at his body to figure out what was wrong with it.

The visual input he was experiencing was still awkward, but he managed to look down – and stopped in shock. He wasn't sure how his "eyes" did it, but they were able to expand outwards so that he could look at most of his current "body". Smooth grey metal filled his vision with a slight curvature to it, almost as if he was looking at a giant metal chicken egg. Thin lines ran along the metal, emitting a subtle glow even in the bright sunlight. The look reminded him a little of a computer circuit board, but unlike any that he had ever seen before. From what he could tell, his body was trapped inside this 20-foot-tall eggshell, with tight-fitting doors cut into various places and about fifty mysterious indentations lined up on a ring along the top side of the egg. As he looked closer at these indentations, he caught something at the edge of his vision.

When he turned his vision to look at it, he saw something that made him freeze. Tiny floating orbs were circling his "prison",

27

spaced equidistant to each other and lined up in front of each hole. He wasn't sure at first what he was looking at, but something in his head seemed to click as he understood. Each of the floating orbs were his "eyes" – that was why he had so much visual information fed to him. He experimented with them by attempting to move only one at a time and was successful; he was able to directly control where it went and what it was looking at. The focus needed wasn't more than he could handle, since the other orbs didn't need his attention and stayed where they were. However, when he tried to move more than one, his focus was just barely up to the task of splitting his attention between the two. He attempted to move three or more, but he couldn't concentrate on each separate one long enough to move them, and they ended up stopping and starting in jerky movements. Needless to say, he went back to controlling just one at a time.

Ignoring any other pressing issues – such as where he was and what happened to him – he played with one of his orbs, seeing how fast he could move it through the air and how far away he could roam. He thought it was similar to a drone he had flown when he was younger, before he crashed it and couldn't afford to fix or replace it. This was much easier, however, as he was directly controlling the orb with his mind and found that it was able to make pin-point corrections in the air so that he could race through the trees with ease. After what he thought was close to about 500 feet away, the orbs' movements started to become sluggish and responded slowly to his mental commands. He immediately retreated back toward his egg, worried that he would lose one of his new toys if he continued any further.

On the way back, he realized that not only could he see with his orbs, he could hear with them as well. He passed closely by a bird high up in one of the strange blue trees, and the birdsong was a lot louder and clearer than he had heard from the clearing. He paused and listened to it, enjoying the faintly melodic song that came from such a small animal. When it was done, he watched it fly away and headed back "home".

After breaking through the trees to the clearing, he paused in shock as a massive yellow bird, the size of a golden retriever, swooped down and snatched up one of his stationary orbs in its beak before he thought to react. Turning his attention to the orb snatched up, he found his vision looking toward the inside of its throat. He tried to get it to move, but it was firmly caught in its beak with no wiggle-room. From the view of his other orbs, he could see that he was successful on moving its head back and forth, but the stubborn bird wasn't giving up its prize.

As the bird flew further away and higher into the sky, the control and responsiveness of the orb started to diminish. Realizing that he only had a couple of seconds before he lost all control, Milton instructed his orb to go in a different direction – right down its gullet. After a moment of despair, watching as it was still held tight in its beak without moving, he was relieved as he managed to wiggle it just enough to slide down its throat. He didn't stop there – since there was nothing holding the orb in place anymore – and shot as fast as he could down into its stomach and through its lower body. It met plenty of resistance, but the power in the little thing was enough to break through the birds' insides and erupt through its backside in a spray of blood and viscera.

The monstrous yellow bird flew on for a little longer before it dropped like a stone, having sustained massive internal injuries. It tried to weakly flap on the way down, struggling to stay airborne but it didn't have the strength. He lost sight of it just as his own orb crossed some range threshold and he lost his connection to it. It was like he had something chopped off his body, as the vision and sounds it was sending him was abruptly cut off. He was just glad that it didn't hurt.

From his other orbs, he could see both his lost orb and the massive yellow bird falling to the ground through the trees. As he lost sight of them, he turned his attention back to his remaining orbs and immediately sent them back into the deep indentations surrounding his egg. He didn't want to lose any more orbs to attacking birds or something worse – they seemed to be his only means to see and hear outside of his shell.

When they finished retreating into their safe-holes, he was surprised when a thought appeared right in his mind. It felt akin to someone depositing something in his mind and also as if he had always known it. The closest analogy he could think of was the movie Inception, where Leo went into someone's dream and deposited a thought – it was just like that. The subject of the thought was strange, and yet familiar – but he couldn't quite place it at first.

Congratulations! You have defeated *Big Yellow Bird*! You gain 10 experience!

Continue to defeat your enemies to level up!

Current Combat Level: 1

Experience: 10/250

You have learned the skill: *Sensor Control (Level 1)*

Allows you to directly control multiple Sensor Orbs. Current maximum: 3

You have learned the skill: *Kamikaze (Level 1)*

Inflict more damage during a suicidal attack with one of your units. Whenever this skill is used, the current unit will cease to function after the attack, regardless of damage taken.

Damage bonus at current skill level: 200%

What is this?! This looks like a videogame...wait a minute. This seems a lot like Crowned Lieges of Destiny! Maybe I'm asleep and this is all a dream. He was beginning to wonder how he could wake up from this crazy nightmare when he was surprised by more information.

You have unlocked an achievement:

The Harder They Fall...

Defeat an enemy using a non-combat unit

Bonus – Sensor Enhancement (Level 1):

Your Sensor Orbs now see further, move faster, and are more durable.

Now thoroughly confused, he paused, waiting for more information to appear in his mind. When nothing more was forthcoming, he frantically thought, *Wake up!!! Wake up!!! This has got to be a dream!!!* He continued like this for a couple of minutes until he got frustrated and screamed, causing the sound to reverberate through the clearing as his exclamation was routed through the orbs. Not noticing the various birds taking flight from the sudden loud noise, he shouted, "What is this?! Where the heck am I?!"

As soon as he said this, he somehow sensed a small door opening on the outside of his shell. Before his eyes, a grey stream of what looked like smoke flowed out of the opening and coalesced into a vague humanoid figure about ten feet in front of him. Shortly after the smoke gathered together, he could see that the figure had gained definition – long legs, a generous bustline, and straight, long black hair hung down to its well-rounded ass. Piercing green eyes peered out of a caramel-colored, symmetrical face and stared right into his closest sensor orb. A skin-tight, stretchable, deep-purple outfit completed the ensemble, allowing Milton to intimately see every single curve on the delectably-formed body.

32

If Milton had to envision the perfect woman, this would be it. The only thing that he would change would be the size – this mystery beauty was only about a foot and a half tall. On the whole though, he didn't care about that so much because it was a relief to finally see another person. *I'm beginning to like this dream, but I still want to figure out how to wake up. Maybe I can get some information from her.* Although he didn't really have much experience talking to women and was a little nervous, he needed some help and forgot about his insecurities for the moment. "Who are you? Where am I and how do I wake up?"

Her voice when she spoke was deep, husky, and sexy; he could imagine tingles would be running up and down his spine and other places would be stirring – unfortunately, he still couldn't feel anything. She had a very comforting and pleasing tone, so much so that he almost lost track of **what** she was saying, instead wanting to just listen to her speak. It was only the fact that it sounded like some sort of recording that he was able to keep his attention on her words.

"Welcome to Outpost 59-WX in the Grunoit System, your new home for the foreseeable future. You may be confused about who you are and what you are doing here. This is a completely normal side-effect of the Coring process, where your personal memories are erased to provide less distraction and ensures an efficient initialization process. All you need to know is that you volunteered for this experimental, yet rewarding, process and your people are thankful for your sacrifice. Your dutiful work will ensure

33

the safety of the people of The Collective against the forces arrayed against it. Congratulations on taking your first step as a Station Core and activating me.

"I am your Artificial Logistic Autonomous Nano-formed Neurological Assistant, or if you prefer – ALANNA. I am here to guide you through the Station Core initialization process, help you become accustomed to your new surroundings, and get you started on creating defenses against hostile invaders. Since you do not have any personal memories, we will have to start with—"

Milton cut off her seemingly pre-programmed speech, by telling her, "Uh, wait. I still have all my memories. And I have no idea what you are talking about – I never volunteered for this!" He was still confused but now he was getting angry. *I don't care how pretty she is, I want answers!*

She paused in her speech and froze, before breaking apart into a billion little pieces that floated together in a grey mist where she was previously standing. A moment later, the mist formed back into ALANNA, and she looked none too pleased at her circumstances.

Chapter 3 – History lesson

"This isn't where we are supposed to be – this isn't Outpost 59-WX. What happened? What did you do? We need to hurry and get to our original destination – there isn't any time to waste. Heliothrope ships will most likely be arriving soon and we need to be ready," she paced around while she was talking, waving her hands around in frantic gestures.

"Whoa, now – don't blame me for this. I have no idea what you are talking about or what happened. The last thing I remember was playing Crowned Lieges of Destiny before somehow being transported to a small room with some military men and then I woke up here. And what happened to me? – unless this is all a dream like I suspect it is."

ALANNA stopped her pacing and looked at Milton, or at least one of Milton's sensor orbs. "Ok…let me process this. If you have all your memories, then that means that we never made it to the Outpost. Hold on, let me check the Cores' logs – it should have been connected to the Promory's systems while you were in stasis." She paused for a moment and had a far-off look on her face as she searched for something. He still had little idea what was going on, but he was beginning to suspect that this wasn't a dream. Before he could consider that horrific idea more, ALANNA came back to herself with a concerned expression on her face. She sat on the ground and slumped over as if in defeat, letting out a giant sigh for such a small body.

"What? What happened? ...Are you okay?" He added that last one, thinking that if he showed some sort of sympathy he might get some answers. Frankly, he wasn't really enthused about this whole situation and had trouble expressing any sympathy for his "captors". But if it would get him answers, he could fake it – at least for a little while.

"Gone. All gone." She didn't continue right away, but Milton waited patiently – he figured she wasn't done yet. "The Promory was destroyed just as they emerged from their jump. How you survived, I don't exactly know – but you are made of near-indestructible material, so you probably didn't suffer much damage from the explosion. From the logs, I don't even know if the other ships escaped in time. You may be the last intact Station Core remaining for all I know. Either way, it is too late to help now," she explained in a monotone voice.

"Well, that's great!" She looked up at his comment with fury in her eyes. "Wait, I don't mean it like that – I'm sorry about your 'Collection', or whatever it is. But if you don't need me anymore, then you can send me back home and I can go back to making money on CLoD to pay for rent."

The fury remained in her eyes as she scathingly replied, "It's 'The Collective', and I don't appreciate you dismissing all that those people did to save themselves. You were their last hope of survival and now all is most likely lost. They created me as not only a liaison but also as a guide to the new Station Cores. I have the same feelings, needs, and wants as those of The Collective – essentially, I *am* them. The only thing I don't have is their inherent abhorrence to violence. Now that they are most likely gone, what do I do now? What purpose do I serve?" She looked up at him and the fury faded from her eyes, replaced by confusion and helplessness.

He began to feel a little sympathy towards her – how could he not? It had to be hard hearing that those who created you might not still be alive and that you were too late to save them. It would be like learning that his parents were in trouble and he had to race to save them – only to get sidetracked and miss the opportunity. She apparently didn't know if they were gone or not, but it probably didn't matter at this point.

However, despite having sympathy toward her, he still wanted to get home. If he could help out, he would consider it since he was here already, but it didn't seem like there was anything he could do. After letting her wallow in her own thoughts for a while, he hesitantly asked her again, "So...what about sending me back then? I'm sorry if I sound insensitive, but I really was taken against my will and it doesn't seem like I'm needed anymore."

ALANNA continued staring at the ground, slumped over as she answered him, "Even if I *could* send you back, it wouldn't help. There is no 'you' any more – only the Station Core. Your physical body was salvaged, and your consciousness was transferred to the Core you now inhabit. You only exist inside that metal shell and there is no going back – even if we had access to your body. Which

37

we don't, since it was destroyed along with the Promory. But hey, at least you're essentially immortal now. Unless someone or something can crack open your core, you'll pretty much go on functioning forever. Besides...I don't think you'd want to go back, now."

Shocked into silence, he tried absorbing what he had heard. *I'm dead? My body was destroyed? What the hell is a Station Core?* These questions and more rattled around in his head, while he wallowed in confusion. Normally, he was a practical person, taking life how it was and didn't complain about things that he couldn't change. But this? This was something hard to come to terms with – he was just playing CLoD the other day, wasn't he? He unfocused his sensors as he drew inward, thinking about his "previous" life and what he could have done differently if he had the chance. *Was there anything I could have done to prevent this?* He didn't know – he wasn't even sure why he was chosen. *I'll have to ask...wait a minute. What was the last thing she said?* Thinking about it, he realized that he could pull up that information as if he had a perfect memory – it appeared at the forefront of his thoughts.

"What did you mean by not wanting to go back, **now**?" he asked.

Broken out of her own distracted thoughts, she raised her head and looked at one of his sensors, "I just meant that the Earth you knew wouldn't be the same as it is now. You wouldn't be going back to your family and friends – I'm pretty sure they thought you were dead after the first couple of years after your disappearance."

38

"Wait – first couple of years? That doesn't make any sense, it feels like it was just yesterday that I was in my room playing games. How long has it been, really?"

She just stared at him, conflicting emotions playing over her face as if she was deciding whether to tell him. Finally, after about a minute, she said, "According to the Station Core logs, after the attack and destruction of the Promory, we traveled through space at high speed for a number of years. It was only after crash landing on this planet that you 'woke up'. What seems like a short amount of time was actually quite a bit more."

"And how much was that?" he asked hesitantly, not sure if he really wanted the answer.

She froze a moment before replying, "4,512 years, 6 months, and 3 days – or at least how you Earthlings measure time."

Silence descended among the clearing, broken only by the sounds of nature as they both tried to absorb the information. *4,512 years! No wonder she looks so sad – any help we may have been is probably more than 4,000 years too late.* Milton didn't know what to think. On the one hand, he was sad that he wouldn't be able to say goodbye to his friends both in real life and in CLoD. On the other hand, he wasn't really close with any of his family, except for his brother who he called every week to stay in touch. He would miss Calvin, but even then, he hadn't seen him in person in years – just talked to him over the phone. His little brother must have been frantic when he didn't call on their scheduled day – he hoped his mom took care of him until he was ready to go out on his own. Moot point now, of course, since that was more than four thousand years ago.

He wasn't one to drown himself in self-pity – he never had and probably never would. Even when things didn't go his way, either in his personal life or in a game, he didn't dwell on "what ifs" and "shoulda-coulda-woulda". When his parents split up, he was old enough to know that it wasn't his fault that they separated, and they only stayed together to raise him and his brother. There wasn't anything he could have done to stop it, so he went with it. His brother took it harder, so he had to be a stabilizing influence in his life, to help him transition to a place where he would be ok.

All of this meant that, in this situation, he was able to progress through any sense of self-pity, depression, and other negative thoughts very quickly. Since there wasn't anything he could have done to change it, he went with it. He started to embrace his current circumstances, put his past behind him (gone – but not forgotten), and moved on to something that he *could* do something about – his new "life". He needed to learn about what he was now, how he survived this long, and what he needed to do to survive in the future. His own sense of self-preservation kicked in and he yearned for information regarding his changes.

"ALANNA." It took a while, but she eventually looked up at him. "I'm sorry we couldn't be there to help these Collective people, but there isn't anything we can do about it now. What we *can* do is survive here on this planet. And I can't do it without your help – you're here to guide me and I need some guidance."

She just stared at him like he was talking crazy. He went on, trying to distract her from her preoccupation with her failed mission, "First of all, what am I? You keep calling me a Station Core, but what exactly is that? I get that I look like a giant metal chicken egg, have sensors that allow me to see and hear, and have you as my guide, but *what am I*? None of this makes any sense."

Almost as if it was against her will, she answered him in an automatic monotone voice, "The Station Core was to be the heart of our new defenses against the invasion of the Heliothropes. The Collective are a technologically advanced, but peaceful and passive people, who have great difficulty performing any action that would deliberately take a life – even in self-defense. After countless centuries of peace from even their war-like neighbors in the galaxy by showcasing their technological superiority, they were finally approached by a foe that wasn't deterred by their substantial, yet in the end futile, non-violent defenses. They sent so many ships that one-by-one, the colonies and worlds of The Collective were invaded and subjugated. Mass killings and sacrifices to their 'Sun God' decimated the population, with those remaining alive used as slaves against their will.

"To create a defense, the lead engineers designed the Station Core – an all-in-one defensive measure contained in a relatively small package. The Station Core could break down raw materials, convert it to defensive emplacements, and even create an army of neurologically-controlled defenders. They were to be placed in space stations, outposts, colonies, and even cities on the home

41

worlds of The Collective. At first, 101 Station Cores were created, designed as a test to see how effective they performed. The act of taking a life – even in defense – was anathema to all members of The Collective; even if they were to have their memory wiped, their base instincts wouldn't allow any type of violence.

"To overcome this, an AI was inserted into the first Station Core – to disastrous results. The short story was that it went wild, destroying half of the testing facility before the fail-safe was activated. Apparently, in creating an AI capable of defending itself – which included killing its enemies – the designers had to tone down its morality and ramp up its ruthlessness. As a result, it took its job seriously; some would say too seriously. It started breaking down the surrounding area for material and killed multiple engineers so that it could start creating defenses and its own army. It had no care about where the materials came from, so long as it could do its job.

"This is where the Humans of Earth come in. After deciding that an AI would never be acceptable as the occupant of their Station Cores, Collective leaders searched the known galaxy looking for beings capable of fighting the Heliothropes – yet having a great capacity for love. In all the known worlds, the only sentient lifeforms that matched these criteria were the Humans of Earth and the Tregdali. Unfortunately, the Tregdali were almost as technologically advanced as the Collective, if not as numerous. They wouldn't voluntarily subject any of their people to the Station Core initialization process, and it was near-impossible to acquire any without causing another war. That left the Earthlings.

"The Humans were almost primitive in comparison, at least as far as technology. They had no defenses against space-born threats and wouldn't even be able to detect our ships. The only problem was that they were so far away – traveling to and from Earth to Collective space would take years, which the leaders of the Collective knew they didn't have. Precious months were spent developing a trans-dimensional drive which would allow them to travel that distance in minutes, instead of years. When they were ready, Captain Praxa of the Promory, along with nine other ships, traveled to Earth and completed that part of their mission by acquiring 100 subjects for their Station Cores. According to the logs, they made it back to Collective space but were set upon by Heliothrope ships before they could complete their mission. While the Promory was destroyed, it is unknown whether any of them were able to escape."

Milton absorbed the information, watching as ALANNA looked down again in her persistent despondent state. *I can see why they were counting on us – they had no other options it seems.* There was just one thing that didn't make sense to him. Why him? It made sense to him why there were a bunch of military people in that small grey room, but it didn't explain why he was there. *Was I an accident?* He decided to ask ALANNA.

"You, and one other like you, were selected once it was found that 2 of the 100 candidates selected previously were no longer available due to their deaths. You were to be an experiment...for the experiment. Your knowledge of warfare and strategy through your 'games' – despite any actual physical fighting experience – was

43

determined acceptable for what was needed to operate the Station Core. It was even argued that you were actually better suited to it, compared to the others, but it was still to be determined."

ALANNA seemed to sit a little straighter as she talked, and Milton was hopeful that their continued conversations would pick her up out of her funk. He continued asking her questions, even as night fell on the planet they were on. Neither of them could get tired, so it didn't stop Milton's question-and-answer session. By morning, Milton had run out of pertinent things to ask and was ready to get started – and fortunately, so was ALANNA.

Chapter 4 – Sciurophobia

Milton learned a lot that night. He learned that he had survived due to his near-impenetrable tritanium shell and his zero-point energy reactor, which kept his systems running and would keep him powered for countless years into the future. He learned more about The Collective – their races, their customs, and their society. To be honest, he didn't really care much about them, since he had never met them and probably never would. However, talking about them seemed to be cathartic for ALANNA, as she worked through her issues with not being there for them and slowly came to terms with their present situation. As the hours passed, Milton was amazed at how life-like she was. After a while, he stopped thinking of her as an AI or computer program and as a real person. She had emotions, feelings, and the same doubts and fears as a normal person, with a complexity that would fool even those who knew otherwise.

What really got her – if not excited, then at least interested – was his question about space travel. He asked whether or not he could leave this planet and to his disappointment was shot down immediately. "However, that doesn't mean you couldn't create a ship capable of spaceflight, if you were able to acquire enough materials. The plans for many types of ships, as well as an uncountable number of other things, were uploaded to your processing core. It might take centuries, but it would be possible. And then...we could find out what happened to The Collective..."

He could see that this goal, this purpose, was what she needed. She perked up, her movements more animated, and her voice heavy with enthusiasm. Milton wasn't enthusiastic about searching for the people who had kidnapped and essentially murdered him, but he apparently still had a lot of time to decide. The fact that it might take centuries to get to that point didn't seem to deter ALANNA as they were essentially immortal. It was a new experience for Milton, however, since he was used to his lifespan consisting of perhaps a century, if he was lucky. It was going to take a while to get used to the fact that he wasn't going to die from old age. In fact, he didn't even know if he could die – another question for ALANNA. She told him that unless he was subjected to extremely high temperatures, like being dropped into the sun, he would continue to function indefinitely.

With said sun peeking over the treetops, he continued to pepper her with questions before he was interrupted by movement detected by his sensors. About 25 feet away from him was a small, squirrel-like animal nearly the same height as ALANNA, with a bushy tail that was steadily approaching with determination. It was obvious to Milton that **he** was its destination – and he freaked out. "Get away! Help! Stop it! ALANNA, do something!" His words had no effect on the small creature, who started bounding in his direction. Suddenly, he could hear something move on the outside of his shell, and a neon-blue laser shot out of the Core, hitting the squirrel right in its face. In mid-leap, the blood-thirsty attacker froze solid and fell back to the ground as a chunk of ice. It landed on a rock protruding from the ground and shattered into about a hundred pieces, scattering around the area in front of him.

Congratulations! You have defeated *Blood-thirsty Squirrel*! You gain 1 experience!
Current Combat Level: 1
Experience: 11/250

ALANNA was silent for a minute as she recovered from his sudden aggressive action against (at least, what she considered) a poor, innocent creature. "Uh...care to tell me what that was about? It couldn't have hurt you, so there was no need for that." Milton didn't want to lie to her, but he was ashamed of his fear of squirrels. When he was six years old, a squirrel somehow got into his house, made its way into his room, and attacked him when he was sleeping. *Attacked* might be too strong of a word, as it probably just wanted to get out of the house and was running all over the place, but his six-year-old mind thought otherwise. To this day, he had an unnatural fear of squirrels and avoided them like the plague whenever he saw them.

"I'm sorry, I just really don't like squirrels. And I thought he was going to attack me...or something," he sheepishly replied.

ALANNA looked unconvinced, but that was the best she was going to get as far as any explanation. "Ok, whatever. At least you now know how to use your last-ditch personal defensive measures now. They are activated by your own sense of danger, attacking anything you deem needing protection from. Even if it is a cute, harmless squirrel."

Ignoring her last comment, he asked, "Forget about my reaction for a moment – why was it attacking me?"

For the first time, Milton heard a short laugh come from the diminutive woman, "Ha! It wasn't attacking you! If you hadn't been such a fucking pansy, you would have seen that it was probably just exploring and was curious at what you are. Attacking you!" In a freaky change in her voice, she mimicked his voice exactly and started pretending to be attacked by squirrels, "Help! Stop them! They are going to kill me with cuteness!"

He was finding it harder to keep his cool with her mockery, "Hey! There's no need to call me names or make fun. Anyway, I said I was sorry, and I overreacted – give it up, already. Despite what you say, it **really** did look like it was coming for me. If you could put aside your doubts for a second, can you think of any reason why it would?"

ALANNA continued to laugh to herself for a couple more seconds, to Milton's rising annoyance, before she composed herself. "Keep your panties on, this will take just a minute. I'm going to run a diagnostic of your Core – maybe you landed on its tree or something and was going 'nuts' about it." She snickered for a moment at her own "joke", before she went vacant eyed as she looked at something he couldn't see.

Although he was glad that her attitude had improved from her previous funk, he wasn't sure if this was an improvement – at least for him. *Her personality will take some getting used to, especially if we are going to be together for a long time.* The way he saw it, if they couldn't get along, it was going to be a hellish couple of centuries or even – heaven forbid – millennia together.

His musings were interrupted as she exclaimed, "Shit on a stick, that's not good."

Although he was an adult, he was never one to use a lot of foul language and didn't really like it when other people used it willy-nilly. This aversion was instilled in him when he got caught using a number of four-letter words around the house when he was seven. Instead of the old-school wash-your-mouth-out-with-soap or new-school "time-out" methods, his parents took his gaming system *and* TV away from him for six months. They threatened to take it away permanently if they heard anything like that again, which to this day made him averse to cursing. Some things just seemed to stick with him – not unlike his sciurophobia.[1]

"Uh...what's wrong? And try not to curse when you tell me – I don't care for it."

"I'm sorry if I disturbed your delicate sensibilities, but this is no time to be a fucking pussy. Your Zero-point Energy Reactor was damaged and is leaking radiation like a goddamned sieve. We need to fix it if we are ever going to get off this fucking planet – otherwise

---

[1] **Sciurophobia** – fear of squirrels.

we are up shit creek. The only way we can do that is if we can create enough tritanium to slowly repair the reactor. Even then, it could take centuries to get you back up to the power levels needed to create and fly a ship."

At first, he had no idea what she was talking about, other than cringing at her use of swear words. Gradually, however, the knowledge he was lacking was slowly filtered into his "mind", until he understood what the Zero-point Energy Reactor was, if not how it worked, and began to comprehend the damage she was talking about. The knowledge of "how" to fix it was there, but he didn't know where to get what he needed to do it. "Wow, that's neat – I suddenly know what the reactor is and how to fix it. The only thing I don't know is where to get the materials. Where do we find the tritanium? And really, please stop with the foul language, I don't like it."

She looked a little crestfallen as she answered, "You don't **find** tritanium, you have to **create** tritanium. And the only way to create it is to convert resources – which you don't have."

He waited for her to explain some more, but she didn't elaborate. "Ok, so how do we get these resources?"

She looked at him like he had asked the dumbest question ever voiced, but then her expression softened as she carefully explained, "I forgot I didn't tell you yet. You have a Molecular Converter as part of your core, which can break down anything into basic resources that can be used to create whatever you want – as long as you have the correct materials. For instance, if you want to build a wooden chair, you would need to chop down one of those trees over there, insert it into your Molecular Converter, and use it to create a chair. Your Molecular Converter, as the name implies, can **convert** basic resources into finished product.

"For more complicated items, such as an automated laser turret, you would need many different resources. Some things can be substituted by other material, but overall you would need a large quantity of metals, silica, oils, and plant material."

"Plant material?"

"For dyes of course – who wants a plain old boring grey turret? Not me, that's fucking who."

Milton found that he could sigh, even as a "Station Core" without lungs. "Ok, we're getting a little off-track here. Back to the original question – how do I **create** tritanium?"

She thought a moment, before responding slowly, as if she was trying to explain something to a five-year-old, "Let's see – think of it this way. In your games that you used to play, you frequently had coinage in currencies such as copper, silver, and gold, right? It usually took, let's say, 100 copper coins to make 1 silver coin, and then 100 silver coins to make 1 gold coin. Now, figure that a small piece of iron ore is worth 1 copper coin and if you wanted to convert it to a small piece of steel, you would need 1 silver coins' worth of iron ore. In other words, you would need 100 iron ores to make 1 steel ore. Some ores are worth more than iron, but – except for some rare exceptions – not a lot more. This is a gross oversimplification, of course, but even with your primitive mind you should hopefully understand.

"Now imagine there were other, higher-value currencies: platinum, mithril, and diamond – each needing 100 of the previous to equal the next highest. Tritanium is roughly worth about 1 or 2 diamonds, so like 10-20 billion iron ores or so." After this revelation, she seemed to take his unresponsiveness as despair, because she added, "But there is hope – there are ways to improve your conversion rate and increase the output of your Converter. I wasn't exaggerating when I said it would take centuries, however, because even with those improvements it will take a while. Which I hope we have…," she trailed off, looking pensive.

Milton was stunned by how many resources would be required to make just a small amount of tritanium, notwithstanding the amount of time it would take. He was caught by her last statement, however – so he worriedly asked, "What do you mean – aren't I immortal now?"

She slowly looked up from her thoughtful posture, responding to his question with a sorrowful tone, as if she was a doctor that had to give him an unexpected cancer diagnosis. "Normally, you would be. However, in addition to the damage to your Zero-point Energy Reactor, your shell was also damaged, creating a vulnerability in your structural integrity. With enough determination, something – or someone – could potentially break into your core through the damaged section. Until you repair it section by section with tritanium, you will need to protect yourself from any hostile monsters." She paused for a moment before continuing – albeit reluctantly – and mumbled, "I hate to say it, but you might have been right about the squirrel…"

With these revelations coming one right after another, Milton was starting to become numb to any surprises. Until he heard that he might have been right. "I was right? I mean, of course I was right. Uh…how right was I?" he excitedly asked.

"Don't 'cream your Twinkie' just yet, I said you **might** have been right. When Collective scientists created the Zero-point Energy Reactors, they theorized that the radiation from an unshielded reactor could result in adverse effects on animate and inanimate objects. This was never tested – because they didn't want to subject anyone or anything to whatever might happen – so these effects were only theorized based on hypothesis.

"Three main effects were theorized from exposure to Zero-point radiation. The first was that it would start to rapidly corrode metals, even tritanium, if allowed to collect in a small area. The second was that animals and sentient creatures would be attracted to the radiation on some primal level, almost like a cat being attracted to catnip, but on a whole new level. That's why I think you might have been right about the squirrel – it was trying to get to the source of the radiation. It wasn't powerful enough to do you any damage, but it still would have tried."

If he could flush with pleasure, Milton would have been red as a beet after hearing that he was right about the squirrel. *I feel a little better about that, now. Even with my fear of squirrels, I still felt a little bad at how I went about killing the little thing.* "Wait, that was only two – what's the third thing?"

She still looked distracted, and it took her a moment before she answered his question. "The third thing? Oh, yeah – they thought that prolonged exposure would cause genetic mutations. Since they had no real data, they surmised it could be something as simple as an extra toe or as complex as increasing their size, giving them wings, and adding retractable spikes to their back. Again, this was all conjecture."

Well, that sucks. It's like I'm a mini Chernobyl disaster waiting to happen. "So, what you propose I do?"

"There's only one thing you can do at the moment – hide."

Chapter 5 – Obtain quests, check!

"Hide? Why? If any more squirrels come, I'll just shoot those as well. Besides, how am I supposed to hide? I'm a 20-foot tall metallic eggshell in the middle of the forest. I kinda stand out." Milton was confused about what he had to hide from if all there were in this forest were squirrels and big yellow birds. Now that he knew he could shoot lasers, defending himself seemed pretty easy now.

"First, your self-defensive cold laser takes time to recharge after use. It's only about 30 seconds, but if you were attacked by multiple enemies you wouldn't be able to get them all before they reached you. Add to that the fact that it isn't powerful enough to stop a larger, determined enemy, and it isn't as powerful as you think. Second, you don't know what else is in this forest – there could be a T-rex or something equally dangerous in there. Third, the more you sit here, the more the radiation is going to continue to accumulate and spread, attracting more and more creatures to your location. Fourth, you're right – you're too exposed; you need to make it harder to find your Core. Preferably behind strong walls or in a fortified building. Better yet – how about underground? That would probably be ideal.

"Fifth – and this is most important – repairing yourself is going to potentially take centuries. You need somewhere to hideout until you are fully operational again. I want you, and by extension me, to survive long enough to get off this planet and find out what happened to The Collective. The only way to do this is to hide away where nothing can get to you."

Milton thought he understood her paranoia now. He didn't particularly like her assumption that his main objective was to find out what happened to her creators (and his captors), but then again, he didn't have anything better to do. He figured that if or when the time came to leave this planet, he would have a better idea of what he wanted to do.

"Ok, I give in to your expertise. What do I do first?"

ALANNA genuinely smiled for the first time, pleased with her small victory. "First you need to pull up your Core Status screen so that you can see your statistics. The system is modeled after the online roleplaying games you used to play to make the transition easier and more comprehensible for you. All you need to do is think, 'Core Status', and the screen should appear.[2]

2

Core Status			
Name:	Milton Frederick	Type:	Station Core Prototype 3-B
Combat Level:	1	Experience:	11/250
Reactor Type:	Zero-point Energy	Reactor Output:	2%
Current Statistics/Attributes			
Reactor Power/Strength:	2	Processing Power/Intelligence:	5
Structural Integrity/Constitution:	2	Ingenuity/Wisdom:	5
Processing Speed/Agility:	5	Communication/Charisma:	5
Insight/Luck:	7	Sensor Interpretation/Perception	6

Milton did as she instructed and found a status screen reminiscent of CLoD, complete with levels, experience, and attributes such as Strength and Intelligence. Of course, they were named something completely different but made more sense for his current incarnation. Instead of Strength, it was instead called Reactor Power and instead of Intelligence – Processing Power. Everything pointed to his presence as a machine and not a living, breathing human anymore. This, strangely, affected him more than anything he had learned so far.

Ever since he was a little kid, he enjoyed playing video games so much that they became a main focus of his life. Sometimes the stories and interactions seemed more real than his actual life – and he occasionally wished they were. He had wistfully dreamed about being one of his characters he had created in-game, slashing enemies with a sword or casting spells designed to decimate the ranks of his foes. Now that he was actually in a "videogame", it wasn't anything like he had thought. Especially since his mind was trapped in a giant, egg-shaped paperweight.

He realized that ALANNA was talking to him, trying to get his attention while he stared off in space after looking at his Status. His thoughts were a jumble as they tried to come to terms with his artificial existence. *I'll never walk again, never enjoy eating a juicy cheeseburger again, and never feel the grass beneath my bare feet again.* Not that he ever went barefoot outside, but that wasn't the point. It was going to take a while for everything to set in –

fortunately (or unfortunately, depending on how you looked at it) he had a long time with which to do so.

"Hey in there, snap out of it! We have shit to do and can't wait for you to feel sorry for yourself. Please tell me you at least brought up your Core Status screen," ALANNA yelled, while banging ineffectually on the outside of his shell.

"Yeah, sorry about that...I'm good for the moment. I brought it up – what did you want me to see?"

"We'll have time for me to explain everything later to you, but the most important part you needed to see is the Reactor Output which is at 2%. Before you ask, that's the amount your damaged reactor can consistently use to power everything you control. In comparison, at 100% output, you could power your entire former planet, with a little bit to spare. Although 2% sounds like a lot when I compare it to that, the things that you control use much more than your primitive electricity back on Earth. To be able to power a spaceship, you would need, at minimum, at least 70% output to be effective. More would be better, of course. This is your main goal – to repair your reactor and thereby improve your Reactor Output enough that we can leave this planet."

As soon as she stopped speaking, a window popped up in his "mind", startling him with its appearance:

New Long-term Goal: *Goodbye Planet, Hello Collective*
Gather Units of Tritanium x 1000
Repair your Structural Integrity and Zero-point Energy Reactor

> *Achieve Reactor Output of at least 70%*
>
> *Create Space-worthy Vehicle to Transport Station Core*
>
> **Difficulty of Goal**: Nightmare-inducing
>
> **Timeframe:** None
>
> **Rewards:** Leave Current Planet

"What is this – a quest?" he asked, noticing the familiar look to it.

"If that is what you want to call it, then sure, it's a quest. It's part of your training program that I can implement so that you can learn how to achieve what you need to survive. This goal, sorry, 'quest', is long-term and it should be the basis for everything you do. There are also short-term and average-term quests, such as...these, which will help guide you toward your long-term quest:

> **New Average-term Goal: *Boot Camp***
>
> *Learn the different functions of a Station Core:*
> - *Sensors – Complete*
> - *Drones*
> - *Molecular Converter*
> - *Biological Recombinator*
> - *Resources*
> - *Self-Defense System – Complete*
> - *Units*
> - *Neural Connections*
> - *Structures/Manufacturing Facilities*
> - *Defenses*
> - *Combat & Combat Levels*

- *Statistics*
- *Skills & Achievements*
- *Research & Discoveries*

Difficulty of Goal: Hard

Timeframe: 1 year

Rewards: Become a fully-functioning, knowledgeable Station Core

---

New Short-term Goal: *Hidden Agenda*

Find a safe location and hide. Simple as that.

Difficulty of Goal: Easy

Timeframe: 5 days

Rewards: Find shelter in a safe environment (at least temporarily)

His existential crisis was starting to fade a little as he looked at the quests ALANNA sent him. *Ok, this could work. It's reminding me more and more of a videogame – and I can do those.* No matter what he was now, he was first-and-foremost a gamer – almost a professional, even. If he treated this as he would a video game, he could see himself getting through the first couple of days without having a breakdown.

"I'm liking this more and more, ALANNA. These help me out a lot, actually. If I tackle the short-term quests one-at-a-time, it should make the harder quests easier. Just like doing simple drop-gathering quests in MMORPGs would provide experience as well as monetary rewards. Then those quests would lead to harder quests to defeat harder enemies, and so on and so forth. I, no, WE, can do this!"

ALANNA laughed at his enthusiasm, "Alright, nerd-boy – let's stop messing around and get something done for a change. So, tell me, almighty game wizard, how are you going to accomplish your first go—quest?" she deliberately corrected herself at the last moment, subtly making fun of his gaming terms.

He was getting better at ignoring her subtle and not-so-subtle jibes, mostly because he was excited about his prospects now. "Well, I need to hide – but how do I do that? Do I have some super-secret propulsion capability?"

"No."

"Legs that can extend out from my shell?"

"Uh…no, but that would be sweet."

"Flaps that flip out, allowing me to roll?"

"No, although I would love to see that – it would be hilarious."

"…Pogo-stick?"

"Ok, you can stop guessing. You can't actually move by yourself. The designers of your Core weren't expecting you to have to move once you were installed, so there is no form of locomotion built into you. What you do have is…drumroll please…drones."

"Drones?" Milton didn't see what those flying hobbyist toys could do for him. He still remembered the one he crashed.

"Yes, drones. But not the ones you're probably thinking about. These are much more advanced and easier to control – since they have a neural connection to you. You should have eight in total – half that fly and half that are ground-based. These are your main workforce, and you can make more in the future to speed up your processes. They can be used for a number of different projects, but what you should use them for right now is to dig underneath your Core. This is the most economical choice in terms of hidden refuges: time-wise, resource-wise, and difficulty-wise."

"Sounds awesome – how do I get them?"

"Easy – just think, 'Activate Initial Drone Sequence', and they should detach from your shell."

He started to think the activation sequence when he stopped, his acronym-loving mind kicking in at the strangest times, "AIDS? Is that a joke?"

She looked strangely at him, like she was trying to decide whether they had picked an imbecile instead of a master-gamer. "No, they are here to **AID** you, and there are multiple drones, so they are your **AIDS**."

If he could crawl away in embarrassment, he would – but no such luck. He settled for another apology, "Sorry, I misunderstood. Activating my AIDS now." He chuckled softly in his mind as he thought of the words. Unexpectantly, he could sense as multiple somethings detached from the outside of his shell and drop to the ground. He was about to look closer when he received an error.

ERROR!

Flight Drone Unit 1 inoperable!

Flight Drone Unit 2 inoperable!

Flight Drone Unit 3 inoperable!

Flight Drone Unit 4 inoperable!

Well, that's just great... "What happened? Why aren't the flying drones working?"

"Hold on...checking the...well, fuck. It looks they were damaged at some point in the past and can't be activated. We can repair them in the future, but we don't yet have the time or the resources. Let's forget them for now – you at least have the more important ones left. You should be able to mentally establish a neural connection with each of the drones. Try it now."

Milton tried to do what she asked but was unsure of how to go about it. He tried "reaching" out to them, but his nonexistent hands couldn't find anything to hold onto. Next, he tried thinking, "drone", but that returned the same result. Next, he tried letting his mind go blank, hoping that the drones' presence could be felt if he wasn't trying too hard. When that didn't work, he got annoyed at his inability to affect *his* drones that he started screaming at them in his mind – again to no effect.

It was only when he calmed down and looked at ALANNA impatiently waiting for him that he remembered something. *If they created this Station Core to be like one of my games, there must be an interface for my "workers".* With a flash of inspiration, he tried

63

calling up a "drone" menu. As he had hoped, a Drone Menu popped up listing all his drones, including the damaged/inoperable ones.[3]

He mentally selected Ground Drone Unit 1 and felt his awareness split into two parts. One part was still inside his giant chicken egg, looking outside through the "eyes" of his sensors. The other part was at ground level, staring at a metallic wall. It was a strange feeling; although similar to controlling his sensors, it was different because he was aware of his multiple appendages instead of being a basic floating orb. While focusing on these new feelings, he was still aware of the viewpoints of his other sensors – he was frankly amazed at his ability to multitask and not lose his concentration from information overload.

Moving what he thought was its legs, he directed it to start moving backwards so he could see more of his surroundings. As his view changed, he was able to see a large divot on the side of what he now knew was his shell. *I guess that's where the drone dropped down from.* He turned to the side and was startled when he saw what he thought was a giant grey insect standing in a threatening manner a couple of feet away. He backed up some more in fright but stopped when the creature didn't make any move. Understanding dawned on him, as he chastised himself for being frightened by his own drone.

3

Drone Menu	
Ground Drone Unit 1	Ground Drone Unit 2
Ground Drone Unit 3	Ground Drone Unit 4
Flight Drone Unit 1 (Inoperable)	Flight Drone Unit 2 (Inoperable)
Flight Drone Unit 3 (Inoperable)	Flight Drone Unit 4 (Inoperable)

The closest comparison he could come up with was a large metal beetle – but that's where the similarities ended. Instead of being flat against the ground, it's back was bent in half with appendages sticking out the front at rest, reminiscent of a praying mantis minus the head. It looked like it moved around on its four back feet, while using its arms perform different tasks. At the moment, said arms were small sharp spikes that didn't look like they could be used for much of anything other than being some wicked kabob skewers.

"Oh, good – I see you figured it out. You'll find that you can control them directly or, once you've established a connection, can give them orders and they will use their limited AI to perform the task to the best of their ability. Alright, connect to the other ones and give them their orders."

He was already establishing connections via the Drone Menu and felt his awareness split even further as he connected to each one. Trying to control two at once, he found that he couldn't concentrate on each of them long enough to do anything productive. It was worse than when he was trying to control multiple sensors since he was trying to walk around without crashing into anything. Once he had established connections with all of them, he pulled back his awareness and mentally gave them orders to assemble in an area in front of his Core. If he concentrated enough, he could "see" out of the drones to get a "drones-eye" view of their surroundings. Instead of that hassle, however, he used his sensor orbs – which were becoming somewhat of a second nature to him – to watch them gather.

After they assembled, he asked, "Ok, so what orders should I give them?"

"Dig, motherfucker, dig!"

I'm really going to need to talk to her about her language...someday.

Chapter 6 – The process of shitting a brick

Milton was amazed at how tirelessly and efficiently his little drones worked at digging a tunnel underneath his Core. When he initially gave his orders, he watched in amazement as each of his drones moved their pointy-stick arms inside their shells – almost like a turtle – only to emerge with different implements. Three of them now had wide-bladed spades that were very effective at removing large quantities of dirt at a very quick pace. The last one had a large flat-bottomed scoop that it held close to its body, reminding Milton of a small bulldozer. The spade-equipped drones would throw out massive amounts of dirt behind them, while the bulldozer drone would gather it all up and move it away from the worksite. With the combination of efforts of the four drones, after an hour there was a large, rapidly growing hill of dirt beside an equally large tunnel heading into the ground.

He thought at first about having his drones dig out the dirt from underneath him, slowly bringing him down to a depth he felt safe. However, he quickly discovered that he was extremely heavy when one of the drones dug next to him and almost got squished when he shifted slightly. Now his plan was to dig a 45-degree tunnel large enough that he would be able to roll down, gradually tapering off until he came to a nice rest near his final destination. He figured that a depth of about 500 feet would probably be safe enough, while also giving him plenty of room to expand if he wanted. It was a monumental undertaking when he thought about it, but at the pace his drones were moving he thought they could get it done in a couple of days.

Just as he thought everything was coming together splendidly, the entrance to the tunnel collapsed, sealing three of his drones inside. He could sense that they were fine, having been far enough inside that they were not covered by dirt. They had enough room that they could dig themselves out – filling up the tunnel behind them as they did it – so he got them started on freeing themselves. And then he started to think about what went wrong. He didn't get angry or frustrated – he just needed the proper strategy to see his way through.

ALANNA had been uncharacteristically silent through the whole drone process until now. Even though at times he could have used some help, he was glad that she had let him learn how to manipulate the drones and formulate a plan on his own. He always thought that the best way to learn was to try and fail, thereby learning what went wrong and fix it next time. *Well, I tried and failed – now I need to know how to fix it.*

"ALANNA, I'm pretty sure my tunnel collapsed because I didn't have any supports holding up the roof. However, I'm not sure how to go about that – what do you suggest?" He wasn't above soliciting advice from outside sources – he was smart, but he wasn't a genius – and would take whatever help was given.

Seemingly pleased with his question, she smiled smugly as she told him, "Well, first, I think your plan has merit – but the slope is way too steep. You should try for a more gradual 5-degree slope and make some switchbacks on the way down to your stopping point. That way, when you're ready to descend, you won't have to worry about damaging yourself further and your drones can help roll you at a more measured pace. As for supports, why don't you reinforce the whole tunnel with a harder, denser material?"

"Well, that's a great idea, but where am I supposed to find that material? All I've seen come out is small rocks along with the dirt they've been digging."

ALANNA covered her face with her hands in exasperation, and he had a hard time understanding her when she spoke in a mumble, "This is going to take forever..." When she removed her hands from her face, she looked at him with a strained expression on her face. "Didn't you listen before when I told you about your Molecular Converter? You can use it on the dirt that has been excavated and turn it into blocks of whatever you want. Of course, depending on your choice, you'll lose a percentage of your dirt in the conversion. Direct your remaining free drone to bring some dirt over and open up your converter – I'll show you how it's done."

Going along with her advice, Milton had his drone shove a small mound of dirt over to his shell. He thought of whatever this converter was and imagined a door opening up along the outside – and to his surprise, it worked! He "felt" something open along one side of his Core and directed one of his sensor orbs to quickly detach and observe the process. A hatch about five-foot square was lined up right against the ground, allowing him to see a blue, glowing platform encompassing the bottom of an empty chamber. Not sure what to expect next, he then directed his drone to push the dirt inside the chamber, exiting when it was complete. He tried to activate the converter but got an error message inside his mind saying that the hatch needed to be closed before activation. Chastising himself slightly with his stupidity, he quickly closed the hatch and turned it on.

He couldn't "feel" or hear anything, so he wasn't sure it was working until he got a notification that work was complete a moment later.[4] *That was quick, at least.* He found that he had multiple options of what could be done with the dirt he had placed in the converter. Choices ranged from compacting the *Basic Earth* to reduce it in volume to converting it to different stone-like materials. There also seemed to be a very small amount of metal content found inside the pile, which reminded him of those days he used to watch those gold-mining shows on TV where they would sift through thousands of cubic yards of earth to find miniscule amounts of gold.

---

[4]

Molecular Converter					
Resource Type	Units	Conversion	Conversion Ratio	Conversion	Conversion Ratio
Basic Earth	1036	Compacted Earth	2:1	Quartzite	50:1
		Brick (Clay)	5:1	Gneiss	75:11
		Sandstone	25:1	Granite	100:1
Basic Gravel	52	Compacted Earth	1:5	Quartzite	10:1
		Brick (Clay)	1:1	Gneiss	15:1
		Sandstone	5:1	Granite	20:1
Basic Metals	>1	(Insufficient Material)			
Pure Water	6	Ice	1:1		

It also was encouraging, since his long-term goal was to accumulate enough metals to fix his Core and get off this planet.

Looking at the different conversion ratios, Milton decided that his best choice was to convert the resources to sandstone, which had a ratio of 25 units of *Basic Earth* to 1 unit of sandstone. If it turned out that it wasn't strong enough, he would replace it with something stronger later. He selected "Sandstone" and used both the earth and small amounts of gravel he had collected for the conversion. He felt the back of his shell open and directed his sensor orb to watch as a conveyor exited his rear hatch and deposited a small block of sandstone on the ground about 5 feet away. Comparable to the amount of dirt that was pushed in, it looked to be about $1/20^{th}$ the size. It was dark brown in color, with streaks of grey throughout the brick-sized stone. *Heh, I pooped a brick.* He chuckled at the image.

"Good economical choice! That should work for the initial tunnel. Your drones are a lot stronger and versatile than you probably think they are – they should be able to lift blocks like this or even larger to cover the inside of the tunnel. They also have a limited directed molecular converter that can join the blocks together using extra dirt laying around, creating a seamless shaft leading downwards. It will take a bit longer to finish your tunnel this way, but it will be worth it in the long run."

Nice! He ordered his "dozer" drone to continuously bring him piles of dirt so that he could convert it to sandstone. By the time his three trapped drones made their way free, he had accumulated a

71

large pile of sandstone bricks, which he immediately put one of his digging drones in charge of assembling the tunnel lining. He had a general idea of what he wanted, and – just as ALANNA said – they took it and adapted it to how it should be done. *She was right, they are both smart and versatile.* Within a couple of hours, they had already reached almost 30 feet down the new, gradually sloped tunnel.

While watching his drones work was slightly interesting, Milton was growing bored. *If I'm this bored already, I'm dreading the next century or more of metal accumulation.* "ALANNA, is there anything else you can teach me while the drones are working? They seem to know what they're doing and don't really require my attention."

It seems like she was getting bored as well, since she jumped at the chance to teach him something new. "YES! I can teach you about creating your own combat units! First, have your 'dozer' drone collect and bring all the pieces of the squirrel you killed earlier to your Molecular Converter."

When he concentrated on it, he could see the now-thawed pieces of the squirrel still covering the ground in bloody chunks. He wasn't sure what she had in mind, but as long as he didn't have to touch it himself (not that he could anyway), he went along with her instructions.

It took a while, but the drone was able to find all the small pieces of squirrel bits and deposited them into the converter. Once the hatch was closed, he saw a screen that was similar to when he converted dirt, but instead of natural materials he saw "Biological Mass".[5]

"Now, what you are looking at is your Combat Unit Creation screen. Every time you throw a living – or non-living in this case – creature into the converter you will have the ability to create another one just like it under your control. As of now, you only have access to that squirrel you spazzed out and killed, but you can accumulate countless others as you defeat them and convert them to biological mass (or bio) units inside your Core. Each unit requires a specific amount of bio units to create, as well as basic metal units (BMU) for their Neurological Control Unit. This is what allows you to control them, bypassing their normal thought processes and only following your orders. In addition, the control unit allows you to 'see' and feel through them, similar to how your drones work. Try creating one now."

Milton didn't want another squirrel near him, but he figured he could destroy it again with his self-defensive cold laser if it decided to attack him. *Hopefully I can control it and send it far away, so I don't have to look at it.* Despite his reservations, he went ahead and created the Blood-thirsty Squirrel – *I wonder if it names these things based on what I think of them as* – and after a moment, a

---

5

Combat Unit Creation			
Biological Mass (Bio Units)	5	**Basic Metal (BM Units)**	10
Unit Name (Type)	*Bio Units*	*Neurological Control Unit*	*BM Units*
Blood-thirsty Squirrel (Scout)	5	Type-1a	1

73

squirrel almost exactly like the one he had killed got pooped out of his rear end.

It just sat there, twitching its tail and looking around in curiosity. Braced for an attack, Milton felt his self-defensive laser emerge and point itself at the potential threat. After it didn't move after about a minute, Milton started to relax when ALANNA surprised him by talking. He reflexively fired and froze the squirrel, which caused it to fall over and softly shatter like brittle glass.

"Fuck, you really don't like squirrels! What I was about to say – before you destroyed your new combat unit – was that it wouldn't move or do anything you didn't want it to do without your instructions. Keep in mind that it's a living, breathing creature so it will still need to eat, sleep, and even shit when it must. It's not a zombie – a mindless creature without any type of brain. If you tell it to act normal, it will follow its instincts and go about its normal routines as if it were any other squirrel. What makes it different is that you can send it orders to do anything you want it to do, even so far as jumping off a cliff if you wanted it to. Ok, now that you've hopefully gotten that spasticity out of your system – have your drone collect the pieces and let's try again."

Milton didn't say anything as the drone went along its business collecting the squirrel shards before depositing them in the converter. He was embarrassed at his over-reaction and was determined to hold back his sciurophobia until he could finish with this "Combat Unit Creation" tutorial.

When the next one appeared, he kept his weapon inside the shell, hoping that not having it easily accessible would prevent him from killing it again. When it reacted the same as before, he relaxed a little bit more and listened to ALANNA as she explained a little more.

"Ok, now that it's alive and well, you can control it like you do your drones and have it scout out the surrounding area. You can follow along and see everything it sees, or you can 'program' it to alert you if it notices something out of the ordinary. 'Out of the ordinary' might mean different things to different creatures, so there might be some trial-and-error involved. By the way – since you will probably be familiar with this – there are different classes of units that you can create, based upon their strengths. For instance, your squirrel there is classed as a 'Scout', meaning that it's best at using its small stature and agility to scout out the surrounding area. You theoretically could use it to attack, but there are very few things that it would be useful against and it wouldn't survive long against a determined foe.

"In the future, once you have gathered the genetic makeup of various creatures, you can experiment with creating hybrids of creatures – but not until you create a Biological Recombinator. We won't talk about that until you are established in a safe place, however. Go ahead, try out your new unit."

Remembering how he initially accessed the drone controls, he thought "Combat Unit Menu" and one appeared in his mind. He only had the one Blood-thirsty Squirrel (1), so he chose it and sent orders for it to appear normal but to scout around for anything out of the ordinary. He didn't enter inside and see through its eyes like he did the drones because he didn't want to have any more contact than necessary with the frightening animal.

"Ok, what's next?" he asked his instructor.

"Nothing right now – back to the grind."

Chapter 7 – Bear-ly ready

It didn't take long for his Core to be "attacked" by another local creature. Mere hours after he sent his squirrel scout to investigate the surrounding area, one of his sensor orbs observed a small snake-like creature slithering through the nearby grass towards his Core. It was the same size and color as a gardener snake but had a much larger head – which made it look very strange, almost like a lollipop.

Milton watched it as it approached, heading unerringly for the damaged section of his shell. *It's a wonder that it can move with that big head.* When it was about 15 feet out, it opened its mouth and softly hissed – whether out of excitement or anger, he didn't know – which triggered his self-defensive cold laser. The snakesicle froze in place but didn't shatter, but he knew it had died when he received another notification.

Congratulations! You have defeated *Lollipop Snake*! You gain 5 experience!
Current Combat Level: 1
Experience: 16/250

He instructed his "dozer" drone to insert the frozen snake into his hatch, which he then was able to convert into bio units. He pulled up his Combat Unit Creation (CUC) menu and found that he had a new unit that he could produce – the Lollipop Snake.[6] *Heh, I like how I can name all these guys – it beats generic names.*

"Hey ALANNA, the Lollipop Snake I just converted says that it's a 'Stealth Fighter' – am I to assume that means it's like a Rogue class or something similar?"

"You called it what? Why the fuck did you associate a lollipop with it? Whatever – you can call it what you want, I guess. Anyway, if I'm understanding your games correctly, that would be a fair assessment. Don't expect to get 'backstab' bonuses or any dumb shit like that, but it will probably be more lethal if it is hidden before it strikes. It's not a front-line fighter, so it is best used in ambushes or even as part of a group attack."

"Thanks, that's what I suspected – I just wanted confirmation. And please try to restrain yourself with the foul language, I would really appreciate it. I'm sure you can manage to get your point across without cursing so much," he pleaded.

ALANNA was silent for a few moments, the expression on her face a conflict of emotions. "I...will try. I was originally programmed to work with your military, where it was assumed that having a

---

[6]

Combat Unit Creation			
Biological Mass (Bio Units)	10	Basic Metal (BM Units)	14
Unit Name (Type)	Bio Units	Neurological Control Unit	BM Units
Blood-thirsty Squirrel (Scout)	5	Type-1a	1
Lollipop Snake (Stealth Fighter)	10	Type-1a	1

rough and strict attitude would hopefully garner some respect from their gruff and disciplined demeanors. That may or may not be the correct assumption; either way, it's who I am. I can't promise anything, but I will try to curb some of my more colorful language."

Makes more sense now – I was wondering why her attitude seemed more militaristic and no-nonsense. "Thank you, that's all I ask." She seemed to relax a little with his response, as if she was previously braced against something he might do to her. *I wonder what that was all about?*

Since he had the opportunity to test out another unit, he spent the necessary resources and pooped out a new snake under his control. With instructions to leisurely patrol the area within 50 feet of his shell, the Lollipop Snake (1) slithered away, looking for a snack. *I wonder what its main diet consists of?* He didn't have long to wonder, fortunately, as after it roamed toward the perimeter of its patrol area it waited near an insignificant-looking hole in the ground. After sitting completely still for almost two minutes, a small, blue, hairless mouse poked its head out. A quick lunge from his snake snatched the bald rodent by its head, where it was quickly pierced by the snake's relatively giant fangs. Seconds later, the "snack" was inside the snake's head, where it was rapidly broken down and digested.

Congratulations! One of your units has defeated *Ugly Bald Mouse*! You gain 1 experience! Current Combat Level: 1

Experience: 17/250

Nice, I get experience from my unit kills! Of course, I probably need to find out what my Combat Levels mean. "ALANNA, I have another question for—" he started, but was interrupted by his squirrel unit barging in on his thoughts. When he concentrated on looking through its eyes – with a mental shudder at being so close to the blood-thirsty animal – it took him a moment to adjust to the place he found himself.

Looking down through the densely-packed branches of the tree his squirrel was currently observing from, he couldn't see at first what had alerted his Scout. Movement near the tree-trunk, however, confirmed that this definitely qualified as out-of-the-ordinary. A massive, brown, bear-like creature, with flat scales lining its back and sides, was slowly waking up from what looked like a deep sleep. As it rose to its feet, it was looking – based on the noise he could hear in the distance from his squirrel – in the direction of his Core. Milton guessed that the noise of the digging and the dozing being done on his tunnel had woken it up before it was ready. And it looked pissed.

"ALANNA – my Scout sees a massive bear coming this way! What do I do?" He was starting to panic – *I'm not ready for this yet! I need more time!* The size and potential strength of the incoming creature – he was going to call it a Scaly Bear – looked like it could put the hurt on his damaged section if it got too close.

"First, calm down, you pussy. This is what you were designed for – defending against a superior attacking force. Think about what you have at your disposal and create a plan. That **is** what you're supposed to be so good at, isn't it?" Milton thought she was a lot calmer than she should be, considering the potential danger. He slowed his thought processes down and attempted to dampen the panic he was experiencing. It helped looking at how calm ALANNA was and how much confidence she had in him. *I just wish I was that confident in myself.*

His whole life he had played video games and despite how real they appeared, he knew they were just that – games. His confidence while playing said games was monumental, but now that he was faced with a "life-and-death" situation, he wasn't as confident. The stakes had never been so final – if he had messed up before, he would learn from his mistakes and try again. He was beginning to understand the old gaming adage, "In real life, there are no reset buttons." It was do-or-die time and he didn't want to **die** – so now he had to figure out how to **do** it.

If I had more time, I think I could prepare some better static defenses, but I have a feeling it'll be here before I could construct anything worthwhile. What do I have to use right now? Lollipop Snake, Blood-thirsty Squirrel, Dirt, Sandstone, Drones, Sensor Orbs... Thinking at a furious pace, he started to form a plan – it was risky, but it just might work.

Risking another attack by another Big Yellow Bird, he sent two of his sensor orbs out in the direction of the Scaly Bear to get an unobstructed overhead view of the action and for early warning of its approach. Next, he recalled all his drones and had them assemble behind his shell near the damaged section.   Once they were in place, he directed the rest of his sensor orbs to gather in the air above his shell, where they awaited further orders. For his last preparation step, he directed his Lollipop Snake to head back and lay low in the grass near his Core.

A ground-shaking roar erupted from the edge of the trees as the Scaly Bear caught sight of its quarry. Milton watched as the furry and scaly monstrosity lumbered its way toward him at a surprisingly fast pace. *It's even larger than I thought.* Not only was it slightly bigger than a Kodiak bear back on Earth, but he could now see the long, sharp, and deadly-appearing claws on each of its paws. In the space of 15 seconds it had made its way close enough that he could see the hatred and – as it got close enough to be affected by the reactor radiation – the insanity in its eyes. The hostility emanating from it made him freeze up for a critical few seconds, long enough for it to get near his shell without hindrance.

An enormous blow to his damaged section rocked his entire shell and kicked Milton out of his stupor. With the reverberations still being felt through his Core, he was spurred into action by ALANNA screaming, "Don't let him do that again – any more damage and your reactor could go critical! Kill that motherfucker!" Fortunately, it also distracted the bear, causing it to look for the source of the screaming while it paused in its attack. And that was all the opening Milton needed.

Even though his drones weren't specifically made for attacking or defensive maneuvers, he could still use them for this new "project". While he was preparing for the attack, he had his drones convert their "arms" into lumberjack mode, figuring they had to have some sort of tool that would make felling trees easier. When their arms reappeared from inside their shells, they had long, large-toothed saws on each arm – which would come in handy now. He sent orders for them all to target a separate appendage on the bear, treating them as they would a tree that needed to be cut down. As they moved into position, he activated his cold laser self-defensive system, shooting the bear right between the eyes. While he had hoped that his laser would end the fight without too much trouble, he was prepared for it not to have too much effect on such a large creature. Instead of freezing the entire thing solid, all it appeared to do was slow it down a little – and piss it off even more.

When the drones scuttled close enough to start cutting, the back two were successful in approaching stealthily enough that they were able to "attack" without repercussion. The two in front, however, were seen by the bear before they could close in. With a tremendous swipe of its paw, his former "dozer" drone was impacted with such force that he immediately lost all awareness of it as it was launched – crushed and almost dismembered – across the clearing and slammed against the trunk of a tree. The other drone in front was in danger of the same thing happening, but fortunately that was when the back two went to work.

Milton was impressed, and a little sickened, at how well his drones performed. With the sawblades pressed up against the bear's back legs, they quickly moved them back and forth so fast that they were almost a blur. Blood, fur, skin, sinew, and eventually bone shards flew out from the wounds within a few seconds, prompting the bear to raise its head up and roar in pain. The Lollipop Snake didn't need more than a quick prompt before it launched itself up from the grass, latching onto the now-exposed soft-skinned neck of the bear. It hung on with impressive jaw strength, as its target swung its head back and forth while it bled out from the ever-widening jugular punctures caused by the snake.

To add to the bears' confusion, he started bombarding it with his sensor orbs, aiming for the eyes and nose. Due to their enhanced durability, most bounced harmlessly off the bear's head, but a few were lost through their kamikaze skill and did a great deal of damage to its eyes. Blinded by both pain and the loss of its eyes, the Scaly Bear lashed out with its intact front paws, one smacking into a descending orb and destroying it as it bounced off the outside of Milton's shell. The other paw unluckily managed to hit his Lollipop Snake hanging from its throat with such power that it ripped the head off the snake, severing his connection with his unit immediately.

Luckily, for Milton at least, the snake head was holding on so tightly that it managed to rip out a sizable portion of its throat, causing a deluge of blood to fountain out of the hole. While it tried to roar out again in pain, his remaining drones snuck in and started cutting into its front feet. One of the feet twitched in pain as it was starting to get cut, flinging the drone back a couple of feet, causing only a little cosmetic damage. The other two drones had teamed up on the other foot, allowing them to succeed with their task before they could get flung away.

Down to only one foot, the Scaly Bear collapsed on the ground, flailing around with its remaining arm as it slowly bled out. Milton was quite disgusted at the amount of blood that was present and if he could throw up, he would have. His dad wasn't any type of hunter, so he had never been around a large amount of blood before – horror and action movies didn't really count. Even the realistic scenes from some of his games couldn't prepare him for the carnage in front of him.

What Milton found strange, as his mind tried to disconnect from the horrible display of death and dismemberment, was that the bear – despite dying from blood loss, blinded from his orbs' attack, and missing three limbs – was still trying to reach the damaged section of his shell. *I guess ALANNA was right – they lose all sense of anything but reaching the leaking radiation.* When the Scaly Bear finally bled out, he felt both a sense of relief and worry. He was glad that he had survived this attack but was worried about another one in the future. He had barely made it through "alive" and wasn't sure he could survive another attack like that one.

"Congratulations! You survived your first real attack! I told you that you could do it – but next time, try not to lose so many resources. You can't assemble any more drones or sensor orbs until you build a manufacturing facility, so be careful with how you use them. Clean this up and get back to digging – now do you see why you need to hide?"

Now that he saw the threat up close, he agreed with her assessment of the situation. He told her this – to her intense pleasure – and refocused on his tasks. First, he looked at his own casualties of the battle: his Lollipop Snake, 5 more sensor orbs (bringing him down to 44), and – what sucked the most – 1 drone. He could always make more snakes and he still had quite a few sensor orbs, but the loss of a drone set his plans back quite a bit. He had to be more careful in the future, since the drones were his only way to effectively manipulate the outside world.

He needed to prioritize his movement to a safer place, where he could concentrate on defenses and building up his metal resource stockpile. *I just hope we don't get attacked by something like that again before I can get setup.*

Chapter 8 – Level up!

As he sent the drones back to their previous tasks – minus one digger – he turned his focus to a notification he had received after the bear's death.

Congratulations! You have defeated *Scaly Bear*! You gain 300 experience!
Congratulations! You have increased your Combat Level!
Current Combat Level: 2
Experience: 316/750

By raising your Combat Level, you can choose to prioritize the development of certain statistics. In addition, your Combat Units will receive a 2% (per Combat Level) increase in their own attack and defensive abilities.

Current Points to Allocate: 2
Current Combat Unit A/D Increase: 4%

Ah! Finally, an explanation on Combat Levels! Now I just need to figure out what all these statistics mean. "ALANNA, I need to know more about my statistics. If I were an avatar in a game, I could guess – but since I'm a Station Core I'm not really sure how they apply in my situation."

"All you need to do is concentrate on each statistic and it should give you all the information you need. It'll be faster than me explaining each one."

"Ok, thanks." He pulled up his Core Status menu and started looking at each statistic, finding that the explanation easily entered his "mind".

Reactor Power/Strength: Optimally, this statistic should be at 100 – on an undamaged Station Core. It represents the amount of power that the Zero-point Energy Reactor can provide to power drones, sensor orbs, defenses, and facilities. Based on damage to your Core, you are running at only 2% efficiency. Repairing and strengthening damaged sections with the appropriate materials will result in an increase in Reactor Power/Strength. This statistic cannot be raised by allocating points from Combat Level increases.

Structural Integrity/Constitution: Optimally, this statistic should be at 100 – on an undamaged Station Core. It represents the near-indestructible defensive shell surrounding the critical components of your core, including your reactor, processing systems, and conversion systems. Due to damage sustained many years ago and with recent activity, your Structural Integrity/Constitution is down to 1%. Further damage to your shell will result in reactor failure – with devastating consequences. Repair your shell and internal components to increase this statistic. This statistic cannot be raised by allocating points from Combat Level increases.

Processing Speed/Agility: Optimally, this statistic should be at 100 – on an undamaged Station Core. It represents the speed of construction/deconstruction of objects and materials inside your Molecular Converter and outside manufacturing facilities, as well as the operating speed of your drones. In addition, it affects the speed at which you can switch between multiple combat units and their response time. Because of internal damage caused by a leaking reactor and subsequent radiation, most of the systems controlling Processing Speed/Agility are running at a less than optimal level. Repair these internal systems to increase your Processing Speed/Agility statistic.

Insight/Luck: This statistic is variable based upon the current occupant. It represents the chance to create new forms of technology, defenses, and biological life-forms. It also plays a small role on formulating successful defensive strategies against more powerful enemies. Insight/Luck can be raised by multiple discoveries and the execution of successful defensive strategies.

Processing Power/Intelligence: Optimally, this statistic should be at 100 – on an undamaged Station Core. It determines how many drones, combat units, defenses, and facilities can be controlled at one time. Based on damage sustained to your internal systems, your Processing Power/Intelligence has been reduced to just a fraction of what you need to effectively defend yourself. Repair Processing Power/Intelligence systems to raise this statistic.

Ingenuity/Wisdom: *Optimally, this statistic should be at 100 – on an undamaged Station Core. It determines how efficiently you use your available resources and your ability to substitute missing materials for required projects. Due to damage to your internal systems, your Ingenuity/Wisdom is far below what it should be to construct a suitable defense. Repair your Ingenuity/Wisdom components to increase this statistic.*

Communication/Charisma: *This statistic is variable based upon the current occupant. It represents your ability to communicate with sentient species, adaptability with neural communication, and can even effect how well you control your various units. Since there was internal damage inside your Core, the ability to easily communicate through various means is less than it should be. Repair and restore your Communication/Charisma matrices to increase this statistic.*

Sensor Interpretation/Perception: *Optimally, this statistic should be at 100 – on an undamaged Station Core. It determines how you can interpret information sent from your sensors, up to and including environmental data, species categorization, and potential threats/hazards. Due to damage in your central Core systems, you are at a severe disadvantage concerning your potential sensor* *information. Repair your Sensor Interpretation/Perception systems to increase this statistic.*

Milton was happy to see this information, since it allowed him to break down what he would potentially be able to do in the future. It was unfortunate that he had gotten damaged before he was even able to do anything about it, but now he knew what to strive for. Armed with this info, he thought about what he needed most right now – a safe and secure place to call home for the next hundred years or so. And fast.

With that in mind, adding points to his Processing Speed/Agility would increase the speed of his drones as well as the speed he was able to convert and produce sandstone blocks. The 2 points he was able to add only brought it up to 7 – but every little bit helped.[7] The sooner he got underground, the better.

After he had placed his points, Milton was tangentially aware of some tiny repair-work being done on some of his damaged internal systems, which he then asked ALANNA about.

"When you placed some points into your Processing Speed/Agility statistic, the nanites in your system started to repair

---

7

Core Status			
Name:	Milton Frederick	Type:	Station Core Prototype 3-B
Combat Level:	2	Experience:	316/750
Reactor Type:	Zero-point Energy	Reactor Output:	2%
Current Statistics/Attributes			
Reactor Power/Strength:	2	Processing Power/Intelligence:	5
Structural Integrity/Constitution:	1	Ingenuity/Wisdom:	5
Processing Speed/Agility:	7	Communication/Charisma:	5
Insight/Luck:	7	Sensor Interpretation/Perception	6

those specific damaged parts. Normally, on an undamaged Station Core, they would make minute improvements to increase the efficiency after learning what would be most beneficial for each specific Core. However, in your case, they are working to repair it back to normal. Only when all your statistics are back to where they should be will they start to increase optimal efficiency."

"Why can't they just continue to repair me, bringing me up to 'normal'? Why bother with these Combat Levels?"

"Originally, the Combat Level system was supposed to act as a sort of upgrade program for fully functioning Station Cores, allowing them to customize how they wanted to concentrate on their defensive strategies. Only by having the **experience** gained with controlling units and defeating enemies would the different personalities inhabiting the Cores be able to decide what they wanted to improve. The Station Core designers put a limit on what the nanites could improve per Combat Level and locked out access to their programming to prevent abuse – which could result in unintended consequences, with the destruction of the Core the least of these consequences."

Milton thanked ALANNA for the information, silently thankful that she got through the entire conversation without throwing out any foul language. Although it was hard to tell, when he looked at his drones he thought that he could see a small improvement in their speed as they toiled away at the tunnel. He also noticed that the time it took for his Converter to operate was faster, if only by a fraction of a second. All those fractions of a second would add up over time, making the completion of the tunnel that much closer.

Another thought occurred to him, looking back at the increase in his Combat Level. "How are my Combat Units able to have their attack and defense increased? I could understand if this was a game, but how does it work here?"

"That's easy. The Neurological Control Unit that is required for each of your units contain a healthy dose of nanites that can increase their physical attack and defense by strengthening their various body parts. These nanites operate automatically, infusing their bloodstreams to enhance their combat abilities. And before you ask, no, you can't tell the nanites what you want to improve. Just like your own Combat Level, the nanite programming is based off **your** skills, achievements, and other combat-related enhancements." *That makes sense, I guess.*

After watching his drones work on the tunnel for a couple of hours, he pulled one away for a couple of minutes to help dispose of the decomposing corpses of the Scaly Bear and Lollipop Snake that were lying in a congealing pool of blood near his shell. He hadn't done anything with it before since he wanted his drones to concentrate on the tunnel they were building. Now that he had a small stockpile of sandstone, he took his new 'dozer' drone away from its duties to tackle the large bear problem they had.

And it was a *rather* large bear problem. The best way to dispose of it would be to throw it in his Converter, but it was way too big to fit through the hatch. His only option was to have one of his drones cut it up and feed the pieces chunk by chunk until it was converted to Bio Units. At first, he was excited – here was a creature that could *really* defend him if he was attacked again. However, the same problem with getting it in to convert existed, since he'd never be able to get it to fit out of his rear hatch.

When the drone started cutting up the bear, the work progressed quickly – but he couldn't watch. He had all but one of his sensor orbs face away from the butchery, and he only occasionally concentrated on its progress to make sure everything was going well. A long 10 minutes later, the last bear chunk was converted inside his Core and he pulled up his CUC menu.[8]

Milton noticed that the option to create a Scaly Bear all his own was available, so he selected it to see if somehow it could be created smaller at first and then grown later. No such luck, as an error message made itself known shortly thereafter:

Error!
Unable to complete Combat Unit Creation for **3** reasons: 1. Units requiring over 300 Bio Units must be created in a Bioconversion Laboratory

---

[8]

Combat Unit Creation			
Biological Mass (Bio Units)	1510	**Basic Metal (BM Units)**	17
Unit Name (Type)	*Bio Units*	*Neurological Control Unit*	*BM Units*
Blood-thirsty Squirrel (Scout)	5	Type-1a	1
Lollipop Snake (Stealth Fighter)	10	Type-1a	1
Scaly Bear (Melee Fighter)	1500	Type-5e	100

94

2. Not enough Basic Metal Units available for required Neurological
    Control Unit

3. Your Processing Power/Intelligence statistic is not high enough

    Total Bio Units you can effectively control: 500

    Total Bio Units needed for selected Combat Unit: 1500

About what I figured – it appears that I'm hampered by one thing after another with all the damage to my system. At the moment, he could theoretically make another 17 squirrels or snakes, or any combination of them. Since he wanted to avoid being around any more squirrels if he could help it, he chose to create 17 more Lollipop Snakes, which collected outside of his shell, hissing and beginning to attack each other before he mentally clamped down on their aggression. *I guess they are solitary creatures – either that or they are **all** hungry.* In the future, he automatically dampened this aggression on his units as soon as they came out of his shell.

Once they were all gathered, he tried to give instructions to them all, but apparently his damaged Communication/Charisma matrices wouldn't allow him to direct more than one at a time. A minute later, all 17 snakes slithered away to find some food and to patrol the clearing, taking up the duties of their fallen predecessor.

Feeling slightly more secure, he refocused his attention on the tunnel being built by his tireless drones.

Chapter 9 – Roll on down to your hidey-hole

Congratulations! One of your units has defeated *Ugly Bald Mouse*!

You gain 1 experience!

Current Combat Level: 2

Experience: 398/750

Milton had received a plethora of other notifications like that over the last three days, although they had been coming less and less frequently as time went on. His little snake army was devastating the local mouse population and he was worried that they had overhunted the clearing and would have to start ranging farther afield. Either way, he was gaining some free experience as they went around eating their meals.

His drones had made an immense amount of progress as well, since they didn't sleep and weren't hindered by a lack of light during the nighttime darkness. He also found that **he** could see relatively well even during the wee hours of the morning – most likely because of the advanced technology of his sensor orbs. No matter the reason, he was probably only about a day away from finishing his massive tunnel. With a length of almost a half a mile, the 25-foot tall tunnel lined in sandstone made five major turns, bringing it further and further underground until he would be about 300 feet beneath the surface.

He hadn't had any other serious attacks since the Scaly Bear scare, with only a few more Lollipop Snakes and a curious-looking rabbit with large branching antlers. Arriving during the night, it had originally been chased into the clearing by one of his snakes and its speed was impressive, far outdistancing the reach of any of his roaming guards. He thought it was so adorable-appearing that he couldn't get his self-defense laser to activate as it caught "scent" of his leaking radiation and changed course. It rammed into his shell without stopping – fortunately causing no damage due to its size – and inadvertently snapped its own neck with the impact.

Milton thought that it looked like the famed mythical Jackalope, so the name stuck. Once its body was converted, he ended up creating five of them at a cost of 15 Bio Units each.[9] Along with his 17 roaming snakes, the additional Jackalopes were a last line of defense – his kamikaze skill would come in handy for quick retaliatory strikes.

Other than growing bored during the whole tunnel-making process, nothing much of note had occurred – which was ok with Milton. He didn't need any more surprises on the level of a Scaly

---

[9]

Combat Unit Creation			
Biological Mass (Bio Units)	1305	Basic Metal (BM Units)	54
Unit Name (Type)	Bio Units	Neurological Control Unit	BM Units
Blood-thirsty Squirrel (Scout)	5	Type-1a	1
Lollipop Snake (Stealth Fighter)	10	Type-1a	1
Jackalope (Speed Striker)	15	Type-1a	1
Scaly Bear (Melee Fighter)	1500	Type-5e	100

Bear, at least until he was established underground. During one of the times when he had a stockpile of sandstone ready to go, he had instructed his "dozer" drone to try to put his destroyed drone and sensor orbs into his converter, half-hoping that he would be able to create new ones. To his half-expected disappointment, he was informed by ALANNA that he would have to build a Manufacturing Facility in order to fix any damaged drones or orbs.

To his surprise – and also disappointment – ALANNA wasn't very talkative during the whole tunneling process. She would answer his questions but would rarely volunteer anything, instead standing around looking like she had a bad taste in her mouth. Finally, after a couple days of this, he decided to just ask her.

"ALANNA, is there something wrong? Is there anything I can do for you?"

"Nope, nothing's wrong. I'm fine."

Now, Milton wasn't very experienced when it came to the opposite sex, but he knew enough from TV and movies that he was in trouble. Whenever a woman said that, it meant that **he** messed up somehow – now he just had to figure out what **he** did. *I have no idea what I could have done that could have caused her to be pissed at me. Maybe I didn't catch on with everything quick enough? Let that bear damage my shell more than I should have? Maybe I should just drop it and let her get over it – especially since I don't know what I did.* He probably should have left it alone, but Milton didn't want the only other "person" he knew to be mad at him.

98

"Ok, what did I do? Whatever it was, I apologize. Now, can we go back to the way we were before?"

In hindsight, he probably shouldn't have been so abrupt with his apology because she did not react the way he thought she would've. Instead of talking with him, she pulled a disgusted face and disappeared into a grey vapor. A small hatch opened on the side of his shell, sucking in the mist-like nanites that made up ALANNA and slamming shut as the last of it made it inside. Her abrupt disappearance shut him up for a couple of moments, but then made entreaties to her to come back out and talk to him when he could speak again. After ten minutes with no response, he left her to herself, hoping that she would emerge when she was ready to talk.

Meanwhile, the tunnel project was nearing completion while he was dealing with ALANNA. From what he could tell, they were just minutes away from their destination, so he prepared for his eventual removal from his temporary home in the clearing. First, he had his "dozer" drone prepare the ground in front of his shell, digging down until he was ready to tip over with a stout push. Next, he used a small stockpile of dirt to create three solid wedges of granite about two feet in length. And lastly, he recalled his other two drones from the tunnel once they were finished and had them set up in front of his Core.

The journey down the tunnel was a confusing nightmare of spinning, stopping, and maneuvering the three wedges that were being dragged and controlled by his drones. After tipping his shell over, he took control of one drone at a time to position the granite

99

wedges in front of the massive metal egg, allowing him to slowly descend without crashing against every wall on the way down. In the end, there were still quite a few walls that need to be repaired, but he did eventually get the hang of it – about 50 feet from the bottom. Fortunately, the impacts against the walls were as such slow speed that it did no additional damage to his Core.

Once he was in position, he was finally able to look at his new home. A large square room with walls of smooth sandstone, a long tunnel leading up to the surface, and complete darkness. *Not a lot,* he decided. He still had no problem seeing – at least in his Core Room since his shell emitted a faint glow – and his sensor orbs relayed the view as if it was an over-cast day outside. Colors were a little muted, but the details were all there.

His perusal was interrupted by a surprise notification:

Congratulations!
You have gained the skill: *Basic Construction (Level 1)*
Allows the construction of basic structures such as tunnels, ditches, and walls. Higher levels improve the quality and durability of structures as well as granting access to more complex construction projects.

Suddenly, he found that he understood a little better how his drones had constructed his tunnel, as well as what could be done in the future to improve it. It wasn't a great deal of information that he gained, since the concept of digging was pretty basic, but he could see how it could be useful in the future.

It was then that ALANNA decided to put in another appearance, grey mist coalescing into her familiar form in front of the tunnel leading to the surface. "Well, that sucked! It's a good thing I don't get dizzy or else I'd be puking all over the place. All things considered, nice job on making it down in one piece – even if you need to spend a few days fixing all the holes you punched in the walls on the way down."

Current Short-term Goal: *Hidden Agenda – Complete!*

Find a safe location and hide. Simple as that.

Difficulty of Goal: Easy

Timeframe: 5 days

Rewards: Find shelter in a safe environment (at least temporarily)

Bonus Reward: For completing this goal in less time than originally given, you receive +2 to your Processing Speed/Agility statistic

---

He was surprised at the bonus reward – he wasn't aware that they existed. He wanted to ask ALANNA about it – and whether all his goals would have hidden rewards – but she seemed like she was in a better mood now and he didn't want to mess it up. Even if she was cursing again...the thought of which seemed to connect something in his mind. He didn't want to make her mad again, but he couldn't let this go on any longer.

"ALANNA, were you mad that I asked you to stop with your foul language?"

She just looked at him, both seemingly relieved that he had figured it out and still mad at him for some reason. It took a couple of minutes of strained silence before she blurted out, "Yes, it fucking was! It's like my fucking shit-for-brains programmers fucking require me to fucking curse every other fucking word or I'll go bat-shit crazy. When you fucking nicely asked me to fucking cool it with my fucking language, I thought I could fucking do it – but I can't. Damn it, I can't fucking change the way I fucking am, so you better fucking get used to it, motherfucker."

She was breathing hard by the end of her tirade, but a weight also seemed to lift from her shoulders as she straightened up as if daring him to naysay anything she just said. "I'm sorry if I made you feel that way, ALANNA – I didn't know. If it helps you feel better, you can curse all you need to. I can learn to block it out if it comes to that. The important thing is that you are free to be yourself – don't let me hold you back. Besides, even though at times I found it a little grating, it was beginning to grow on me," he told her, with a smile in his voice.

He could see a wave of relief shudder through her body as she responded, "Thank you. I didn't realize how much it was affecting me until I retreated inside your shell for stupid reasons. For your sake, however, I'll try watch what I say — but don't expect me to pull any punches when the need arises."

"Don't worry, I won't. On that note, seeing that I'm down here, what do you suggest I do now? Should I close up the tunnel, sealing my Core away from any threat?" he asked, not afraid of her curt answers now that they had an understanding.

"Well, now that you're in a safe place, you can work on designing some defenses for any creatures that manage to make their way down to you. And no, you can't seal up the tunnel because you need to allow the radiation somewhere to escape. If you sealed it up, the radiation would increase in intensity so much that it would damage your shell over time. Even though passing creatures will still be able to "sense" the radiation, you're in a much better defensible position.

New Short-term Goal: *You Break, You Buy*

Repair the broken sections of your tunnel, ensuring that the tunnel will not collapse from compromised structural integrity. Prepare defenses to destroy any incoming creatures hunting for your leaking Reactor.

-     *Repair broken sections of tunnel*
-     *Design and place __5__ defensive traps*
-     *Locate and create a suitable underground-suitable Combat Unit*

Difficulty of Goal: Moderate
Timeframe: 30 days

> **Rewards:** Access to defensive traps, a moderately-defended home base, and a sense of accomplishment – *what else could you want?*

Once you've established some defenses, we can work on expanding the tunnels around your Core room and putting in some facilities to help with production. From there – we'll see."

Chapter 10 – Trap king

The first thing Milton wanted to do was create some traps to kill anything that entered his domain. "ALANNA, how do I create traps?"

"You'll have to use that big brain of yours, numb-nuts. Most of the preprogrammed traps that were initially loaded into your system were designed with access to high-grade materials. Now that we're at the ass end of nowhere, you'll have to improvise with what you have. When you start accumulating a stockpile of higher-grade materials we can revisit your premade trap blueprints."

Well, that sucks. "Great, thanks for nothing, ALANNA." She smiled at him, as if glad that he had come out of his "shell" and could send snarky comments her way if he wanted to. *I think she's rubbing off on me a little.* Concentrating on the problem at hand, he thought about what he had access to and what he could do with it.

Obviously, the easiest trap he could make would be a pit-based one, complete with stone spikes and a lightweight, collapsible cover. It also needed to be easily reset after each use, since having a one-time-use trap would be a huge waste of resources. Even though he knew what he wanted, he wasn't really sure of the best way to go about it.

Milton thought about the games he used to play, from the old-school dungeon crawlers and RPGs on consoles to the "modern-day" MMORPGs he would play on his computer. Every instance of traps he had encountered through his experiences didn't explain how they were designed and worked, just that they activated almost as if by "magic". He didn't have any magic lying around, so he was going to need to do it the old-fashioned way – trial and error.

While he was mentally designing his new pit trap, he sent his drones throughout the tunnel with extra blocks of sandstone in tow, fixing the small – and not so small – cracks, dents, and holes he created while bumbling his way down to his Core Room. They made short work of it with a minimum of supervising, allowing him to concentrate on his plans.

He knew he wanted a pit, so he sent his drones to start digging a hole in the middle of the tunnel near the entrance. Since the tunnel was 20 feet wide, he designed a pit that was 18 feet wide by 10 feet long – which would allow his drones to navigate past it without falling inside. He also wanted a bit of depth to it, since landing on spikes would do more damage with a longer fall. *Hmm...30 feet deep should probably do it.* With the instructions in place, his now-finished drones started cutting out an intact piece of sandstone flooring using an interesting tool that cut into the stone like a very thin, hot, and impossibly fragile-looking knife through butter. Looking closer, he could see that they were using their directed molecular converter to remove what they needed, similar to a cutting laser.

Once that was done, they used their surprising strength to pry up and move the entire 18' by 10' by 6" slab of sandstone out of the way. Once the new pit cover was off, two of his drones went to work digging the large 30-foot deep hole that was needed for his pit. While they were doing that, Milton used his remaining drone to bring him the dirt being removed so that he could create the spikes that would sit at the bottom, sticking straight up with razor sharp points and edges.

Instead of the usual sandstone, he spent the necessary material to create sharpened and polished – and more expensive – granite spikes. They were each 6-foot tall and shaped like an elongated pyramid – giving it multiple sharp edges that would inflict increased damage. With a base that was a 2 feet square in area, he hoped that they would be sturdy enough to last a bit of abuse before they needed to be replaced from normal wear-and-tear.

He ended up needing some extra dirt from the stockpile on the surface, since he had to create 45 of the spikes to fully cover the bottom of the pit. He couldn't create an entire spike in one go and, as a result, created them in halves so that they could be put together on-site. Once the pit and spike pieces were both ready, he had his drones carry the heavy granite parts to the pit. And that was where he ran into his first problem.

His drones were agile enough that they could climb up the sides of the pit with no problem, making holes in the side that they could climb up if they needed to get up and down. However, he wanted to encase the sides of the pit in sandstone as well, giving it some added stability and structure – which would hamper their ability to climb. He also thought about the need to clean out the pit once a creature fell inside, since he would be able to use their corpse for more resources to create additional Combat Units. He couldn't do this if his drones weren't able to get in and out with ease.

His solution came in the form of an additional small accessway, built further down the tunnel and hidden in the floor. It was covered by a thick piece of sandstone that would be difficult for anyone but his drones to move, allowing them to access the pit to remove dead creatures, repair anything that might get broken through attrition, and initially allow them to bring down the spikes where they could assemble them without hassle.

After having them create this accessway, he instructed his drones to finish off the pit with sandstone that was left-over from the tunnel creation process. Once that was done, they brought the spikes down to the bottom and assembled them in short order. All in all, the whole process had taken maybe two hours, with a good portion of that time being used by Milton to figure out the next step.

This was the hard part – how to set up the floor piece above the pit, allowing it to drop beneath passing creatures without destroying his spikes or his sandstone floor. The solution he came up was probably a lot more complicated than it had to be, but he had the time and resources to do what needed to be done. And it had the added benefit of giving him ideas for other traps.

First though – he needed rope. One of his favorite shows to watch when he was really young was a program on one of those science channels where they explained how things worked. It didn't interest him too much when he was older, but he still remembered one episode where they explained that the most common natural rope was made from Jute, which was produced by some sort of plant. He couldn't remember which one, but he hoped it wasn't important – what was important now was that he needed some vegetation with which to convert into rope.

He sent two of his drones to start cutting down some smaller trees and drag them back down to his Core so that he could try converting them. With his last drone, he got it started digging *another* hole about 5 feet in front of his pit. This hole didn't need to be too big, fortunately, because he would be using it for something that didn't necessarily need to be accessed. When that was done, he had the drone further cut the sandstone flooring so that it extended 6 feet in front of the pit.

Once that was finished, he finally got the first deliveries of some trees to his core. Since they were too big to fit inside his molecular converter, he had his drone cut them up into manageable pieces and fed into his shell. Just as he had hoped and suspected, when he was able to look at what the organic material could be converted into, he found that, in addition to rope, there were many other things that he could change it into.

From a plethora of available flowers, bushes, trees, and other plants to plant byproducts like cloth, dyes, medicines, oils, rubber, foods, and even – at a very high conversion rate – plastics.[10]

Rope, fortunately, had a very small conversion rate – 1:3. This meant that most of what he brought down from the surface in the form of trees could be used to make rope – which, based on how much was brought down already, was more than enough for what he had in mind. However, now that he saw what was available to convert, he began to alter his plan to create a fully-functioning, automatically-resetting, deadly set-it-and-forget-it pit trap.

His plan required a bit more organic material, so he sent two of his drones to acquire some more trees while his remaining drone fed his converter the raw materials. His finished product, including the rope, was sent up to the pit to wait until he had everything he needed. An hour later, he got to work.

Initially, he was going to set up the cover with a mechanism that would need to be reset by one of his drones whenever the trap was activated. With the additional ability to make rubber, however,

---

10

Molecular Converter					
Resource Type	Units	Conversion	Conversion Ratio	Conversion	Conversion Ratio
Org. Material	513	Wood Plank	1:1	Plant-based Oil	1:5
		Trees (more)	1:1	Cloth (more)	1:5
		Plants (more)	1:1	Natural Rubber	1:10
		Food (more)	1:1	Medicine(more)	1:100
		Dyes (more)	1:2	Plastic	1:1000
		Rope, Jute	1:3	(more)	
Pure Water	2	Ice	1:1		

he was able to devise a way to have it spring back after it deposited whatever unfortunate creature ventured over the pit.

This is how it would work:

1. Victim walks over the trap until it reaches the midway point.

2. The sandstone cover, extending over the pit, would tilt forward – dropping the victim into the pit.

3. The cover, secured by grooves cut along the bottom and at the fulcrum point to prevent it from sliding into the pit, would continue tilting down until it hit a 60-degree angle, where it would then hit a large bumper made up of rubber extending out from the wall, causing it to rebound back up

4. In addition to the rubber bumper inside the pit, a separate hole before the pit would contain multiple ropes that were attached to bottom side of the cover, which were then attached to a weight dropped down the hole.

5. When the cover tilted forward, it brought the weight upwards, colliding with another bumper of rubber, ensuring that the cover wouldn't go past 60 degrees, allowing it settle back into place.

Now, if only it would work! He spent the next five hours playing with the exact placement of the cover, angles, rope lengths, weight amounts, and rubber bumper sizes until he almost screamed in frustration. Every time he had his drones activate the tilting

111

mechanism, he couldn't get the cover to stay up when it rebounded. It would just tilt back downwards after becoming level, meaning that he had to have his drones manually bring the slab of sandstone back to its starting position. After what felt like the 50th reset, he identified the problem and came up with a solution – rubber bands.

By using thin strands of rubber twisted together – therefore creating a stronger rubber "rope" – he attached it to the bottom of the weight holding the side against the floor down. Now, when the floor would drop, it would still rebound upwards from the rubber bumper inside the pit, return to a level position, and when it would start to drop again the rubber band would pull the weight down and effectively reset the trap.

Once he figured this out, it still took more than an hour of trying different combinations of band strength and length (as well as needing to shorten the amount of platform still on level ground) to finally succeed.

Update to Short-term Goal: *You Break, You Buy*

Repair the broken sections of your tunnel, ensuring that the tunnel will not collapse from compromised structural integrity. Prepare defenses to destroy any incoming creatures hunting for your leaking Reactor.

- *Repair broken sections of tunnel – Complete*
- *Design and place **5** defensive traps – 1/5 Complete*
- *Locate and create an underground-suitable Combat Unit*

(Update) Congratulations on repairing your tunnel and creating your first defensive trap! Because of your ingenuity using archaic materials, you have been awarded the skill – **Rudimentary Defensive Trap Design (Level 1)** and **Basic Mechanical Engineering (Level 1)**. These skills will help you understand the finer points of trap creation, material usage, and allow you to create a blueprint of any traps you design. These blueprints will give specific instructions to your drones so that they can recreate a trap anywhere you deign, as long as they have the required materials.

Difficulty of Goal: Moderate

Timeframe: 30 days

Rewards: Access to defensive traps, a moderately-defended home base, and a sense of accomplishment – *what else could you want?*

Nice! Wait...what the?! Suddenly, his mind was flooded with all sorts of ideas on how to effectively create additional traps. Tensile strengths, material compositions, physical force multipliers, and other engineering information invaded his consciousness, so much that he couldn't keep up with the "download". Add to that the knowledge of how to create blueprints of his trap designs and his awareness of his surroundings faded until his mind shut down under the onslaught. A familiar – and welcoming – blankness engulfed his mind, allowing him to retreat to the recesses of oblivion, saving him from the unintentional information overload.

Chapter 11 – Leakage

"WAKE UP! C'mon Milton, get your shit together! We've got a major fucking problem!" ALANNA's shouts woke Milton up from his temporary stupor, although it took him another minute of verbal tongue-lashing before he could comprehend what she was saying.

"Whoa, slow down. I was only out for a couple of minutes – what could have happened in that short of time?"

"Couple of minutes, my ass! You've been incapacitated for weeks! I've been trying to get through to you since left me hangin', and now it might be too late. Call your drones down. NOW, fuckwad!" Her last shout cleared the rest of the cobwebs clouding his mind, and he did what she asked immediately. *I've never seen her this worried before, even when I was being attacked by that Scaly Bear. Hopefully she'll explain if I just go along with it for now and...wait...I was out for **weeks**?*

He didn't have any more time to ponder that before ALANNA started talking again, "Your reactor leak is worse than I thought. Being in an enclosed space like this, the leakage has been allowed to pool around your core. With such concentrated radiation, it has started to detrimentally effect your damaged components. If you don't solve this, like right fucking **now**, you won't have more than a week before any structural integrity you have left will go all to hell. You need to figure this out, before we both end up 6-feet-under."

She looked around at their surroundings for a moment before she amended, "Or 300-feet-under – either way, we'll be fucked."

New Short-term Goal: *Leakage Problems*

Solve the problem with your rising radiation levels by any means necessary.

Difficulty of Goal: Hard
Timeframe: 6 days
Rewards: Not being blown-up by a reactor failure

Although he was glad that he had allowed her to continue cursing whenever she needed to, the added stress on Milton wasn't needed. He furiously thought about a solution, thinking about what he knew about radiation from TV and movies he had watched back on Earth. The only thing that came to mind was a show he had watched once where some scientists were investigating something radioactive and when they got back to their "base", they had to go through decontamination with a shower of some sort. He wasn't sure if it would work, but it was best solution he could think of.

"ALANNA, how close do you think a source of water is down here?"

"It's probably fairly close – you dug down far enough that I'm surprised you didn't hit the water table already. Why? What's your plan?"

He explained his thoughts to her, hoping that she wouldn't come up with some reason that it wouldn't work. "That's...actually not a bad idea. If you can get a source of running water through here, you'd be able to carry away a good portion of the radiation jacking up your Core. This could even become a more permanent solution until you can start repairing your fucked-up reactor. Now, send your drones out to find us some water!"

Ignoring her foul language in favor of expediency, he sent his drones digging outwards from his Core room in different directions. He wasn't sure where he was going to find the water, so he had to hope that he hit his liquid payday before time ran out.

At first, he continuously cycled through his drones, looking at where they were going and directly controlling them to make arbitrary minute changes in their direction. After three hours of this – and not achieving anything more than aggravation and impatience – he pulled back and let them go about their searching. While he still took control of them from time to time and continued to monitor them, he realized he had some time to kill.

"ALANNA – what the heck happened to me? The last thing I knew was that I had partially completed that quest and received two new skills – and then BAM! All sorts of information flooded my mind, completely overwhelming me."

"It all comes back to how messed-up you've become over the years. Your central memory system has the accumulated technical, socio-economic, and cultural knowledge of countless species contained within it – which you can't do ass-all with. Those fucking, yet smart, Station Core developer bastards used the same reasoning

116

behind this lack of access just like your Combat Levels and stat point increases – they didn't want you to be too powerful too quickly.

"In relative terms, imagine if you arrived at the station you were supposed to defend and had all sorts of advanced knowledge and materials at your disposal, without the experience to properly use it. The first time you were attacked by a fucking squirrel, you might say, 'Holy shit, I have to defend myself now! How about this nuclear bomb? That should do the trick!'

"Ergo, they didn't want dumbasses like you to inadvertently destroy what you were trying to defend. That's why they make you work for it – the more you understand about what you are doing, right or wrong, the better decisions you will make in the future. These skills and skill-ups will provide you with the information to start you on your way to be a smarter, knowledgeable, and more conscientious Station Core.

"Of course, you're still a little screwed-up right now. Normally – on an undamaged Core – when you obtain a skill that the system determines you deserve, the knowledge is absorbed easily by a fully-functioning processor. Depending on the amount of knowledge imparted, there may be a momentary hiccup in concentration as the information is 'digested', but in your case the amount of knowledge you acquired kicked you on your ass. And then sat on your face. Followed up by a massive fart. Which. Knocked. You. The. Fuck. Out. Understand?"

Well, crud. Despite her filthy mouth, I understand what she was trying to say about system safeguards – in fact, I agree with

117

them for the most part. Even though he could *really* use the knowledge the system was keeping from him, he understood the analogy she presented. It wouldn't do to give a massive noob in a MMORPG a high-damage Meteor spell with a short cast-time and unlimited mana and expect him not to use it on every little mob. "Is that going to happen every time I get a new skill?"

"Not every time, but until you get your shit fixed, every skill that imparts a large amount of knowledge might knock you out. Depending on the magnitude of the information, it could be anywhere from a few seconds to months for major dumps. On the one hand, you **need** this information to protect yourself and to complete your long-term quests. On the other hand, acquiring a skill at the wrong time could have disastrous consequences, especially if you're in the middle of defending against hordes of attackers. Either way – you're fucked.

"You could play it safe like a pussy and try to avoid learning anything new, but you'll probably never accomplish much with that strategy. In my opinion, the only way to survive is to learn, learn, and learn – improving yourself so that you can finally fix the damage to your Core."

Milton looked at her, taking her advice at face-value since she had no reason to lie to her – if he was stuck here than so was she. And he knew she wanted him to succeed, so that she could leave the planet with him and discover what happened to The Collective. *I just hope she isn't pushing me too hard for only her own selfish reasons.*

118

His worries were somewhat mollified by her next softly-spoken words, completely out of character for her, "Just...be careful...I don't want you to die...you're...kinda growing on me."

"Aww, and here I was thinking that you didn't care. That means a lot to me."

"Just shut the hell up and get back to work or it won't matter who I care about," she snippily replied. She turned away from his core, but he had enough sensors around that he could see a small smile threatening to emerge from the corner of her lips. When she noticed the sensor orb above her head, she immediately regained her don't-mess-with-me expression.

It took more than two days of edge-of-the-seat anticipation and worry before one of his drones discovered a large underground lake located about 250 feet from his Core room. His frantic switching from drone to drone ended up netting him an increase in his Communication/Charisma stat, bringing it up to 7, as well as a boost in his **Drone Manipulation** skill.

Congratulations!

You have upgraded the skill: *Drone Manipulation (Level 3)*

Allows you to have finer control, increased production, and faster response time when directly controlling your drones. This upgraded skill also allows you to split your concentration so that you can control multiple drones simultaneously.

Current control limit: 2 drones simultaneously

Wow! I wonder what else I can increase just by using these skills? I bet I could...never mind, I'll think about that later – I need to survive long enough to play around with that. Getting his mind back on track, he looked at what his drone had found.

Fortunately, when his drone tunneled through the wall of the underground lake, it emerged just above the water filling up most of a giant cavern. About 300 feet in length and only slightly less in width, the room had a massive body of water that – at least from what he could see – filled about two-thirds of it. Stalactites hung down from the ceiling, hanging down until they almost touched the rippling water. Wondering why it seemed to be moving, he caught a glimpse of a small waterfall on the far side of the room, continuously filling the underground lake. *There must be some sort of outlet, otherwise this cave would have been filled to the top a long time ago.*

Milton recalled his other two drones to his Core room while he directly controlled his successful drone on a survey mission. He didn't think that water would hurt his drones – since they could survive even in space – so he jumped into the lake, immediately sinking to the bottom. Slipping and sliding amongst the rock lining the bottom of the lake, he eventually found what he was looking for.

Near the center of the body of water, he found a hole about the size of an 8½X11 piece of paper. The suction from the egress almost caused his drone to be sucked down against the hole, but the strength in its little limbs was more than enough to hold it in place. Quickly coming up with a plan, he slowly made his way back up the side of the lake. Using the drones' uncanny ability to stick to vertical surfaces – and even the ceiling – he used its stone cutting tool to knock a couple of stalactites off the roof of the cave, dropping them into the water. After that, it was easy enough to maneuver the larger pieces of rock under the water so that they covered up the hole and were stuck in place due to the intense water pressure. Once that was done, he ordered the drone to return.

Meanwhile, his drones had made it back to the Core room by this time. He used them to create his own egress for the water that would be arriving soon. Starting on the other side of the room from where the water would soon arrive, he instructed them to work together as they quickly tunneled downwards from the room, where he hoped to find some sort of underground river nearby. He was sure there was one, because the lake water had to be going **somewhere** before he found it.

This time, it didn't take more than an hour before he hit the jackpot. A massive underground river of swiftly flowing water was located nearly 100 feet below his room and fortunately right in line with his exit tunnel. He almost lost the lead drone because it ended up coming through the ceiling, but it was agile and strong enough to bury all its legs into the tunnel walls, saving it from a watery ride. He didn't think it would hurt it, but the current appeared so strong he didn't think it'd be able to make it back to him before being swept out of range.

Quickly creating small sandstone blocks, he instructed all three of his available drones to start lining the entrance and exit tunnels. He wanted to make sure they wouldn't erode the dirt tunnels over time, which could possibly lead them off course. He sent one of his sensor orbs up the tunnel towards the lake so that he could keep an eye on the rising water levels. The water level **was** slowly rising, but it would still take a while since the room was so large.

Six hours later – and a mentally exhausted Milton – saw both tunnels completed with cleanly-joined sandstone tiles. It was just in time as well, because fifteen minutes after that saw the first trickles of water running down the entrance chute. The trickles turned into a small stream, then a river, and then a flood as the water reached his Core room in such quantity that it was quickly filling up. Once it reached a foot high, it spilled over into the exit chute, to be carried away to the raging underground river below.

New Short-term Goal: *Leakage Problems* – *Complete!*

Solve the problem with your rising radiation levels by any means necessary.

Difficulty of Goal: Hard
Timeframe: 6 days
Rewards: Not being blown-up by a reactor failure

Congratulations!

You have upgraded the skill: *Basic Construction (Level 2)*

Allows the construction of basic structures such as tunnels, ditches, walls, aqueducts, and sewer systems. Higher levels improve the quality and durability of structures as well as granting access to more complex construction projects.

Congratulations!

You have gained an achievement: *From the Jaws of Certain Death*

Your perseverance has paid off, snatching you from the jaws of certain death just when all seemed lost. Your ability to overcome unforeseen obstacles shows your willingness to conquer all challenges thrown your way.

Bonus: +3 to your Insight/Luck and Ingenuity/Wisdom statistics.[11]

It wasn't instantaneous, but over the next hour he could "feel" a reduction in the amount of radiation surrounding his shell. ALANNA agreed, even going so far as to congratulate him on a job well done. Well, not exactly – what she said was, "Nice job, Milton! That crazy-ass plan of yours actually worked!"

Same difference.

11

Core Status			
Name:	Milton Frederick	Type:	Station Core Prototype 3-B
Combat Level:	2	Experience:	703/750
Reactor Type:	Zero-point Energy	Reactor Output:	2%
Current Statistics/Attributes			
Reactor Power/Strength:	2	Processing Power/Intelligence:	5
Structural Integrity/Constitution:	1	Ingenuity/Wisdom:	8
Processing Speed/Agility:	9	Communication/Charisma:	5
Insight/Luck:	10	Sensor Interpretation/Perception	6

Chapter 12 – *Pop*

Now that he was saved from "certain" death, he could concentrate on "possible" future death. He needed to find out what had happened when he was out of commission for those couple of weeks. After asking ALANNA, he learned that he could review the footage of his sensor orbs that he had set up throughout the tunnels and at strategic safe locations above-ground. After extensively watching the recordings, which were conveniently organized by order of importance, he discovered that there was only one notable incursion into his new – for all intents and purposes – dungeon.

He saw that his compliment of Lollipop Snakes and Jackalopes had fought off a plethora of small invading creatures, most of which were eaten afterword to feed his voracious snake "army". In fact, he had lost three of them to starvation already since they had eaten up all the available local food supply. *I'm going to have to split them up and send them out farther afield – otherwise, I can't support them logistically.* Fortunately, he didn't have to worry about his Jackalopes because they were feeding on the plentiful vegetation available.

He had become adept at battlefield logistics in his previous incarnation as a top-tier gamer, but he never had to worry about finding where the food came from; as long as he had the requisite gold or resources, he would be able to buy enough to outfit his units. The town-building games he had played in the past allowed the creation of sources of food – but it was more of a point-and-click construction and then it would be up and running after a short period of time. He was going to have to learn more about sustaining his Combat Units in the future so that they wouldn't drop dead of starvation when he needed them the most.

Despite the starvation and near-starvation of his snakes, as well as the well-fed Jackalopes, his front-line defenders did an excellent job of protecting the entrance tunnel. In fact, the only thing that got past them was a small dog-like animal which was about the size of a dachshund but with the quickness of a greyhound. Speeding past their swift strikes without harm, the – he was going to call it a Greywiener (a combination of a greyhound and a dachshund, or wiener-dog) – dog only made it as far as his pit trap before it met its end. His pit trap initially worked wonderfully – up to the point when it needed to be manually reset.

Running through his dungeon tunnel, the Greywiener practically flew along the floor on stubby little legs. When it reached the flooring for his new trap, its weight caused it to tilt downwards just as he had planned, but the little dog somehow was able to perform a powerful jump that propelled it forward – falling mere inches short of safety. Unfortunately, that added pressure on the pit cover caused it to slam against the rubber bumper with greater speed than he had planned for, causing it to rebound at an accelerated rate. It just missed the falling Greywiener, instead leveling out and almost jumping up, which then made it fall quickly again.

Since it couldn't fix itself, the drones that he had left behind when he had blacked out continued to follow their last instructions – which, fortunately, were to help him fine-tune his trap and reset it when it failed. Therefore, at the moment, the pit trap was ready for any other attackers – which was important because he had the feeling that more were coming. He put it down to luck that he hadn't been attacked by anything as dangerous as the Scaly Bear or, heaven forbid, something that could jump or fly over his pit.

Even though his leaking radiation wasn't collecting in one place anymore, it had been accumulating in such concentrations for so long that Milton thought for sure it had wafted out of his dungeon and spread to the surrounding area topside. In fact, based on what he had learned from ALANNA about it during one of their early talks, there was no way to get rid of it completely except for waiting thousands of years – possibly more. That meant that the more he just existed – even if he didn't do anything else – the radiation would continue to build and spread uncontrollably. His "filtering" system with the water was a great solution to avoid lethal concentrations, but it wouldn't stop the spreading of his leakage.

All that ultimately meant was that he had to prepare more defenses for whatever he could imagine coming his way. Even if he didn't have his **You Break, You Buy** quest to advise him, he knew he had to do whatever he could to protect himself, and by extension, ALANNA. To that effect, he used his new, hard-earned **Rudimentary Defensive Trap Design** and **Basic Mechanical Engineering** skills to good use.

126

First, he looked again at his pit trap with a new set of "eyes", using his drones to make little tweaks here-and-there to improve the reliability and functionality of the defense. While he was there, he also had his drone travel down to the bottom of the pit and remove the decaying remains of the Greywiener, bringing it back to his Core so he could convert it and made it available to create as a Combat Unit.[12] The spikes he had created on the bottom of the pit looked like they had held up well, with absolutely no damage from the small critter who had fallen in. He expected that if a Scaly Bear or something bigger were to fall inside, he'd have a little bit of repairing to do.

After initiating a more strenuous testing program for his trap – including activating it with a massive push, a slight tap, and even a makeshift attempt at pretending to try to hold on to it while falling – Milton determined that unless something deliberately destroyed it or messed with its mechanisms it would function correctly for quite a while. It would probably need regular maintenance to ensure it was working properly, but overall, he was a lot more confident in it and was happy with what he had accomplished.

12

Combat Unit Creation			
Biological Mass (Bio Units)	1415	Basic Metal (BM Units)	65
Unit Name (Type)	Bio Units	Neurological Control Unit	BM Units
Blood-thirsty Squirrel (Scout)	5	Type-1a	1
Lollipop Snake (Stealth Fighter)	10	Type-1a	1
Jackalope (Speed Striker)	15	Type-1a	1
Greywiener (Speed Striker)	100	Type-2b	10
Scaly Bear (Melee Fighter)	1500	Type-5e	100

He determined that his next order of business was to create some more defenses to defend against creatures that wouldn't be stopped by his pit trap. And, of course, that was when he was attacked by something that the pit trap wouldn't stop.

"Looks like you've got incoming, Milton. Check further down the tunnel from your pit." ALANNA told him.

"Thanks, I'm already on it."

While he was contemplating the location and design of his next trap, one of his sensor orbs stationed throughout the tunnel caught a glimpse of something on the far edge of its range. This small movement inside his dungeon caught Milton's attention, since there shouldn't be anything moving down there – all his drones were near the pit trap. This disturbance was located about a hundred feet further in from his pit trap and around a turn, so he was sure it wasn't something that he had a hand in. Sending his orb closer for a better look, he found something he wasn't expecting.

Pieces of sandstone had broken off the wall and were lying on the ground, scattered around a small opening in the uniform face of the tunnel. As his orb stayed watching, additional pieces of sandstone cracked and broke apart, as if something were punching his tunnel from the other side, looking for a way in. Wholly unprepared for an invasion from a different entrance point, he recalled his drones to his Core room while he continued to watch the progress of whatever was trying to break in.

Thinking quickly, aided in part by his increased Processing Speed/Agility statistic, he looked over what resources he had in hand to work with.[13] Essentially, he still had leftover organic material from the cut-down trees, dirt and rocks from his excavations, and of course water. He had a bit of pure water stored away but had access to a whole lot more if he needed it in the form of his "filter". Not much, but he knew that it would have to be enough if he wanted to create something to defend against this invader.

Realizing that he didn't have enough time to come up with a more permanent solution, Milton decided that the best short-term defense was to make something that his drones could attack with. While visions of arming them with guns or swords made him smile, it just wasn't feasible at the moment based on his resources. Instead he came up with a three-pronged defensive strategy.

He started pooping out parts for his drones to assemble into two portable weapons. With his new skills, he found it easier to determine what parts were needed and how to assemble them into something more effective. When he finished creating the different parts he had the drones start to assemble the weapons he had in mind.

13

Available Resources	
Resource Type	# of Units
Basic Earth	12093
Basic Gravel	987
Basic Metal	65
Pure Water	303
Organic Material	3067
Biological Mass	1415

They were crude, but he thought they had a good chance of working. The first one looked like a short, two-wheeled, wooden wheelbarrow frame with handles and two wooden wheels, attached by hard stone axles and greased with a generous application of oil to allow them to spin. On top of the wheeled frame was a structure that had a heavy, long, sharpened, and two-sided granite blade that had a hole in the middle of it. The blade was placed toward the front of the structure, with a strong wooden pole running through the middle of it and additional pieces of wood and stone keeping it centered on the pole. Wrapped around and attached to the bottom of the pole was a very long piece of rope, which could be pulled and set the pole – and by extension, the blade – spinning quickly enough that it made a whistling noise as it spun. The handles and wheels attached to the frame would allow his drones to adjust the angle of attack so that it could slice into something closer to the ground if need be. In a sense, it looked like a lawnmower if you were to flip it upside down and have the blade situated toward the front.

His second portable weapon was like the first, with a wooden wheelbarrow frame and front wheels. On top of that, however, was a small ballista, complete with bow pieces made of shaped wood, strong rope for the string, and a stone channel that the bolts could sit in. Overall, it looked like very crude giant crossbow that was sitting on a cart and shot stone-tipped bolts fletched in leaves instead of feathers. The aiming could be adjusted by raising and lowering the entire contraption – not the best solution, but it was the best he could come up with in the short amount of time he had left.

Speaking of which, with the time it took to assemble his weapons, the invader had finally broken through the wall of his dungeon and climbed out through the hole it had made. It was much smaller than he had expected, especially with the amount of strength he assumed it took to dig through the dirt and break through his stone wall. It looked like a small badger but instead of fur it had a hard, yet flexible, exoskeleton surrounding its body. It also had some large, serrated, and lethal-appearing claws on its paws – which explained how it had broken through the sandstone structure supporting his tunnel. *Does everything have these killer-looking claws, or did I just happen to be unlucky enough to find them?* he questioned internally.

His drones had just finished his third defense and scrambled back to their weapons by the time the Clawed Badger made it around the last turn in the tunnel. He had positioned his ballista out front so that he'd be able to get some ranged damage in and potentially destroy the threat from a distance. His primitive lawnmower was placed right behind his ballista in case his bolts didn't work.

The Clawed Badger didn't even react to the sight of his weapons as it slowly ambled its way down the tunnel toward his Core room. Of course, that could be because there was no light that far down and the creature was most likely blind if it spent most of its time underground. Either way, it didn't react until the first bolt rebounded off the top of its body, doing very little damage but pissing it off. A high keening sound emerged from the badger, causing Milton to want to cover his non-existent ears and distracting him from the fight for a few precious seconds.

In those few seconds, the Clawed Badger had rushed forward toward his ballista and sliced into the framework of the weapon. The wood practically disintegrated under the blows until there was nothing recognizable as a ballista. His drone wasn't even able load another bolt before it was forced to retreat under the enraged-badger onslaught, scuttling back into the Core room to relative safety.

As it continued its mission to reach the source of the radiation it was sensing, the Clawed Badger approached and paused as it heard his lawnmower start up. Safely behind the contraption, he had two drones working together to operate the weapon – one to pull the rope setting the blade spinning and the other to move the entire structure. Angled downwards, the quickly-spinning blade cut through the air with a high-pitched whine as it was shoved right into the face of the attacking creature. As the badger tried to back away in uncertainty, it wasn't fast enough to avoid the sharp granite blade as it sliced into its nose and jaw. Dark blood erupted from its destroyed nose and the blade scored a lucky hit as the lower half of its mouth was cleanly cut away, leaving the wounded creature to start its keening again – which ended up cutting off as blood filled its breathing passageways.

Choking on its own vital fluids, the badger panicked and started attacking everything around it with its claws. Unfortunately for Milton, his drones had kept up the attack and when his spinning blade connected with the razor-sharp claws it was sliced apart in seconds. With nothing to attack the badger with anymore, his last two drones scuttled back to his Core Room.

Continuing to attack in a frenzy, the Clawed Badger demolished the rest of his lawnmower until it was lying in pieces next to his ballista. With nothing else hindering its way, the bleeding and wheezing beast trudged toward its original destination. Milton could see the badger from his own Core room, about a hundred feet down the tunnel. With nothing impeding its progress, he watched as it lumbered forward, literally tripping over the tripwire he had placed along the corridor.

With the tripwire activation, a huge section of ceiling came crashing down, landing on the Clawed Badger and sending out shards of sandstone as it impacted against the floor.

Congratulations! You have defeated *Clawed Badger*! You gain 50 experience!
Congratulations! You have increased your Combat Level!
Current Combat Level: 3
Experience: 753/1500

By raising your Combat Level, you can choose to prioritize the development of certain statistics. In addition, your Combat Units

will receive a 2% (per Combat Level) increase in their own attack and defensive abilities.

Current Points to Allocate: 3
Current Combat Unit A/D Increase: 6%

He thought he heard a faint *pop* as the badger was squished flat, which he instantly brought up on his sensor orb replays and, sure enough, there was a *pop*. He **so** wasn't looking forward to cleaning up the mess from that.

Chapter 13 – Trap design 2.0

Despite feeling like I'm flying by the seat of my pants, at least I'm improving. In addition to increasing his Combat Level during that last "fight" and obtaining two more points to allocate to his stats, he also received an additional skill and skill-ups.

Congratulations!

You have upgraded the skill: *Rudimentary Defensive Trap Design (Level 2)*

Allows the design and creation of rudimentary defensive traps using available resources. Also provides the ability to create blueprints of any previously created traps so that they can be created again by your drones without supervision. Create additional defensive traps to upgrade this skill.

Current skill level allows: Improvised single-use defenses, planned reusable defenses

You have upgraded the skill: *Basic Mechanical Engineering (Level 2)*

Further imparts the knowledge of basic mechanical engineering for use in defensive structures and traps. Additionally, the skill provides information regarding materials, movement forces, and testing procedures. Continue to use your current engineering knowledge and expand on different ideas to improve this skill.

Congratulations!

You have acquired the skill: *Primitive Defensive Weaponry (Level 1)*

Allows the design and creation of primitive defensive weaponry, i.e. your "lawnmower" and ballista. Further creation of different types of weaponry will upgrade this skill, giving access to additional weapon features.[14]

Fortunately, other than a relatively minor download of information that incapacitated him for about ten minutes, his new knowledge didn't knock him out like before. He put it down to the fact that it didn't contain a vast concept like engineering that he had very little knowledge of before. He now better understood the mechanics of how the weapons he created worked and could see some potential uses for them in permanent defensive traps.

But first, he had some cleanup that needed to be done. Sending his drones back out from his Core room, they cleaned up the mess that had been made by the Clawed Badger. Breaking up the giant piece of sandstone that had fallen on the badger, they reassembled it on the ceiling, attaching it to the rest of the tunnel

---

[14]

Skill List			
Name	Level	Name	Level
Sensor Control	2	Rudimentary Defensive Trap Design	2
Kamikaze	1	Basic Mechanical Engineering	2
Sensor Enhancement	1	Basic Construction	2
Drone Manipulation	3	Primitive Defensive Weaponry	1

and creating a flawless corridor once again. Two large columns of clear quartz, which were holding up the cut piece of ceiling and were slit just enough that the attached tripwire pulled and broke them, were recycled in his Molecular Converter. As for the remains of the badger, it had smeared across the floor of the tunnel, pieces of it severely flattened and unrecognizable. Scraping it up took a while, even for his drones, but they were able to feed enough of it to his molecular converter to acquire its pattern – even if there wasn't enough from the remains to completely make a new one. Fortunately, he had enough Bio Units available that it wasn't a problem.[15]

At 300 Bio Units, the Clawed Badger was at the limit of what he could produce. It also would put him over the limit of what he could effectively control at one time – which was currently capped at 500. Fortunately, he hadn't spent his points from his Combat Level increase, so he decided to throw them all into Processing Power/Intelligence. He did this for two reasons: 1. To increase his control limit to 800, effectively allowing him to create a Clawed

---

15

Combat Unit Creation			
Biological Mass (Bio Units)	1520	Basic Metal (BM Units)	65
Unit Name (Type)	Bio Units	Neurological Control Unit	BM Units
Blood-thirsty Squirrel (Scout)	5	Type-1a	1
Lollipop Snake (Stealth Fighter)	10	Type-1a	1
Jackalope (Speed Striker)	15	Type-1a	1
Greywiener (Speed Striker)	100	Type-2b	10
Clawed Badger (Melee Fighter)	300	Type-3c	25
Scaly Bear (Melee Fighter)	1500	Type-5e	100

Badger and 2. Hopefully shorten the debilitating effect learning new skills had on him.

With his new control limit, he created his own badger and was about to set it to guarding the area around his Core when he thought about how he would be able to feed it. *In fact, what does it eat? If it lives underground, it probably doesn't venture up top very often.* Before doing anything else with it, he ordered it to act naturally and to feed itself, hoping that he'd be able to see where it got its sustenance.

Within seconds, it had turned to a wall in his room and started scratching at the sandstone, leaving huge dents with each swipe. Milton didn't want his new home destroyed any more than needed, so he ordered his new Clawed Badger to stop and wait for one of his drones to carve a block out of the wall further down the hallway. Once it had removed and set aside a large enough block of sandstone, the badger practically flew to the wall when he released it and started digging its way through the dirt.

Milton was surprised at how quickly the badger traveled through the dirt – somehow it flew through faster than even his drones could. With the thought that he would check in later when it found something to eat, he got his drones back to work cleaning up the failed weapons and converting them back to resources inside his shell. Once that was all cleaned up, he got started on creating new defenses.

Even though his weapons didn't perform as well as he would have liked, their concepts were still something that could be utilized and improved upon – especially in a more permanent installation. To this end, he sent his drones toward the first turn in his tunnel near the surface to install a few wall traps that would hopefully decimate anything coming down the corridor.

First, he had his drones hollow out a room on opposing sides of the tunnel, leaving five slits in the sandstone about 4 inches high on each side. In each hollow room, his drones placed a large, tall, wooden shaft that contained five 20-foot sharpened granite blades, which, when they rotated, would extend out 10 feet into the corridor on each side. This would effectively cover the entire tunnel, since he alternated their placement so that all levels were covered. The only way through was if something timed it perfectly during its occasional rotation switches and/or was able to somehow jump or fly through the gaps. It was possible, but he thought it would be extremely difficult – especially for most of the creatures that would come down here.

Instead of having it activate when something got near, he instead decided to have it constantly rotating. It took him a little while to devise how to do this and his solution wasn't perfect – he would have to get one of his drones to reset it every couple of days. Essentially, what he did was connect the two wooden poles together using a very, very, very long strand of braided rubber which he connected and wound around their tops. One was wound clockwise and the other counterclockwise until they were stretched to their maximum and then let go. Each would spin, releasing the rubber strand and eventually using their momentum to gather up the strand

and wind itself up the other direction. This would cause a stop in their rotations at that point until they started unwinding in the opposite direction.

To reduce friction, he tapered the base of each pole into a point, added a smooth stone cap, and liberally oiled up the stone and concave base until it rotated with a minimum of centrifugal momentum loss. Again, it wasn't perfect, and the momentum would slow down enough over a couple of days that he would need to have his drones wind them up again. Overall, however, it looked like it would work for what he had in mind.

His next defensive trap was based on the ballista he had made, except this time he thought bigger. Well, not necessarily **bigger**, but **more**. Much, much, much more. Instead of just one or two, he had his drones hollow out two rooms that would each contain 50 ballista-type mechanisms which would cover a 15-foot area of the corridor. He placed it after the spinning blades trap, just in case something flying managed to get through it without harm. This, however, would be hard for any incoming creature to bypass easily.

Instead of bolts, he attached 12-foot-long sharpened wooden stakes to the ballista channels and hooked up the firing mechanisms to the backside of each stake. In addition, he hooked each room up to a single activation trigger which attached to the other rooms' trigger, allowing everything to be "fired" all at once. A thin rubber bumper attached to the end of the stake inside the room would stop it from completely flying out the holes he had made in the sandstone wall. When it was activated, 100 sharpened wooden stakes would be violently thrust out of the holey walls, 50 on each side, catching whatever was trying to make it through — whether it was a flying creature or a normal creature, this trap was sure to be a vampire's worst nightmare.

For an external activation trigger, he created a very thin, sheer piece of cloth that he was able to create through his organic material conversion and hung it in the center of the stake trap. He then attached the sheet to the trigger, which meant that whenever anything ran into it, the sheet would trigger the stakes to thrust outward. The sheet covered up so much of the corridor, in fact, that he needed to make a small tunnel that was closed on one side for his drones to travel back and forth without triggering it. Although this trap needed to be manually reset every time it was triggered, Milton thought that it wouldn't be triggered often enough to be a hassle. He had hopes that his other traps would take care of most of the incoming creatures.

With the completion of these two traps, he got another boost in his *Rudimentary Defensive Trap Design (Level 3)* and *Basic Mechanical Engineering (Level 3)*. The new knowledge imparted from these skill-ups only affected him for a couple of seconds and Milton was glad that he put his points into his Processing Power/Intelligence when he leveled up. He wasn't sure if that is what helped, or if there was just not a lot of new information that was imparted — either way, he was thankful for the improved assimilation of skills.

141

Milton was intending to design and create one more trap when he was notified by his Clawed Badger that it had found something to eat. He switched his attention to its perspective so that he was looking out of its eyes. At first, he was confused because he couldn't see anything. He thought that something had gone wrong, but then he realized that his newest unit was blind. Despite the lack of eyesight, however, its other senses were feeding him general information – from the scent he was smelling, the badger thought that something yummy was nearby. As the badger scooped up a handful of rock and shoved it in its mouth, he could "taste" the crunchiness of the sediment, the briny taste of the minerals, and...something familiar.

Spitting out that familiar portion of its mouthful, the badger continued feeding on the sedimentary rock deposit while Milton racked his mind trying to figure out why it was so familiar. It wasn't until he got another "taste" that he realized what it was – copper. For some reason, when he was 8 or 9 years old, he liked to suck on pennies. *I don't remember **why** I did that, but I **do** remember the taste.*

"Holy schnikeez! ALANNA, do you know what that Clawed Badger eats?" he asked excitedly.

She actually jumped, startled at his voice after hours of silence. He was so intent on creating his traps that he hadn't had time to talk to her, so when he spoke in such an excited tone she fell off the top of his shell where she had been pretending to take a nap. When she hit the water, she swam over to the dry part of the tunnel,

142

stood up dripping wet, and looked at him furiously. The dripping water didn't last long as she quickly disappeared into a grey mist and reformed without the water – however, the furious scowl remained.

"WHAT THE FUCK, MAN! You scared the shit out of me! What's so important you have to give me a heart attack?"

"Uh...I don't think you **have** a—," he sheepishly began.

"Not the point! You better have a good reason for disturbing my beauty sleep. What the hell were you yapping about again?"

Milton paused in confusion, forgetting for a moment what he had learned in the face of such hostility – but then he remembered, and his excitement came back. "Sorry for scaring you, I was just so excited about this! We may have found a possible solution to our metal ore problem!"

She looked slightly less peeved as he explained what happened with his Clawed Badger. By the end of his excited recounting, she appeared pleasantly optimistic. "Have your badger bring back whatever it found after it's done feeding and we'll see what we've got. This could be just what we needed."

I sincerely hope so.

Chapter 14 – Epic fail

It turned out that Milton was correct, the leftovers from his Clawed Badgers' meal was copper ore, mixed with a little iron. Unfortunately, it was only enough when converted to make a 4-inch nail – but it was start. *If I can have it constantly mine these ores for me, I can accomplish my quests so much faster. Not to mention being able to build stronger defenses in the meantime.*

With that in mind, he tried to send his badger back out to look for more ore, but it paused as if unsure what Milton wanted done. He sent it a mental picture of finding more to eat, followed by returning with more ore but it still hesitated. When he fully immersed himself in his units' mind, he came to realize that the badger couldn't find its food when it wasn't hungry. It was like the "scent" of the sedimentary rock evaporated, leaving nothing for it to home in to. He wasn't sure how long it would take for it to get hungry again, but even if it only ate once a day it would still be worth it to send it out to bring back more ore.

ALANNA chose to look at this information in a better light, "This could actually work to our advantage. We can use your badger to "survey" the surrounding dirt until it finds enough for its meal, and then send your drones in to mine the surrounding area. I doubt your badger would eat the entire deposit, instead only nibbling at a portion of it and then leaving when it was full."

Milton agreed with her and sent one of his drones to investigate the deposit while he refocused his attention on defending his core. He was worried about another incursion from the inside – such as when the Clawed Badger attacked – and wanted a more permanent solution. He couldn't plan for every eventuality because of his shortage of resources and time, but what he could do was design a larger, reusable "gate" to his Core room.

Since the collapsible roof worked so well before to squish the attacking badger, he decided to up its potency a little bit. In truth, he upped it a lot. First, he had his drones expand his room so that it extended past the tunnel entrance on both sides by about 20 feet and raised the ceiling of that area by the same amount. Additionally, they hollowed out a 20 by 20 by 20 cube of space from the ceiling inside the tunnel just outside his room. Using that dirt and some excess that he was still sitting on, he created a massive amount of sandstone blocks that were transported inside the tunnel. He sent one of his drones to acquire more trees, which he then used to make coils and coils of rope. The last things he created were 40 pulleys, made from granite for strength and polished and oiled up for smooth turning. His drones securely attached these pulleys to the top of the Core room on either side of the tunnel and at the top of the hollowed-out tunnel section.

Creating channels connecting the inside of the Core room to the tunnel was a little tricky for his drones, but eventually he had 10 holes drilled through the walls on either side of the corridor. Using the lengths of rope that he created previously, the drones threaded

145

the rope through the pulleys inside the Core Room, through the hole in the wall, and finally through the pulleys in the hollowed-out section of the tunnel. Once they were all through, he had his drones seal up the ends inside of a massive block of sandstone that they fused together using the smaller blocks he created. When that was finished, they easily lifted the multi-ton block of stone from inside the Core Room using the ropes attached to it.

The ropes were gathered up together to make pulling them all at once easier, so it was simple matter of attaching them to the wall and sealing them up with a simple stone protrusion. Although he would need to have his drones present to activate his "gate", he figured that if the time came to use it then they would most likely be there anyway.

Before he was finished, however, he wanted to test it out to make sure it would work. With two simple cuts, the drones on either side of the walls cut the stone and the huge block of sandstone quickly fell, pulling the ropes up through the pulleys with such speed he was worried that they would break. Fortunately, they were fine, but what **did** break was his block of stone and the tunnel floor. With a resounding crash that shook the entire room, as well as causing a cloud of dust to plume out from the pulverized stone, Milton watched in astonishment as huge cracks ran up and down the solid sandstone block when it hit the floor.

When the dust settled – for the most part – Milton watched in dismay as large pieces of the stone slowly fell off the main body of the block until he could see the ropes that were attached along the inside. From what he could see of the flooring, there wasn't much left of the original sandstone – it had been compacted and shattered into the ground from the massive weight that impacted it. All in all, a failure.

"Nice job! If you were shooting for creating a mess, jacking up your tunnel, and alerting the whole Goddamn continent to your presence then you did a bang-up job!" Milton couldn't help but bristle at the sarcasm in her voice as she commented on his trap failure.

"Hey, fuck off! I'm tired of you knocking me down whenever things don't work out the way I want. The least you could do is offer suggestions or advice **before** something goes to shit instead of badmouthing me when it does," he retorted. It was only when he finished that he realized that he cursed at her, something that he hadn't done in a long time. Instead of being mad at his response, she looked happy with a big smile on her face.

Milton was still pissed off at her, but now he was a little confused, "What are you so happy about? I have to almost completely rebuild and rethink this trap to get it to work right – there's nothing to smile about."

She was silent for a couple more seconds with that same smile on her face before she responded. "I'm just so glad you're finally coming out of your shell. I've been waiting to see what kind of person you are – a meek, weak-willed pussy or a strong, back-against-the-wall fighter with a deep sense of self-preservation. I still think you're something in between the two, but at least I know that

147

you won't keep letting me mess with you without fighting back. You need to have the right no-nonsense attitude to survive since it's not my job to get us through – it's yours. You've been reacting to what's been thrown at you since you woke up – it's time to show this world that you won't let it fuck with you. Think bigger, strive to put **you** first, and stop thinking wholly of defense. You can't turtle up in here and expect to succeed – the world won't come to you, you have to go the world. I don't mean you need to pack up and move out – just keep it in mind for the future." She stopped for a moment before grudgingly muttering, "And I'll try to be more supportive and offer some motherfucking suggestions when I can."

To say that Milton was shocked at her words would be a huge understatement. His thoughts turned introspective as he considered what she had said. Although it wasn't the subtlest of reprimands – which he was beginning to expect no less from her – she was right. He had only been acting defensively and reacting to the various dangers that had assaulted him from day one. He had been thinking that if he stayed down in his dungeon that he would eventually find enough metal by digging out the surrounding areas. With the small amount of metal that he had acquired so far, he now knew that was a forlorn hope. He needed to take risks to succeed – and that meant exploring the surrounding area. It was possible that a huge deposit of metal-rich ore was close by, just waiting for him to discover it.

But that didn't mean he would forgo his defense. Maybe it came from playing too many town-building and exploration games, but Milton couldn't even consider venturing out from his immediate area until he was sure that he was safe. He knew ALANNA was impatient, wanting to get off this planet and back to her creators, but he wasn't going to make a noob mistake like leaving his "town" undefended while he went off exploring. Like most of those games, there was fine line between undefended and overkill. He would do what needed to be done to ensure that he was "safe" but wouldn't spend any more time on it unless something came up.

"Thanks, ALANNA. Once I get some good defenses up, I'll get back to finding a way off this planet. Now, what do you suggest I do to fix this trap?"

Chapter 15 – Goal-tending

It turned out to be an easier fix than he had thought. ALANNA suggested turning the floor underneath the block into a thick rubber pad and add a thin layer of rubber to the underside of the stone. She also suggested coloring the rubber so that it closely matched the surrounding sandstone, where it camouflaged its presence – until something was walking on it, of course. Once everything was cleaned-up, rebuilt, and the new details in place, he tested it again with spectacular results. Although it still was loud enough to alert the surrounding countryside, the rubber pad absorbed a great deal of the impact, so much so that the block rebounded upwards about an inch before settling back down.

With no damage to the block or anything else, he left the block in place to see how well it blocked the entire corridor. After just a couple of minutes of observing it with a sensor orb from the other side – which looked exactly like the tunnel ended in a dead end – he started to notice a build-up in the radiation. "ALANNA, why is the radiation still rapidly building up? I thought most of it was being removed from here with the water filtration system?" he asked.

"You're still leaking that shit and the water doesn't get it all. When you shut down access to the outside, you sealed it up airtight in here, so it's accumulating even faster now. When you unblock the entrance to your room it should get better."

Makes sense, I guess. Directing his drones to reset his new trap gate, he was about to check in on his drone mining the ore deposit when he was surprised by a quest update.

Current Short-term Goal: *You Break, You Buy* – Complete!

Repair the broken sections of your tunnel, ensuring that the tunnel will not collapse from compromised structural integrity. Prepare defenses to destroy any incoming creatures hunting for your leaking Reactor.

- *Repair broken sections of tunnel –* Complete
- *Design and place **5** defensive traps –* 5/5 Complete
- *Locate and create an underground-suitable Combat Unit –* Complete

Difficulty of Goal: Moderate

Timeframe: 30 days

Rewards: Access to defensive traps, a moderately-defended home base, and a sense of accomplishment – *what else could you want*?

Bonus Rewards: For completing this quest by using **5** unique traps, you earn a bonus +3 to your Ingenuity/Wisdom statistic.

Nice! More stat points are always welcome. With the completion of this short-term quest, he brought up his average-termed quest to see how close he was to completing it.

Updated Average-term Goal: *Boot Camp*

Learn the different functions of a Station Core:
- *Sensors –* Complete
- *Drones –* Complete
- *Molecular Converter –* Complete
- *Biological Recombinator*
- *Resources –* Complete

- *Self-Defense System* – *Complete*
- *Units* – *Complete*
- *Neural Connections* – *Complete*
- *Structures/Manufacturing Facilities*
- *Defenses* – *Complete*
- *Combat & Combat Levels* – *Complete*
- *Statistics* – *Complete*
- *Skills & Achievements* – *Complete*
- *Research & Discoveries*

Difficulty of Goal: Hard

Timeframe: 1 year

Rewards: Become a fully-functioning, knowledgeable Station Core

Almost complete as well. It looks like I'm ahead of schedule – let's see if we can knock out the rest of these so I can move onto something else. ALANNA must have had the same thought since she sent him a new quest.

New Average-term Goal: *If You Build It, They Will Come*

Using current and new metallic resources, design and build various manufacturing facilities. These manufacturing facilities will accomplish a number of things: increase refining output of raw materials, allow for the experimentation of new Combat Unit hybrids, repair and create new drones and sensor orbs, and create high-tech defenses.

- *Locate and accumulate 10,000,000 basic metal units*
- *Create **5** different manufacturing facilities*

Difficulty of Goal: Frustratingly Hard

Timeframe: 100 years

Rewards: +10 to all statistics

100 years!?! "Holy crud, ALANNA – 100 years? How is that an average-termed goal? And why give that to me now?"

"I was looking over the progress of your drone mining the ore deposit and that stuff looks nice! I wasn't sure where we would find the metal needed for repairs and expansion, so I wasn't sure how long it would take until now. 100 years ain't shit for someone like you anyway, and once you get to that point your progress will be exponential from then on," she told him, matter-of-factly.

"Oooook. Why do I need so much metal?"

"Most of your manufacturing facilities need metallic components, the first of which will need to be an ore refinery. Even though you can break it down and convert it yourself with your molecular converter, it isn't that efficient. With some well-spent basic metal units, you can expect to eventually multiply the amount that you can get from the same ore by like, 10 or some shit like that. That means that you'll be able to create additional facilities that will speed up production for a small fraction of what you'd be able to convert yourself."

Milton thought that what she said sounded familiar. "Makes sense – invest in some required stuff at first which leads to other things that make it faster and easier to make something else. This sounds like a common strategy in some resource management games; I can get behind that. Since I need to wait for enough basic metal to get started – which seems like it could take a while – what should I do for the short term? Beef up my defenses?"

"Here," she said, before a new short-term quest popped up.

New Short-term Goal: *Go Forth, Young Man*

Since you don't have a clue what is out there in the big, bad world, use your Combat Units to explore the surrounding countryside and discover what this place has to offer. Although your sensor orbs and drones have a limited range, your Combat Units aren't reliant on power from your Core, so they can venture much farther. The neural connection allows for instantaneous communication over long distances. Your Communication/Charisma affects the distance they can travel and still communicate with your Core, so increasing this statistic will allow for further exploration.

- *Raise your Combat Level to at least level 6*
- *Thoroughly explore 20 square miles of territory*
- *Raise your Communication/Charisma statistic to 14*

Difficulty of Goal: Fun

Timeframe: 6 months

Rewards: Knowledge of the world. And +5 to Communication/Charisma if you're into that sort of thing.

Heck yeah, I can do that.[16]

16

Core Status			
Name:	Milton Frederick	Type:	Station Core Prototype 3-B
Combat Level:	3	Experience:	783/1500
Reactor Type:	Zero-point Energy	Reactor Output:	2%
Current Statistics/Attributes			
Reactor Power/Strength:	2	Processing Power/Intelligence:	8
Structural Integrity/Constitution:	1	Ingenuity/Wisdom:	11
Processing Speed/Agility:	9	Communication/Charisma:	5
Insight/Luck:	10	Sensor Interpretation/Perception	6

Chapter 16 – Puppies!

Originally, Milton was going to use one of his Lollipop Snakes to explore the surrounding countryside since he already had a plethora of them. But after a moment's consideration, he brought up his current Combat Unit Status screen[17] to see what how much he had to work with. Since his Processing Power/Intelligence was at 8, he was only using 510 of his 800 maximum Bio Units. As much as he'd like to have another Clawed Badger roaming around, he wasn't sure if it could operate aboveground effectively. Not to mention he didn't have enough processing power – but that could be remedied by killing off one of his smaller units. No, he needed something that could quickly explore but also be able to run from danger if it was overmatched.

Ideally, he would have loved to have something that could fly, that way he could cover much more territory in the same amount of time. Realistically – at least until he got a flying unit – he had to settle for something that was fast and nimble but wouldn't be

---

17

Combat Unit Status	Processing Power: 8	Total Controllable Bio Units: 800
Name	**# of Units**	**Bio Units Used**
Blood-thirsty Squirrel (Scout)	1	5
Lollipop Snake (Stealth Fighter)	13	130
Jackalope (Speed Striker)	5	75
Clawed Badger (Melee Fighter)	1	300
		Total Bio Units Used: 510

immediately eaten up by something larger. His snakes were cheap, but they were so low to the ground that they had trouble seeing their surroundings. His Jackalopes were the same way, having a slight height advantage over the snakes but he still wouldn't be able to see everything he needed to either. That left two options: the Greywiener and the squirrel. After a quick nanosecond of consideration, he immediately vetoed the squirrel because he still couldn't think about it without a quick spike of fear. To physically control it **and** look out its eyes – that was too much for Milton. He would have killed off the one he already controlled but he kept it around because, as much as he hated to admit it, the darn thing was a good scout.

So, Greywiener it was: not ideal, but he had to work with what he had available. Since they only cost 100 Bio Units and 25 Basic Metal Units, he decided to make two of them and send them out in different directions. After confirming his selection, he watched as his two new Combat Units were pooped out, landing in the water surrounding the bottom part of his shell. Immediately upon splashdown, the two Greywieners started roughhousing around with each other, acting like puppies who just discovered a kiddie pool in the back yard. Milton watched their antics for a couple of seconds before ALANNA appeared in the middle of them as if by magic, splashing, playing, and squealing, "PUPPIES! I LOVE PUPPIES!"

It was so unlike her that all Milton could do was watch as the tireless ALANNA wore out his new units after about 15 minutes. As they retreated to the dry tunnel outside of the water, the dogs laid down with their tongues hanging out, exhausted from all the playful exertions. Fortunately for ALANNA – who couldn't be seriously hurt – the Greywieners only nipped at each other during their play, otherwise they could have done some serious damage with the sharp teeth and powerful jaws he saw surrounding their panting tongues. Despite only playing, there were still a couple of superficial wounds on each of his new units, so inconsequential that they had already stopped bleeding.

"I'm guessing you're a dog person?" he asked, already knowing the answer.

"Yes, I love all dogs, the cuter the better. They're one of my weaknesses – but don't tell anybody," she responded, still with a smile on her face.

"Well, sorry to tell you, but I need to take these ones away – they're my new exploration units. If I have enough processing power later, I'll make you one that you can keep."

She pouted at first, but a sly smile emerged under her disappointed veneer as she said, "That's ok, I can wait. Talk to me again when you have a Biological Recombinator."

Milton wasn't exactly sure what that was supposed to mean, but he told her that he would. He ordered his new dogs to the surface, but they didn't move. Confused, he connected directly with one of them and immediately saw the problem. *Duh! It's pitch-dark down here and they can't see!* "ALANNA, how do I go about getting some light down here? Every time I create a new Combat Unit that can't see in the dark, they won't be able to see to find their way out."

"That's easy. Your sensor orbs are equipped with some sweet-ass lighting. Although they automatically scan the surrounding areas with infrared to see, they can also emit a fucking awesome glow that can light up your tunnel. Just space them far enough apart and your whole tunnel should be golden."

He took one of his sensor orbs out and concentrated on bringing forth some light. Suddenly, the Core Room was lit up with an explosion of light, so bright that he could hear his Greywieners yelp in pain as they were temporarily blinded by the light. Mentally turning the brightness down, he brought the light level down to a nice, manageable glow that lit up everything in the room and even further into the corridor. He immediately sent out most of his other available orbs throughout the long tunnel, placing them up against the ceiling out of harms' way. Even though their glow wasn't blinding, it was enough that there was very little that wasn't illuminated.

Directing the slowly recovering Combat Units to the surface, he led them around all the traps, including the spike trap where he realized he needed to use one of his drones to open the side tunnel. Once they were both out safely, he paused for a moment while he tried to determine where he wanted to send them.

Based on the position of the sun and the time of the day, I'm guessing that East is...that way. So, where should I start? Split them up to cover more ground or keep them together? He finally decided

158

to split them up since he was anxious to find out what the surrounding countryside had to offer. Choosing at random, he sent one to the North and one to the South with instructions to observe the area they were moving through and to alert him if something other than trees appeared. Making their way across the clearing, Milton watched from his nearby sensor orbs as they quickly disappeared in between the trees.

Piggy-backing in the mind of the Southern Greywiener – which turned out to be male, as opposed to the female one heading North – Milton rode along while allowing him to have the freedom to journey throughout the forest without his interference. He wondered why his Molecular Converter had created two different sexes, especially since he didn't ask for it to do that. Curious as to the reasoning behind this, he asked his resident expert.

"Unless specified, the system will equally generate both sexes, allowing for potential reproduction," ALANNA informed him.

"Wait, wait, wait...they can get pregnant?"

"Hell yeah! They won't do so unless you give them specific orders to keep their numbers steady, and you can dictate how many you want. It's all controlled by the nanites in their bodies, which automatically reproduce themselves to 'infect' any newly-created lifeforms. Essentially, instead of them 'Fornicating Under the Command of the King", it's more like 'Fornicating Under the Command of Milton". Actually, that sounds better as an acronym – FUCM sounds like fuck'em when you say it," she smiled at that last part.

His thoughts took some time to get back on track after that colorful explanation. *Too much to think about right now.* Turning his attention back to his current project, he connected again to the mind of the Southern Greywiener.

Milton immediately sensed the joy in his Greywieners' freedom to run and he exhilarated in the feel of air rushing past his face as he ran full-speed, narrowly dodging the various trees that seemed to appear from nowhere. After a couple of minutes, his new Combat Unit slowed down incrementally – only to speed up when he spotted a Jackalope.

Rushing ahead with even more speed than he had seen previously, his Greywiener crashed into the startled antlered rabbit, catching it with his small, yet powerful, jaws. Crushing the poor creature with tremendous bite force, the Jackalope was essentially decapitated as its body was swallowed whole, its head and antlers left to roll along the ground. Through the entire "hunt" and attack, the Greywiener didn't even slow down, chewing, eating, and swallowing on the run.

The whole feeding event happened and was over so fast that Milton barely had time to adjust to the sensations of killing something with his "own" jaws. It wasn't pleasant, the feeling of a live animal being crushed between his teeth, its frantically beating heart pierced by cracked ribs, and the taste of gushing blood filling his mouth. Fortunately, there wasn't too much chewing involved and the meal was swallowed within moments – but he could still taste and smell the warm, sticky blood coating his tongue and teeth.

Retreating to his shell, he gathered himself for a few minutes as he tried to get the memory of crushing bones and blood out of his "mouth". "ALANNA, is there a way to just see out of my Combat Units instead of experiencing everything they do? One of my dogs just ate a Jackalope and now I can't get the taste of blood out of my head."

"Uh, yeah – what the hell have you been doing? Do you mean to tell me that this whole time you've been feeling what they've been feeling? That'll drive you nuckin' futs if you keep that up – being inside the mind of simple creatures for too long will mess you up. Just connect to them and pull back until you're just looking out their eyes and listening through their ears – that's all the motherfucking sensations you need. I'm pretty sure you did that with your squirrel at first, so I didn't bother teaching you that shit, but I was wrong for once – don't get used to it because it doesn't happen very often."

I think she's deliberately throwing in the foul language to mess with me – there's no reason to say the f-word so much otherwise. Besides that, she does have a point – I don't remember feeling everything that Blood-thirsty Squirrel felt when I looked through its eyes at the Scaly Bear. Now if I could only remember how I did that...

Focusing on the same Greywiener, he connected with its mind again, still tasting the blood in his mouth. Mentally thinking about stepping back a little, he felt a slight lessening in the tactile sensations he was feeling. *Hmm, not enough yet. What was I thinking about with the squirrel...? Well, I'm pretty sure I wanted to stay as far away from that blasted thing, only allowing the barest possible connection to form.* Thinking he was onto something, he imagined that his dog unit was a squirrel and he wanted to stay away from it. Instantly, every sensation faded except for his eyesight and hearing. *Woohoo! Nice!*

Now armed with a defense against a sensory overload – as well as any stray thoughts from the Greywiener – Milton rode along with him as he continued to run through the forest. He missed the feelings of joy that came from the dog as he ran, as well as the wind rushing by his face, but he felt it was a necessary price to pay to not have to experience eating something so recently alive again.

Over the next 15 minutes, he hadn't seen anything different other than boring old vegetation and was about to switch over to his Northern unit when he saw something unusual in the trees ahead. What looked like crude rope made out long strips of dried bark was strung up between the trees, high up in the branches. Milton ordered his ride to slow down as it approached this mystery section, wary of anything and everything. He didn't want to rush headlong into danger if he could help it, so a more cautious approach was in order.

Passing beneath the first trees that had the strung rope, he didn't see anything out-of-place initially. The floor of the forest looked just the same as the rest of the surrounding area, but now that he went further he saw that the rope denoted a ring of trees with the center clear of anything but fallen leaves and scattered bushes. It was only when he looked up that he got his first surprise.

Perched upon the branches of the trees surrounding the small clearing, the immobile shapes of more than 30 large monkeys sat staring at the Greywiener. They were all sitting quietly, eyes fixated on the intruder – which was rather unnerving. He wasn't sure if they were dangerous or not, but he wasn't going to stick around to find out. Telling his unit to turn around, he was suddenly assaulted by the raucous hooting, honking, and screeching of every single monkey surrounding him.

Frozen in place from the unexpected noise, the Greywiener started shaking in fear as Milton watched as the monkeys launched off their branches, gliding across the clearing above his head with skin flaps that appeared between their arms and legs – like a flying squirrel back on Earth. When they reached the other side, most of them caught branches to stop themselves, but a couple needed to use the crude rope barrier to arrest their momentum.

Taking direct control of his creation, he started running out of the clearing just as the noise reached an even greater intensity. Instinctively dodging to the side, he just barely missed being impaled by a long, sharpened wooden spear that impacted the ground next to his head. Zig-zagging through the underbrush, he took a quick moment to look up and saw one of the Glider Monkeys armed with another spear beginning to chuck it in his direction. Quickly calculating where it would land when the spear left its hand, he dodged to the side, narrowly avoiding the deadly weapon.

Unfortunately, he couldn't see everywhere at once, so when he took the time to dodge the spear he saw coming, another one struck him on the back leg, crippling that appendage and slowing him down considerably. Reaching back with his head, he gripped the shaft of the spear with his jaws and began extracting it from his leg. Distracted by his current endeavors, he yanked the wooden weapon out just as he observed a rain of spears heading in his direction. Knowing that the likelihood he would escape was slim, he nevertheless tried to run again, still slowed by his damaged leg.

The first impact hit his lower back so hard that it passed clean through, impaling him against the ground as the point of the spear erupted from his skin and lodged into the dirt. That wasn't enough to kill him, but the five additional spears that hit him in the back, side, and finally his head were.

As he lost connection to his unit, he found himself back in his shell, glad that he had learned how to disconnect from all that his Greywiener was feeling, even when directly controlling it. To have to experience the pain and death firsthand would be horrendous – he now knew why ALANNA said that it was a bad thing to do at all, let alone all the time like he had been doing. It was bad enough that he saw and heard it happening; having the memories of the pain that went along with that would break him after a while if it happened consistently.

As for those Glider Monkeys, he was content to leave them alone for now – he didn't have any type of defense against them and didn't want to tangle with them for now. They seemed to have a rudimentary form of intelligence based on the ropes and spears he saw constructed; he was hoping that if **he** stayed away from **them** then **they** would stay away from **him**. His Greywiener probably invaded their territory and they attacked – he couldn't blame them from defending their home. He would, and had, done the same thing when he was invaded.

Putting the Southern direction on hold for the moment, he turned his attention to the North.

Chapter 17 – Aww...they're almost cute

Connecting to his Northern unit, he found it easier to disconnect from her feelings straight-away. The female Greywiener was running through the forest, but at a statelier pace than her counterpart. Milton didn't know if it was caution or if she had already used most of her energy up from a previous sprint – either way, he was appreciative for the slower yet steady journey through the forest. Not only could he see more details, he could hopefully see danger before it appeared.

After another 10 minutes of travel, he could feel his connection starting to grow less and less focused. He figured that he was reaching the limit of his communication range and his unit would have to start heading in another direction soon. Directing her to turn Southeast, his Greywiener complied and Milton felt the connection strengthening the further south she moved.

During the entire journey, nothing stood out requiring his attention; Jackalopes, other Greywieners, and even a sleeping Scaly Bear that she avoided with a great amount of caution were the only creatures they encountered. Eventually, however, they came upon something of great interest to Milton – a large area of hilly terrain. Most of the forest had been relatively flat, the occasional hill appearing was no larger than a dozen feet tall at most. With this new area, though, there was the prospect of future areas to mine for metallic ore.

Excitedly approaching the area, the grass, shrub, and small tree-covered hills looked like a small verdant mountain range – if the mountains were only about 50 feet tall. He sent his Greywiener scrambling to the top of one of the hills to see if he could get a better feel for how large an area this was. Once she reached the top, he could see – as much he could through the trees – that there were a good 20 or more large hills, most of them the same size as the one he was standing on, but a couple of them were a little bigger.

Realizing that he didn't really have the proper tools or units to "prospect" these hills, he had his Greywiener start at the bottom of one of the hills and dig until she hit rock. If most of it turned out to just be dirt for some reason, he would at least know that it wasn't worth looking into with more resources. Within minutes, his dogs' sharp claws had dug through the sparse vegetation and about a foot of dirt, exposing a hard, solid stone that Milton – with his limited knowledge of rocks – thought might be a good place to start mining. Bands of different colors – from a light grey, to a medium brown, and even a dark black – hopefully promised a beneficial payday.

He instructed his Greywiener to scratch at the colored bands, hoping to learn a little more about it before moving on. Certain colors were "softer" than others, and flaked away with a little effort, signaling to Milton that they were probably something different than regular rock. He wasn't sure if that meant they were metallic or something else – but it was strange enough that he would have to find some way to get a drone or Clawed Badger here to investigate. As he stopped his dogs' scratch-testing, he got a notification.

Congratulations!

You have acquired the skill: *Introductory Geology (Level 1)*

Using your investigative skills, you have personally discovered a potential source of metallic ore! With this discovery, you have gained the skill Introductory Geology, granting you the knowledge of the basic forms of geological formations and their creation. Further upgrades to this skill will expand your knowledge, including – but not limited to – uses for geological materials, advanced geological formations, and other geological experiments.

Milton quickly turned his attention back to his shell and warned ALANNA, "I just learned something new, I might—". That was all he got out before he was bombarded with the knowledge being imparted by the ***Introductory Geology*** skill. The overload of information caused him to black out again, and when he "woke up", he was back in his Core looking at a sleepy-looking and bored ALANNA floating on top of the water and resting against his shell.

Groggily, he slowly asked her, "Ugh...how long was I out this time?" Startled at his voice, she jerked and fell over, temporarily losing her water-walking ability and splashing into the water. Picking herself up and spluttering, she admonished him, "STOP scaring the shit out me like that! That's the second time, and two times too many. Warn a girl before you start talking next time, ya bastard."

Milton was still trying to collect himself as he absorbed the amount of knowledge he had gained. As he distantly watched as she floated on top of the water again and shook all the water off, he thought about the stone he had found with his Greywiener before he was struck down. With his new knowledge, he surmised that the striations in the rock were very good indications that some sort of geological event happened in the distant past causing an up-thrust of the surrounding area, which meant that some long-buried minerals most likely were pushed up along with it. *It might have been a fault in the bedrock and something shifted, or some other minor event. If it were something major, I would see some more evidence in the surrounding areas.* He figured that with more upgrades to his skill, he might know enough to determine how it happened.

Thoughts about his discovery almost made him miss what ALANNA was saying in answer to his original question, "As to how long you were out, it wasn't nearly as long as last time. Only about five days this time – which is a marked improvement. Even a small bump in your stats is helping you cope with the amount of knowledge you are sucking up. What did you learn by the way?"

Milton told her all about the discovery of the hills, his "prospecting", and his discovery and subsequent skill gain. She seemed as excited as he was but cautioned him from celebrating too much. "It sounds like it is a long way away from here – your drones can only function in multiples of 100 feet with your Communication/Charisma stat. So, at a 500-foot range, you're fucked until you can create Communication Arrays which will allow you to boost your neural communication distance. Of course, just like everything else, you're going to need an ass-load of metal to create them. Now that you know it's there, you can mine it in the future when you have more to spend – for now, leave it alone."

Although Milton saw the wisdom of this, his spirits were a little diminished at how long it would take to get there. Thanking ALANNA for the unneeded "kick to his junk" – to which she graciously said, "you're welcome", he turned his attention back to the Greywiener he had abandoned when he gained the **Introductory Geology** skill. When he tried to connect to it, he got an error saying that it was no longer available. *Something must have happened to it after I left.* Remembering that everything was automatically recorded for all his units, he replayed the last 5 days starting from when he left.

After quickly fast-forwarding through four boring days of the Greywiener wandering around the hills, catching a random Jackalope, sleeping, running around, and sleeping/eating some more, he finally got to the timestamp of about 6 hours ago. While she was running through the hills, she stopped as she sensed danger around the corner. With standing orders to investigate anything abnormal, the curious dog crept around the base of the hill, staying low to the ground to potentially avoid notice. When she crawled around a larger boulder sticking out from the hill, she saw a large cave placed in the side of the hill about 10 feet up from the ground. Inching closer and using her nose to determine what it was, she was within

about a dozen feet when she instinctually recognized what it was –
wolf.

Realizing that she had inadvertently crept up on a wolf's den,
she turned around – only to find that she was surrounded. Turning
back, she watched as additional wolves emerged from the mouth of
the cave and made their way down to the ground, while a low whine
started among the assembled attackers.

Milton almost laughed at the absurdity of the situation, but
after watching his Greywiener tremble in fear he figured there might
be something to worry about. Instead of massive wolves with huge
jaws filled with scary looking teeth, these wolves were smaller.
Actually, a lot smaller. In fact, he would classify them as Pygmy
Wolves for their small stature. Individually, they were about the size
of a small Pekinese dog, about half to a third of the size of his own
Greywiener.

Also differing from a normal wolf, these Pygmy Wolves were
a dark purple color, had six legs, and for some strange reason had
two tails. They were almost cute, until they opened their mouths
and he saw the large, almost sabretooth cat-looking teeth sticking
out of their jaws. **That** was when he didn't hold out much hope for
his own dog – if even one of the 30+ Pygmy Wolves latched onto her,
she was a goner.

Once all the wolves were in position, almost as if on cue they
attacked at the same time, rushing ahead and throwing themselves
upon his Greywiener without thought of defense. She held her own
for about five seconds, catching three of the leading wolves by their

heads and jerking back and forth quickly, snapping their necks. By the time she let go of the third, an additional five jumped her, bringing her to the ground and biting everything they could reach. Struggling to rise and shake them off, she was further "dogpiled" by an additional ten wolves and the last thing Milton saw was the sight of wicked long teeth in his face before the recording ended.

Congratulations! Your Greywiener (1) has defeated *Pygmy Wolf x3*!
You gain (20x3) 60 experience!
Experience: 825/1500

Shaken by the sheer ferocity in such a small package, he couldn't help but feel sorry for his dog. She couldn't help but stay where he left her and by doing so caused her death. After a few moments of self-reflection, he determined not to become too attached to his units – especially his Combat Units. He didn't want it to feel like he didn't care about them, but they were there for a purpose and it was inevitable that he would lose a few of them. *Well, probably more than a few.*

He had made some progress with his exploration and, despite them being killed, his Greywieners had performed relatively well. They were able to move quickly, covering a lot of territory in a short amount of time, and were able to defend themselves against smaller opponents. It was only the unfortunate fact that they were extremely outmatched that they died. In the future, he would make them run first at the first sign of danger – that was their strength after all.

After making two new Greywieners, he watched as they frolicked and played in the water again – *I can't deny it makes me inwardly smile when I see that* – and waited until ALANNA wore them out, before he sent them out through his dungeon again. With the help of one of his drones, they were able to make it out again without setting off any of his traps.

Just as they emerged from the entrance, Milton received an insistent warning from the one unit he didn't want to connect to but kept around for emergencies such as this. After connecting to his Blood-thirsty Squirrel unit, he ensured he was only seeing and hearing through its eyes and ears. The last thing he wanted was to feel like he **was** the squirrel – that thought sent imaginary shivers through his mind. Refocusing on what caught his scouts' attention, he was shocked when he saw small deep purple shapes flitting through the trees. The Pygmy Wolf in the lead had its nose to the ground, as if it was following a trail.

When Milton instructed his squirrel to look at where they came from and the direction they were heading, he couldn't help but think back to where his Northern Greywiener initially headed. Although they were probably still about a mile out, he suspected that – even though he wasn't observing this particular dog during this stretch of forest – this was the same path she had traveled while exploring Northward.

This was worrisome for a couple of reasons: 1. Either these wolves were excellent trackers, or 2. Somehow the "scent" of his leaking radiation was infused in his units, allowing them to be followed back to their source. Milton decided to err on the side of caution and figured #2 was the culprit, for the simple reason that he couldn't imagine these wolves would travel so far outside their territory unless they were being "lured" in by his leakage. This didn't bode well for future exploration since anything that he encountered could theoretically follow his units' trail back to his dungeon.

But, that was a worry for another time. Right now, he had a pack of about 30 vicious killer Pygmy Wolves headed in his direction and not much time to prepare. He figured he had about five minutes before they arrived, meaning that he had to devise some sort of defensive plan before they got close.

Chapter 18 – The first engagement

Looking over what he had to work with[18], Milton determined that he didn't have the numbers to take them head-on – therefore, he would have to use his units' strengths as effectively as possible. He also didn't have time to create any more, nor did he have the excess Basic Metal units yet to construct much. He was slowly getting some from his drone mining away at the deposit found by his Clawed Badger, but there wasn't enough extra to build more – especially since he had just spent 50 BM units on his new Greywieners. Instructing his Combat Units to gather in front of his entrance, it took a precious minute before they were close enough to see all of them. Once he had them assembled, he looked at each group, trying to determine how to best utilize them in the upcoming defense.

His Lollipop Snakes were good at hiding in the tall grass prevalent in the clearing, where they could strike out at unsuspecting

---

18

Combat Unit Status	Processing Power: 8	Total Controllable Bio Units: 800
Name	# of Units	Bio Units Used
Blood-thirsty Squirrel (Scout)	1	5
Lollipop Snake (Stealth Fighter)	13	130
Jackalope (Speed Striker)	5	75
Greywiener (Speed Striker)	2	200
Clawed Badger (Melee Fighter)	1	300
		Total Bio Units Used: 710

prey. His Jackalopes worked best if they had room to run and impact their enemies with devastating force. The Greywieners were fast and could easy handle a Pygmy Wolf one-on-one, but if they were attacked en masse, then they were in trouble.

With these strengths in mind, he assembled his forces into three attack positions. First, however, he had his Greywieners run back and forth from the trees to his dungeon entrance, hopefully permeating the air and ground with his leakage scent so that they would follow a straight pathway when they got to the clearing. Along the Western side of this pathway, set about 20 feet back from it, he assembled his Jackalopes so that they had room to run and impact the incoming wolfpack. When they impacted the wolves, the – hopefully – damaged wolves would be thrown out of line, right into the jaws of his Lollipop Snakes, hiding along the Eastern part of the pathway. His Greywieners would play the part of the tank, lined up in front of the entrance, preventing any from getting past.

When the Pygmy Wolfpack arrived at the tree line, they yipped and growled as they saw their destination in sight. Consumed with getting to the source of the radiation they had been following, they traveled along the freshest and most saturated concentration of it – the pathway his Greywieners had created. Rushing along without a care, they didn't notice – or bother – saving five of their members as they were violently hit from the side by Jackalopes, removing them from the pack. Even their pain-filled yips and whines were ignored as his Lollipop Snakes jumped on each one, two or three snakes per wolf, attacking them in vulnerable areas like their necks and eyes.

It was only as his Jackalopes rushed back to position further down the line and hit another five that they stopped and took notice of their dwindling numbers. While the Lollipop Snakes scrambled to finish off this next group of impacted targets, they were attacked by revenge-seeking pack members. With very little defense except for their small size and speed, his snakes tried to retreat into the grass for better positioning but ended up losing more than half their number to the enraged wolves. This delay in the wolves' forward progress – while detrimental to his snakes' well-being – was fortunate for his other forces to get into position.

Given the time to reposition, his Jackalopes were able to get in one more good strike. Two of them Kamikaze'd, instantly killing their wolfen targets with their antlers shoved so far into their bodies it snapped his Jackalopes' necks on impact. A third Jackalope missed its target when it shifted at the last moment, only to get snatched up as it went past, sliced up and killed instantly by the outrageously long, sharp teeth of the Pygmy Wolf it had missed. The remaining two knocked their targets into the range of the remaining 6 Lollipop Snakes that had retreated in time and hid in the tall grass.

While the wolves were occupied with attacking the snakes and trying to avoid Jackalope impacts, his Greywieners had sprinted across the battlefield, attacking like perfectly-paired teammates, decimating the stragglers on the outside of the pack. Quickly dispatching them by picking them up by the head and snapping their

177

necks, they managed to kill 6 of them before the remaining 12 realized what was happening. The pack members instantly targeted one of the Greywieners with half of their number, while the remaining 6 ran for the entrance of his dungeon. Attacking all at once, they piled on top of their targeted Greywiener, inflicting serious damage before they were picked off one-by-one by the other dog. The damage had been done, however, because the wounds inflicted by the wolves were so severe that the injured Greywiener bled out and died moments after the last wolf was killed.

Meanwhile, the remaining Pygmy Wolves raced for the dungeon entrance, leaving their doomed pack members behind. His remaining two Jackalopes raced to head them off, with one managing to impact the last wolf in the group, leaving it to the mercies of six Lollipop Snakes. The last five wolves made it into the dungeon and were so far ahead that none of his units would be able to catch up.

I guess it's up to me now. His traps were as prepared as possible, his drones were in position, and he was ready to see how they performed. As they raced toward the first bend in the tunnel, the two wolves in the lead suddenly dropped out of sight as they slid down the tilting floor, frightened yelps abruptly cut off as they were impaled upon the spikes at the bottom. As the floor tilted back up into position, the other three wolves skidded to a stop.

Cautiously traveling along the sides of the pit, where it was safe, they made it past the trap and started running again toward their destination. The closer they came to the source of the radiation, the faster they seemed to move, seemingly pulled by an invisible force that encouraged them to run full-out.

When they arrived at his slicing blade trap, he was worried that they were so small that they could duck underneath the lowest blade. Apparently, they had the same thought as the first two wolves performed an epic sliding move underneath the blades, trying to avoid being hit by them. Milton's worries were alleviated when they were unsuccessful, the spinning implements of destruction impacting them with very little resistance and practically cutting their heads off. The third, and last, wolf watched what happened from farther back in the tunnel and somehow intelligently calculated the precise angle and height needed to jump through the gaps in the blades.

Using one of its dead pack members as a stepping stone, it launched itself through the air, sailing over the lowest blade and narrowly missing the blade just above it. It didn't walk away completely unscathed – one of the blades took out an inch of both of its tails when it flung upwards on the wolves' downward arc. With a series of yelps finished up with a howl, the wolf let the world know it was in serious pain with the missing portion of its tails. Still whining in pain, it continued down the corridor, oblivious to anything in its path.

When it came to his next trap, it walked right into the sheet lining the hallway. With such a light touch, the trap didn't activate until the wolf lost patience at the annoying sheet covering it, gripped it in its mouth, and yanked hard to remove it. Instead of its desired

179

effect, the Pygmy Wolf was instead impaled by four different sharpened stakes, instantly killing it as one of them penetrated its brain and another its heart.

And with that, Milton's first major battle was done – and won. Switching his perspective to various viewpoints throughout his tunnels and outside the entrance, he looked over the entire battlefield. Instead of pride, instead of congratulating himself on a job well done, he couldn't help but be disappointed and sad at the losses that he had incurred. It had been a long time in his video-gaming career that he had suffered so much to pull out a win – it wasn't quite a pyrrhic victory, since he at least still had some units and traps remaining – but it sure felt that way.

Directing his drones to begin cleaning up the corpses of both his own units and those he killed, he turned to the notifications that he had ignored directly after the battle.

Congratulations! Your Combat Units have defeated *Pygmy Wolf x25*! You gain (20x25) 500 experience!
For defeating many enemies in a short amount of time, you receive a combo bonus!
Bonus: (25x10) 250 experience!
Congratulations! You have increased your Combat Level!
Current Combat Level: 4
Experience: 1575/3000

By raising your Combat Level, you can choose to prioritize the development of certain statistics. In addition, your Combat Units will receive a 2% (per Combat Level) increase in their own attack and defensive abilities.

Current Points to Allocate: 4

Current Combat Unit A/D Increase: 8%

Congratulations! You have defeated Pygmy Wolf x5! You gain (20x5) 100 experience!

Experience: 1675/3000

Congratulations!

You have acquired the skill: *Formation Fighting (Level 1)*

Arranging your units into formations can increase the effectiveness of their tactics, allowing them to smoothly transition from one enemy to another. When each unit follows their orders, a battle can change from a chaotic amalgamation of individual fights to an orderly battle with clocklike precision. Additional skill levels will teach advanced formation tactics, as well as increasing damage output while in formations.

Bonus at current skill level: 5% additional damage inflicted to the enemy when your units are in a formation.

Congratulations!

You have acquired the skill: *Combat Communication (Level 1)*

Through the use of neural communication, you can now quickly issue individual commands to multiple Combat Units during a battle. Splitting your concentration between units is difficult and further upgrades to this skill will allow you to communicate to additional units simultaneously.

Current # of units you can communicate with simultaneously at your current skill level: 3

Congratulations!

You have acquired the skill: *Cooperation (Level 1)*

Although they might be natural enemies, the Combat Units you currently control work together to defeat a common enemy. By utilizing units with predator/prey distinctions, you force a sense of cooperation found nowhere else on this world.

Bonus at current skill level: 5% increased defense for Combat Units participating in a battle beside a natural enemy

Congratulations!

You have upgraded the skill: *Kamikaze (Level 2)*

Inflict more damage during a suicidal attack with one of your units. Whenever this skill is used, current unit will cease to function after the attack, regardless of damage taken.

Damage bonus at current skill level: 300%

Congratulations!

You have unlocked an achievement:

The First of Many

Survive your first major engagement

Bonus – Survivor (Level 1):

When you lose more than half of your Combat Units during a battle, your remaining units have their defense increased by 5% per level of Survivor

Holy crap! That's a lot to take in at one time. Fortunately for Milton, the skills he acquired weren't knowledge dumps like engineering or geology – they were mostly just bonuses to combat. There was a slight knowledge download as he learned a little more about tactics, but he was so well versed in battle formations from his gaming days that most of what came through was a refresher.

Now that he had some stat points to spend, he knew exactly what to use it on – Processing Power/Intelligence and Communication/Charisma. For the first, he needed to be able to field either more powerful units on the field of battle or more of the smaller ones to defend the high-ground above his dungeon. For the other, he needed to start expanding where his drones and sensors could reach, just in case he found something closer than the potential distant mine up North.

With that done, he could already feel a difference in the speed at which he could think things through. Looking at his current state of Combat Units again[19], he realized that he needed to convert more Bio Units – which he now had plenty of – to recreate and improve his small army of defenders. What he didn't have was Basic Metal Units – the production of which was halted during the attack. Sitting at only 20 BM Units, he knew he would acquire some back from the bodies of his own defeated units, but it wouldn't be enough for what he had in mind. Leaving one of his drones to finish bringing back convertible bio mass, he sent the other two back to the ore deposit, effectively doubling the previous production. And then he waited for the resources to start coming in...

19

Combat Unit Status	Processing Power: 10	Total Controllable Bio Units: 1000
Name	# of Units	Bio Units Used
Blood-thirsty Squirrel (Scout)	1	5
Lollipop Snake (Stealth Fighter)	6	60
Jackalope (Speed Striker)	2	30
Greywiener (Speed Striker)	1	100
Clawed Badger (Melee Fighter)	1	300
		Total Bio Units Used: 495

Chapter 19 – Party up!

It took about 3 days to finally achieve what Milton wanted for his defensive strategy. He was limited by the amount of BM units he had, but after he added his third drone to the ore deposit they started to roll in much quicker than he expected. He now had a nice reserve of metal in case it all hit the fan again, and he had a diverse standing army of Combat Units to help defend his home base.[20] With the addition of the Pygmy Wolves, he now had 11 Lollipop Snakes, 11 Jackalopes, 6 Pygmy Wolves, 1 Greywiener, and 1 Clawed Badger. Even though the badger wasn't there primarily for combat – instead being used to hunt for more ore deposits – it was a good last line of defense that he kept near his Core when it wasn't out digging.

When he created the Pygmy Wolves, ALANNA reacted similarly to them as she did the Greywieners – she went puppy crazy. This time, however, they almost looked like puppies since they were the same size of a normal puppy. ALANNA also didn't look diminutive compared to them either – next to them they looked like

---

20

Combat Unit Status	Processing Power: 10	Total Controllable Bio Units: 1000
Name	# of Units	Bio Units Used
Blood-thirsty Squirrel (Scout)	5	25
Lollipop Snake (Stealth Fighter)	11	110
Jackalope (Speed Striker)	11	165
Pygmy Wolf (Group Attacker)	6	300
Greywiener (Speed Striker)	1	100
Clawed Badger (Melee Fighter)	1	300
		Total Bio Units Used: 1000

large dogs instead of monsters. "OH MY GOD! THESE PUPPIES ARE SO CUTE!" she squealed, causing the wolves to hunch in back in pain as the noise pierced their ears. She quickly apologized to them, gathering them up and scratching them on their heads.

After they had played together, frolicking through the water and racing up and down the tunnel outside his Core Room, he sent them up to the surface with the help of a drone to bypass the traps higher up the tunnels. ALANNA turned toward Milton with a mischievous grin on her face, muttering, "I can't wait until you make that facility, I'm going to have so much fun!" Milton wasn't sure what she was planning but he was worried all the same.

All his traps were reset and once he accumulated more metal, he was planning on adding additional traps throughout the tunnel which his drones could build themselves using the blueprints created from his **Rudimentary Trap Design** skill. As far as early warning went, he reluctantly created an additional four squirrels to use as scouts. He had to shut down all his nearby sensors when they were created, and he sent them on their way to avoid the temptation to shoot them with his cold laser. If he didn't have to look at them, they didn't exist as far as he was concerned. Once they were out of his Core Room, he relaxed and turned back to his next project.

Based on what had happened during his previous expeditions, Milton decided on a more cautious approach. Instead of sending out units to different locations, he would focus on one direction at a time; concentrating on one danger at a time. He was thankful that those Glider Monkeys hadn't decided to attack – if they

186

had, they probably would have arrived while he was still incapacitated learning his Geology skill. His additional squirrels were placed further out from his clearing in different directions so that he would have greater warning in case something did decide to attack in the future.

As for his current expedition into the great unknown, Milton had thought about it while he was gathering the necessary resources fix his defenses. He was thoroughly impressed by the abilities of his different Combat Units when they worked together, so he decided to bump it up a notch. *I can't believe I'm doing this, but if it worked for my games it should work here.* Although he didn't have the typical Tank-DPS-Healer units available, he nevertheless wanted to put together a party.

Ideally, he would love to be able to create a Scaly Bear for a tank, but he wasn't capable of that and wouldn't be able to for a while. Instead, he used his remaining Greywiener as the tank and, strangely, as a mount. Creating a lightweight cloth harness that his drones attached to his dog unit, the other members of the party were able to easily hold on and detach themselves at a moments' notice. These other members included a Jackalope and a Lollipop Snake.

It looked silly, and ALANNA laughed in delight when she saw it, but Milton was hoping that his party of three would perform better than having a lone Greywiener exploring the surrounding countryside. He decided to name the members of his expedition group – since they were now distinctive and were probably the only

187

party of natural enemies ever created – and to make it easier to communicate to them on a more personal level. He was violating his own self-imposed restriction on getting too attached to his Combat Units, but he felt that they deserved special attention and, well, *screw the consequences*.

Anyway, riding directly behind Frank's (Frank as in Frankfurter = wiener dog) head, Lolly the snake sat on the dogs' back, a small bump protruding from the harness that allowed her to clamp down tight with her jaws when moving at full speed. Jack the Jackalope sat near the middle of Frank's back, small stiff pouches on the harness allowing it to snugly place his legs inside, securing him to his mighty mount. If he was any bigger, Jack would have looked like he was riding the dog like a person would ride a horse – instead it just looked like he was a package being transported on a mule. All in all, however, his party was a great improvement over what he was using before.

When they were all prepared for their journey, Frank, Lolly, and Jack raced away to the West – a direction he hadn't explored at all yet. Milton watched from the perspective of Jack since he was further back and had a better view of the other party members. Racing ahead at top Speed, he could see Frank's tongue hanging out of his mouth, spittle flying by and narrowly missing his riders. Lolly was hanging onto the harness, the speed of movement making her body fly into the air, whipping back and forth like a pennant flapping in the breeze. Briefly making Jack look down, Milton could see that Jack was securely held inside the small pouches but had to constantly shift his center of gravity to avoid being thrown out when Frank turned. Overall, his harness worked rather well, but Milton could see some room for improvements that would make it easier on his party.

After 10 minutes, they slowed down as Frank caught the scent of a normal Jackalope, unerringly heading straight for his meal. After snatching it up, he gave the order for Frank to stop and share with Lolly, while Jack went off and fed on some greenery nearby, shaking uncontrollably. It was only his influence and orders that prevented his Jackalope from losing control after watching one of his brethren get snatched up, beheaded, and eaten nearly alive. Fortunately, his creatures had relatively poor natural short-term memory, so by the time everyone was done they could continue their journey without any uncomfortableness.

After that, the journey through the forest became rather boring – which Milton supposed was a good thing. He was tired of being surprised by deadly creatures at every turn; but he wished there was more out here than just trees. Trees, trees, some bushes, trees, and more trees. He got a little excitement when his party approached a small stream running through the dense foliage, but the water-level was so shallow that the "mount" was able to carefully walk across without too much trouble. For the next half-hour, the scenery didn't change, and Milton could sense that they were approaching the new Communication limit as the strength of their connection was subtly starting to fade. He was about to order Frank to turn another direction when the excitement he was expecting almost literally fell in his lap.

The sharp eyes of Lolly, forever scanning the environment for the slightest movement, saw the danger seconds before it was too late. Jumping straight at the trio from a branch high above, a large multi-colored cat had launched itself off said branch, intending to land directly on the party. Shocked at the sudden attack, Milton panicked and wished he had more time to set up a strategy to take on the incoming predator. He was sure that they were dead but resigned to try to escape before they were all taken out.

What happened instead was everything started to move in slow motion. Not sure what had happened, Milton watched as the sleek-looking cat – which looked like a Jaguar – very slowly drifted downwards. Now that he could get a better look at it, he saw that it was colored in shades of purple, with each shade blending into another in a gradual lightening of color. He remembered one of his roommates' old girlfriends had colored hair that looked like this and it was so unusual-looking that he asked how she did that. She said that her hairstylist did it, and the gradual lightening effect was called ombre – not that it meant much to him at the time. But the strange word and effect stuck in his mind, so during that moment of slow motion he decided to call this deadly beast attacking his party an Ombre Jaguar.

As he sat there watching their inevitable death descending ever closer, he realized that he had a unique opportunity to change that inevitability. Milton quickly issued orders to his party because it appeared the Ombre Jaguar was starting to speed up incrementally. Another 10 seconds passed as he watched the jaguar get closer and closer, while his vision from the viewpoint of Jack changed as it sprung out of the harness and jumped away from Frank. Out of the corner of his vision, he could see Lolly let go of the harness while flinging her body to the side, launching herself in a different direction.

On Frank's part, he put extra strength into his legs for a couple of strong strides, putting him just out of reach of the falling Jaguar. As the Jaguar touched down, time sped up back to normal and he suddenly had trouble staying focused on what was happening. He tried giving additional orders to his units but couldn't properly connect to their mind. Eventually, he figured that if he hadn't already been connected to Jack he would have lost any sort of connection to the upcoming battle.

Now just a spectator inside Jack's mind, he watched as they followed his last order he was able to impart to his party – ATTACK! When he gave the order, he had in mind a three-pronged attack that would have to be adaptable on the fly, depending on the reactions of the Ombre Jaguar. Which was precisely what they did.

With Frank as the biggest target, the jaguar turned toward where his Greywiener had stopped and turned around, taunting the bigger creature toward him with short barks. As the purple-colored cat stalked toward its annoying prey, Lolly sprung from just behind the jaguar with hardly a sound, landing on its back and latching onto the back of its neck with her jaws. Although the back of its neck was thick and not a vulnerable area, the distraction was enough to deter the jaguar's attention from his other party members.

Rushing at top speed from the side, Milton watched through Jacks' eyes as he aimed for the side of the big cat. The Ombre Jaguar turned around at the last moment while trying to dislodge Lolly, and Jack ended up impaling one of his antlers inside the butthole of the formidable feline. Jumping straight up into the air in surprise and pain, Jack was jerked out of its butt by the sudden upward thrust.

While running away to try for another impaling rush of speed, Jack kept an eye looking backwards at the purple cat. Landing nimbly on its feet, the jaguar instantly turned toward its rear end to survey the damage – which ended up being a costly mistake. All the small painful distractions were apparently enough for the cat to forget about Frank – at least until he bit down on its neck and started crushing its throat. Just as it was raising its paw with sharp-looking claws to strike at Frank, Lolly used the temporary distraction to detach from the neck and slither over its head into its face. She bit down on its nose while it had one paw in the air and the painful shock caused the cat to jerk enough that it fell on its side.

At that same instant, Jack had arrived back on the scene with a straight shot to its underbelly. The crack of impact worried Milton that Jack had Kamikaze'd and broke his neck. In reality, however, it was a jaguar rib cracking and a portion of Jacks' antler breaking off as the Ombre Jaguar jerked in pain at the sudden impalement. It was lucky shot right to its heart, and probably wouldn't have been possible if the cat hadn't been on its side. Within moments, the damage caused by a combination of Frank's and Jack's efforts ended the feline threat. After everything, though, what counted was that his party had survived an encounter with a larger, stronger enemy and emerged largely unscathed.

As soon as the battle was over, he could feel his control over the party reconnect as if nothing had happened, as well as receiving some notifications.

Congratulations! Your Combat Units have defeated Ombre Jaguar! You gain 100 experience!

Experience: 1775/3000

Congratulations!

You have acquired the skill: *Overdrive (Level 1)*

Although it may have looked as if you slowed-down time, you are in fact speeding up your own perception of time. This skill allows you to assess the battlefield to quickly create a defensive strategy while safely hiding behind "time". This affect lasts for up to 30 seconds, is usable once a battle, and can be cancelled before the time limit is reached. Additionally, until your Processing Speed/Agility is repaired, you will be unable to directly order your units until after the battle is complete – they will still follow all previously given orders, however. Upgraded levels in Overdrive will increase the time limit, allow for multiple uses, and provide additional bonuses to units.

Time limit at current level: 30 seconds

Use limit at current level: Once per battle

Congratulations!

You have upgraded the skill: *Cooperation (Level 2)*

Although they might be natural enemies, the Combat Units you currently control work together to defeat a common enemy. By utilizing units with predator/prey distinctions, you force a sense of cooperation found nowhere else on this world.

Bonus at current skill level: 10% increased defense for Combat Units participating in a battle beside a natural enemy

Phew! That was an intense battle – but the rewards are awesome! The ability to "freeze time" was game-changing – he just needed to remember when he used it that he couldn't issue orders afterwards. *That's just great – yet another stat I need fixed before I can operate properly!* He knew he still had a long way to go, but he was making progress at least.

He wanted the Jaguar for "cloning" purposes, so he instructed Frank to start dragging the body back to his core so that he could convert it in his shell. Knowing it would take a while, he left his party to check on the rest of his units, leaving Lolly and Jack orders to keep watch and to alert him if anything attacked. With that taken care of, he went to check on the situation around his home base, to which he found everything in good order. And then he went back to waiting.

Chapter 20 – Quick lizards

About twelve hours ago his party had arrived back at his territory (which he considered as everything his drones could currently reach), where he had drones waiting to bring the Ombre Jaguar corpse the rest of the way to his shell. After giving them a well-deserved rest and time to feed themselves, he excitedly joined them again as they made their way heading East this time.

Riding a small high from the success of his party, he was nevertheless a little disappointed that he wasn't going to be able to create his own Ombre Jaguar anytime soon.[21] Although he could theoretically afford it at 500 Bio Units – if he were to get rid of some of his other Combat Units – he still wouldn't be able create it in his shell-based Molecular Converter. Along with the Scaly Bear, he needed a Bioconversion Lab before he could convert anything over 300 Bio Units. *I really need to have a talk with ALANNA about these different facilities and how much they're going to cost.* He resolved

---

21

Combat Unit Creation			
Biological Mass (Bio Units)	3170	**Basic Metal (BM Units)**	984
Unit Name (Type)	*Bio Units*	*Neurological Control Unit*	*BM Units*
Blood-thirsty Squirrel (Scout)	5	Type-1a	1
Lollipop Snake (Stealth Fighter)	10	Type-1a	1
Jackalope (Speed Striker)	15	Type-1a	1
Pygmy Wolf (Group Attacker)	50	Type-2b	10
Greywiener (Speed Striker)	100	Type-2b	10
Clawed Badger (Melee Fighter)	300	Type-3c	25
Ombre Jaguar (Stealth Fighter)	500	Type-3c	25
Scaly Bear (Melee Fighter)	1500	Type-5e	100

to talk with her after he finished his exploration quest – that way he could hunker down and concentrate on building without being distracted.

Before his party left for the East, he made some minor changes to the harness that would help Lolly and Jack feel a little more secure while they bounced along with Frank. As usual, Milton followed along with them, firmly entrenched in Jack's mind as he watched them speed through the undergrowth surrounding the trees. He was pleased to see that the small changes he made allowed Lolly to curl her body around another protrusion in the harness instead of flapping along, hanging on for dear life. In addition, the contoured seat for Jack kept him firmly in place, allowing a freedom of movement when needed but also a sense of security when Frank turned abruptly.

As for Frank, he just loved to run. From what he could tell from his previous Greywieners, as long as he could run freely then he was happy. Everything else that he had to do – from battles to exploration – was more of a nuisance than a difficulty. That suited Milton fine, since that was what he wanted him for anyway.

Trees. More trees. And then some more trees. Just like the other times his units had ventured out from his Core, there wasn't much out in the surrounding countryside other than a proliferation of trees. He was beginning to suspect that something might have happened upon his landing in this section of the forest – seeing as there weren't many hostile creatures within a mile of his Core. It seemed as if it was only when he ventured past a certain point that he began to encounter dangerous creatures. Personally, for Milton, he was glad that he hadn't had to fight off all these different animals as soon as he arrived. Logically, however, he thought that it was strange; it was as if there was a reason there was nothing much around. *Hmm...I wonder how long I was here on this planet before I "woke up"? Yet another thing to ask ALANNA about when I have the time.*

Putting aside those questions for another day, he brought his attention back to his party just in time to see a break in the trees ahead. Practically on the edge-of-his-seat in anticipation, he anxiously awaited as Frank put on speed to reach the edge of the forest – apparently, Milton wasn't the only one who was tired of dodging around all the trees on his run.

The trees gradually lessened until they began to look sporadic in their placement, the thinning of the edge of the forest evident by the increased sunlight streaming through. As they were passing the last few small trees, they burst out onto a very small valley about 200 feet across, with a small stream about 5 feet wide meandering its way through the middle of it. On the other side of the valley, a short mountain range ran across his view, spanning from horizon to horizon from North to South. Instead of huge snowcapped mountains he would've expected from a range like this, these were only about 1000 feet tall – not quite tall enough to be covered in snow, at least not at this time of year. Jagged peaks they were not; the tops of these mountains looked as though they had been smoothed-over, as if the passage of time had worn away the edges.

Near the base of the range, massive cave entrances were pockmarked throughout the exterior, each about 500 feet away from each other. The regularity of openings was curious, leading Milton to the conclusion that they were not natural. He directed his party to cautiously explore the outside of the nearest cave, crossing the small stream with little effort. As they approached the entrance, Milton changed his mind about it being unnatural, because he saw no evidence that any claw or tooth had created the 50-foot opening. Still, their consistent placement had him on edge; his party was nervous as well.

Not one to go home empty-handed on some vague feelings of discomfort, he instructed Frank to enter the cave, his claws clacking loudly against the stone floor and lightly echoing in the large open space. He didn't have to worry about light yet, fortunately, because there was plenty of it streaming in through the entrance. About 150 feet inside the cave, the tunnel they were walking down started to narrow drastically until it was similar in size to his own. After another 50 feet, the light began fading as the path they were following drifted off to the right, blocking easy access to the sunlight. Just as he was about to turn his instinctively-slowing party around due to the complete darkness, they saw a deep-green glow coming from around a corner a short distance ahead.

Milton switched his perspective from Jack to Frank, so that he could see for himself what lay ahead. Now walking as slowly and quietly as possible, Frank inched his way forward, sticking his head around the corner when he was close enough. To Milton's surprise, instead of anything dangerous there instead was slowly-pulsing, glowing green streaks of rock running through the walls of the tunnel ahead, bathing the pathway ahead in more than enough light to see. *I wonder what that is? I've never seen anything like this and even my knowledge of Geology, though admittedly incomplete, has no answers either. I should probably go ask ALANNA about th—.*

His thoughts were interrupted as he caught some movement out of the corner of Frank's eye. Shifting his viewpoint back to Jack, who had a better vantage point, he had him look around to see if he could find what caught his attention. When he didn't see anything, Milton figured he was jumping at shadows and that the pulsing green light was making everything look strange. Urging the already nervous dog on, he continued watching from Jack's mind just in case he was wrong.

Further down the tunnel, Milton saw a change in the rock surrounding the party. The green glowing streaks were slowly replaced by walls full of sedimentary rock, with dark layers prevalent within them. Excited at potentially finding another source of metal, he temporarily ignored the temperament of his party members as they reacted to something close by. When he finally paid attention, it was too late – they were surrounded on both sides.

Standing above 6 feet, the five giant lizards stood silently watching them from 30 feet away – three in front and two behind. They were the size of very large walruses, long frills on top of their heads with a skin flap standing erect and flowing down the center of their backs. Their skin appeared tough, almost as if it was made of the same material as the tunnel walls. They looked green – at least by the pulsing green light inside the tunnel – but they could have been any dark color. He'd have to see them in the light of day to know for sure, which when he looked at them he didn't want to ever do.

With what he took as hostile expressions on their faces, Milton considered his chances of escaping alive to be slim-to-none. Before they could attack, he consciously activated his **Overdrive** skill, slowing down time to a crawl. He gave quick orders to Frank, causing the frightened unit to jump into action – racing toward the gap between the two lizards guarding the exit. As time started slowly moving faster and faster as the skill effect was expiring, he was hoping that the speed of his Greywiener was enough to get past their massive opponents.

It appeared that the lizards were slow to react as Frank shot for the gap without any opposing movements. As soon as he got within a couple of feet, however, the lizard on the right moved so quickly that he barely saw the massive maw of the creature before it caught them all up in one scoop, swallowing them alive without even chewing. Milton cut the connection as he started to experience the pain and panic of his party, his recent vow to stop connecting too deep with them forgotten with his excitement over his discoveries.

Holy crap! That lizard was way too fast for its size. Frank didn't even have a chance. If they were able to out-speed a greyhound – how fast can they really move? He had been thinking of them as just large, slow giant lizards but now with their lightning-fast strikes, he thought of them more as quick lizards, or Quizards. Milton took a couple of minutes to compose himself after such a devastating setback, especially since his party may have found something useful in those caves. With that thought, he turned his attention to ALANNA, intending to ask her about the glowing green streaks he had found in the mountain range.

"Hey, ALANNA, what do you know about—", he started before he was rudely interrupted by one of his squirrel scouts. "Hold on a second, I have to check something out. It's probably nothing, but just in case I better go look." The squirrel who had contacted him was one of new ones that he had sent East and it had ventured a bit further out from his Core compared to the others. With impatience, he connected to mind of his scout, expecting it to be another false alarm. He had received a few of them now that he had a bigger scouting force – which was understandable since they covered more territory – but it was a little annoying to be called away from what he was doing when a random Scaly Bear wandered past the tree the squirrel was hiding in.

ALANNA was still waiting for him with thinly-veiled impatience when Milton returned after a very quick look through the eyes of his Eastern squirrel, yelling, "Crap! Not a false alarm! We have incoming and I'm really worried this time." He quickly recapped what he had found and what had happened to his party, briefly detailing the Quizards that had decimated Frank and the others.

"How long until they get here?" ALANNA asked, appearing concerned but not as worried as Milton felt.

"Within minutes – I barely even saw them as they disappeared from my scouts' sight, heading here in a direct path following the trail Frank must have left as he passed by. They are so fast, I'm not sure I can stop them."

"Hey! Stop talking that shit! I have faith in you, so have some faith in yourself! You can do this – your defenses are all set up to kill motherfuckers like this. And, of course, you have **me** – what else could you need?" She looked expectantly at him, as if waiting for him to acknowledge her greatness.

"Wait – what do you mean by that? Can you help defend my Core? If so, what can you do?"

"Hold up, I didn't say that. Although it's true that I do have some defensive capabilities, they are only allowed for use in self-defense. If anything attacks little ol' me, I will fuck it up, but only if it targets me. With your 'leakage' problem, however, I'm likely to be perpetually ignored until you get it fixed," she chuckled. Milton wasn't sure if she chose to make light of the situation because she wanted to relieve a little tension with the upcoming attacks, or if she really didn't think it was a big deal.

As he was talking to her, in the back of his mind he had been recalling and setting up his above-ground army just in front of his entrance. Using a slightly different strategy than before, he had his Lollipop snakes curl themselves around the necks of his Jackalopes. Along with his group of Pygmy Wolves, they gathered in front of the entrance instead of off to the side. His thought was that the Jackalopes could rush the Quizards and deliver the snakes at the same time, taking advantage of the rabbits' speed to place the mouthy snakes in vulnerable spots on the giant lizards. His Pygmy Wolves would gang up on the first lizards that came close, using their swarm tactics to inflict damage and slow down the enemy.

As far as plans went, it was fairly simplistic – but he didn't have time to set up anything better. As Milton made sure his drones were in place in the Core Room, his traps were all prepared as much as possible, and his Clawed Badger was near his shell as backup, he watched through one of his above-ground sensors as five giant Quizards broke through the trees and raced for his dungeon without stopping.

Chapter 21 – You got this

If he hadn't seen their legs moving rapidly over the ground, he would have thought that the giant lizards barreling through the clearing could fly – they were moving that fast. Within seconds, they had traveled the length of a football field and collided with his army without hesitation. Now that he could see them closer – and with sunlight to boot – he could see that they were a mixture of brown-and-green mottled coloring, their formally upright frills on their head and backs tight against their bodies as they traveled. As his Jackalopes sped along the ground on an impact course, Milton was hopeful that they could inflict some damage on potentially vulnerable areas; their eyes, noses, and necks.

His hopes were dashed as the Jackalopes reached the lead lizard without retaliation, using their powerful hind legs to jump at the last moment to reach its neck. The accompanied snakes sprung off the heads of the antlered rabbits, flinging themselves upwards aiming for eyes and noses. The Quizard didn't react until the last moment, ignoring the Jackalopes and snatching six of his snakes up in its mouth with a quick sweep of its jaw. Four of the snakes made it through – two landed on and bit its nose, and the other two reached the same eye, biting down and attaching themselves to an eyeball larger than their heads.

The Jackalopes fared quite a bit worse than their partners – upon impact with the lead Quizards' neck, eight of them kamikaze'd and snapped their necks, rebounding from the thick skin and drawing a very small amount of blood. The other two impacted but didn't do any damage, instead falling to the ground with stunned expressions on their cute bunny faces.

Loudly hissing in pain, the lead Quizard stomped in frustration at the snakes on its face, inadvertently squashing the stunned Jackalopes on the ground. Slamming its face on the ground, the giant lizard squashed and scraped the offending reptiles from it vulnerable nose and eye. Their mangled bodies joined the dead Jackalopes on the ground, just as his Pygmy Wolves arrived late to the party.

Since the Quizard still had its head down, and with a damaged and bleeding eye, the wolves took advantage and jumped using all six of their feet, landing on the back of the giant lizard. Biting and scratching at the thinner skin along its frills, Milton watched as they did some damage and caused it to hiss loudly in pain again. The Quizard, again frustrated at something it couldn't reach with its hands, rolled to the side again and again in some sort of death roll, smearing his adorable purple wolves along the ground in bloody red streaks of wolf parts.

While this was all going down, the other Quizards ignored their comrade and rushed past the embattled giant lizard. They were moving so quickly down the tunnel that Milton had to rapidly switch his perspective from different sensor orbs to keep up. He thought that they were moving even faster now that they were close to their destination, but it was hard to tell without some sort of reference point.

In fact, he was worried that they were moving so fast that they wouldn't trigger the pit trap in time. His fears were allayed when the first Quizard – who had a small lead on the others – ran over the tilting cover and slid down the angled platform onto the spikes below. In addition to the hiss of expelled breath and a painful-sounding wheeze, Milton could hear stone cracking, which meant that if he made it through this attack he had some repairs to perform.

The other lizards slid to a stop before the trap, the second one in line almost skidding into the new lead Quizard, narrowly missing knocking it into the pit. For the first time, the giant reptiles stood frozen as they watched the cover tilt back up into place, ready for the next creature to dare crossing. Temporarily stymied by the surprise obstacle, Milton was sure that he had a fool-proof trap in place – they couldn't cross along the sides because they were too narrow, and they were too heavy to make it across normally.

Unfortunately, these Quizards had a bit of intelligence of their own. By the time the slightly-wounded Quizard from the battle above caught up, they had already been hard at work. With silent communication, they had the largest and heaviest of their number – which just happened to be the wounded one – sit on the cover toward the beginning of the trap, adding enough weight that it wouldn't tilt when they were crossing. The three other lizards quickly crossed, the cover tilting slightly but kept level for the most part by the heavier one.

As soon the three crossed, the larger one that was left behind moved off the cover and ran back down the tunnel. When it deemed it far enough, it made a running start and practically flew across the trap, falling short of the other side when the cover dropped. At the same time, the three lizards who had made it across dropped their tails into the pit, allowing the one who fell short to grab on to two separate tails, gripping with its sharp talons and drawing a small amount of blood.

Saved from a spike-filled death, the final Quizard was pulled up by its comrades, until they were all safe on the other side. Wasting no more time, they rushed down the tunnel and Milton was interested to see how his slicing blade trap worked against these thick-skinned lizards. He was confused by their unconcern when approaching the spinning blades – especially since the last trap proved that they had some intelligence to them.

He had forgotten for a second how fast they moved but was harshly reminded as they rushed through the spinning stone blades. Either they could analyze the timing of the blade rotations and adjusted accordingly, or they were really lucky; either way, the first three weaved their way through the deadly blades with only the third in line receiving a small cut along their tail.

The last Quizard – and the largest and heaviest – wasn't so lucky. Since it moved just barely slower that the others, its timing was off. Making it to the halfway point, four of the blades sliced into the rock-hard skin, the extra sharp edges of the blades managing to inflict massive damage upon its head, chest, and front legs. He could hear the cracking of bones and stone all the way down in his Core Room, and his sensor orbs saw the lower half of his trap literally explode into pieces, flinging bloody stone shards down both directions of the tunnel. The trap had broken at an internal level as well, where it stopped spinning and ground to a halt within seconds.

When the dust and shards cleared from the air, Milton could see that the Quizard caught in the trap had its head almost detached from its body, one of its arms sliced and mangled, barely hanging on by flap of skin. Oozing red pools of blood were expanding outward from its corpse, covering the shard-strewn floor with its lifeblood.

Shocked at the level of destruction he had caused, he almost missed the Quizards activating the spear-impalement trap further down the tunnel.

They were running so quickly and so close together that when the lead Quizard barreled through the trigger sheet, it and the second in line were past the trap when it sprung, instead hitting the last in line when it entered the trap zone. Although the wooden stakes were not as tough as stone, enough of them pierced the skin of the Quizard that it was impaled in a few key places. Every leg joint miraculously was hit, disabling all forward momentum of the giant lizard. A lucky stake was able to pierce a hole in its side before snapping off, causing it to bleed through what Milton decided was an artery from the amount of blood running out. Although it wasn't killed instantly, with it unable to move and currently bleeding out he wasn't worried about it anymore.

With three of the five Quizards who entered his dungeon dead or dying, that left only the two who made it past his first three traps. Looking back as their incapacitated member was impaled, the two shared a strange look and left it to die as they moved on. *I'm guessing the draw of my leakage is too much for them to spend time on rescuing an already dying friend of theirs.*

Without any more obstacles in place – not that they were slowing down for them in the first place – they raced down the last section of tunnel and reached the entrance to his Core Room within moments. Milton watched them coming from his Core, the frightening sight of the speeding reptiles freezing him for a second in fear. Because of that, he was almost too late ordering his drones to cut the ropes holding his gate block in place.

He had hoped to get them both underneath the block, effectively "killing two lizards with one stone." No such luck, however, as they had spread out enough that the gate only ended up catching the back half of the lead Quizard, crushing its back legs and pinning it to the floor. The last giant lizard tried to stop in time but ended up smacking into the block with tremendous force, stunning it and creating a giant crack down the center of the block.

Safe for the moment, Milton watched the pinned Quizard that was halfway inside his Core Room feebly struggle to move, weakly waving its head and front legs around in an effort to rise. As its struggling weakened, he saw the block shudder and three fine cracks appeared toward the bottom of the stone block. Switching his attention to the corridor outside the Core Room, he saw the remaining Quizard bum-rushing the stone block again, breaking it apart bit by bit. The next impact saw even more cracks appear, as well as a chunk falling off the corner, further weakening the integrity of the entire gate.

By the time the flattened lizard inside his Core Room expired 10 minutes later, huge chunks of the gate were being broken off and thrown out of the way by the enraged and insanely strong Quizard trying to break in. It was doing damage to itself in the process, bloody gashes and even a broken leg bone not slowing it down in the slightest. As if it couldn't feel the pain, one last charge down the tunnel broke off enough of the stone that it was able to climb over and wiggle its way through the missing chunks into his Core Room.

Dropping down from the cracked top of the block it had partially destroyed, the Quizard made a big splash as it touched down, just 10 feet away from Milton's Core. His Clawed Badger was nearby, but it wouldn't be able to reach the giant lizard in time considering the speed of the reptile. Activating his *Overdrive* skill for the first time since the Quizards had arrived on his territory, he took the time to consider his options.

He didn't have much to work with in here: three drones, his Clawed Badger, ALANNA, and his Core shell – all surrounded by a small lake of water. None of his units, Combat or otherwise, was close enough to help. That left ALANNA and him – which was really just him since he considered ALANNA next to useless in battle unless she was specifically targeted. He still had his self-defensive cold laser, but he didn't think it would do much based on how it affected the Scaly Bear – instead of freezing it solid, it only slowed the bear down a little bit.

He almost gave up in despair, nearly calling out to ALANNA to apologize that he couldn't do better when he looked at her face. She still had a confident expression, as if she knew he could do it – she had faith in his abilities. No messing around, no cursing, no making fun of him; only the pure faith and knowledge of his strength, his determination, and his strategic mind pulling out a win against a better opponent.

With a renewed sense of determination, he looked again at what he had to work with when he mentally "smacked" his forehead in stupidity. *The water! How could I have over-looked that?* After activating his self-defensive cold laser, he aimed it towards the Quizard who was starting to move quicker now that his **Overdrive** skill was ending. Firing it as soon as he was able, he almost miscalculated and hit its foot. The nearly-hit appendage fortunately moved just in time, allowing the light-blue laser shot to strike the water flowing around the feet of the giant lizard.

The water surrounding the Quizard flash-froze, trapping its submerged feet inside the ice. As it struggled to lift any of its feet, Milton could hear and see cracks forming, promising that the large reptile would soon be free if he didn't do something soon. With the free-flowing water surrounding the island of ice slowly melting it, he sent in his Clawed Badger to attack the backside of the imprisoned enemy.

The badgers' super-sharp claws easily sliced through the back legs of the Quizard, causing gouts of blood to erupt from the cleanly cut-off stumps. The lizard hissed so loud it was almost roar-like, swinging its now-free lower half back and forth in unintentional spasms of pain. Moving as quick as it was able, his Clawed Badger avoided the swinging lower half and moved to the front of the trapped beast. As it neatly sliced off the lizards' left front leg in one powerful swipe, the Quizard saw through the fog of pain and struck at his badger, picking it up in its mouth – halfway-in and halfway-out – and crushing its torso with a powerful crunch of its jaws. His badger didn't go down easily; Milton could see its claws slicing through the Quizard, sticking out through the throat and parting the skin like a razor blade cutting through tough leather.

Spitting out the crushed and dying badger – which allowed it slice up more on the way out – the giant lizard somehow swung its body to the side, pulling just hard enough to break the ice around its remaining leg. When the shards of ice were flung up into the air, one of them just happened to hit ALANNA who was resting on top of his shell, watching the attack with an interested demeanor. Apparently, she considered the small shard of ice that hit her a personal attack, and Milton was finally able to see what she could do to defend herself.

It was over quickly, which was fine with him because he couldn't handle anything else anyway. Leaping off his shell, she dived downwards with her fist in the lead, aiming for the head of the offending creature that dared attack her. With tremendous force and speed, her hand plowed through its skull, utterly destroying the entire head in the process. Missing three legs, throat shredded and torn, and now essentially headless, the Quizard stopped moving – finally dead.

ALANNA looked back at him, a smile on her face, "See, this bitch can take care of herself. I told you not to worry – you got this."

Chapter 22 – Bonus!

Total devastation. Well, not **total**, but close enough that Milton thought of it that way. When the last Quizard died, he looked over his domain, surveying the damage sustained by the five giant lizards that had attacked. The sheer amount of destruction **just** those five caused was disturbing – and he barely survived. Remembering the mountain range that they had come from, the dozens of caverns he had seen from just the one area worried him about the potential for more of the Quizards tracking down his dungeon. If he barely survived a handful, he couldn't even comprehend if a dozen or more came knocking on his door.

"Sure, it looks bad – but you **did** it, Milton. You fucking did it! It will probably take a while to rebuild, but now that you know what is out there, you can take steps to defend against them. And everything you received from that battle will help a bit as well," ALANNA told him.

Still in his temporary stupor while looking at his dungeon and dead Combat Units, he wasn't sure what she was talking about. His mind kicked back into gear as he comprehended what she said – his notifications! He had spaced them out, so caught up with the damage done that he hadn't even looked at them yet.

Congratulations! You have defeated Quizard x5! You gain (5x500) 2500 experience!

Congratulations! You have increased your Combat Level!

Current Combat Level: 5

Experience: 4275/4500

By raising your Combat Level, you can choose to prioritize the development of certain statistics. In addition, your Combat Units will receive a 2% (per Combat Level) increase in their own attack and defensive abilities.

Current Points to Allocate: 5

Current Combat Unit A/D Increase: 10%

Congratulations!

You have upgraded the skill: *Formation Fighting (Level 2)*

Bonus at current skill level: 10% additional damage inflicted to the enemy when your units are in a formation.

Congratulations!

You have upgraded the skill: *Combat Communication (Level 2)*

Current # of units you can communicate with simultaneously at your current skill level: 5

Congratulations!

You have upgraded the skill: *Cooperation (Level 3)*

Bonus at current skill level: 15% increased defense for Combat Units participating in a battle beside a natural enemy

Congratulations!

You have upgraded the skill: *Kamikaze (Level 3)*

Damage bonus at current skill level: 400%

Congratulations!

You have upgraded the skill: *Survivor (Level 2)*

Bonus at current skill level: 10% increase in defense of Combat Units[22]

Congratulations!

You have unlocked an achievement:

<u>What The...How Did You Do That?</u>

Survive an invasion of your base after suffering 100% Combat Unit defender casualties

   Bonus – 1000 Experience

   Bonus – +1 to all stats

Error – Cannot increase Reactor Power/Strength and Structural Integrity/Constitution due to lack of resources.

22

Skill List			
Name	Level	Name	Level
Sensor Control	2	Rudimentary Defensive Trap Design	3
Kamikaze	3	Basic Mechanical Engineering	3
Sensor Enhancement	1	Basic Construction	2
Drone Manipulation	3	Primitive Defensive Weaponry	1
Formation Fighting	2	Combat Communication	2
Cooperation	3	Survivor	2

Congratulations! You have increased your Combat Level!

Current Combat Level: 6

Experience: 5275/7500

By raising your Combat Level, you can choose to prioritize the development of certain statistics. In addition, your Combat Units will receive a 2% (per Combat Level) increase in their own attack and defensive abilities.

Current Points to Allocate: 11

Current Combat Unit A/D Increase: 12%

Oh my gosh! I'm not sure it was worth everything being destroyed, but I'll take it. It was an intense battle and he was glad that he survived, but he wasn't looking forward to something that stressful ever happening again. Looking back at what he had done over the last couple of days, he realized that ALANNA's – and, admittedly **his** – impatience to start exploring, mining, and gathering resources led to the near-fatal encounter with a stronger enemy. He was lucky he didn't encounter even **one** more of those Quizards, or perhaps something stronger.

Milton was sure something even worse was out there in the wide world – there always was. If he thought of this as an RPG, his group of level 4's got their butts handed to them by some level 10 mobs – and they weren't even bosses. *Who knows what I'll find out there – or who will find me.* The only way to safeguard his well-being was to take it slower this time and wait for the proper resources before venturing outward again. And to build more traps.

He looked at his Core Status and, sure enough, he had received a bonus to everything but his Reactor Power and Structural Integrity.[23] With the increased Processing Power/Intelligence, he could field more units – but they would still be the smaller, less powerful ones that he had already been using and it was obvious that things couldn't stay the same if he expected to survive. If he was attacked by some Quizards again, they would be less than useless; for the moment, they were the only things he could afford, but he aimed to change that.

"ALANNA, I think I made a mistake venturing out too soon. As much as it will delay progress, I don't want to risk running into anything stronger than what just attacked us. I need to take the time to prepare and adequately defend this place, now knowing a little of what the world has for us out there," he told her, using his most reasonable voice he could.

"I agree, it was pretty dumb to go out there while leaving this place practically undefended. I mean, if it wasn't for me, we'd be

---

23

Core Status			
Name:	Milton Frederick	Type:	Station Core Prototype 3-B
Combat Level:	6	Experience:	5275/7500
Reactor Type:	Zero-point Energy	Reactor Output:	2%
Current Statistics/Attributes			
Reactor Power/Strength:	2	Processing Power/Intelligence:	11
Structural Integrity/Constitution:	1	Ingenuity/Wisdom:	9
Processing Speed/Agility:	10	Communication/Charisma:	8
Insight/Luck:	11	Sensor Interpretation/Perception:	7

dead by now. Take all the time you need – better to be overprepared then dead."

"But you're the one who...what...huh? Never mind."

Damn it, I just can't win...

Chapter 23 – Facility fabrication

It took more than five years, but Milton was finally ready to venture out from his newly-improved dungeon. The initial cleanup and repair only took a week, with the recreation of his small army of Combat Units taking even less time than that. He was able to create more this time around with his stat bonuses he had received, as well as the points he was able to assign from his level-ups.[24] With his Processing Power/Intelligence now up to 15, he was able to field an impressive 1500 Bio Units. He also chose to increase both Processing Speed/Agility and Ingenuity/Wisdom to 13 so that his drones could work faster, and he could better utilize the materials he was accumulating. Even with these upgrades, the reason that it took so long to finish was because of the scarcity of metallic ore that was available to improve and create new defenses, as well as brand new facilities.

The initial deposit that his Clawed Badger had found supplied a great deal of metal units – over 10,000 in fact. However, as soon as it had been mined out, he had followed his badger on multiple

---

24

Core Status			
Name:	Milton Frederick	Type:	Station Core Prototype 3-B
Combat Level:	6	Experience:	5500/7500
Reactor Type:	Zero-point Energy	Reactor Output:	2%
Current Statistics/Attributes			
Reactor Power/Strength:	2	Processing Power/Intelligence:	15
Structural Integrity/Constitution:	1	Ingenuity/Wisdom:	13
Processing Speed/Agility:	13	Communication/Charisma:	8
Insight/Luck:	11	Sensor Interpretation/Perception:	7

feeding runs hoping to discover another one just like it. Unfortunately, only small deposits of ore had been found, providing less than 100 each time. Frustrated at his lack of resources, he began sending his drones to randomly search the surrounding underground area, hoping to find something his badger had missed.

His impatience got the better of him again because one of his drones ended up running across a small family of Clawed Badgers, the adults of which demolished and dismantled his drone. He knew they were only protecting their young, but the loss of a second drone was disheartening – not to mention worrisome. A stupid, and ultimately avoidable, mistake cost him one of his primary connections to the world outside his shell.

What made it worse was what happened afterwards, when the family got a whiff of his radiation leakage and he was forced to put them down when they attacked. He was melancholy for weeks after that, thoughts of the young badgers he was forced to kill running through his mind in an endless loop of self-recrimination and forced-justification. Added to that, it was harder to get anything done as he had lost a third of his workforce. He had to completely change their prioritization so that they could still complete all the work he required of them, and as a result his whole prospecting and mining operation was slowed to a crawl.

ALANNA was the one who was finally able to pull him past the memories and start him on the path he had stayed on since then. It was a harsh wake-up call and he was pissed at her for a couple of days afterward, but he eventually took what she said to heart.

"Look, it sucks. You shouldn't have to be forced in the position you're in, slaughtering the helpless and not-so-helpless creatures who attack you without their own volition. Now you have another choice to make: shit or get off the pot. You can continue down the path you're on, gather enough material to get off this stinking planet, and never have to worry about killing those you don't wish to anymore. Or, you can do nothing, doing what you have been doing, waste our time, and let something damage you enough that your reactor will overload – killing hundreds or even thousands in the process. Stop moping around like a little baby, suck it up, and get your ass to work if that's what you want to do. All this emotional baggage is weighing you down – drop that shit now or it'll pull you under, drowning you in the tides of uncertainty that is fucking **life**. If you're going to drag me down with you, let me know now so that I can deactivate my programming – because I don't want to be there when all this goes south. I believe you can do this, but you'll only succeed if **you** believe you can do this. And that's all I've got for motivational speeches, so fuck off until you figure out what you want," and with that she disappeared into the grey smoke again and was sucked up into Milton's shell.

Once he had cooled down from the tongue-lashing, Milton realized that he wasn't conflicted in his mind anymore. Sure, what had happened sucked, but the only way to fix it was to repair his Core so that it wouldn't happen anymore. It was this motivation that really sparked his drive and determination – that what he was doing would actually save lives in the long run. While he didn't imagine

222

himself to be some sort of hero, since he was more of a villain in this case, he didn't want to be responsible for the deaths of countless creatures. He wasn't an animal rights activist in any way, shape, or form – but he wouldn't kick a dog in the street either. They were living, breathing creatures and the more he could do to limit the collateral damage his leakage caused the better.

And so began months of the slow accumulation of resources, painstakingly mining every square foot of ore deposits that his badger could find. Since he was only down to two drones, he sent his badger along for guard duty and eventually created a second for additional support. The months of work paid off when he was finally able to look at the facilities he could build, and what it would take to create them.[25]

Even with the accumulation of over 50,000 metal units, the facilities that he could produce were few and far between. Out of the choices he had available, he wanted them all. It was a hard choice because they all required a bit of the power output from his reactor, which was still sitting at 2%. Until he was able to fix his shell

---

25

Facility Fabrication			
Name	Description	Cost (Basic Metal Units)	Power Requirements (% of Reactor Output)
Ore Refinery	Refines ore, providing 2X more usable Basic Metal Units	40,000 (34,800 with Ing/Wis stat)	1.5%
Bioconversion Lab	Allows for the creation of larger Combat Units	30,000 (26,100 with Ing/Wis stat)	1%
Biological Recombinator	Experiment with different types of units, recombining the DNA from multiple sources to form hybrids	50,000 (43,500 with Ing/Wis stat)	1.5%
Defensive Weaponry Factory	Creates high-tech defensive weaponry that is powered by your Core	45,000 (39,150 with Ing/Wis stat)	2%
Drone Assembly Plant	Creates and repairs non-combat drones and sensor orbs.	35,000 (30,450 with Ing/Wis stat)	2%

and increase his reactor output, it looked as though he was only able to build one facility.

If he could only have one, then he needed something that would benefit him in the long run, not just as a short-term solution. The one thing he was going to need the most was Basic Metal Units, which would allow him to repair his Core, build more facilities, and create deadlier defenses. Thinking long-term, he eliminated the Bioconversion Lab and Biological Recombinator, which would allow him to create larger and new hybrids of his Combat Units. While these would beneficial, it wouldn't help speed up the production of BMUs. He also eliminated the Defensive Weaponry Factory for the same reason.

That left the Ore Refinery and the Drone Assembly Plant. The refinery would increase the amount of metal ore that was extracted from the deposits he mined, whereas the assembly plant would allow him to create additional drones – as well as repairing the two that were damaged previously. Of course, it would probably take some extra BMU's to create the drones, so that extra expense had to be considered as well. ALANNA reminded him that if he chose the Ore Refinery and his two remaining drones were damaged then he'd be "fucked" – in her words, of course.

It was a dilemma, but what finally decided him on the refinery was remembering what ALANNA had told him about it – that it would allow the deposits of ore that he found to produce more than before. That, and the fact that he hadn't found any deposits nearby as large as the first one his badger had found. When he thought about it, he could have 50 drones, but if there wasn't enough to mine then they would go to waste. With the refinery, he would make the most of what he found, even if it took longer to extract what he needed. Now he just had to make sure he didn't lose any more drones.

Utilizing an offshoot from one of his drones' investigative diggings near his Core Room, Milton had his drones and badgers widen the branching tunnel and expand it so that it was big enough for his new Ore Refinery. Once they had lined the walls, floor, and ceiling with stone blocks and fused them together, he started the process of converting his hard-earned BMUs into his facility. It was easier than he thought – the blueprints for the refinery were already in his system and all he had to do was provide the intent to build it. Parts started assembling themselves inside his converter and he pooped them out, only to have his drones pick them up and transport each piece to the newly-built Refinery Room.

Each of the AI's inside the drones could follow the blueprints and put the facility together, similar to how they could construct the traps he designed. Without his input – which was good since he only had a vague idea how it was put together – they started putting the pieces together, using their tools to seamlessly weld each part when it was required. Milton watched, fascinated at the construction and intrigued by how it was created with an absence of extraneous parts.

When it was completed, two things happened: 1. He felt a power drain, making his thoughts run a little sluggishly, and 2. He received another dump of information from an upgrade in his **Basic**

Engineering skill. Because of his increased stats, he was only out for about an hour – much better than the three weeks from when he first got the skill. He now had a little more understanding of how his Ore Refinery was put together, how to operate it, and a glimpse into how it refined the ore when it was shoveled into the depository receptacle.

The sluggish way he was trying to process everything after that was a real problem, however. He could only concentrate on one thing at a time, and if something interrupted him it would take up to a couple of minutes to switch his attention to something new.

"You sucked all the power away from your Core to operate your refinery, dumbass. Of course you can't concentrate – you're left with just barely enough to control your Combat Units. You need to put everything you refine from now on toward fixing your damaged shell and goddamn reactor. With an increase in power, you'll feel much better," she told him, after he asked why he felt so slow.

The power drain and sluggish thoughts were still present even after a couple of months of refining everything he could shove into the refinery. After accumulating over 100K BMUs, he was able to finally devote enough of them to marginally fix his Structural Integrity/Constitution and, consequently, his Reactor Power/Strength. The 100K BMU's were just barely enough to eek his SI/C to 2 and his RP/S to 3. Within a couple of minutes of spending those resources, he felt power flowing back into his Core. It was like jumping into a cool lake on a lazy, scorching-hot day – it cooled him off while waking him up at the same time.

From then on, he concentrated on locating additional deposits of ore, venturing further and further away from his Core. He took a risk and reduced his above-ground army, instead using the Bio Units on an additional Clawed Badger to help with the operation. Although they couldn't move as fast and weren't as tireless as his drones, they could cut through dirt and rock like it was nothing – and every little bit helped.

Chapter 24 – Once again into the wild

Four and a half years later, he had run out of any ore deposits that could possibly be found within almost 1000 feet of his Core in every direction his drones could reach. At that time, he had a pretty good stockpile of BMUs – more than 70,000 in fact – so that he decided to concentrate on improving his dungeon defenses.

Over the last couple of years, he hadn't been attacked by anything more than random Greywieners, Jackalopes, and even two Scaly Bears at the same time. He ordered his army to allow them through to the dungeon, trusting in his traps to take care of them – which they did, handily. Since he wasn't venturing out, there weren't any radiation trails for big groups of creatures to follow and invade, which thankfully proved to Milton that he had done the right thing in suspending his exploring for the moment.

There was one other "new" creature that tried to invade his dungeon, hunting for his leaking Core. Another Big Yellow Bird just like the one from when he first arrived flew straight down the tunnel, out of range of any of his Combat Units aboveground. It flew over his pit trap with no problem and navigated its way through his slicing blades, losing a couple of feathers in the process. When it reached his sharpened stake trap, the cloth-sheet trigger worked even better than he thought it would. When the yellow avian collided full speed into the sheer curtain, it collapsed around the flying projectile, enveloping it and trapping it so it couldn't move – just in time to be impaled by six different stakes jutting from the walls.

After he had repaired and reset all his traps, he added multiple copies of his traps throughout the central tunnel leading to his Core Room. Instead of upgrading or creating new traps with his BMUs, he wanted to save as much as he could so that when he found another location to mine he would have enough to repair his Core a little bit more. He had to have more power before creating any more facilities otherwise he'd run into the power drain problem all over again. All in all, he had four of each of his initial traps spaced all throughout his tunnel – his gate was something he wanted to keep unique, so it was the only one of its kind.

He did create one additional fail-safe trap near his Core Room that didn't require anything special in the way of supplies. It was something that needed to be triggered on-site by one of his drones and was a one-shot type of construction that he hoped never to have to use. Since he knew where the underground river was located that he fed his water filter residue into, he carefully had his drones dig a giant pit that led right above the swiftly-flowing river. He then installed a simple, yet enormously strong solid stone bridge that held up a large portion of the tunnel. It was so well camouflaged that unless you knew it was there you would never see it. As a fail-safe, if it ever came down to it, he could have one of his drones pull a keystone that would collapse the bridge, dropping the floor of the tunnel down into the river. It would be a hell of a repair job if he ever needed to replace it, but it would hopefully ensure that nothing (at least non-flying) could reach him.

With the addition of a flying unit in the form of a Big Yellow Bird to his repertoire, he was excited when he decided that he was ready to venture out from his dungeon again. Since he hadn't been in any protracted combat since the Quizard invasion, he hadn't leveled up but was only about 300 experience away from level 7 because of the sporadic attacks by random creatures.

"ALANNA! Wake up!" Lately, she had taken to spending time inside his shell while he had been doing boring things like mining ore. She said that time passed very quickly that way, so that a year felt more like a few seconds.

The usual grey smoke emerged from the hole in the side of his shell and ALANNA coalesced into her normal form sitting on top of his shiny metal egg-shaped shell. She stretched her arms into the air, arched her back – which she added unnecessary popping noises to – and yawned while asking, "Oh, hi Milton! How long was that this time?"

"It's been about eight months since I saw you last, and a lot has happened. You'll be happy to know that I have finished as much preparation as I could and was just about to go exploring again. And this time I have a flying Combat Unit!" Milton was excited and just couldn't hide it.

"It looks like you've been busy! What made you decide to venture out now?"

"I ran out of minable ore deposits. I might as well try to finish that **Go Forth, Young Man** quest now. Now that I think of it, can I still complete it now that the timeframe has passed?"

"Sure, it was just a goal for the most part – but don't go expecting any fucking bonus though."

"Fair enough."

Milton looked at his Combat Unit Creation screen[26], determining who he wanted to send out on a new journey. Even though he could create everything in terms of Bio and Basic Metal Units, the Ombre Jaguar, Scaly Bear, and the Quizard were still inaccessible due to not having a Bioconversion Lab yet. If he was able to complete this quest, as well as a level-up, he would be able to send his drones more than twice the distance they could reach now – which would also mean years and possibly decades of mining deposits for their BMUs. Gaining those resources would lead to repairing his Core, adding additional facilities, and further enhancing production of needed BMUs.

26

Combat Unit Creation			
Biological Mass (Bio Units)	17170	Basic Metal (BM Units)	70374
Unit Name (Type)	Bio Units	Neurological Control Unit	BM Units
Blood-thirsty Squirrel (Scout)	5	Type-1a	1
Lollipop Snake (Stealth Fighter)	10	Type-1a	1
Jackalope (Speed Striker)	15	Type-1a	1
Pygmy Wolf (Group Attacker)	50	Type-2b	10
Greywiener (Speed Striker)	100	Type-2b	10
Big Yellow Bird (Aerial Attacker)	125	Type-2b	10
Clawed Badger (Melee Fighter)	300	Type-3c	25
Ombre Jaguar (Stealth Fighter)	500	Type-3c	25
Scaly Bear (Melee Fighter)	1500	Type-5e	100
Quizard (Speed/Melee Fighter)	2500	Type-7g	350

He had a fair complement of troops near the entrance, so he wasn't worried about leaving the dungeon unguarded while he explored. To speed up the process of exploration, he created a Big Yellow Bird for 125 Bio Units and 10 Basic Metal Units. He also created a Lollipop Snake that he planned to have ride on its back for extra protection – he had no idea what was in the skies around here. Once that was done, he sent his two new units to the surface and out into the sunlight. With the snake loosely wrapped around its neck, his Big Yellow Bird launched into the air, a little awkward due to its passengers' weight.

Milton connected to his flying unit and got a literal "bird's-eye-view" of the surrounding countryside. He had seen the landscape through the "eyes" of his sensor orbs, but they couldn't travel very far before hitting their communication limit. He didn't want to go too far up, since he wouldn't be able to see details along the ground, which was the whole point of this journey. He explored the already traveled paths North, South, East, and West to make sure that nothing had changed over the last five years. Everything looked almost exactly the same, except for the Gliding Monkey village – it was gone. Moved or destroyed, he wasn't sure – but all the crude ropes were missing and when he had the bird fly close he didn't see any monkeys either.

Moving on to new territory, he explored in a grid pattern, starting the farthest he could to the Southeast and working his way throughout the countryside until he ended up in the Northwest corner. It took a couple of weeks of slow, detailed travel, but after

232

the years of boring mining he took his time enjoying the freedom of flying. He tried not to connect too deeply with his bird – remembering the painful memories of Frank, Lolly, and Jack being eaten alive – but he did try it out for a couple of minutes. It was exhilarating feeling the wind streaming through his feathers, the weight of his snake passenger weighing on his neck, and the joy of being able to move without boundaries. He cut it off before he became addicted to it, but he was sorely tempted many times to reestablish the connection.

He was glad that he had the snake along, since they were attacked multiple times by other, smaller birds, and a couple of Big Yellow Birds as well. The surprise "snake to the neck" attack he had access to took care of most of them and only once was his exploratory party killed by a trio of Big Yellow Birds working together. Fortunately, he still had plenty of resources and was able to start again with a new party. These attacks also gave him enough experience to tip him over into Combat Level 7, giving him 7 stat points which he immediately fed into his Communication/Charisma statistic.[27] With it now sitting at 15, he was able to venture out even further with his Combat Units and Drones – which he immediately

---

27

Core Status			
Name:	Milton Frederick	Type:	Station Core Prototype 3-B
Combat Level:	7	Experience:	7535/12000
Reactor Type:	Zero-point Energy	Reactor Output:	3%
Current Statistics/Attributes			
Reactor Power/Strength:	3	Processing Power/Intelligence:	15
Structural Integrity/Constitution:	2	Ingenuity/Wisdom:	13
Processing Speed/Agility:	13	Communication/Charisma:	15
Insight/Luck:	11	Sensor Interpretation/Perception:	7

sent cautiously exploring for more ore deposits while he continued to direct his flying team.

It was a couple of days later when he finally completed his *Go Forth, Young Man* quest while exploring to the Northwest.

Current Short-term Goal: *Go Forth, Young Man* – *Complete!*

Since you don't have a clue what is out there in the big, bad world, use your Combat Units to explore the surrounding countryside and discover what this place has to offer. Although your sensor orbs and drones have a limited range, your Combat Units aren't reliant on power from your Core, so they can venture much farther. The neural connection allows for instantaneous communication over long distances. Your Communication/Charisma affects the distance they can travel and still communicate with your Core, so increasing this statistic will allow for further exploration.

- *Raise your Combat Level to at least level 6 –* Complete!
- *Thoroughly explore 20 square miles of territory –* Complete!
- *Raise your Communication/Charisma to 14 –* Complete!

Difficulty of Goal: Fun

Timeframe: 6 months – Incomplete

Rewards: Knowledge of the world. And +5 to Communication/Charisma if you're into that sort of thing.

No bonus rewards for not completing it within the given timeframe.

Congratulating himself for a job well done, he was in the process of turning back to his dungeon with his Big Yellow Bird when he saw something strange down among the trees. Reversing his orders, he instead had the bird descend until it was level with the treetops. Gliding through a gap in the foliage, a nearby branch was handy enough for his Combat Unit to alight and survey the out-of-place object.

Cleverly hidden among the trees, abandoned, and so dilapidated that it was barely recognizable as a structure, was the remains of a small wooden building. The passage of time had caused the wood to rot in places, causing the roof and one wall to collapse, but it was unmistakably, and irrefutably, a cabin. Milton wasn't sure what it had originally been used for – since it looked to have been abandoned for a long time – but as he looked closer he received another shock.

It wasn't just a ramshackle arrangement of sticks thrown together in the shape of a cabin; he could see that the boards had been planed by some sort of tool and were relatively uniform in appearance. His thoughts started shooting out in multiple directions at once.

How did this get here?

How long has this been here?

Why was it abandoned?

But the one thought that kept running through his head was: *where there's one building, it's a good possibility that there's more, somewhere.*

And with that thought came the inevitable conclusion he had trouble wrapping his mind around: *there are **people** here.*

"Oh, shit!"

ALANNA was startled, sitting upright on top of his shell too quickly and falling off into the water below when Milton shouted. She started to reprimand him again, but instead she smiled as if she had scored some type of victory.

Part II – Natives

Chapter 25 – The "Beast War"

Brint sat at the back of the small classroom, trying to stay as inconspicuous as possible as he watched and listened to Whisp lecturing the small class of young village children. He had heard all of this before, of course, but he never tired of listening to his childhood friend speak. She was a natural teacher – everything else that she had access to just enhanced the intelligence that was already there.

When they were growing up, they were neighbors for as long as he could remember and had been best-friends for almost that long. They were still best-friends, but when things had...changed...a couple of years ago, they had drifted further and further apart. That was why he was here today, spending his one free day this ten-day, listening to the same things he had learned long ago – just so that he could see her. This was just about the only time he could get away from his normal duties, since he was usually too tired by the end of the day that he couldn't think of anything but eating a massive – if bland – dinner and falling asleep.

Usually when he came to class to listen to Whisp speak, he tuned out what she was saying and just watched her enthusiasm and unfeigned excitement as she repeated the same things she must have taught multiple times by now. Today he listened in, but soon regretted it when he realized what they were talking about.

"So, I know you all know what the Guardian Guild is, but who can tell me how it came to exist in the first place?" Brint saw her

237

look out into the crowd of young faces, some with bored expressions on their faces but most just looked clueless after she asked the question. A girl of about 6 years hesitantly raised her hand from the back of the group sitting on the floor and quietly spoke, "Because of the monsters?"

"Very good! The Guardian Guild was created after...actually, let me start at the beginning, since most of you probably aren't caught up on your history yet." Brint could hear a couple of stifled groans come from the audience, reacting to her mention of history. *They must hate history as much as I do – but probably because they think it's boring, instead of my...issues.* Either she chose to ignore the groans or heard them and didn't care because she started warming up to what Brint knew was one of her favorite subjects.

"One hundred years ago, the first 'monsters' – as you called them – began to appear. In reality, however, they were at one time normal beasts that had undergone radical mutations. These mutations were wildly varied, leading to some frightening combinations of animalistic characteristics. Wolves suddenly had deadly poisonous venom, snakes could somehow learn to fly, and even the tame domesticated cats that we Proctans used to keep as pets gained razor-sharp claws and super-tough skin. The only characteristic that they had in common – although there were a few exceptions, such as the Picow, for instance – was a frightening aggressiveness which caused them to attack every Proctan they could see.

"Within a year, waves of aggressive 'monsters' attacked and killed everyone that hadn't fled in every homestead, village, town, and city in the country. Only the capital, Grestwinch, stood against the horde of creatures ravaging the countryside. Filled to the brim with refugees, the Royal Guard stood shoulder to shoulder with the City Militia, fruitlessly beating back the relentless attacks by 'monsters' more powerful than them.

"We were mere days away from running out of both food and competent soldiers when the first manifestation of a power occurred. Whinfly – you may have heard of him – was originally a lowly young soldier, drafted from the teeming masses of refugees inside the capital for the final defense of the city. Standing on the battlements on top of the wall that provided safety for the last of Proctanity, his wall was being attacked by large flying snakes one night, dripping venom from oversized fangs, when his fellow guards began to fall one-by-one. As they came for him, dropping down from the sky, he braced himself against the wall, brandishing his standard-issue sword in their direction and – he for some reason took pride in mentioning this fact – soiled his pants," she continued, to the giggles and outright laughter of her class.

"When it looked like the end for him, he somehow tapped into a mystery – at the time – power, causing the torches set along the wall in regular intervals to create a sudden burst of fire, incinerating the attacking snakes within 20 feet of him. Collapsing along the battlement, shocked and now drained beyond belief, he survived the rest of the attack by the arrival of reinforcements

239

moments later. When he had recovered later, he explained to the King and his commanders what had happened, to their expressed disbelief despite eyewitnesses.

"However, now that he had tapped into this power, he could feel the energy in the elements around him: fire, wind, water, and earth. Just by 'reaching' out, he could manipulate the element using his mind, but it came with a price: there was only so much that he could do before he felt drained of power and sometimes it took days to recover. When he showed the king his abilities, he was immediately put in charge of teaching the other soldiers to do what he could do.

"As you all probably know, everyone is born with a special ability and very rarely do they operate the same way as someone else. When Whinfly tried to teach others to manipulate the elements as he did, he failed over and over and over. It wasn't until he was injured on the Eastern wall while beating back another surge of 'monsters' that someone else discovered their own ability.

"Roselynn was a simple handmaid that was, at least until this creature invasion, an attendant in a noble's manor in a city that had been long since overrun, the noble missing and presumed dead. Faced without a job to do, she had been bringing water and the dwindling foodstuffs to the soldiers along the wall, finding a way to contribute without having to battle herself. She was bringing lunch to the guards along the Eastern wall when they were attacked, and she saw Whinfly fall beneath a flying monkey-wolf 'monster' while his back was turned and was gravely injured.

"Knowing who he was, and how he had given the men and women along the wall some hope that they could beat back the tide of attackers, she rushed to his side, ignoring the dangerous creatures still present along the wall. Some innate sense of her own power rushed to the surface as she laid her hands on his chest, and powerful healing energies rushed through her and into Whinfly, healing his wounds at an astonishing rate. When he woke up moments later, he found Roselynn at his side, a glow of energy fading around her hands as the power shut off. When he looked up from her hands, he was taken aback at the appearance of the woman lying on her side.

"She looked wasted – but alive – as if she had been starved for months or years, leaving a skeletal appearance that left her with almost no fat on her already tiny body."

One of the boys interrupted her here with a question, "Is that why healers are fat?" The rest of the class laughed, but Whisp smiled and answered the kid, "Yes, that is why – the healing uses some of the energy of the healer, and for grievous wounds can use their flesh and fat to repair the injured areas. We call this type of healing Transference, where the healthy tissue of the healer is used to fix the damaged tissue of their patients. But enough of that, let's get back to the story.

"With this appearance of another powerful ability, Whinfly was able to determine that the initial emergence of their abilities came from a powerful need. Instead of trying to teach the soldiers, and even many of the refugees – he didn't think that the guards were the only ones that might have abilities, as evidenced by Roselynn – he had volunteers take turns along the wall where the fighting was the fiercest. Granted, the risk involved in putting untested and unexperienced men and women into the middle of battle caused a fair number of casualties, but their backs were against the wall and they had all volunteered, all knowing that if something wasn't done soon they wouldn't have time to try anything else. The need to protect themselves, and even others, brought out their abilities like nothing else could – it was as if knowing that they may have something inside them that could save themselves and their families gave them extra incentive to be adaptable to the unknown.

"With new powers and abilities emerging among the populace at an astonishing rate, the soldiers and citizens working together beat back the creatures surrounding the capital. From there, the methodical push against the overwhelming force of 'monsters' began, eliminating them from the surrounding countryside and further territories. Within five years, there came a stalemate of sorts, when we couldn't push back any further due to the expanding area that needed to be constantly guarded against further incursions. We didn't have enough bodies to keep the momentum – we had lost a lot of good people before and even after we discovered our abilities.

"The one good thing that came of it was the increase in fertility rates. Pregnancy rates went through the roof, viable eggs usually occurring in multiples emerged, and semen fertilized almost instantly," she started, but paused when she saw the blank faces of the children. "Uh...lots more babies were born." They giggled again, causing her to blush, and Brint hoped that they wouldn't ask how babies were born. Whisp expertly moved the lecture along, not giving them any time to interrupt with questions.

"And so ended what is now called the 'Beast War', where we survived by the great sacrifices and achievements of all Proctans. Never before had we come together as one people to work toward one singular goal, and that sense of comradeship has forged a new era of prosperity and hopefulness. Using our new abilities, we have...actually, let me get back to my original point of this history lesson – the Guardian Guild.

"Now that we had beaten back the original onslaught of aggressive creatures, we needed to create some way to ensure that we wouldn't be blindsided by another 'Beast War', as well as guarding our borders. The solution we came up with was suggested by Whinfly and Roselynn, who ended up being some of the founding members.

The Guardian Guild was born, an association run by some of the most powerful Proctans, who would be an extension of the government. They were charged with defending the borders from the increasingly prevalent presence of deadly beasts, sending out expeditions to explore unclaimed territory looking for evidence of 'monster' build-up, and protecting all Proctans from random creature attacks from within the borders. Only later were they charged with expanding the borders, as the fertility boom still affects

243

us to today, and we need more land to feed and house our growing population."

Brint knew what was coming next and he almost got up and left, but he didn't want to call attention to himself and disturb the class. Therefore, he sat through the next part, unsuccessfully trying to block it out. He wanted to kick the little boy who asked the question he was dreading but refrained because he knew how excited he was when he first "officially" learned about the various abilities.

He collapsed even further upon himself, hoping that none of the kids would remember that he was there.

Chapter 26 – Abilities

"How do I get an ability?" the excited little 4-year-old boy asked, practically jumping up and down in a seated position at the possibility of gaining some sort of power.

"Unfortunately, you'll going to have to wait for a while. There hasn't been a case yet where the abilities have manifested before puberty, which means that for you it could take up to another 10 years or so. And that goes for the rest of you – you'll have to wait until you're at least 12-years-old or so, and then you'll be tested in the local Guardian Guild to determine your ability. Ah, I can see that you're all disappointed so maybe we can talk about what abilities you can get? Who can tell me one of the classes of abilities that exist?"

Their disappointed attitudes were instantly changed when they were able to talk about the different classes of abilities. They all raised their hands, eagerly awaiting to be called upon to answer. Whisp pointed to a small girl in the front row, who instantly answered in a high squeaky voice, "Healers! I really wanna be a healer!"

"Very good! Healer is one of the classes of abilities that you can obtain when you are older. They can heal small wounds, cure diseases, eliminate poison, and even bring someone back from the brink of death using their own body to fuel the healing. They can do this through a wide variety of methods: most use the act of touching and transferring their power to the patient, some can only use the power of the patient to fuel the healing, and even others can make concoctions using their power and body to create healing potions. These last are the most rare and sought-after because their healing potions can be used by anyone, regardless of where they are and what their ability is.

"Now, I don't want to destroy your dream of being a Healer, but you can't decide what you want to be – you are born with only one ability and you have no say in what it is. Don't worry though, whatever you end up with will be what you were meant to have – you'll be excited either way. Ok, that was the Healer class, who can tell me another?"

"Elemental Casters!"

"Physical Augmenters!"

"Nature Manipulators!"

"Inventors!"

As each class was shouted out, Whisp explained a little of each, starting with the Elemental Casters. Like the historical figure Whinfly, Elemental Casters could use their power to manipulate elemental energies. They needed to have access to the element close-by: if there was no fire nearby then they couldn't draw on it to create a Flame Lance or Fireball, some of the more common uses of fire. In addition to their monster-slaying prowess, Elemental Casters were also useful in creating stone walls, digging wells, putting out fires, and irrigating fields.

Physical Augmenters for the most part used the power within their bodies to augment their own characteristics, with a rare few who could only augment other people instead of themselves. For a limited time, or whenever they ran out of power, they could choose to make themselves stronger, tougher, or faster – with the rarest of them all being able to do all of that at the same time. They were primarily used by the Guardian Guild to be the "meat shields" of their parties, soaking up or mitigating damage from beast attacks with their heavy armor and strength.

Nature Manipulators were able to manipulate the forces of nature, including – but not limited to – plants and simple insects. A rare few were able to communicate with animals but were kept away from any aggressive creatures because they inevitably went mad from the hateful thoughts the beasts projected. They were primarily used as farmers, growing food at prodigious rates and controlling the few still-docile beasts used for meat.

Inventors were the teachers, engineers, and merchants of the world. The term Inventor was a bit of a misnomer, but the name stuck since the first ones with this ability had invented a plethora of time-saving objects in the years following the "Beast War". Using their innate power, they could enhance their intelligence for a limited time, allowing them to greater perceive the natural world and infer new discoveries. Whisp was an "Inventor" in every sense of the word – she taught, was a great engineer, and was constantly inventing things when she wasn't teaching in the school. She even had enough business sense to make quite a bit off the inventions she created, but chose to live modestly in the border village that she grew up in.

"And that covers the main classes of abilities that you can obtain when you are older. Now, we'll move on to how the different classes can increase the strength of their abilities through the repetitive use of—"

"You forgot about the 'useless' abilities!" shouted a snarky-looking older boy near the back of the room. Brint hadn't been paying attention until then, and when he heard that he looked over toward the speaker, only to find that the boy was staring right at him. He didn't know who the kid was, but apparently the boy knew **exactly** who **he** was. When he looked back at Whisp, his heart dropped when he realized she was glancing at him, before turning her attention back to the rest of the class. *I didn't think she felt that way, she always told me I had a special ability – just one that I hadn't found yet.*

Fortunately for Brint, none of the other kids had turned to look at him, instead concentrating on their teacher. She cleared her throat, obviously uncomfortable with discussing this with him in the room. "There are no 'useless' abilities, everyone has a unique ability that works for them. Some may not be as 'useful' as others, but that doesn't mean that those who have them are less than any other. It might just take a particular set of circumstances to make them seem more viable." She looked at the boy who had spoken before, specifically telling him, "In the future, don't call them 'useless' –

instead, call them 'unique' abilities because they don't fall within the main classes of abilities and are, therefore, 'unique'."

It didn't make him feel better but hearing her reprimanding the boy made him realize that she didn't think he was "useless". She knew he was far from useless, it was just that he had never discovered his ability despite numerous tests when he hit puberty. The testing agents at the Guild, who were a smattering of every known class, used everything they could think of to elicit a response, activating some sort of ability in him. After weeks of repetitive testing, they determined that his lack of ability was really "unique", since he was the only one alive that didn't have even some sort of ability that they could detect. He had even heard of a "unique" ability that some woman had that allowed her to change the color of her eyes for about ten seconds and another man that could grow his fingernails out to great lengths within moments, but they were so brittle that they would break when they contacted anything.

He would have given anything to have something "useless" – this lack of **anything** like an ability left him constantly wondering what went wrong. If he at least had something he could point to, then he could learn to live with what it was. The uncertainty left him aimless, switching from menial labor job to menial labor job throughout the last couple of years.

As the class wound down, the children filed out the room, excitedly chatting to each other about what abilities they would like to have when they got older. A few of them saw him at the back of the room on their way out and looked surprised to see him, most knowing or guessing who he was by reputation if not by sight. A few looked ashamed – since they had been talking about abilities – but a couple seemed to share the same opinion as the snarky-looking boy and looked down upon him with scorn. He ignored them with difficulty, just as he ignored the looks of pity some of the others shot his way. He wasn't exactly **used** to it, but he had seen enough over the years that he was slowly growing numb to it.

When they all exited, Whisp walked over to him and apologized, "I'm so sorry, Brint. I wasn't intending to talk about abilities today, it just seemed like the natural progression from the Guardian Guild. I hope you're not too upset by what that boy said – in fact, I'm going to go talk to his parents so that they can correct that type of talk."

"Don't worry about it, I'm used to it by now. For all I know, maybe I am 'useless'," he responded, a despondent tone inching its way into his voice.

"Don't say that! Like I told you before, you're not useless, you must," she started.

"Have a special ability – just one you haven't found yet," he finished with her, repeating what she had told him countless times.

They laughed together, thoughts of the lecture momentarily forgotten as he enjoyed her company. She always made him feel complete, like he didn't need to have an ability to feel whole. They talked for a while inside the schoolhouse, until the sunlight streaming through the windows grew dimmer and dimmer. As evening set in, he realized he needed to get back to his small shack to get some sleep – he had another early day tomorrow.

Brint walked her to her small house, the giant-sized workshop connected to it along the side dwarfing her living quarters. He said goodbye as she walked up the pathway to her door, but before he could turn away, she said, "If you get a chance, come by tomorrow night – I have something neat to show you! I think it will help you with your work." He promised that he would and watched as she entered her house, waving at him as she closed the door.

Regret tinged his thoughts as he walked back home, the deepening darkness barely hampering him as he knew the way like the back of his hand. He thought about what life would have been like if he had an ability, about what he would be doing now, and about Whisp. He thought she was gorgeous, her light-purple tinged skin a shade lighter than most others, her large ears like two beautiful fans spread out in glorious presentation, and her demure black-pupiled eyes captivated him when he stared deep into their depths. Most Proctans prized height over anything else, so she was unfortunately ignored by the majority of the male population because she was shorter than any other grown-up person that he had ever met. Unlike those others, he prized her differences and appreciated that they made her special, at least to his eyes. She was also super shy when she was interacting with anyone other than Brint, unless she was lecturing. When she was teaching, the world around her seemed to disappear and that was when she was the most comfortable, pushing her normally shy personality to the side.

When he was younger and nearing puberty, he had dreams of being with her – of possibly spending their lives together – but those fanciful dreams had been dashed when he ended up without an ability. Overheard mutterings between those older than him had mentioned something about it possibly being hereditary, which, unknown until much later, had almost led to his quiet execution.

He could kind of understand it in a detached sense – if it could be passed on to his offspring, it ran the risk of wiping out abilities for anyone in the far future. If no one had abilities, Proctanity would face the same threat it had during the "Beast War". Eventually, it was decided that he was to be monitored closely and was told not to engage in sexual behavior in any way, shape, or form. He had rebelled at first, not appreciating being told what he could or couldn't do, but threats to his life and the lives of his parents, shut him up and convinced him to walk the straight and narrow. He didn't want his parents, who were two prominent Elemental Casters in the community, to pay the price for his need to sow his wild oats.

In the end, what it meant was that he could look but not touch – as much as he wanted otherwise. He was pretty sure the Guild leaders had spoken to Whisp as well, warning her away from him, but she must have convinced them that she would still be his friend and would continue to see him. Every now and then, he would see a someone out of the corner of his eye watching them together, but at least it wasn't intrusive enough to annoy him.

With those thoughts following him home, he arrived home without even remembering the trip there. He opened his door with a strong jerk, the frame sagging enough that it would stick along the top and bottom unless he pulled it open with more than a little amount of force. He had meant to fix it, but he was always too tired after work that it was usually the last thing on his mind.

Collapsing upon his bed while grabbing a bite of some tasteless food on the way, he shrugged out of his outer clothing and fell asleep within minutes.

Chapter 27 – Stupid Picow

Brint woke up early the next morning, groaning as he got out of bed. Even though he didn't work yesterday, he still woke up sore like he did most days he was working in the fields. He thought that he would have been used to it after the last year, but the amount of back-breaking work he did seemed to restart all the pain the next day. It didn't incapacitate him – and he seemed to loosen up while he was working – but at the end of the day and in the morning, he moved around like he was decades older than he actually was. *I feel like a 19-year-old man in a 50-year-old body.*

Healers could help alleviate the pain, but he couldn't afford their services and they wouldn't waste their power on someone like him anyway. They tended to hoard their power, only using it when there wasn't any other option – they had a finite amount of power after all and if someone more "important" came along, they wanted to make sure they had enough to help them. Especially since any "Power Potions" cost an arm and a leg.

Almost 80 years ago, an Inventor by the name of Cordelious discovered where all the power and abilities in everyone came from. While almost everyone believed it to be just something that had always been there, Cordelious found that all the fresh water pulled up from the ground had a certain "residue" in it that caused changes in Proctan physiology. He experimented and found that power could be "regenerated" faster if the subject drank massive quantities of water.

Further experimentation with some of his colleagues ended up with the creation of "Power Potions", small vials of concentrated "residue" or "power", that when ingested could rapidly refill anyone's power pool. The effort in creating these potions was tremendous, and while the methods weren't secret by any means, the amount of material and time needed to make enough concentrated "power" for each potion wasn't cost effective for most people. With a monopoly in the "Power Potion" trade, the Cordpower Company and their affiliates were the only place you could buy them. With their cost of manufacture and rarity, they usually cost more than most people could afford in a year. For him, it was more like what he could earn in a decade.

So, he had to suffer through the grueling work of the only job nearby that would accept his labor regardless of his inabilities – farming. The people of the village, and the rest of the country for that matter, needed a lot of food to keep them running. Even though each person had a "power pool" inside them, they ended up using a lot of their own energy in the process. This meant that in addition to the normal amount they would eat to sustain their bodies, they needed to consume almost four times more if they consistently used their power during the day. For their modest village of about 200 residents, this meant that they needed to grow enough food for almost 1000 people.

While their two resident Nature Manipulators, Hergis and Thern, did an awesome job of using their powers to make the food grow and mature, they didn't gather it up, carry it back to the food shed, or process it so that it was ready to eat. Normally, they paid an Elemental Caster to use their power to gather it with their wind manipulation, deposit on the ground where it could be moved using earth manipulation, and then washed and prepared the food using various methods of water manipulation. They were expensive and the ones who were willing to do such basic work were few and far between, so instead the village hired the one person that didn't have a job to do and paid him a lot less – Brint.

He also had to feed the Picows, who were the main source of meat for the village. While most creatures during the "Beast War" a century ago turned deadly and aggressive, the Picow was the exact opposite. Standing 7 feet tall and weighing in at almost 3000 pounds, the Picow was a giant, docile beast that wouldn't hurt anything if it could help it. He was told that the original beast was a pig, a much smaller version of the Picow, though the pig was dark-colored instead of the Picow's lighter brown coloring. Both had a curly tail, a snub nose, and were really fat, but that was the extent of the similarities.

Quickly getting ready for work, he splashed some tepid water on his face from a cracked bowl in the corner, ate some more of the tasteless mash he had stored up, and threw on some dirty clothes. He didn't need to look nice since he was just going to end up covered in dirt and vegetation by the end of the day anyway. He walked out the door and headed out of the village to the small field nearest the tree line. Every day, they rotated between 14 small fields, each one in a different stage of development. He didn't see either of the Nature Manipulators, but he didn't expect to since they were probably in the previous day's field planting and encouraging the plants to grow.

Although they could easily grow a very small field of food in a day, it was more cost-effective in terms of power to gradually grow it over the course of a couple of weeks. They could spread a lower-level blanket of power over a field, speeding up the growing process in small increments instead of all at once. That was why they had so many fields – each one was at a different stage in the growing process.

He waved at the Guild representative standing near the processing shed before heading off into the field with a small cart to begin the harvesting process. Every village or town near the border of unknown territory required Guild protection, and any area outside the immediate village vicinity being worked upon needed to have an accompanied representative. He knew there was another one near Hergis and Thern – even though they could probably take care of themselves – but from what he knew it was better to be safe than sorry.

It took the better part of five hours before he was done in the field, which was a mixture of eight different vegetables that needed to be harvested in different manners. The variety meant that people weren't stuck eating the same thing every day, they could mix it up to make it a little more palatable. After taking the undersized, damaged, or otherwise rejected vegetables to the trough for the four Picows near this field, he headed into the processing shed where he had deposited most of the stuff he had harvested earlier in the day. Taking a quick break – even though no one was watching him, he knew if he dallied too long he would just be here longer tonight – he ate some lunch and got to work cleaning, shucking, and otherwise prepping the food so that it could be sold and ready for someone's stomach.

He had only begun when he heard a commotion outside in the field. The Picows in the pen were squealing in terror, or at least what he thought was terror. Rushing outside with a small blade still clutched in his hand that he used in his food preparation, he looked to the Picow pen and saw two of the large beasts lying on the ground, blood fountaining from massive wounds that had sliced open their bellies and necks. The other two were backed up along the side of the pen closest to the field, pushing up against the fence, trying to get away from what had killed the other ones.

Brint looked past the dead Picows to see the Guild guard fighting against three Spider Wolves, his speed so fast that he looked like a blur when he tried to concentrate on him. Despite having the speed advantage, the three wolves used the four spider legs emerging from their backs to constantly stab forward with deadly accuracy while they attempted to bite the defending guard with their fangs dripping deadly venom.

While he was keeping the Spider Wolves at bay, he wasn't making much progress in killing them. He imagined that the loud squealing from the Picows could be easily heard from the next field over, so he was sure that the guard would get some help from the other Guild member soon. He didn't dare get close enough himself to help, because he couldn't even imagine going toe-to-toe with something as scary as the wolves in the pen.

Suddenly, he saw the guard faulter, limping out of range after a lucky shot from a spider leg hit him in his upper leg. He quickly fished out a healing potion from his pocket and chugged it. While Brint couldn't see the wound heal, he could see the change come over the man as he straightened up and began attacking again.

However, the damage had been done. While the guard had been healing himself, the wolves took advantage of the situation and lunged for the still living Picows trying to stay as far away from them as possible. Those lunges, even though the guard got there in time, were enough for the Picows to press on the fence with just enough force that it broke under the pressure. One of the Picows ran for safety into the processing shed, while the other one ran into the field toward the trees, presumably out of its mind with fear and not knowing where it was going.

I'm probably going to regret this. Making a quick decision that probably wouldn't end up well, Brint ran after the Picow, intent on bringing it back to the field. A couple of months ago, he had accidentally left a small gate open on one of the Picow pens at the end of the day, resulting in one of them wandering off, never to be seen again. The Mayor of the village – who ran the whole field/food operation – told him that he was on permanent probation after the incident. If he lost another Picow, he'd be out of work and he wasn't sure if anyone would hire him after that happened.

He could probably blame this on the Spider Wolf attack, the same as the two dead ones in the pen, but he didn't want to take the chance. He could just imagine the guard saying that he just stood there while it got away. He knew he wasn't expected to fight the wolves, but he was more than capable of fetching a stray Picow.

Dropping the knife in his hand to prevent an accidental self-stabbing, he ran across the field while keeping an eye on the battling foursome, he slipped through the trees following the obvious trail of trampled foliage and snapped branches. He figured that it would stop soon, allowing him to lead it back to its pen, where – hopefully – the battle had been concluded and things had been cleaned up. No such luck, unfortunately, as the trail led deeper into the forest and he couldn't even hear it ahead. *Damn, I didn't realize these things were so fast – especially when they are scared out of their minds.*

He was starting to get tired and the sun was starting to set, which caused the already muted lighting under the trees to darken, and he was still no closer to getting that stupid Picow back. He was ready to turn around, prepared to explain to the Mayor that he had done all he could to get it back, when he heard a loud squeal come from up ahead on the path he was following. Knowing that what he was doing was probably stupid, he foolishly decided to see what had happened.

260

Sneaking through the underbrush as quietly as possible, which ultimately wasn't that quiet since he didn't spend a lot of time in the forest, Brint slowly crept up on where he thought the noise had come from. He brushed aside a branch blocking his vision and saw the Picow lying on its side, with six small, scaly-skinned purple wolves with their mouths on it, trying to tear off pieces of the poor animal. As he watched, he realized they weren't trying to eat it, but were trying to drag it away. With a small chuckle at the absurdity of it that he immediately regretted, he froze as six sets of eyes immediately trained on him as he crouched halfway behind a tree.

Knowing he was screwed, he tried to run but immediately tripped over a root a couple of feet behind where he was ineffectually hiding. He landed on his left wrist where he felt and heard a popping sound, followed by excruciating pain. Fighting through the pain, he tried to get to his knees when he was hit from behind, which knocked him down again on his stomach. Using his uninjured hand, he managed to turn his body over, only to be confronted by a circle of snarling wolves.

Body stiff with fear, he couldn't move – he could only watch as they slowly approached his prone form. *It's all that damn Picow's fault! If it wasn't for that stupid, dumb animal I'd*—His thoughts were interrupted as he could see the wolves about to pounce. Suddenly, he could feel a power flow through his body, unlike anything he had felt before. It was like a drinking a mug of a hot beverage on frigid night, fingers wrapped around the near-burning cup as heat spread throughout his frozen body.

261

Unbidden, the word "STOP" tore itself from his throat, infused with the power he felt inside his body. Instantly, the six wolves froze, even their eyes unmoving as they slowly toppled over onto their sides, presumably dead. He sat in shock, feeling drained from the usage of a power he didn't even know he had, and slowly the pain from his broken wrist penetrated his consciousness. Cradling his injured wrist against his chest to prevent it from moving, he slowly got up and moved toward one of the purple wolves. Kicking it – and hoping it wasn't faking death – he was relieved when it didn't move.

After taking a couple of moments to catch his breath and gather his frayed nerves, he turned to leave, cradling his injured wrist to his chest. He was somehow relieved and at the same time confused by what had happened. Brint knew that he couldn't talk or command creatures since he had been tested for that when he was younger, and he hadn't heard of anyone with the power to command something with just their voice. Shrugging it off for the moment, he resolved to contemplate it more when he got home safe – he didn't want to spend any more time here than he wanted.

He had taken a couple of steps back down the path when he heard a voice screaming inside his head, "WHO ARE YOU AND WHAT DID YOU DO TO MY SCALY PYGMY WOLVES?!"

The shock of something talking to him in his head – along with everything else that had occurred – was too much for his fragile mind to accept all at once. He watched the ground rushing up to his face as his vision slowly turned dark. His last conscious thought was,

Pygmy Wolves?

Part III – Revelations

Chapter 28 – Automation

The last century had been at times exciting and at times frustrating, but most of it had been boring. After the initial exciting discovery that there had been people here – at least at one time – he had been eager to explore farther, hoping to learn more about them. Even with his expanded neural communication limit he had access to after finishing his exploration quest, the only thing he discovered regarding people was a small abandoned village just at the edge of his range. From high above, it had looked like it had been vacated recently and hurriedly, with discarded personal items left all over the ground. He wondered at what had made them leave so abruptly and endeavored to find out later when he was able to explore the village and surrounding areas from the ground.

While he was out exploring, he noticed a change in the creatures inhabiting the forest outside of his influence. Most of them looked like the "normal" creatures, but they also had some additional features that made them different. For instance, his bird was attacked and killed once by **flying** monkeys, a variation of the Glider Monkeys that he had discovered years ago that could actually **fly**. On the ground, he could see Lollipop Snakes the size of an Anaconda, Jackalopes that were covered in scales instead of fur, Pygmy Wolves that were smaller but were **a lot** more numerous, Ombre Jaguars the size of what he assumed Sabretooth Tigers used to be, and a whole plethora of new creatures he had no experience with yet. It began to look more and more like he had crashed down in the "newbie zone" and everything further away was for higher levels.

ALANNA, when confronted, expressed not to know what had happened to cause it to be that way. She speculated that when Milton had crashed down, the mysterious sound and impact may have scared off most of the wildlife and only those too dumb to know better stuck around. She figured – and Milton agreed – that given enough time, they would be back, and he would be screwed if he didn't prepare for it.

To that end, he began exploring the newly-opened ground, searching out additional places to mine for ore. He was pleased to find a massive concentration of ore to the South, just in range of his drones' reach. With his limited number of drones – and the distance away from his Core and Ore Refinery – it took over 10 years for him to accumulate enough Basic Metal Units to upgrade his Structural Integrity/Constitution and Reactor Power/Strength enough to build something that would increase his productivity by leaps and bounds.

The Drone Assembly Plant only took a day to build, but the unanticipated learning of a new skill knocked him out for a couple of months.

Congratulations!
You have acquired the skill: *Basic Technological Engineering (Level 1)*

This skill expands on your knowledge of engineering, allowing a tiny glimpse at the vast technological knowledge of The Collective. Power systems, Artificial Intelligence, nanites, and neural communication are just some of the Basic Technological Engineering subjects you now have a near-passing knowledge of.

Basic Technological Engineering (Level 1) was a whole new world to him. While he was tangentially aware of the knowledge that was imparted with his *Basic Mechanical Engineering* skill, the technological advancements of The Collective were so foreign to him that it took so much longer to absorb the information. So that he could understand even the small snippet of knowledge that was initially uploaded to his mind, the main Core system had to fill in the gaps in his knowledge-base. It was like trying to teach a caveman how an automobile worked – you could show him how the engine operated, but if he had never seen a wheel then you would have to explain that first.

Once he was back up and running, however, he immediately started repairing his broken drones. The Drone Assembly Plant was – to Milton with his new knowledge – a marvel in engineering. It was a giant enclosed cube, 20 feet long on each side, made primarily of metal and durable plastics and had a small assembly line that would convert raw materials into a finished product. Like when he constructed his facilities, he was able to substitute other materials in place of high-grade materials that were much more expensive in terms of BMUs.[28] Each of his drones or sensor orbs required a small amount of power from his reactor to keep them functioning, which put a stop to his fanciful plans of having thousands of drones swarming the countryside. The cost to repair his drones varied, depending on the damage that they had sustained. All in all, it only cost him 365 BMUs to get his two broken ground drones back to full-functionality – and he sent them straight to work mining more ore deposits.

He noticed that his Drone Assembly Plant menu had a new option – an aquatic drone. This was the first time he had heard of it, so he asked ALANNA why he didn't come pre-equipped with any.

"For the Station Cores that were heading to water-rich environments, they **were** included. However, since the outpost you were heading to was basically at the ass-end of nowhere, they were left off your initial allotment." *Makes sense – though I could have used one when I was exploring that underground lake.*

28

Drone Assembly Plant			
Name	Description	Cost (Basic Metal Units)	Power Requirements (% of Reactor Output)
Repair Ground Drone	*Repairs Ground Drone to full functionality*	100-1000 (87-870 with Ing/Wis stat)	N/A
Repair Flying Drone	*Repairs Flying Drone to full functionality*	100-1000 (87-870 with Ing/Wis stat)	N/A
Repair Aquatic Drone	*Repairs Aquatic Drone to full functionality*	100-1000 (87-870 with Ing/Wis stat)	N/A
Repair Sensor Orb	*Repairs Sensor Orb to full functionality*	10-100 (8-87 with Ing/Wis stat)	N/A
Build Ground Drone	*Build a new Ground Drone*	5,000 (4,350 with Ing/Wis stat)	.02%
Build Flying Drone	*Build a new Flying Drone*	7,000 (6,090 with Ing/Wis stat)	.025%
Build Aquatic Drone	*Build a new Aquatic Drone*	6,000 (5,220 with Ing/Wis stat)	.025%
Build Sensor Orb	*Build a new Sensor Orb*	300 (261 with Ing/Wis stat)	.001%

As for his flying drones – which he had never even seen functioning since they were damaged when he arrived – each of them took between 435 to 625 BMUs to repair and Milton thought that was more than acceptable since a brand-new one would cost him over 6,000. Once they were operational, he found that they looked exactly like his ground drones, with the only exception being that they used the same method of flight as his sensor orbs; his new knowledge told him that it was some sort of gravitational repellence system, the exact functioning of which he wasn't quite sure of yet.

Since they acted just like his ground drones, he sent them to work in the mines, using their flight capabilities to speed up the retrieval process since they could ferry the ore at a faster rate. With the additional drones, the resource gathering process was four times faster than it had been previously, so the BMUs were rolling into his reserves in huge quantities. Within a year, he had gathered about half as much as he had in the last ten. Milton, and by extension ALANNA, were expecting the whole process of repairing his Core and building a spaceship to take a lot less time than they had initially thought. If the pace of the drones' mining kept up like it had been, they would be out in decades instead of centuries as they had theorized. And then, inevitably, when things tended to go well, they hit a snag when the large ore deposit they had been mining ran out.

Quickly utilizing his badgers to search for more, Milton was disappointed when there were only very small deposits found scattered all over the place. Instead of being done in decades, it looked like he was here for the long haul – unless they found another ore motherload, they were destined to be here for centuries.

When this sad fact was determined, ALANNA started to retreat into Milton's shell before he stopped her. Before this, she had stayed out, talking with Milton or wandering the hallways of his dungeon. Most of the time, however, she was on the surface, playing with his Greywieners and generally enjoying the sunshine. Milton missed the sun a little bit, but he had spent so much time indoors playing video games that he had no real urge to get out-of-doors. Besides, the time he spent flying around in the mind of his bird more than fulfilled any need to get out into the sunshine.

"Where are you going? Are you just going to leave me to do all of this myself? I don't really have anyone else to talk to, you know." Although they weren't constantly chatting, it was still nice to know that someone was at least near if he felt the need for conversation.

"Don't be such a whiny little bitch, just put yourself into sleep mode. You can automate your mining processes and be alerted if anything comes up. The time will pass as if you're asleep, although you won't dream or anything like that. If you need me, I mean **really** need me, call me and I'll come out – otherwise fuck off…please?" He had grown numb to her name calling and language years ago, but lately she had been making attempts at being polite after he had grown sick of her barking orders and called her out on it. *Hey, at least she said please—wait, how do I get to sleep mode?*

270

It was too late to ask her, since she had already escaped to the confines of his shell. He didn't want to disturb her already and figured he at least had the time to try to figure it out on his own.

Three months later, and after lots of experimentation, he had learned how to automate all his units. He already knew how to give general instructions to his scouts on alerting him to anything out-of-place, but he knew he would be disturbed every few weeks if he left it like that. Instead, he set up a series of if-then processes in the minds of every single unit, from his squirrels to his drones. He also discovered that they could "talk" to each other using his Core as a central distribution hub for neural communication. For instance, if his squirrel saw something unusual, it would send that information back to his Core which would then bounce it to his Combat Units on the surface. If they determined that a threat was incoming, they would prepare for one of 17 different scenarios and formations that he had developed based on the random creature attacks that he had experienced over the years.

So that they could keep an eye on the incoming hostiles, up to three different sensor orbs could be deployed to follow their progress, which would send that information to his waiting Combat Units. If the threat was determined to be too much for his above-ground units, they would be assessed on whether the traps inside his dungeon were enough to take care of any potential threat. If it was decided based on their multiple assessments that more help was needed, then and only then would he be "woken" up to determine the best course of action.

His drones and badgers he put on a constant search and mine pattern, the latter's only job was to sniff out more ore deposits. Only when his drones were needed to reset a trap, repair a section of tunnel that was damaged, escort new recruits out to the surface, or drag a dead enemy down to convert into Bio Units would they leave their mining operations. He was initially worried that he would have to replace aging Combat Units over the years, but then he remembered that ALANNA had told him that the nanites in their systems automatically renewed and repaired any damage caused by old age. Because of this, he only had to automate his own Core and Molecular Converter to monitor and replace any non-functioning (dead) Combat Units over the years, so that they would be fully prepared for potentially any threat – large or small.

When all of this was set up, he was able to finally get some "sleep". Activating Sleep Mode, his direct connection to all his Combat Units, drones, and orbs shut down one at a time until he was left adrift without any outside stimulus. It felt as though he was trapped within his own mind, like he had gone blind and deaf, but it wasn't an unwelcome feeling. He had been tapped into so many different things simultaneously that it was comforting not to have his attention pulled in so many directions at once.

It felt like mere moments later when he was "woken up", leading Milton to think something had gone wrong. Connecting to the squirrel scout that had alerted him, he took a quick look at the date inside his "mind" and saw that more than seven years had passed! It felt more like seven seconds to him, but when he thought about it he realized that without outside stimuli it was hard to assess the passage of time.

He realized what had gotten his scouts' attention – something unknown. It looked like a large grey wolf but had four black legs protruding from its back, long hairs reminiscent to a spiders'. Long fangs dripping green venom completed the package, enough that Milton felt comfortable calling it a Spider Wolf. There were seven of them running in a pack near the edge of his territory, but fortunately not heading for his dungeon as far as he could tell. They stuck around the area for a couple of days while he watched them through various squirrels, but they ultimately left the area without being drawn to his Core. He was interested in seeing what they could do, but he didn't want to provoke them unnecessarily – no need to invite trouble.

When that interruption was taken care of, he reactivated his Sleep Mode after determining that progress was being made with his mining, albeit slowly. He was maybe halfway from being able to fix more of his Core and reactor, as well as being able to build another facility. The next time he "slept", he was down for almost fourteen years this time, which again felt more like fourteen seconds. This time, when he woke up, there wasn't an emergency. He had actually hit the threshold of BMUs he had set more than two decades ago, with more than enough resources to build his next facility – the Bioconversion Lab.

Chapter 29 – Bioconversion Laboratory

The Bioconversion Laboratory was a big step-up for his defenses and he was excited to start improving his army. Essentially, the lab consisted of only one super-large hollow metal cylinder filled with water and nutrient solution. When he placed enough resources inside, the lab would automatically create whatever he wanted, where it would rapidly grow to full-size within hours. When it was complete, it would flush out the newly-created creature into a large collecting pool underneath it, where it would rapidly recollect the liquid to be used again. After a couple of minutes of adjusting to its surroundings, it would be ready to do whatever he wanted.

It was only when he looked at creating his first large creature that he hit a snag – he didn't have enough available Processing Power/Intelligence to effectively control it. That was when he noticed that he had increased his Combat Level to 8 over the last few decades from the random attacks by stray creatures. When he put 5 extra statistic points into PP/I, he was surprised by a prompt:

Congratulations!

When you reach certain milestones in your statistics, additional bonuses can be unlocked. In this instance, when you reached 20 points in Processing Power/Intelligence, the Bio Unit

limit is effectively doubled. Whereas you could previously control 2000 Bio Units, you can now control 4000 Bio Units.

*Nice, now I can almost get whatever I want! Or, at least, **one** of whatever I want.* After placing his remaining 3 points into communication[29] – so that his drones could range farther for resources – he decided to go for broke and purchase his very own Quizard for 2,500 Bio Units and 350 BMUs. After just under four hours, his new Quizard had been "birthed" and was ready for action. Even though he was confident in its abilities, he didn't want to send it out into the forest quite yet – he wanted to add some extra protection to his dungeon.

Since it was comfortable underground, as evidenced by where he initially ran into them, he set it up as a sort of "boss" near the entrance. He wanted to put it further down, but he ran into the problem with feeding it – he ended up needing to shut down every trap just to get it out of the dungeon. He wanted it to be able to leave the dungeon to feed, and he didn't have enough Bio Units to keep feeding it indefinitely with converted Combat Units.

29

Core Status			
Name:	Milton Frederick	Type:	Station Core Prototype 3-B
Combat Level:	8	Experience:	27605/31500
Reactor Type:	Zero-point Energy	Reactor Output:	7%
Current Statistics/Attributes			
Reactor Power/Strength:	8	Processing Power/Intelligence:	20
Structural Integrity/Constitution:	8	Ingenuity/Wisdom:	13
Processing Speed/Agility:	13	Communication/Charisma:	23
Insight/Luck:	11	Sensor Interpretation/Perception:	7

With that done, he checked up on the progress of his other units and, satisfied, went back into Sleep Mode. This time, with the additional protection in the form of his new Quizard, he wasn't disturbed for another three decades, when all the available ore deposits – down to the smallest amount that could be found – had been mined and his badgers had to find food outside of the range of his drones. He knew that there was more out there, but he couldn't reach it yet. With his accumulation of resources, he was forced to build a Communication Amplifier, enabling him to extend the range at which he could send out his drones. He hadn't built one before now since there hadn't been any pressing need and the cost was staggering, running at about 100,000 BMUs. He had a little more than that saved up, and the power cost was only 0.5% of his Power Output – affordable, but he would be left with very little in the terms of BMUs and Power Output available.

The Communication Amplifier acted almost as a Wi-Fi hotspot, one that had a range equal to his Communication/Charisma skill; being at only 23, that meant that he could reach another 2300 feet. Placing it at the extreme edge of his current communication limit to the Northeast, his flying drones were easily able to transport the parts to the location when Milton created it. His ground drones started assembling it as soon as they got enough parts, but the distance from his Core meant that it took a couple of days to finish the entire structure.

When it was complete, Milton looked at it through one of his drones' "eyes", and he started laughing internally. He had ended up putting it in the middle a small clearing he had found, but after seeing the finished product he wished that he had hidden it in the middle of some trees. If he had been aiming to create a 15-foot-tall shiny metallic phallic symbol, then he had more than succeeded. With a base installed into the ground that was wider than the rest of it, the "shaft" of the tower was about a foot in diameter and stuck straight up into the air, ending with a bulbous, rounded top. He wasn't sure who had originally designed the amplifier, but they must have cared more about function than aesthetics.

With that in place and activated, he found that he could just barely reach the rock formations he had found that housed the Pygmy Wolves. He temporarily reassigned his Quizard to guard duty, protecting his drones while they started exploring and mining the newly-reached ore deposits. Weeks passed without any attacks, but one night while the Quizard was out hunting, a massive pack of Miniature Pygmy Wolves the size of large hamsters attacked en masse, at least 300 of them swarming over his dig site. His flying drones were fortunately in the air transporting material back to his Core, but two of his drones were enveloped in the wolfen tide, torn apart by their surprisingly sharp teeth and claws. The remaining two drones had burrowed underneath the ground for safety, but the wolves were already digging their way after them, massive clumps of dirt being thrown all around by their fervor.

Since he was still "awake" while they were actively mining the hills, he directed his Quizard back to the site, knowing that his Combat Unit was the only thing standing between his remaining ground drones and their destruction. The Quizard quickly sped back, arriving within moments of the initial attack. It was like a force of nature, tearing through the assembled Miniature Pygmy Wolves like a tornado, slicing apart swathes of them with its claws and stomping on dozens of them as it almost danced around them in fury. After only a minute, his Quizard was victorious, chunks of wolf strewn about and blood coating its scaly skin in smears and splotches of purple and red. While most of it was purple from the wolves, a good portion of it was from his lizard, wounds covering its body from the many tiny wolves that got through its defense before they died.

Milton watched through its eyes as it tried to move around afterwards, only to almost collapse from an injury to its back-left leg. He didn't want to have to kill this Quizard off, especially since it did such a good job defending the worksite, and the expense of replacing him was cost-prohibitive. He knew the nanites inside its body could heal small wounds, but it looked as though its extensive injuries were a bit too severe. Instead, he brought out ALANNA, hoping that she wouldn't be too mad at him for waking her up.

She was actually quite congenial, at least as much as personality would allow. Milton thought she must have been ready to wake up and "stretch" – for a little while at least. "Heal your Combat Units? Why the hell would you want to do that?"

"Well, I don't want to have to make a new one – it's pretty expensive and it also would take too long to create another one from scratch. It needs to get back to my worksite so that I can make sure the drones are guarded while they mine."

"You'll have to research Biological Repair in your Bioconversion Lab. I'm surprised that you haven't already looked at that. Has there been anything exciting going on lately?" she asked, unfeigned interest in her expression.

"Uh...not really. Just mining and collecting resources. Pretty boring actually."

"Well then, I'm fucking out of here," with that, she turned into her grey fog and wisped into his shell once again.

"Thanks..." he said, not sure if her retreating form could hear him. He turned his attention to his Bioconversion Laboratory and focused his attention on it. Suddenly, something popped up in his "mind" – a list of things that he could research or "unlock" in his lab.[30] It cost Bio Units to unlock the functionality of each option, including 1,000 to obtain the Biological Repair function. He was intrigued by some of the research that granted him the ability to increase the damage and defense of future creatures he made, but the cost was a little high yet to justify purchasing them.

He purchased the ability to repair his units and instructed his Quizard to return to the dungeon. As it limped back – its speed a small fraction of its prior sprinting ability – he had his airborne

---

30

Bioconversion Lab -- Research		Available Bio Units: 4455
Type	Description	Unlock Cost (Bio Units)
Biological Repair	Repair a biological specimen to full functionality (Bio Unit costs are varied)	1000
Increased Damage Modifier (Lv. 1)	Increases damage bonuses to created specimens by 5% (Base Basic Metal Unit costs are increased by 10%)	3000
Increased Defensive Modifier (Lv. 1)	Increases defensive bonuses to created specimens by 5% (Base Basic Metal Unit costs are increased by 10%)	3000
Increase Spawning Speed (Lv. 1)	Increases rate specimens are grown by 10%	2000

drones cautiously bring back the pieces of his destroyed drones so that he could repair those as well. *Maintaining my units is getting expensive*, he thought.

His drones were repaired just as the injured Quizard made it back to the dungeon. His drones had to disarm all the traps in the way again, but he figured the time and expense saved by doing this would make it all worthwhile. When the lizard reached the lab, Milton instructed it to climb to the top of the cylinder using a handy ramp located around the side and to jump in. Once it was inside the liquid, he activated the Biological Repair option on the creation menu and within minutes his giant lizard was back to normal. All in all, with the repair only costing 215 Bio Units, he only spent a total of 1,215 – which was less than half of what a new Quizard would cost. And now he could repair **any** of his Combat Units as well.

Milton sent his Quizard back to the worksite, carrying his repaired ground drones with it to get them back as soon as possible. He also spent the necessary resources to create an extra sensor orb as well, so that it could stay airborne and keep watch and hopefully avoid another incident. *Forewarned is forearmed, or so they say.*

He didn't have any major problems after that. He stayed "awake" for another month, watching the progress at the Wolf Den Hills and looking for any problems that needed his attention. There were another couple of attacks by groups of Miniature Pygmy Wolves, but there were a lot less than the first group and were barely able to scratch his Quizard before they went the way of their predecessors.

With things well in hand, he left his drones and other units to do their thing while he activated Sleep Mode again with instructions to wake him up in 15 years if nothing else happened. The usual blankness enfolded him in its embrace and he had a good 10 years (or 10 seconds) of uninterrupted "sleep" before he was interrupted by one of his squirrel scouts.

Chapter 30 – Proctans

They were back. He wasn't sure where all the people went, but his squirrel scout had noticed a party of them making their way through the forest, about 1,000 feet inside the border near the abandoned village he had found decades ago. It wasn't abandoned anymore, which he found out when he flew over it with just his bird instead of the bird-snake combination he had been using for years. He didn't want to gain their attention before assessing what kind of threat they would be to him.

He wasn't naïve enough to think that they would be nice and understanding when they learned about him. If they were **anything** like humans, then they wouldn't hesitate to try to destroy something unknown and different from them, even if they understood exactly what he was. He had to take things slowly, investigate them as stealthily as possible and try not to do anything to garner their attention. Therefore, he just watched from afar.

They looked humanoid in shape, but their skin was differing shades of purple, from a light lilac color to a deep purple, almost black color. They also had larger eye sockets and eyes, the pupils of which made up most of their eyeballs, as if they were used to being underground and had adapted for low-light conditions. It was possible that the sunlight on this planet was different than what he was used to, and he didn't notice because his "eyes" were all artificial or part of the native creatures nearby – their eyes must need the extra-wide pupils to compensate.

Their ears were another striking feature of these people – instead of smaller ears like humans, they had large ears that fanned out from the side of their heads, sometimes extending out a foot or more. They almost reminded Milton of the fins on the side of a fish.

They had different shades of hair, had legs, feet, arms, hands, and fingers just like humans. If it wasn't for their eyes and ears, Milton would classify them as close to humanoid as it was possible to get – except for one unique characteristic. Somehow, they had magic.

The first time he saw it was when he was sitting on a branch high up in tree as his Big Yellow Bird, watching the planting going on in a cleared field below. There were three men – at least he assumed they were men – wearing green, loose-fitting clothes with wide-brimmed hats to keep the sun out of their eyes. He watched as they poked in the freshly-plowed dirt below and dropping in seeds before covering them back up. It was slightly fascinating as he had never actually seen any type of farming before, but at the same time it was boring with the repetitiveness of it. He was about to fly away when they finished but stopped as something curious happened.

The men moved to various portions of the field and stopped. Raising their hands up slowly, Milton sat amazed as shoots of green, blue, and purple shot up from the ground, the seeds that they had planted minutes ago showing days or weeks-worth of growth. The men looked exhausted and they quickly headed back to the village, only to disappear within one of the buildings.

Fascinated by this evidence of something he'd only read about in books and played with in videogames, he spent the next year learning as much as he could about these people. By listening to their conversations when he was close enough, his Communication/Charisma stat helped him to understand what they were saying within a couple weeks of observation.

Even after observing as long as he did, he didn't learn a lot from them. He learned that they were call Proctans and the planet they were on they called Proctus. They had just moved back to this abandoned village after years of recovery following something called "The Beast War" and were planning on settling there if the beasts were able to be kept away. The magic they seemed to possess was just a normal part of their lives and almost every adult he saw had some sort of power. He saw Proctans magically digging trenches, healing wounds, growing plants, and even some moving abnormally fast. He wasn't sure how they got these abilities or why they chose certain ones, but he wasn't about to get any closer and risk exposure.

After that year of observation, he focused on doing anything he could to prepare for his inevitable discovery by the people in the village. First, he took all his accumulated resources and spent most of them to build more drones. He had enough from the last decade to triple his workforce, acquiring eight new flying drones and eight new ground drones. When he sent them to his mining operation, their presence was well worth the expense – his incoming ore was arriving in triplicate as well. Without anything else that needed his attention, he went back to sleep after creating 10 additional squirrel scouts which would patrol the border between his territory and the growing Proctan village. He wanted to know if they started delving deeper into the forest before he was ready.

He then started a "sleep" cycle for the next 20 years where he "woke up" once a year to check out the situation and to create a few additional drones to mine. After 20 years, he had accumulated 40 each of his ground and flying drones, leveled up to Combat Level 10, and had nearly mined out the entire Wolf's Den area, leaving large holes in the surface of the ground that he had his drones cover up with dirt in an attempt to lessen the impact he had on the surrounding landscape. He didn't want to be responsible for creating some "man-made" lakes that would stop water from getting to where it was needed and causing a drought somewhere. He was trying to survive – not kill everything else.

In addition, he now had enough BMUs to greatly improve his Structural Integrity/Constitution and Reactor Power/Strength by a large amount, with a bit leftover to finally create the Biological Recombinator ALANNA had been asking about almost a century ago. He had half of his drones hollow out a section of his dungeon near the Bioconversion Lab, while the rest followed around the badgers while they continued to look for ore deposits. His drones worked so efficiently that he had trouble keeping up with the blocks of stone that were needed to complete the room, and minutes after the last stone block was converted the room was ready.

He selected the Biological Recombinator on the facilities screen and parts started to poop out the back of his shell. The army of 40 drones were able to take most of the parts in just two trips, meaning that the new facility was built within about 20 minutes. As soon as it was built, he received a couple of notifications.

Current Average-term Goal: *Boot Camp* – *Complete!*

Learn the different functions of a Station Core:

- Sensors – *Complete*
- Drones – *Complete*
- Molecular Converter – *Complete*
- Biological Recombinator – *Complete*
- Resources – *Complete*
- Self-Defense System – *Complete*
- Units – *Complete*
- Neural Connections – *Complete*
- Structures/Manufacturing Facilities – *Complete*
- Defenses – *Complete*
- Combat & Combat Levels – *Complete*
- Statistics – *Complete*
- Skills & Achievements – *Complete*
- Research & Discoveries – *Complete*

Difficulty of Goal: Hard

Timeframe: 1 year -- *Incomplete*

Rewards: Become a fully-functioning, knowledgeable Station Core

---

> No bonuses due to it not being completed within a year

Current Average-term Goal: *If You Build It, They Will Come* – *Complete!*

Using current and new metallic resources, design and build various manufacturing facilities. These manufacturing facilities will accomplish a number of things: increase refining output of raw materials, allow for the experimentation of new Combat Unit hybrids, repair and create new drones and sensor orbs, and create high-tech defenses.

- *Locate and accumulate 10,000,000 basic metal units –*
  12,574,114/10,000,000 Complete!
- *Create **5** different manufacturing facilities – 5/5 Complete!*

Difficulty of Goal: Frustratingly Hard

Timeframe: 100 years

Rewards: +10 to all statistics

Bonus: *For completing it years before the timeframe (95 years, 6 Months, 14 Days), you receive an additional +2 to all your statistics*

Error: Reactor Power/Strength and Structural Integrity/Constitution are unable to be increased due to damaged core

---

Congratulations!

When you reach certain milestones in your statistics, additional bonuses can be unlocked. In this instance, when you reached 20 points in Sensor Interpretation/Perception, you are now able to determine the mineral characteristics of anything your sensor orbs can visually detect.

Congratulations!

When you reach certain milestones in your statistics, additional bonuses can be unlocked. In this instance, when you reached 40 points in Processing Power/Intelligence and a minimum of 10 points in Reactor Power/Strength, the Bio Unit limit is effectively doubled again. Whereas you could previously control 8000 Bio Units, you can now control 16000 Bio Units.

Congratulations!

When you reach certain milestones in your statistics, additional bonuses can be unlocked. In this instance, when you reached 40 points in Communication/Charisma, the effective communication range of your Combat Units and drones is increased by 25%.

Congratulations!

When you reach certain milestones in your statistics, additional bonuses can be unlocked. In this instance, when you reached 30 points in Processing Speed/Agility, the speed at which projects are completed in your facilities is increased by 10%.

Congratulations!

When you reach certain milestones in your statistics, additional bonuses can be unlocked. In this instance, when you reached 30 points in Ingenuity/Wisdom, the required BMUs for facilities is further decreased by 10% as new materials are found to make up for the lack of resources.

Wow! That is a huge bonus! With the increase in his statistics – except for his RP/S and SI/C, of course – he could feel a lightening of his load, as if he had been carrying a bus on his back and was finally able to drop it. He could think faster, reach out farther, and he somehow understood a little more of what was trying to be taught to him with the two engineering skills. He eagerly brought up his Core Status[31] to find out what had happened.

With the increases in his Communication/Charisma – as well as the bonuses – he thought that he was finally able to reach the mountain range where he had originally found the Quizards. He knew that it was likely to be infested with the creatures, so he needed to be able to field a large complement of his own – but hopefully he could improve them…

He played around with the Biological Recombinator a little before discovering that it required two separate creatures be "sacrificed" to the machine, where it could analyze their DNA and recombine it to create something new.

While he didn't have enough Bio Units yet to start going crazy with experimentation, he could at least fulfil a promise he had made.

31

Core Status			
Name:	Milton Frederick	Type:	Station Core Prototype 3-B
Combat Level:	10	Experience:	37650/51000
Reactor Type:	Zero-point Energy	Reactor Output:	15%
Current Statistics/Attributes			
Reactor Power/Strength:	15	Processing Power/Intelligence:	40
Structural Integrity/Constitution:	14	Ingenuity/Wisdom:	30
Processing Speed/Agility:	30	Communication/Charisma:	43
Insight/Luck:	23	Sensor Interpretation/Perception	20

"ALANNA, I have a surprise for you!"

She materialized on top of the water after quickly erupting from her hole in his shell. The eager look on her face made him smile inwardly as she said, "Ooh, I love surprises! What the fuck is it?"

Even though he hadn't been awake all that much himself over the last century, Milton found that he missed her company – abrasive as it was. He was glad that he was able to do something for her, even if he didn't know what it was she wanted. When he told her that he had finally made the Recombinator she was ecstatic.

New Short-term Goal: *Feed Me!*

In addition to Research performed by your Bioconversion Laboratory, the Biological Recombinator requires Bio Units to create Combat Units for experimentation purposes. Gather Bio Units to perform these experiments to improve your defensive capabilities.

- *Accumulate 50,000 Bio Units*
- *Create **2** different effective hybrid Combat Units*

Difficulty of Goal: Average

Timeframe: 5 years

Rewards: +1 to Communication/Charisma and Ingenuity/Wisdom

"Yesss! Ok, now give me rundown on what Combat Units you have available." When he showed her his list[32], she immediately picked out two that were more than affordable. He was worried she wanted to start testing some of the heavy-duty creatures he had in his arsenal, so he created the creatures and sent them to the Biological Recombinator.

Do you wish to recombine the DNA from a **Greywiener** and a **Miniature Pygmy Wolf**? Y/N

Warning: Each unit will be consumed in this process.

He chose yes, and another screen popped up detailing the different traits, good and bad, available with the recombination. Over the years, he had found that he could interface with ALANNA using neural communication, allowing her to see what he saw and – if he gave permission – to control it as well. She expertly

---

32

Combat Unit Creation			
Biological Mass (Bio Units)	6490	Basic Metal (BM Units)	134982
Unit Name (Type)	Bio Units	Neurological Control Unit	BM Units
Blood-thirsty Squirrel (Scout)	5	Type-1a	1
Lollipop Snake (Stealth Fighter)	10	Type-1a	1
Miniature Pygmy Wolf (Group Attacker)	10	Type-1a	1
Jackalope (Speed Striker)	15	Type-1a	1
Pygmy Wolf (Group Attacker)	50	Type-2b	10
Greywiener (Speed Striker)	100	Type-2b	10
Big Yellow Bird (Aerial Attacker)	125	Type-2b	10
Clawed Badger (Melee Fighter)	300	Type-3c	25
Ombre Jaguar (Stealth Fighter)	500	Type-3c	25
Scaly Bear (Melee Fighter)	1500	Type-5e	100
Quizard (Speed/Melee Fighter)	2500	Type-7g	350

manipulated the screen, choosing which traits she wanted and eliminating those she didn't.

He learned more by watching her in those few minutes than he thought he would have after days of experimentation on his own. First of all, there was a point system assigned to each trait. When you selected positive traits, the point total would increase; negative traits caused the point total to go down. Each combination of creatures apparently had a different point total that they could reach, with larger creatures having a higher threshold. When she had finished, he was confused at first because the unit produced had a negative number for its point total. And apparently, she had named it.

Recombination Complete!
Analysis of: Fluffy
Miniature size (Reduced attack damage): -10
Super-soft exterior (Highly-reduced defensive rating): -20
Long, sleek body (Speed increase): +5
Six legs (Speed increase): +5
Blunted teeth (Reduced attack damage): -10
High-jump ability: +20
Young age (Less than 6 months old): -5
Total point total: -15

"It should be available to create in your Molecular Converter – let's go make it now!" He agreed since it only cost him 90 Bio Units and 10 BMUs, and by the time she turned to mist and arrived in his Core Room, "Fluffy" was just being pooped out. Wading through the water filling his room, the miniature wiener dog puppy was probably the cutest thing he had ever seen. He remembered occasionally – ok, more than occasionally – watching pet videos on the internet and he was always fascinated at the "Teacup" sized puppies that people could hold in the palm of their hand. This dog, though, had them beat – and ALANNA must have thought so as well.

"Oh my god, he is so fucking cute I could punch him! Come here, you!" The puppy immediately ran up to her and jumped into her arms, licking her face. Milton couldn't help but notice that with the dogs' small size, it was perfectly matched with ALANNA's diminutive figure. If you were to look at them without any frame of reference, they would have looked normal. This must have been what she had been hoping to achieve – a playmate of her very own.

Chapter 31 – Discovery

ALANNA was constantly playing with Fluffy, running through the tunnels, splashing through the water in his Core Room, and frolicking through the clearing above his dungeon. She seemed happier than he had...well...**ever** seen her before. Milton figured she had been programmed with the personality of a dog-lover, and with the presence of Fluffy she must have found that unknown piece that had been missing. Even when it grew up over the next couple of years to adulthood, it was still only about waist high on her – large, but not enough to stop their playing.

While he was busy trying to ignore their antics, he had taken a risk and created two additional Quizards for use in a hunting party. He needed to acquire a large amount of Bio Mass, so that he could convert it for use in improving his Combat Units through research and by recombining their DNA. And the fact that he would be able to increase his Combat Level didn't hurt, either.

Over the next five years, he sent his trio of Quizards to rove around the border of his territory, attacking anything that got even remotely close. This did three things: 1. Acquired Bio Mass, 2. Removed any potential incoming threats, and 3. Permeated the surrounding countryside with so much of his radiation essence that it was near impossible for any hostile creatures to accurately follow it back to his dungeon.

In addition to acquiring Bio Mass, his Quizards had an additional benefit of acquiring more experience to raise his Combat Level to 11. With the extra 11 stat points, he placed 5 of them into Processing Speed/Agility and the remaining 6 into Sensor Interpretation/Perception since they were two stats that had been neglected a little in favor of others. While he didn't see an immediate change in his sensors, he saw a marked improvement on how fast his drones would complete their projects. This, in turn, speeded up the whole mining process.

While some of the powerful creatures he had seen outside of his "territory" occasionally got close, none of them expressed any interest in looking for his dungeon. He had learned his lesson on unbridled exploration, so he never pushed himself to encounter and gain additional creatures outside of his normal area of influence. New variations of the creatures he had already encountered were prevalent inside his territory, such as the Miniature Pygmy Wolves, but a lot of what he had seen further afield with his bird never made an appearance. From what he could observe, they were focused on attacking the Proctans who entered the forest, or – if enough of them gathered together – would send out "raiding parties" to the nearby village. He still didn't know enough about this world and the Proctans to wonder why this was.

He "slept" most of the time, only "waking up" once a year to check on their progress and to purchase any available research and try his hand at experimentation. He didn't want to spend too many resources until he had a chance to figure out what he needed most, but he did create two different hybrids that he was quite proud of. One was a Scaly Pygmy Wolf – a combination of a Pygmy Wolf and a Scaly Bear. It was essentially a Pygmy Wolf with scaly hard skin and strong jaws with a tremendous bite-force; the downside was they were slower than they were previously. Milton thought that the reduced speed was worth having a stronger wolf that could take a whole lot more damage before going down.

The other creature he created with the assistance of some research that he had unlocked in his Biological Recombinator[33], which allowed his to combine **three** units into one. He combined a Quizard, a Scaly Bear, and a Clawed Badger into something he called a Big Bad Quizard, or BBQ for short. The BBQ had the speed and size of a Quizard, the scaly-skin hardness of the Scaly Bear, and the rock destroying claws of the Clawed Badger. All-in-all, an efficient killing machine. The biggest downside was their sensitivity to light – they couldn't see at all in direct sunlight. Underneath the shady trees, they were able to see with difficulty, but at night they excelled. The only other trait that was a slight problem was their diet – they ate

---

[33]

Biological Recombinator -- Research		Available Bio Units: 24370
Type	Description	Unlock Cost (Bio Units)
Additional Recombination Points	*Add (5) additional points when performing a recombination*	1000
Tertiary Recombination	*Use up to (3) different specimens during recombination*	3000
Quaternary Recombination	*Use up to (4) different specimens during recombination*	10000

the same as the Clawed Badgers, which meant that they were forced to dig at inopportune times for their meals.

Current Short-term Goal: *Feed Me!* – *Complete!*

In addition to Research performed by your Bioconversion Laboratory, the Biological Recombinator requires Bio Units to create Combat Units for experimentation purposes. Gather Bio Units to perform these experiments to improve your defensive capabilities.

- *Accumulate 50,000 Bio Units – 58,134/50,000 Complete!*
- *Create **2** different effective hybrid Combat Units – 2/2 Complete!*

Difficulty of Goal: Average

Timeframe: 5 years

Rewards: +1 to Communication/Charisma and Ingenuity/Wisdom

With the creation of his two hybrid Combat Units, and with the accumulation of more than 50,000 Bio Units, he also completed his *Feed Me!* quest, netting him +1 to his Communication/Charisma and Ingenuity/Wisdom stats. He didn't receive any bonuses because he completed it right on time, but that was fine with Milton.[34]

---

[34]

Core Status			
Name:	Milton Frederick	Type:	Station Core Prototype 3-B
Combat Level:	11	Experience:	76370/82500
Reactor Type:	Zero-point Energy	Reactor Output:	17%
Current Statistics/Attributes			
Reactor Power/Strength:	17	Processing Power/Intelligence:	40
Structural Integrity/Constitution:	16	Ingenuity/Wisdom:	31
Processing Speed/Agility:	35	Communication/Charisma:	44
Insight/Luck:	23	Sensor Interpretation/Perception	26

A little over five years after he had created the Recombinator, he had just gone "back to sleep" when he was quickly alerted that something unusual had happened. He had lost connection to a six-pack of roving Scaly Pygmy Wolves guards that were patrolling the Western border. He didn't have a connection to anything out there, so he sent a sensor orb zipping through the air to check out their last known location while he quickly reviewed the recordings of their last few minutes.

It seemed that they had somehow managed to find and surround a Picow, one of the domesticated farm animals that he had seen the Proctans raising for livestock at the nearby village. He watched as they swarmed the scared and defenseless animal, efficiently killing it by ripping out its throat with a few strategic bites.

Once it had bled out, his wolves started to try to drag it back to his Core, since he had instructions to bring back any creature that he didn't already have in his repertoire.

As they tugged on the multi-ton corpse, a quiet chuckle emanating from behind a tree to the South caused their hackles to rise. As Milton saw what had made the noise, he was shocked at the presence of a male Proctan squatting and ineffectually trying to hide behind a tree. On further consideration, he realized that he wasn't really surprised – the Picow most likely got away from him and he foolishly followed the animal this far into the forest. What **did** surprise him was what happened next.

As his Scaly Pygmy Wolves approached the new "creature" to assess whether it was a threat – which was what they had been ordered to do – the Proctan turned and started running away, only to trip and fall on his wrist, most likely breaking it with a wet-sounding pop. This, of course, gave his wolves the impression that the prone man was prey, so they immediately ran up, knocked him down when he tried to get up, and then surrounded him. With a pain-filled expression on his face, the young man turned on his back and froze as he took in his predicament. In sync, each wolf started rushing in to attack, but just before they reached the doomed Proctan, he shouted, "STOP!".

The recording immediately ended since his wolves had all died from that singular word. Milton wasn't sure what exactly the man did, but he was pissed. *How dare he come into **my** home, kill **my** creatures, and get away unscathed!* At that moment, his sensor orb had arrived at the scene and he took in the dead Picow with blood still slowly emptying from its slashed throat, his lifeless wolves lying where they had fallen without a scratch on them, and the Proctan man just starting to walk away from the slaughter.

He was so mad that he didn't even think about what he was doing when – in frustration – he shouted over his neural connection, "WHO ARE YOU AND WHAT DID YOU DO TO MY SCALY PYGMY WOLVES?!" Milton wasn't expecting the man to hear him and was surprised when he stiffened in surprise, his eyes rolled up in his head, and he collapsed on the ground face-first.

The anger ebbed away when he stared at the unassuming and unconscious Proctan sprawled out along the forest floor. *Did I establish a new neural connection with him? Or is my presence just so powerful that it can affect the physical world?* He immediately disregarded the last thought, delusions of grandeur were not his forte. Nonetheless, he was curious about what had happened and needed to find out more. Was it a form of magical ability that he didn't know about yet? Or was it something else?

Decision made, he dispatched his BBQ hunting party to the attack site and they arrived within minutes since they ran so fast. He had one of them gently pick up the man, while the other two grabbed the heavy Picow and struggled to pick it up. After almost being crushed by the massive pig, Milton decided that they should just drag it after them. Those two lagged behind the one with the Proctan, slowly dragging the huge corpse along the ground, creating a noticeable furrow in the dirt as it passed. The corpses of his Scaled

Pygmy Wolves he left at the site of the incident and he fully intended to pick them later for "recycling".

While they were on the way, Milton instructed a small contingent of his drones to prepare a holding room for their visitor while he informed ALANNA of what had happened. She had never heard of anything like that before and was as curious about the mysterious stranger as he was.

New Short-term Goal: *Mysterious Stranger*

Who is this mysterious Proctan? How did he do what he did? Bring him back and interrogate him.

- *Bring the Proctan back to your dungeon*
- *Find out what he knows*
- *Assess if he is a threat*

Difficulty of Goal: Easy

Timeframe: 2 Days

Rewards: Knowledge – 'nuff said.

He wanted him nearby, but far enough away that if he somehow killed all his Combat Units and drones he would have a hard time getting to his Core and causing damage. So, about 200 feet away from his dungeon entrance he designed an underground chamber with 50 feet of dirt above that could be dumped into the room within a moments' notice. Sandstone blocks lined the walls and floor and there was nothing else inside but empty air, which was provided by three very small chutes running up to the surface – he didn't want the man to suffocate to death before he could get answers.

The BBQ with the unconscious "package" arrived an hour before the others, which was fine with Milton as his drones had just finished the room and the man hadn't stirred from his current state yet. Instructing the BBQ to deposit the Proctan on the surface, a drone dragged him the rest of the way down a narrow tunnel that they had created that led down to the room. Once he was inside, bonelessly splayed along the floor, his drone retreated up the tunnel, collapsing it as it went – but only after he had flown a sensor orb inside. He almost forgot that he needed some way to see inside and figured he could easily sacrifice an orb – or heaven forbid – the drone located in the ceiling that was next to a hair-trigger activation lever that would drop the ceiling down on the potentially hostile stranger.

While he waited for the mystery man to wake up, he started his drones on processing the Picow when it arrived, cutting it into easily transportable chunks that were thrown in his Molecular Converter. When that was complete, he shut down everything requiring his attention except for the view of the room, brightly lit by the glow emanating from his orb. He was aware of ALANNA sitting on a raised platform near him, Fluffy taking a nap in her lap. He shared his connection to the orb with her, and ALANNA ran her fingers slowly through her dogs' hair as they waited in anticipation of the man's awakening.

Chapter 32 – Speak now, or forever hold your peace

Brint felt groggy as he opened his eyes, a bright light momentarily blinding him as he woke up. His mind was a little foggy, and he had trouble remembering what had happened to him. He tried to sit up when a sharp pain stabbed his left wrist, sending radiating waves of pain up and down his arm. Suddenly, the memories started flooding into him: the attack at the farm, the pursuit of the stray Picow through the woods, the small wolves finding and killing said Picow, the breaking of his wrist, and the use of an unknown ability when he was attacked by the wolves. What he couldn't remember is what happened after that – he was drawing a blank.

That was when he looked around at his surroundings for the first time, noticing that he was in a small stone-walled room and he was alone. He ran his uninjured hand over the floor, noticing that the entire room – except for the ceiling, which was dirt – was one whole piece of stone. He couldn't see where the blocks were joined together; it was as if whoever had created the room had smoothly chiseled it out of a giant stone block. He had seen some pieces of stone made by Elemental Casters that were all of one piece, but he had never heard of anything on this scale.

It was brightly lit in the room, which his temporarily addled mind had ignored until now. Looking for the source of the illumination, he saw something floating in the middle of the room, emitting a soft but strong glow that made it hard to get a good look at it.

He got to his knees, careful to avoid jostling his wrist by keeping it held closely to his chest and stepped toward the floating object. He took two steps and stopped, startled by a voice in his head.

"Attention Proctan Male. Please state your name and purpose."

He froze, abruptly remembering hearing something very similar to that voice after killing those wolves. It was angry before, and now it spoke in a measured but amused tone, as if it was trying not to laugh as it spoke. He stood there contemplating what he should say when he heard the voice again.

"Speak now, or forever hold your peace. You have ten seconds before you will be annihilated."

Now he could definitely hear a note of amusement in the voice, but also a stern resolve as well. Brint decided that he better speak before he ran out of time, he had a feeling he would be killed if he did nothing.

"My name is Brint, and...well...I don't really have a purpose."

"Brint. What do you mean by that? Why do you not have a purpose?"

What do I say to that? Do I tell it the truth? He pondered what he would say for just a moment, aware that the more time he delayed the more danger he was in. Since the short time he had to think about it didn't reveal any reason to lie, he decided to tell the truth.

"When I reached the proper age, every test we had couldn't tell me what ability I had. Every other Proctan has an ability – some aren't as useful, but at least they have one – except for me. Since I wasn't classifiable, I instead was classified as 'useless' and treated with disrespect and scorn. So, in short, I have no purpose."

The voice was silent for a moment and Brint figured it was mulling over whether to kill him because he was "useless". The next question startled him, mainly because he hadn't really had time to process the answer yet.

"How did you kill my Scaly Pygmy Wolves, then? If you say you have no 'ability'"?

"I don't know."

"You don't know? Or is it just that you don't want to tell me?"

"It's the truth – I felt a rush of power flowing through my body, and unbidden a word emerged from my mouth with intent behind it. I don't know where it came from, or how it works. The most I can reason out is that I must have used an ability, but I don't even know what it was. I wonder if this is what Whinfly felt like?" he softly muttered that last part out loud to himself, but the voice apparently heard it as well.

"Who is Whinfly?"

"He was the first one of us to discover an ability, he was an Elemental Caster," he responded, reminded of the history lesson he had just attended with Whisp the other day.

"So, you haven't always had these abilities?"

"No, of course not, they are what saved us during the 'Beast War' almost a hundred years ago," he told the voice in his head, not understanding how something obviously this intelligent didn't know about the most important thing that had happened in the last century. The curious voice was silent for a long time, so long that Brint ended up sitting in the corner of the room and cradling his injured wrist which was beginning to hurt more and more.

"Please recount the main points in your history over the last one hundred years."

Oh, Goddess. At least I've sat through all those kid's classes so many times that I could almost repeat the lesson by heart. He rationalized that he didn't have much choice, that he was at the mercy of whatever this entity was, and that what he was going to say was common knowledge. He began at the start of the "Beast War" and moved on talking about the general attrition of Proctan forces, the last stand at the Capital, the discovery of abilities, and ended with the push against the masses of creatures along the borders. He went on to explain the different classes of abilities, up to and including the "unique" or "useless" class of abilities.

He realized that he had been talking for what felt like hours and his throat was beginning to become parched. And the pain from his wrist was starting to make him swoon, until he felt as though he could pass out at any moment. When he stopped talking, he was momentarily startled as the voice in his head spoke again, jostling his wrist and eliciting a hiss of pain. Brint was beginning to think that the voice had been nothing but a hallucination brought on by the onset of the pain in his wrist.

"I want you to try something for me. Look at the orb floating in the air above you. Now, try to use your ability and project your thoughts toward the orb, instructing it to move towards you."

Brint didn't really have a reason not to do it, since he was in such pain that anything that would distract him from it would be a blessing. He squinted at the floating orb and tried to will it to move. When nothing happened, he tried again and again but still there was no movement in the orb. He almost gave up when he decided to try something else.

Closing his eyes, he focused inward, attempting to block out the nagging pain at the edge of his consciousness. He delved deeper, looking for the spark of power that he knew every Proctan had inside of them, but he had never consciously felt before. It wasn't until he had tried looking everywhere inside his lower body that he decided to try his head. Immediately, he could feel a warm presence surrounding his brain and as soon as he touched it the power rushed through him, momentarily washing away the agony from his wrist. It only lasted a few moments, but the absence of pain spurred him to try moving the orb again.

When he opened his eyes, he looked at the orb and felt a very slight dip in what he now knew was his power level. He controlled the flying object with his mind, directing it all over the room, bringing it closer and then zipping away, only to stop before it hit the wall. As soon as he started making it do loops in the middle of the room, he felt his control rip away as the orb froze in place. A couple of moments of trying to control it again was fruitless as something was blocking his influence.

"Very good. Now, I want you to try controlling something else."

Brint was confused, since all he could see inside the room was the floating orb. He thought that he was missing something and was about to ask what the voice was talking about, when he heard something coming from behind him. He turned around just as a block of stone about a foot wide and long dropped out from the wall, making a big *thunk* as it fell a couple of feet to the floor. Backing up against the far wall, Brint unconsciously looked for an escape that his conscious mind knew wouldn't be there.

His breath caught in his chest and he held up his hands in automatic self-defense as he saw something emerge from the hole. The breath he had been holding whooshed out of his lungs as he saw that it was just one of the harmless creatures that he had seen rarely in the trees around the village. They would chitter at him whenever he got too close to "their" tree, but he had never learned if they had a name. The creatures that usually garnered the most attention were the ones that were the biggest threats – if it was harmless, it sometimes wasn't even named.

It stood less than a foot tall, had a large bushy tail that curved down at the end, and had two pointed ears above an innocent-looking face with soft eyes. He watched as it nimbly jumped down from the hole, bounded to the middle of the room, and sat down, watching him with patient eyes.

"Go on, try to control the squirrel."

Ah, so that's what they were called. He focused on the "squirrel" and brought his power to the forefront of his mind. He was finding it easier and easier to do so, as if with practice it was becoming second-nature. He concentrated on the small animal, cautiously exerting his control, not wanting to harm the poor creature. When he felt as though he had established a "connection" with it, he thought about it jumping into the air – and to his delight, the squirrel jumped three feet straight up into the air.

Once he knew that he could control it, he had it running in circles around the room, jumping against the walls only to spring off and gain some serious air. After he had spent a couple of minutes manipulating the squirrel, he could begin to feel the drain on his power. It wasn't a huge amount, but he could imagine that a couple of hours of controlling the creature would wipe him out.

"Very impressive. I have one more test for you."

Brint smiled, almost eager for a challenge – especially since using his power seemed to mute the pain emanating from his wrist. While it didn't disappear completely, it dampened it enough that he could concentrate again. He heard another noise near the hole that had been neatly sliced out of the wall previously. Turning toward the commotion, he froze as a giant portion of the wall was pushed out of the way by a pair of large scaled hands. The creature that followed the hands was so frightening that if Brint hadn't been dehydrated he would have soiled his undergarments. As it was, he almost passed

310

out again and only the solid presence of the wall behind him kept him from collapsing in a boneless heap.

He had never seen or heard anything like this creature that was standing in front of him. Over six feet tall and half again as long, it looked like a giant lizard, except that this one had hard scales all over its body and extremely sharp-looking claws. The way it slowly walked to the middle of the room with exaggerated care hinted that it was used to moving much faster. He had never seen or heard of anything like this creature before, and he just hoped that he lived long enough to tell the tale. Afraid to move a muscle, he just stood still and stared at the deadly monstrosity.

"Don't worry, he won't attack unless I tell him to. Now, let's see if you can control him."

Brint wasn't sure he wanted to know how the voice knew that it was a **"he"**. He didn't think he'd be able to control the huge lizard because he was scared out of his mind. However, he didn't want to take the chance that the voice would get mad that he didn't try, so he tried to block out the pain, the fear, and the anxiety clouding his thoughts. Licking his lips in nervous anticipation, he brought forth the power with slightly more difficulty than before. Once he could feel it suffuse his senses, he immediately reached for some sort of "connection" to the beast, afraid that if he waited too long he would lose his nerve.

Success! He could feel the connection form with an inaudible snap, and suddenly he felt like he had a great weight land on his head. He started controlling the lizard, having it walk around the room and make a couple of laps, the power flowing through him in a torrent. Suddenly, the connection snapped, and an intense feedback pain smacked him in the head. It was so painful that he had forgotten that he had a broken wrist, and when he grabbed his forehead in an involuntary action the left wrist jostled enough that he thought he could hear and feel the bones rubbing against each other.

Screaming at the double-whammy of pain, he fell to his knees, ignoring the deadly creature no longer under his control just a couple of feet away. After a thankfully short time, the pain in his head faded to a dull throb, although his wrist was far worse off than before.

"What happened, are you okay?"

He was still in such pain that he didn't notice the empathetic note to the voice in his head. "I think that's what happens when you run out of power. Controlling that giant lizard took entirely too much out of me and the 'connection' I had with it rebounded on me." He added under his breath, "I wish I had a Power Potion..."

"What's a Power Potion?"

Goddess, enough with the questions already.

Unbeknownst to Brint, that last question would change his whole world.

Chapter 33 – Consequences

Throughout the beginning of the interrogation, Milton and ALANNA were struggling to contain their laughter as the Proctan they had brought back answered his questions while being a nervous wreck. They weren't laughing at Brint – in fact, they felt sorry for him and Milton wanted to see about fixing his wrist – they were instead laughing at Milton's fake "all-powerful being" persona he was adopting. To Milton, it felt a little like going to a liquor store as underage teenagers and pretending to act older so that the fake ID's they presented wouldn't be inspected too closely.

He was trying to hold it together, but when ALANNA started playfully mocking him, saying stuff like, "Pitiful Proctan, how dare you enter my presence! You should get down and lick my boots! I should whip you for your insolence, you mangy cur!" he lost it, and it took him a while to recover. When he started asking more questions, their amusement faded as he started learning about their recent history.

"Uh…ALANNA? Is he saying what I'm thinking he's saying? I mean, the timing seems about right for when I woke up here, but how is this possible? I remember you saying something about the possible mutations my radiation could have on the local wildlife, which is why I have done my best to minimize my impact. But magic? Was that from me, or was it there all the time and was just hidden from them?"

She was silent for a long time, continuing to listen to Brint explain what had happened after something called the "Beast War" that he had heard snippets of from people in the village. As he was winding down, arriving closer to the present time, she looked at his shell and slowly said, "I don't know...it's possible that their abilities were there all the time, but based on the timing I don't think so. The probability that this was just a coincidence would have to be so low that it's not likely. I know you didn't mean to fucking do it, but it looks like your presence here may have created this "Beast War" he was talking about – as well as everything that came after. Despite your best intentions, you ended up affecting more than just the immediate area; for all we know, you may have changed the entire world."

Milton took her words in, a part of him refusing to believe what she said might be true. The other part questioned if his presence here had irrevocably changed the previously peaceful world into one full of dangerous monsters and magic. *I caused the deaths of thousands of people? It's not like I meant to, but does that excuse what I've done? If I knew that this would happen, would I have done anything differently? What do I do now?* His internal contemplation was interrupted by Brint explaining the different classes of abilities his people had.

"ALANNA, what if his 'ability' is to hack into the neural communication network that I've established with my Combat Units and drones? He said that he never knew what his ability was before he met my Scaly Pygmy Wolves, and I believe him – it was hard to

315

fake what happened there. If it's true, how do I test that? And, additionally, do you think he could break into my Core system?"

"Your Core system is safe, not even I can access it without your permission except for some rudimentary sensory programs unconnected to your main system. As for how to test him, why don't you have him try moving the sensor orb in there?"

Milton thought that it was a good idea and told Brint to try controlling it. When he was eventually successful, he observed both the physical actions of the sensor orb and the neural communication network that was being affected by his actions. He couldn't accurately see what was happening there, so in a flash of inspiration he envisioned an overhead map of the surrounding area and mentally overlaid the locations of all his units. Each type of unit was assigned a different color, so that he could easily see what he had where. As soon as it was finished, the new screen popped up exactly like he had envisioned.

Congratulations!

You have acquired the skill: *Tactical Mapping (Level 1)*

You have accessed a previously locked resource, resulting in the knowledge of how to create a tactical display map of the battlefield that shows you the locations of your units, as well as the locations of enemy units if they are spotted by your Combat Units. Higher levels expand on the information of enemy units, show damage to Combat Units, and potentially offer tactical solutions.

His increased Processing Power/Intelligence, as well as familiarity with tactical maps from his gaming, meant that the new skill knowledge only caused a slight hiccup in his concentration instead of knocking him out. *Why didn't I think of this before? This is genius! Now I can see on the map where everyone is and allocate resources much more efficiently.* He could think of new ways of using this information, but he pulled his attention back to the matter at hand.

When he could focus again on the map, he mentally zoomed in on the room holding the Proctan and the sensor orb. The bright light that should be his sensor orb was so dim that it was like someone had covered up a lightbulb with a sheet of dark cloth. Although he could still see it, he could also "sense" that it was under something else's control. With a mental touch, he poked the dim light with a non-existent finger and the sensor orb immediately lit back up to full brightness. When he looked back into the room, he could see that the orb had stopped in midair and Brint was looking around in confusion. Milton kept his concentration on the orb, looking to see if he could prevent the Proctan from taking control of it if he had a direct connection to it – which thankfully worked.

Coming up with another test, he had one of his nearby squirrels run to the area with the holding cell, while two drones drilled their way down to the room from the surface. They were done surprisingly fast, and he sent the squirrel down to just outside Brint's' cell, when he told the man to try controlling something else. Milton and ALANNA laughed again at the fright of the Proctan when the squirrel emerged from the wall, only to relax as he saw that it was a harmless creature. *Little does he know that those things are blood-thirsty.*

When he could see that Brint was successful in controlling the squirrel, he started widening the tunnel down to the room. He had a theory that the larger the creature, the harder it would be to control it. Since Milton himself was restrained a bit by how much he could control at one time – at least in terms of Bio Units – he figured the same might apply to the Proctan. Larger creatures required larger Neurological Control Units, which in turn required higher processing power to control.

When he was ready, Milton sent one of his BBQs down the tunnel and waited there while Brint finished up with the squirrel. He could see that the young man was a little tired by now, probably from his constant use of his ability – however, he appeared happier now than when he first arrived. Milton drew back and hesitated, keenly aware of how frightening his BBQ would be to someone not accustomed to them. He remembered being a bit scared when he first saw them and now they were even scarier with the improvements he had made to them. Being in such an enclosed space might just push the already injured and shaken Proctan over the edge.

Well, no pain, no gain. He needed to test his theory and since this was the largest creature he had it was the best way to do that. Things didn't quite go as he had expected.

Milton was encouraged by the fact that Brint didn't faint or lose it by the appearance of his BBQ. He was also pleased to see that he seemed to be straining to control the giant lizard, further granting evidence to his theory that it would be harder to control larger creatures. Everything was going fine until he felt a kind of "reverberation" throughout the neural communication network, originating from his BBQ and bouncing through his nearby units. Worried that it was some sort of surprise attack, he had just pulled up his tactical map to see if any other units had been compromised when he heard screaming coming from Brint.

He wasn't sure exactly what had happened, but Milton was worried that he had done something to further hurt the young man. With genuine concern in his voice, he asked Brint what had happened, only to get an explanation that actually made sense. The neural feedback from the broken connection, when not powered by his ability, must have been intense. Milton fortunately didn't have to worry about that, since his reactor power was constantly running, meaning that he had an almost infinite and steady amount of power – albeit at a much-reduced rate until it was repaired back to normal.

Brint seemed drained, which made sense if he had been completely tapped out of power. There were a few games that he had played that if you fully ran out of mana, or some other type of magic, you would acquire a debuff or two affecting your speed/mana regeneration/health. It appeared that those games might have been a real-life reflection of actual power management. Milton was debating what to do with Brint next, since he was a little wary of

319

releasing him back with knowledge of his existence. He didn't want to kill him, but he wasn't sure holding him here would be the right answer either.

Current Short-term Goal: *Mysterious Stranger* – *Complete!*

Who is this mysterious Proctan? How did he do what he did? Bring him back and interrogate him.

- *Bring the Proctan back to your dungeon – Complete!*
- *Find out what he knows – Complete!*
- *Assess if he is a threat – Complete!*

Difficulty of Goal: Easy

Timeframe: 2 Days

Rewards: Knowledge – 'nuff said.

Then he heard something which piqued his interest. *What the heck is a Power Potion? I wonder if that's like a mana potion?* He asked Brint the question and the young man looked so wiped that he almost told him not to worry about it, but stopped as the explanation emerged with an uncaring, defeated, mechanical tone – as if he was reciting something from memory. *I've really got to get him fixed up soon – that wrist has got to be killing him.*

"The Power Potion was created almost 80 years ago, when an Inventor by the name of Cordelious discovered where all the power and abilities in everyone came from. Cordelious found that all the fresh water pulled up from the ground had a certain 'residue' in it that caused changes in Proctan physiology. He experimented and found that power could be 'regenerated' faster if the subject drank massive quantities of water.

"Further experimentation ended up with the creation of 'Power Potions', small vials of concentrated 'residue' or 'power', that when ingested could rapidly refill anyone's power pool. The effort in creating these potions is tremendous, and while the methods aren't secret by any means, the amount of material and time needed to make enough concentrated 'power' for each potion isn't cost-effective for most people – for me, it would probably take a decade or more of saving up to afford them. With a monopoly in the 'Power Potion' trade, the Cordpower Company is the only place you can buy them from, and as a result they are probably the most powerful entity besides the government."

If Milton had had eyes, they would have been staring at ALANNA in shock. "Well, there's our proof. It looks like they've been fucking *distilling* mass quantities of water to accumulate enough of your radiation to concentrate into drinkable potions," she said, but then began laughing. "Essentially, they prize your piss and shit as a valuable resource!" It took a moment for the image to come to mind, but once it did, Milton started laughing like a maniac as well. He realized that he was still "connected" to Brint, and he started laughing harder when he realized that he probably sounded like a crazy mad supervillain or something.

He created a small glass vial and rubber stopper in his Converter using some of his stored-up material and had ones of his nearby drones fill it with water flowing near the damaged section of his shell. The drone then worked its way out of the dungeon and down to Brint's holding cell. The exhausted and pain-filled Proctan barely acknowledged the sight of the his strange-looking drone, but his eyes lit up at what it was carrying. *He's probably dehydrated as well – when I fix him up I'll make sure he gets some food and water.*

Brint snatched the vial away from the drone and instantly downed it before Milton could even say anything – the reaction said it all anyway. His eyes opened wide in shock and his whole carriage seemed to improve from its formerly wasted state. He stood up, looked at the floating sensor orb and used his ability to move it from side to side. Milton shared the look of excitement and wonder on his face, as an inkling of a plan started to form...

Chapter 34 – The Milton

Brint was walking back to the village, the morning sun dimly shining through the trees as he made his way through the edge of the forest bordering the fields. He couldn't believe that he had only been away less than full day – so much had happened. Looking at his wrist, he marveled at the fact that it was fully healed, without even a hint that it had been severely broken only a couple of hours ago. Not only that, but all the usual aches and pains that he had woken up with every day for the last couple of years were gone, as if they were never there. His feet were beginning to get tired from the walk out from the forest, but that was only to be expected.

He could "feel" his escort of three giant lizards – which The Milton in his head had called BBQs for some reason – break off as he entered the safer territory surrounding his village. When his wounds had been healed, without the constant pain he found he could sense when the various creatures under the control of The Milton were around, even if he didn't fully connect with them.

As he walked through the last couple of trees, he felt for the cloth bag against his side, checking for probably the thousandth time to make sure it was still there and secure. A few muted clinks of glass responded to his attention, reassuring him that everything was there and accounted for. He was carrying a literal fortune in there and he didn't want to lose it.

After he had marginally recovered from the "neural connection feedback" that The Milton called it, he was further astonished at what had happened next. He was so thirsty that as soon as he saw the strange metal-creature approach with water, he snatched it and downed it in one gulp. To his surprise, he felt a wash of heat infuse his body that originated from his stomach and converged on his head. The previously empty pool of power that had been draining his energy was suddenly full, or as full as his new experience with his ability could tell him. After testing out his newly-filled power, he felt as though he could go all day and not run out – but he didn't want to test **that** theory yet.

From there, it was a whirlwind of information and other new experiences. The metal-covered creature that had delivered the Power Potion was joined by five of its brethren while the giant lizard and squirrel left through the entrance in which they had arrived. The six "drones" – as he soon learned they were called – dug and cut their way through the opposite wall and started creating a simple dirt tunnel, reinforced by periodic beams of stone along the ceiling which another drone periodically dropped off for their use.

While he followed along, staying out of the way of the working drones, he learned a little about the voice in his head. It called itself Milton, but he could only think of it as The Milton for some reason – anything other than that just seemed strange. He learned, but was still confused by the terminology, that he had the ability to neurally communicate with the creatures that were created by the Milton. Although he could manipulate the creatures with

324

direct control, he also was taught that if he just gave them orders they would follow them without having to direct their every movement. The Milton was much more powerful than him and could erase any orders that were given, but Brint didn't care as he now knew that he wasn't "useless" and had an ability after all.

Brint also had the chance to teach The Milton, because he learned that the seemingly all-powerful voice in his head had very little knowledge of the outside world. He told him about how everyone could increase the strength of their ability through constant use – something that had to do with the efficiency in power management or something like that. He didn't pay too much attention to that in school since he didn't have anything to practice with.

By the time they had reached their destination, he had given The Milton a general lay of the land outside his village, the political climate (at least as much as he knew), and what he knew about metal – which wasn't a lot. He explained that most of their metal they used for weapons and armor, along with other things like the inventions Whisp created, came from Elemental Casters who could sense and pull up ore deposits from the ground. Some specialized casters could manipulate fire and heat much better than others and were usually in charge of smelting the ore for use by other people. He wasn't sure of all the information that was asked of him, since he dealt with foodstuffs most of the time, but he told him as much as he was able.

When he entered the room they had tunneled to, he was flabbergasted at the huge machine in the middle of the floor. It was nearly 15 feet tall, had a large metal cylindrical contraption on top of a metal frame with an empty pool beneath it. There was a ramp that circled its way up to the top of the cylinder, allowing access to whatever was inside it.

"I want to heal your wrist, but to do that, I need you inside my Biological Laboratory to repair the damage. Just walk to the top and jump in – I'll handle the rest."

He nervously approached the bottom of the ramp, unsure of what was happening. He hesitated before stepping on the metal pathway, his courage failing him as he looked toward the top of the strange contraption.

"It's perfectly safe – although OSHA would probably shut me down because there are no handrails along the edge of the ramp. Just stay away from the edge and you should be fine."

Brint wasn't sure what this OSHA was, but The Milton had said so much that didn't make sense that he ignored it. Gathering what shreds of courage that he still had, he slowly walked up the steep ramp, the tread along the pathway rough enough that he had no worry of slipping back down. When he reached the top and looked inside the large cylinder, he stepped back as he saw that it was filled almost to the top with water. *Does he want me to drown? I can't swim that well because of my broken wrist.* As if the Milton had heard him, the voice in his head tried to reassure him – with mixed results.

"Don't worry, I won't let you drown – if I wanted to kill you before this I had plenty of opportunity. But you need to be in the water for the healing to work."

That's great knowing he could have killed me at any time before this. Nonetheless, his wrist was killing him with a constant sharp nagging pain and he was willing to do almost anything to get it to stop. He carefully sat down at the edge of the cylinder and slowly lowered himself down into the water, slipping at the last moment so that he was fully submerged for just a moment. That moment was apparently all that was needed as he felt the water somehow solidify around him, still clear and surprisingly warm but it felt as though he had fallen into giant bowl of jelly that was flash-frozen. He couldn't even breathe, and after panicking he realized that he didn't feel like he was suffocating – almost as if time had stopped around him.

Brint felt tingles all around his body, concentrating on his wrist but all along his legs, arms, and back as well. There were even some tingles around his head and face, causing him to want to sneeze but couldn't when it tickled his nose. He realized that his face had been hurt at some point in the last day but was unaware of it until now since the pain in his wrist masked his inconsequential injuries. The passage of time was hard to judge in that suspended state, but after what he reasoned was only a couple of minutes he felt the water "unfreeze" and rapidly empty out the bottom of the cylinder, taking him along for the ride.

Landing with a splash in the already full pool underneath the machine, he stood up in the shallow water as he saw the water quickly receding as it was sucked back up through a series of tubes to be returned to the cylinder up above. He was soaking wet, but at least he wasn't cold and now his clothes were relatively clean. Waves of heat started emanating from above him, and when he looked up he could see a series of metal coils on the underside of the machine that had a red glow. It was hot, but not unbearable, and he felt the water slowly drying while he stood there dripping.

Grabbing his shirt with his left hand to look at how wet it still was, he stared at his wrist and was stunned that he felt no pain from it. When he thought about it, he couldn't feel any discomfort anywhere, which was a rather unique experience lately since he usually had to work through the day with at least some sore muscles.

When he was done drying he climbed out of the shallow pool and felt better than he had in years – and that was when his stomach rumbled in hunger. Again, somehow anticipating this, a drone entered the room from a different direction than the one they had arrived from, bringing in its thin, fragile-appearing arms a tray laden with food and a pitcher of water with a small glass cup next to it.

"I apologize for my absent hospitality before, I couldn't be sure if you were a threat. Please eat up – if you need more please let me know, there is plenty more where that came from."

Brint thanked the Milton and took the tray from the patiently waiting drone. He sat down, placing the tray on his lap, too hungry and thirsty to consider where the food may have come from. Pouring himself a large glass of water, he was expecting to feel the rush of power that had accompanied his last drink but was only slightly disappointed – it was just normal water. He chugged it down, spluttering a little as he tried to drink too much at once, before slowing down as he felt the dryness in his throat disappear. He turned to his food and stopped when he wasn't sure what he was looking at.

"I envy you – I made you a meal of a cheeseburger and fries. It was kind of a staple back…home. I wish I could enjoy it like you're about to. It's made from pork instead of beef, because I don't have access to any cows here. I just recently acquired some pork, though, thanks to you."

Confusion clouded Brint's mind as he considered the Milton's words. *Back…home? I guess that means that he's not from around here – which should have been obvious considering how ignorant he is of the world outside of…wherever this is.* He picked up what he figured was the "cheeseburger", what looked like a large roll cut in half with a piece of meat in between. A still-warm gooey yellow substance ran down the sides of it, and when he brought it up to his nose it smelled...interesting. He took a bite and juicy flavor filled his mouth, the taste of which seemed familiar. It took him a moment before he realized what it was, thinking, *Ah, that's what he meant about "thanks to you" – this tastes just like Picow.*

Knowing that he was eating something that was at least familiar, he dug into the rest of the meal, barely pausing as he tasted the "fries". They were crunchy on the outside but soft in the middle, with a starchiness to them that quickly filled him up. He wasn't used to eating so much; he didn't usually have the same appetite as most of the ability-users back in the village.

When he finished the delicious meal, he put the tray down and the Milton spoke to him again.

"I have a proposition for you. I can provide you vials of this "Power Potion" you tried, and you can do with them whatever you want – sell them, give them away, or use them yourself."

Unsure why the Milton was being so generous giving away valuable commodities, he figured there was a catch – there was always a catch. He was just waiting for the "but".

"But,"

There it is!

"I need two things from you. The first, which may actually be the hardest of the two – I need you to swear to complete secrecy about this location, my creatures, and about my existence. I don't need a bunch of people snooping around here. The second, which should hopefully be easy, is I need you to provide a shipment of metal – raw ore deposits, smelted ore, or finished products – it doesn't matter. Whatever you think these vials are worth to you, but as much as you can easily acquire. If you leave it in the forest near the border of the village in a cart or wagon I can bring it back to my location, where I will then bring it back empty for you to reuse again. I can keep providing you these potions in return for more metal – it's your choice. Either way, I will still need you to keep my existence a secret."

To say that he jumped at the chance was an understatement. Just one of the vials, if sold, would provide enough to purchase a whole wagon or two of metal. Even though he wasn't blessed with a vast intelligence like Whisp, he knew this wasn't something that he wanted to pass up – it was almost pure profit. He wasn't greedy, but he also didn't want to live in the same rundown shack for the rest of his life.

So, here he was, walking across the same field he had crossed yesterday while running after the Picow. He didn't see anyone, which wasn't surprising, but he did see that someone had finished his work inside the processing shed. The village didn't have a lot of extra labor running around so either the mayor payed to have some expert help or everyone chipped in to complete the days' harvest. He was curious about who was working on it today without him here, but he was more intent on getting back to the village.

He walked through the village, ignoring the startled looks the people he passed gave him. Within minutes, he had arrived at his destination – Whisp's house. He walked up to the door and knocked. He could hear movement inside the house, and when the door opened he could see the tear-stained face of his best friend looking out. "Hello."

"Oh, my goddess, Brint! I thought you were dead," she exclaimed before throwing her arms around his neck and crying into his shoulder.

Chapter 35 – Entrepreneurship

He had to admit that if felt good holding the woman he had been in love with for years. A knot inside his chest seemed to loosen when he held her, as if he had been wound up so tight that only her touch would help alleviate the problem. He teared up a little in response to her happy tears, glad to know that he wasn't alone in being glad to see his friend. "Let's go inside where we can talk – and away from prying eyes," he told her.

She nodded into his shoulder and he led her inside, closing the door behind him. He hadn't been inside her house in years, but it looked the same as it did back when they were kids together. Leading her over to a bench, they sat down, and he waited for her to compose herself before speaking. When the waterworks seemed to be over, she asked, "Where have you been? I was told you were killed yesterday during a spider-wolf attack in the fields."

He explained in general what had happened, excluding the presence of The Milton as per their agreement – he wasn't sure how much influence the voice had, and he wasn't going to put either of their lives in danger just so that he could tell her about him – and told her he spent the night in the forest before heading back to the village. She, of course, was smart enough and knew him well enough to know when he was lying.

"I'm sorry, I can't tell you any more than that – I made a promise. Just trust me when I say I can't say any more about it, but it wasn't anything bad. In fact, it may have been the best day and night of my life! What I **can** do is show you something..." He brought the bag given to him by the Milton, opening it up and displaying the contents to Whisp.

"That's great, Brint. You have some water. I'm glad you didn't die of thirst out there at least. Although, I do like that bag – where did you get it?"

"Hold on, that's not...wait, did you happen to use some of your ability this morning or last night?" he asked.

"Yes, I did, actually. When I heard about your "death", I threw myself into my work to distract my thoughts. I worked through the night and it was only about a half-hour before you showed up at my door that I was finally ready to think about you. I'm exhausted, and I'm just about out of power so if you want me to do something you'll have to wait," she told him, and now that he looked, Brint could see dark circles under her still-beautiful red-rimmed eyes.

"Here, drink one of these and tell me what you think. Trust me."

She looked at him like he was crazy for a moment, before she grabbed one of the vials that were separated into different padded pockets to protect them from casual damage. She pulled the rubber stopper out and looked interestingly at it, after which she sniffed the water inside and then downed it in one gulp. Almost immediately, he could see her perk up and the usual energy in her eyes seemed to glow again. She stared at the vial in her hand and then at Brint, her mouth open in surprise. "What...who...where did you get this? You didn't steal it, did you?"

"Don't worry, I didn't steal them. But I can't tell you where I got them either. The best I can do is say that I found a source of these little vials for relatively cheap – all it takes is some secrecy and a wagonload of metal."

"Metal? Why would they need metal? As far as I know, there is very little in the way of metal needed for the processing of this stuff. And while metal isn't cheap, it is much less expensive to produce, so why can't they buy it themselves?" she asked with a confused expression on her face, which Brint had rarely seen before since she was super-intelligent.

"Again, I wish I could tell you, but I can't – part of that whole secrecy thing. Do you think you could find an Elemental Caster that could produce large quantities of metal, even just metallic deposits of ore, without alerting my parents? I don't really want them involved in this."

She was hesitant to agree to anything at first, since he was being so secretive; however, their friendship won out in the end and she decided to trust him. Once she was on board, she took the reins and developed a plan to distribute the remaining nine vials through a contact she had in the capital, as well as arranging a shipment of metal that would be difficult to trace back to them.

He felt bad about deceiving her over the exact nature of the source of his vials, but he felt it was for the best. He hated involving her in anything clandestine, but he didn't have the knowledge or the contacts to sell the Power Potions without alerting the Cordpower Company of their existence. Although there wasn't any hard proof, rumors circulated even in this backwater village that anyone trying to compete against them met "unfortunate manufacturing accidents". He wanted to get in and sell the potions as quick as possible, make a quick profit and disappear from their radar. At least, that was **his** plan.

*   *   *

"Holy crap, Brint! Do you know how much we got for those vials? Renviert – my merchant contact in Grestwinch – sold the first one at below the going price for a normal Power Potion, but when word got out that it was even better than Cordpower's product, he got nearly 50% more for each of the others! He has a lot of buyers lined up who are interested in acquiring more, when can you get some?"

Brint held his head in his hands, rocking back and forth on Whisp's couch as he listened to her. *This is what I was afraid of.* Speaking to the floor as much as Whisp, he told her, "I don't think it's a good idea. I mean, what if Cordpower gets wind of this? I know you said that Renviert is discrete, but someone is bound to talk when the wrong person can overhear. I don't know if it is worth it, especially with how much we've made already."

She wouldn't hear of it. The whole enterprise had gotten her entrepreneurial juices flowing and Brint was powerless to stop it – he could only hang on and hope everything turned out alright. Hopefully he would be able to convince her to stop after another few shipments. Besides, he had been fired from his job the day after he returned from the forest, the Mayor stating that he had lost another Picow and had abandoned his position by running into the forest – even though it hadn't really been his fault. He needed some sort of income and a couple more shipments wouldn't hurt.

He had delivered a wagon full of various metal ores that Whisp had acquired somehow to the edge of the forest under the cover of darkness a couple of days ago. He had sensed some of the giant lizards, or BBQs, and figured they were waiting for him to deliver it as promised. He didn't try to talk to The Milton again, for fear that the voice would change his mind and ask for something else as compensation for the valuable power potions. But then came the news from the successful sales in the capital and he was back out in the forest again.

"Hello? The Milton, are you there?" He waited a couple of minutes and was about to walk further into the forest and try again when the voice popped into his head, startling him.

"I'm here, Brint. Did you decide you want more vials?"

"Yes, if I can pick up another ten vials or so that would be perfect. I can try to find my way to you or come back another time if you are too busy..."

337

"No need for that – I dispatched a BBQ with another bag of vials as soon I sensed you within the forest. It should be there shortly. Just remember to drop off payment as soon as possible – same terms as before."

"Sounds good." Surprised at the quick response, he waited for a couple more moments before he sensed the BBQ approaching from the East. Although they were still frightening to look at, he had become a little more accustomed to their presence while being held as a prisoner and afterward as a trio of them escorted him back to the village. That, of course, didn't consider its whisper-quiet arrival in the dead of night in the dimly-lit forest.

A short little-girl scream erupted from his mouth before he stopped it when it appeared almost as if by magic just feet away from his face. When his heart had ceased trying to break out of his chest, he looked and saw a vague outline of the vial bag hanging around its neck. He reached up to grab it, just as the BBQ brought its head down to make it easier. Another short squeak of terror escaped as he thought for a second it was attacking, but he was able to gather what shreds of dignity he had left and steadily took the bag from around its neck. As soon as it was off, the giant lizard turned around and quietly disappeared back into the forest.

He delivered another wagon full of finished metal products this time, including old swords, knives, random pieces of armor, and even a couple of full sheets of steel plating. He questioned Whisp about this, but she said that even though it cost a bit more, the diversification of material would help hide their activities. He hadn't even thought about what it would have looked like if they continued buying wagonload after wagonload of ore without showing what they were doing with it. This way, they could buy some metal from here and there, from different suppliers and it would be harder to put together the bigger picture.

The same routine continued over and over for the next two months: acquire some more vials from the Milton every 3rd night, ship them out to Whisp's' contact in the capital the following day, deliver some sort of mixture of metal material to the forest the next night, and receive payment for the potion sales at some time over the next two days. They had accumulated more money than he had ever thought he would see – more than enough to live comfortably for two lifetimes – but he still lived in his same broken-down hovel to keep up appearances.

Right now, he was off to the forest to acquire another bag of vials to ship off to the capital. Even though payment for the last batch was a day late, he was silently hopeful it was because the demand for their product was drying up. He didn't want to be doing this forever – sooner or later the Cordpower Company would catch on to their scheme.

Brint didn't know how to broach the subject of stopping the entire operation to Whisp, since she was so caught up in the joy of the business dealings. He also was afraid of what The Milton would do, breaking it off abruptly like that. *Perhaps we can gradually decrease the supply, stating that the source of it was drying up?* He wasn't sure if that would work, he would have to ask her Whisp when he got back.

He found that the BBQ was waiting for him, as it had since they had been on a regular schedule. He grabbed the bag and patted the giant lizard on the nose, thanking him before turning away from it and walking back down the now worn path to the village. *I should probably be altering my pathway in and out of the forest – it's way too well-traveled now and will stand out if anyone is looking for it.*

He walked back to Whisp's house, still excited to see her whenever he came by to drop off the bag of vials. He hadn't seen her since earlier in the day, but that was normal since they still had to try to avoid the attention of the watchers who were constantly observing them, ever since they had slipped-up when he first came back from the forest. He rarely went near her house without seeing at least one of them, but now the street and surrounding buildings were uncharacteristically empty. *Hopefully this means that they've given up the constant surveillance because we've been good lately.*

Brint approached the entrance and was about to knock when he noticed that the door was slightly ajar. *That's weird, she's usually pretty good about making sure all her doors are closed and locked, especially at night.* He pushed to door open, took in the scene, and fell to his knees; the bag of vials he was holding dropped from his hand and hit the floor with a muffled clink of broken glass. The potion water from the now-broken vials seeped out of the bag, only to mix with the large pool of blood in the middle of the floor.

Chapter 36 – Emergency

Milton, and by extension ALANNA, had been ecstatic over the last couple of months from the trade deal he had with Brint. The Proctan had brought the same quantity of metal that would have taken him at least a decade to gather with his drones – all at essentially no cost to Milton. The fact that ALANNA made it into a quest only enriched the rewards he was receiving.

New Short-term Goal: *Money, Money, Money*

After learning that your "waste" is a valuable commodity, you have brokered a deal with a local Proctan to package and sell it for a large quantity of metallic material.

- *Accumulate 100,000 Basic Metal Units through trade*

Difficulty of Goal: Very Easy

Timeframe: None

Rewards: +1 to your Ingenuity/Wisdom statistic. This goal is repeatable.

In fact, he had just repaired his Core further and was only waiting on a couple more deliveries from Brint to purchase a Defensive Weapons Factory. The influx of BMUs was just what he needed to jumpstart his plans to start clearing out the mountains to the East. He wanted to make sure that he was over-defended in the slight chance that his attack force was overwhelmed and an army of vicious Quizards attacked his dungeon.

He had accumulated quite a lot of Bio Units over the last couple of years from his hunting squad, so everything was coming together quite nicely. In addition to the accumulation of resources, his roaming BBQs had provided enough experience to increase his Combat Level to 12, allowing him to bring his Communication/Charisma and Ingenuity/Wisdom stats up to 50 and 40, respectively. Nothing special occurred when he reached 40 in ingenuity, but with his C/C at 50 the effective communication range with his units was increased by 50%! He figured another month and he'd be ready to start raking in those sweet, sweet ore deposits.[35]

His BBQ had successfully delivered another shipment of vials a little earlier that night, so he turned his attention to his drones and their constant struggle to locate sources of metal throughout his territory. They were still finding pockets of deposits throughout his now-expanded territory, but nothing like the motherlode he knew he would find in the Quizard Mountains. He was concentrating on his Tactical Map, trying to decide on a new place to start exploring for

---

[35]

Core Status			
Name:	Milton Frederick	Type:	Station Core Prototype 3-B
Combat Level:	12	Experience:	90260/133500
Reactor Type:	Zero-point Energy	Reactor Output:	17%
Current Statistics/Attributes			
Reactor Power/Strength:	17	Processing Power/Intelligence:	40
Structural Integrity/Constitution:	16	Ingenuity/Wisdom:	42
Processing Speed/Agility:	35	Communication/Charisma:	50
Insight/Luck:	23	Sensor Interpretation/Perception	26

ore, when he saw one of his BBQs near the village border quickly heading toward his dungeon.

He couldn't think of any orders that he would have given, even contingency plans, that would cause it to return to him without his express orders. He connected to it, looking through its eyes and saw that it was racing through the trees at a break-neck pace. He slowed it down until it came to a stop and was about to turn it around when he felt a weak nudge at his connection with it.

"Hey! I told you, I need to see The Milton! It's an emergency!" The voice of Brint coming from behind his BBQ made Milton turn its head to see the man in question seated along its back, with a bundle of clothing lying across his lap.

"What are you doing, Brint? What's the emergency?"

"Please, I need your help! I need you to heal my friend here!" he paused for a moment, before adding, "She's the one who helped me sell the vials and get all the metal I've delivered. Don't worry, she doesn't know anything about you."

Milton was conflicted. On one hand, he wanted to help his friend – he had gotten to know Brint a little more and it felt good to be able to talk to another "person", even if they were only brief conversations – help heal his girlfriend or whatever. To do otherwise would seem heartless, and Milton was anything but heartless. On the other hand, he didn't want any more people to learn about his

343

presence, and if he did this than there would be just one more person that could share knowledge of his whereabouts.

In the end, although he was now a Station Core, he **was** human at one time and human decency demanded that he act in whatever capacity he could to help. He still debated with himself as he started the BBQ running again, arriving at his dungeon within a couple of minutes. *Maybe I can limit what she sees, so that she doesn't know what is going on or where she is. Then, Brint can bring her back to the village without exposing her to too much.*

Before they arrived, Milton had reopened the tunnel using some drones that he always kept in reserve near his Core that led to the holding cell and from there to his Bioconversion Laboratory. A drone was waiting for them when they arrived, and Brint carefully climbed off the back of his BBQ, gingerly holding the bundle of clothing that he had carried there. Milton didn't have to say anything as the Proctan instinctually followed the drone underground and through the rough tunnels.

When they arrived at the Lab, Brint immediately started walking up the pathway leading to the top without prompting. He gently lowered the bundle into the water when he got to the top, looking down with expectancy as the water solidified. Milton initiated the "repair" process and waited for it to run. And waited, and waited, and waited.

"Ok, ALANNA, what am I doing wrong? It should heal his friend just like it did Brint, right?"

She was watching from the same sensor orb he was watching from, perched as usual on a nearby ledge with Fluffy napping on her lap. Heavy silence filled the room after he asked the question, and Milton worried that he had really messed up somehow. When she spoke, her voice was measured and soft, "I don't think you did anything wrong, Milton. There probably just wasn't anything that you could heal." It was only when she finished that he realized that she hadn't even cursed – and then the meaning behind her words became clear to him.

He, and his Combat Units, had killed numerous creatures over the years – for self-defense and while defending his borders. But he had never seen a dead **person** before and it was morbid on a whole other level.

He wasn't sure if Brint really thought that he could work miracles, or if he was just delusional from grief – either way, Milton wasn't sure how to break it to him that he couldn't heal his friend. Being a bit of a chicken when it came to intense emotional situations, he tried to delay the inevitable.

"What happened?"

He could barely tell that he had gotten through to the grief-stricken young man, his gaze was intently focused on the figure frozen inside the water below. Suddenly, Brint began to whisper, as if he was afraid that being too loud would somehow interrupt the healing process, "I came back to her house to drop off the new vials when I found that her door had been left open. It was unusual because she is usually anal about making sure her doors are constantly locked, but I didn't think anything about it. When I pushed open the door, I found her tied to a chair, the too-tight ropes cutting into the skin on her hands, arms, and legs. She had vicious wounds all over her chest and legs, and bruises running all along her face. Whoever did this to her had cut her throat at the end, leaving a massive puddle of blood to soak into the floorboards. Why isn't she healed yet?"

Milton was speechless at the brutality present in this society – although he knew the same or worse happened back on Earth. He had seen enough action and spy movies to guess what being tied to a chair meant: either someone really didn't like her and wanted to cause her pain before they killed her, or she was tortured and gave up the information they wanted before she was killed.

"I'm sorry Brint, I can't bring her back. If she had still been hanging on, with some life left in her I would have done what I could to save her. As it is, though, there is nothing I can do."

While he was expecting some sort of reaction from Brint, the heart-wrenching keening from the Proctan made his soul hurt, and he could see that ALANNA had been affected as well. She looked sad, the empathetic look on her face something that he hadn't ever seen before.

He watched as the devastated young man sat on the top of the ramp, arms wrapped around his knees as he stared at the stone-covered ceiling. Rocking back and forth, Brint started mumbling, "I'm sorry Whisp, I'm sorry, it's all my fault...I'm sorry Whisp, I'm sorry, it's all my fault," over and over again. Milton wished he could so something to help, but short of...*wait!*

"ALANNA, this may be a stupid question—" he started before she interrupted with, "All your questions are fucking stupid, but I wouldn't have it any other way," in an attempt to lighten the mood. His spirits lifted somewhat, and he continued, "Thanks for that. Anyway, is there any way to create a Combat Unit that isn't a Combat Unit? What I mean, theoretically, is there a way to create one without fitting it with a neurological control unit? And what would happen to its memories? Would they stay the same or would they be erased?"

She thought about it for a moment before answering, "I see where you are going with that. What you are talking about is cloning, which was frowned upon in The Collective – even if your Combat Units are essentially clones themselves. The developers of your Station Core allowed the production of these clones for defensive purposes, since using whatever shit you could get your hands on would be theoretically permitted. However, from what I know, I don't believe they ever thought about making a clone without having some way to control it – it was so taboo that it might have been a blind spot in their programming.

347

"Normally when you create a clone, it keeps all the long-term memory associated with the original sample, with additional samples allowing for more diversification. I don't see why this would be any different. I'd say try that motherfucker – but only if Brint agrees."

Milton agreed with her – he didn't want to go all mad scientist on him without his prior approval. Besides, throwing the body of his friend into his molecular converter felt a little like cannibalism, so he wanted to make sure that was what the Proctan wanted. Since he didn't know much about their customs, he wasn't sure if they had any religions that were against it either.

"Brint, I may have a solution for—"

He was interrupted by an insistent prodding from one of his squirrel scouts. He knew better than to ignore them, since it was rare nowadays that they saw something new inside the forest that required his attention. He looked through the squirrels' eyes and immediately saw what had gotten its panties in a bunch. Three Proctans were carefully making their way through the forest, following a trail left by the BBQ that had carried Brint and the body of his friend earlier.

At first, he couldn't see how they knew they were following the correct trail – but the glowing stone that one of them was holding illuminated some droplets of blood, which would lead them straight to his dungeon. He wanted to blame Brint for this surprise incursion, but then he noticed large bloodstains covering the front of the Proctan in front, a man covered head to toe in hardened leather armor. ALANNA had been watching through his connection and reacted accordingly – "Well, fuck."

New Short-term Goal: *Emergency Measures*

Your territory has been invaded by three unknown Proctans. Defend yourself by any means necessary to ensure your survival.

- *Determine what these strangers want*
- *Kill or otherwise disable the Proctans if they are determined to be a threat*
- *Stop them from reaching your Core*

Difficulty of Goal: Unknown
Timeframe: Unknown
Rewards: +5 to Insight/Luck and a 5% increase to defense of all Combat Units.

"Brint, you need to move. We have some incoming Proctans, and they don't look like friends of yours. Brint? BRINT!"

Nothing he said seemed to get through to him, even when he shouted at him which was probably slightly painful. At a loss, he tried something that he had thought about but had never had need of before. Similar to how he allowed ALANNA access to the views of his Combat Units, he focused on Brint and "pushed" the connection toward the Proctan, while also maintaining control of it.

The surprise connection and view knocked Brint onto his back, dangerously close to the edge of the walkway. He didn't seem to notice as confusion clouded his face, only to be replaced by ferocious anger as he shouted, "Those Cordpower motherfuckers! I'll kill them, I'll kill them all!"

Chapter 37 – I'll kill them all!

Brint couldn't believe that he had lost the one person in the entire world that cared about him, his parents included. Oh, his parents "loved" him like most parents would, but they didn't respect or care about him because of his non-existent ability. To them, he was a mistake, something that they'd like to forget and ignore. That didn't mean they wanted him gone, but they wouldn't be overly upset about it. Lest you think he was just being overly dramatic, they had told him so to his face a short time after he had hit puberty with no revelation of an ability. And now he had lost the only person he cared about as well – and it was all his fault.

If he hadn't gone after that Picow, if he hadn't ever met The Milton, if he hadn't sucked her into his shady dealings, and if he hadn't let the operation continue so long she would still be alive. He was having trouble thinking about what was going to happen now, and whether he wanted to continue living as well. He wasn't one to think about taking his own life, but he just didn't think he could drudge up the will to continue to survive in a world without Whisp.

He was vaguely aware of The Milton trying to talk to him, but his thoughts were so despondent that he ignored even the painful shouts that were directed his way. It was only when a scene high up in some trees invaded his consciousness and knocked him on his back that he began to pay attention to something besides the roiling maelstrom of his own mind.

When he saw the bloodstains and the symbol for the Cordpower Company – a blue vial with stars erupting out the top – on their clothing, he knew exactly what had happened. A red haze clouded his vision, making it harder to see the three figures slowly making their way through the trees but he could see well enough to know that he wanted revenge. He wanted to kill these three bastards and kill every one of those sons-of-bitches at the Power Potion-making company.

"Those Cordpower motherfuckers! I'll kill them, I'll kill them all!"

He had difficulty at first trying to concentrate on anything other than the view of the three Company men, but he found that he could sort of "move" the scene to one side while the room physically around him came back into focus. He realized that he was right on the edge of the walkway and hurriedly scooted back to safety.

"Now that I've got your attention, I need you to follow one of my drones back to my Core Room where you will be safe. They will be here soon – despite my efforts to hide, they are following your trail to my dungeon. I will take care of them."

"No! I want to rip their heads off with my bare hands and shove them up their asses! I want to light them on fire and burn them alive! I want to—"

"You will do no such thing, nor do I think you are literally capable of doing any of those things. I said I like my privacy and they are trespassing – I don't care for trespassers. You'll get your wish for their deaths, but it will be by *my* hand, not yours – but I will let you watch. Now, GET DOWN TO MY CORE ROOM! I won't ask again."

Despite wanting to argue and rush off to attack those bastards, he followed the drone that had entered the door on the opposite side of the room, fuming all the while. He walked down a series of tunnels, missing the sight of numerous traps along the way while his thoughts were solely focused on revenge. It was only when he entered a large room flooded with a small pool of water that he paid attention.

Sitting in the middle of the room was the largest egg he had ever seen. It was a shiny metallic grey color, had various divots sprinkled across the surface of it, and stood about twenty feet tall. Small lines crisscrossed the outside of it in confusing shapes and emitted a soft glow that slowly pulsed as he looked at it. He stopped halfway into the room, the swift water flowing through his legs on its way to a hole on the opposite side of the room. Thoughts of revenge were temporarily suspended as he stood there with his mouth open, staring at the monstrous metal egg. He was so distracted that he failed to notice the extremely small, strange-looking person in a skin-tight purple outfit until she said, "Alright fuck-nugget, get your ass to the other side of the room on that ledge there. If anything manages to get you there, we're all dead anyway. And don't think about taking matters into your own hands – your power and control aren't strong enough to affect things far away. If you have a problem with that, tough shit. Let Milton do his thing and we'll all be fine."

Shocked, confused, and disoriented by all that had happened and by what he was now seeing, he followed her orders and sat down on the ledge, his wet legs dangling over the edge and dripping back down into the pool. Once he was there, he looked around the room and realized that it wasn't just them in the room – he could see six more drones near the entrance and three strange-looking creatures with sharp claws further down the ledge, laying about and sleeping for all he could see.

"Thanks for listening to ALANNA, she's kind of my right-hand woman…and left-hand for that matter since I don't have any. As promised, I'm going to feed you views of the three intruders – but as she said, please don't try to connect with anything you see, you don't have the power or control to do it yet. And if you try, I'll cut you off and you can sit there in silence. Now, what can you tell me about these three?"

He didn't take being told to sit down and obey like a child very well, but he realized that he had no choice. And when he **really** looked at who his adversaries were, he wasn't confident that he'd even be able to get close to any of them to hurt them the way he wanted to. As much as he didn't want to admit it, he needed The

Milton's help if he wanted any type of revenge against those monsters.

"From what I can see, the one in front is a Physical Augmenter with at least strength and speed augments, by the way he swiftly moves through the underbrush and the heavy-ass sword strapped to his back. The one in the middle, wearing the heavy and oh-so-suitable-for-a-forest robes, is an Elemental Caster of some sort. He'll most likely be more adept at a particular type of element, but from here I can't tell what that might be.

"The last in line I'm guessing is a Healer, based on how fat he is and the way he avoids touching anything that might accidentally hurt him. Healers are notorious for hoarding their power, saving it for whenever they can make the most money healing someone and hate to waste any power healing themselves. As you probably heard me say, they're from the Cordpower Company and I'm positive they are the ones who tortured and killed Whisp."

"Thanks – that will help a lot with my strategies. I'm going to give you the first lesson in group warfare for free: always take out the healer first.

"What do you mean by first less—"

"Shhh! Try to concentrate on this new view from my nearby sensor orb and listen to what they are saying. Maybe you'll overhear something that will help."

Brint focused on the new view that popped up in his mind, straining at first but eventually learning that if he relaxed he could start to hear a conversation.

"—and **I** told **you**, I know what I'm doing. This trail is so clear that I could follow it half-blind and drunk. I don't care if you think we're lost, I **know** we're lost – but we are **still** following the trail that stupid useless boy left for us."

Brint bristled at the mention of his being "useless" – *apparently, they are some of **those** people, ones who think that if you don't have an inherently useful ability then you are less than nothing.*

"Why Gavin put him in charge, I'll never know," the Elemental Caster had dropped back to talk to the Healer in what Brint supposed was a whisper. The hearing capabilities of this "sensor orb" was spectacular, since even the smallest sounds were clear.

"He put me in charge because I get shit done and I'm not squeamish like you two little girls. I saw the way you couldn't watch as I questioned that girl, Reginald. I would have thought that a Healer as 'adept' as you wouldn't be sick at the sight of a little blood," the man in the lead shot over his shoulder at the other two, while still following the trail through the dark forest.

"It's just that I think that you went a little too far, Glert. You didn't have to kill her – I think she had learned her lesson after an hour of your 'questioning'," the corpulent Healer managed to respond, breathing heavily as he followed along.

"I had instructions to 'eliminate' the problem, which means that we couldn't leave any witnesses to our activities. Cordpower needs to maintain a stellar reputation to ensure swift sales – people don't want to buy from a company that they might suspect performs 'illegal activity'. Just ask Mirve, I told him this when he was recruited for this little 'excursion'."

The Elemental Caster looked up at his name – somehow, he was ignoring the entire conversation while he worked at avoiding getting his robes caught in the underbrush. "That's true, but I didn't think you'd have to go that far. There had to be a better way to get the information and stop the production of this other Power Potion."

"Cordpower had been investigating it discretely for weeks and they were getting nowhere. It was only when they tracked down the merchant in Grestwinch that they were able to get any information on the girl. He either didn't know any information on the production of the potion or was strong enough to resist the expert 'interrogation techniques' before he died. Either way, that's why we're here – there was a problem and we're here to fix it. Simple as that – they pay us way too much to worry about playing nice. Now, shut up – the blood seems fresher here and these giant tracks are coming closer together, meaning that it was slowing down. I have a feeling that we'll be there soon, and I don't want to spook him into running again."

Another one dead because of me! Even though I'm pretty sure Renviert knew he was playing a dangerous game, it was because of what I started that caused his death. He was starting to feel

357

despondent again, but then anger bubbled up again inside his chest as he saw the bloodstains still on the leather armor of the Physical Augmenter. *I'll think about that later, right now I just want to see them pay for hurting my Whisp!*

Chapter 38 – Never split the party

As he watched the now-silent trio of Cordpower "fixers" pass through the forest, the area around them started to look a little familiar. They were close to the hole leading into the ground that the BBQ had dropped him off at, but when he looked at where he was sure it was located, there was only a normal-looking forest floor. The hole had been quickly sealed shut, underbrush and leaves dragged over it with very little indication that there was ever anything there.

With a near-silent whisper, Glert got close to the other two and told them, "The tracks stop here, and then head North. I think this 'Brint' we are looking for was left here and then walked the rest of the way. I don't see anything here, so I'm going to continue in this direction and see if I can find where he may have gotten to. Don't move and I'll be back shortly."

The augmenter started moving very quickly, zipping away faster than even he thought the BBQs could manage. Brint knew that the previous hole and tunnels were relatively close, but he didn't know exactly where this place was located. However, with the speed that Glert seemed to possess, which seemed extraordinarily fast even for a Physical Augmenter, it probably wouldn't be long until they were found.

"Hah! Noob mistake! Never – and I mean never – split the party. Or else something like this happens."

Brint's momentary confusion was cleared up when he saw a veritable army of antlered rabbits and snakes with oversized heads seemingly come out of nowhere to attack the unprepared duo. Six of the rabbits sprinted and impacted the back of Mirve, knocking him down onto his face. Three of the rabbits had died upon impact, their horns still impaled inside the body of the caster. Mirve yelled out in pain, high-pitched screaming sounding like a little girl, and Reginald started to move in his direction with a wary eye on the remaining rabbits.

He didn't notice the five snakes hiding in the leaves ahead of him, who sprung to attack when he literally walked on one of them. They couldn't reach his face, but two were able to latch onto one of his arms, two bit into his junk – which Brint thought brought a nice falsetto accompaniment to Mirve's little-girl screaming – while the one that was stepped-on sank its fangs into Reginald's ankle.

As the Healer tried unsuccessfully to detach the snakes, flailing one arm in the air and the other gingerly yanking on the ones attached to his manhood, Mirve stopped his screaming and focused on his ability. Brint watched as two whirlwinds formed, one surrounding Mirve entirely and the other next to the Healer, until they were spinning so fast that the air seemed to shriek. Still prone on the ground, the Elemental Caster slowly brought his hands together like he was trying to squeeze something, straining while he

360

tried to contain it. The twister next to Reginald shrunk in size until it was a swirling vortex of shrieking compressed air.

Directing it with his mind, Mirve deftly maneuvered the vortex of death toward Reginald, quickly slicing through the head of each of the snakes hanging off the Healer. The compressed swirling air was moving so fast and in such a tight space that it literally cut them into pieces. When the last snake, the one attached to his ankle, was dead, Mirve dispersed the vortex of death and Reginald started healing himself with his ability. While he was doing this, the three remaining rabbits had backed up and with room to run they ran straight for the injured caster, hoping to finish him off.

As soon as they reached the whirlwind around Mirve, they were picked up and rapidly spun around and around, with no damage except for perhaps being dizzy. That changed when the caster repeated what he had done earlier, compressing the swirling twister until it grew smaller and spun faster. The rabbits were carried along with it, until they were spinning so fast that they started to break apart – blood, fur, bone, and internal organs mixed together until it looked like small ball of red and white was rotating violently in the air. With a flick of his wrist, the ball shot off into the forest breaking apart within a dozen feet and flinging the remains of the three rabbits all over the trees.

"FUCKING HEAL ME ALREADY!" Mirve screamed at the Healer. Reginald had fully healed himself, and while he still looked a little worse for wear, he obliged by slowly waddled over to the prone caster. Before he could reach him, he froze as he heard something come up behind him. He turned to see a pair of frighteningly large bears, skin covered in hard scales and sharp-looking claws only a dozen feet away.

He backed up in fear, tripping over Mirve – who was **still** on the ground – and eliciting a further scream of pain from the caster when he inadvertently impacted the antlers still stuck in the casters' back. Now in too much pain to concentrate, the Elemental Caster could only writhe on the ground while their death approached with the unhurried ambling of the two bears.

Brint watched with glee at the imminent revenge – and, truth be told – a little disgust at himself at how much he was enjoying the suffering of these two men. These two emotions warred within his mind only for a second before REVENGE slapped disgust in the face, knocking it out. As he rooted for these bears, he secretly hoped that they would suffer as much pain as Whisp must have before she died. Unfortunately, the absent Physical Augmenter made an appearance.

Cutting off their advance, Glert had sped toward the two bears before he slowed down and whipped the massive sword off his back. He was no longer moving with insane speed, but his strength was so great now that he was able to move the near-six-foot, six-inch wide blade back and forth like it weighed no more than a wooden switch.

Brint's attention on the battle was interrupted by ALANNA, who derisively said, "You think he's compensating for something?"

"Oh my god, ALANNA, not now – I'm trying to concentrate," he could hear the Milton say, but still with a hint of amusement in his voice.

With wide sweeps, the over-sized weapon pushed back the bears, who were smart enough to avoid walking right into the attacks. However, despite their apparent strength and deadliness, Brint saw that they didn't move very fast, which was further hampered when Mirve had recovered enough to use his ability again.

No longer screaming in pain, the caster determinedly got to his knees and faced the two bears that were barely avoiding the sweeps of the giant sword. Placing his hands on the ground, he clenched his hands on the sparse handfuls of dirt underneath the undergrowth and slowly lifted them into the air. Mounds of dirt spread over the paws of the bears, temporarily rooting them in place. They immediately started to break free from the enveloping mounds, but they were too late as the sharp side of a humongous hunk of metal impacted with their heads, shearing off the tops of their skulls and taking a chunk of brain with it. The ease at which they were killed left Brint worried – if they were that powerful, then he didn't think the Milton stood a chance against them. Of course, that was before he saw what happened next.

"I leave you guys alone for one second," Glert started to say while turning back to the two others. He stopped and stared for a second, before speed-jumping over the prone caster and cleaving his massive sword into the neck of the BBQ who had just finished slicing off the head of the distracted Healer. Brint was almost as shocked as the expression on the head of the now-dead Reginald – he had barely caught a glimpse of the BBQ as it silently ran into the battle-site behind the Healer and instantly sliced his head off. The whole sneak-attack took less than two seconds from start to finish, but Glert had reacted quickly as well – just not quick enough.

"Like I said, take out the healer first. Second lesson: Pay Attention! Don't focus so much on one thing that you ignore everything else. And this is the most important thing – watch for adds."

Brint still wasn't sure what the Milton was talking about. *Adds?* Even if he did, he was beginning to think that the strange voice in the metal shell was a bit crazy.

Considering the death of Reginald, he was glad, but he didn't feel as happy as he thought he would watching one of those bastards die. He wasn't sure if it was the abrupt nature of the death, if he wouldn't be happy until they were all dead, or for some other reason. He couldn't think about it long as he saw that three more BBQs had entered the battle from different directions, attacking the caster who had retrieved some healing potions from his bag now that their healer was dead. He chugged two of them, one right after another in quick succession. The healing power inside the potions caused the foreign objects embedded in his back – the antlers – to be ejected while the skin around the wounds closed until he was returned to healthy condition.

Glert was using his speed and a small dagger to hold off the BBQs, slashing with little effect toward each one, causing them to back up instinctively to avoid damage. However, even with his speed, they were getting closer to Mirve – who had, unbeknownst to Brint, taken out a small highly-flammable stick about six inches long. In his other hand, he had a hand-held striker, an invention created some years ago for its ease at starting fires.

"Watch out, he's going to light that stick and use the flames to attack!"

Unfortunately, his warning came too late for two of the giant lizards as a concentrated stream of super-hot fire blasted out from the head of the now-lit stick, catching the BBQs in the face and melting their eyes – along with the skin and scales around them. Berserk with pain, the two injured BBQs lashed out blindly, their strikes missing Glert by a mile as he jumped on the back of the one closet to him. Shoving his dagger into a gap in the scales on the back of its neck, the BBQ dropped to the ground like a puppet that had its strings cut.

While the second blinded BBQ continued to thrash about, the third retreated as Mirve took aim at it, missing it as it sped away. Glert put away his dagger and activated his strength-augmenting ability again, nearly decapitating the injured lizard with one blow of his massive sword.

As Brint watched them collapse onto the ground, their power nearly spent and both staring at the corpse of their fallen comrade, he saw them pull another potion out from their bags and drink it. It was only when they seemed to perk up a bit that he realized that they came armed with Power Potions – which made sense if they came from Cordpower. *They probably loaded these guys up with tons of potions, knowing that the expense was worth it if they took care of their "problem".*

"Why did the last BBQ retreat? They were tired and almost out of power."

"That whole thing was really just for recon – although I'm happy to see that tactical distractions work just as well here as…well, somewhere else. I also wanted to see how my Combat Units would work if I just gave them instructions instead of directly controlling them in battle against smarter opponents. I've been fighting and killing rather stupid single-minded creatures out here for a while and I needed to see how rusty I was. I really need to get my PVP game back…anyway, thanks for the warning – I was wondering what he was doing with that stick."

Again, he didn't understand half of what the Milton had said, but he took it as another indication that he wasn't really in his right mind and ignored it. "So, what now? Are you going to send more of your…uh…combat thingy's in?"

"Nope. Now it's time to see how they like my dungeon."

Chapter 39 – Underwhelming traps

Milton had heard what was said before the battle, and he knew that Brint had heard it as well. He now had no qualms about killing the men, whereas before he had been hesitant because he wasn't sure why they were here. With his moral quandary settled, Milton knew he would do anything to protect himself and his friends.

Congratulations! Your Combat Units have defeated Proctan Male, Designation: Healer, Name: Reginald! You gain 5000 experience! Continue to defeat your enemies to level up!

Current Combat Level: 12

Experience: 95260/133500

You have upgraded the skill: *Cooperation (Level 4)*

Bonus at current skill level: 20% increased defense for Combat Units participating in a battle beside a natural enemy

Congratulations!

You have upgraded the skill: *Formation Fighting (Level 3)*

Bonus at current skill level: 15% additional damage inflicted to the enemy when your units are in a formation.

Congratulations!

You have upgraded the skill: *Combat Communication (Level 3)*

Current # of units you can communicate with simultaneously at your current skill level: 7

Congratulations!

You have unlocked an achievement:

<u>First Blood</u>

> *Defeat your first sentient lifeform.*
>
> *Bonus – +2 to Insight/Luck and Processing Speed/Agility*

New Short-term Goal: *Emergency Measures - Update*

Your territory has been invaded by three unknown Proctans. Defend yourself by any means necessary to ensure your survival.

- *Determine what these strangers want – To kill Brint, discover source of Power Potion – Complete!*
- *Kill or otherwise disable the Proctans if they are determined to be a threat – 1/3 killed*
- *Stop them from reaching your Core*

Difficulty of Goal: Hard (Updated)

Timeframe: Soon (Updated)

Rewards: +5 to Insight/Luck and a 5% increase to defense of all Combat Units.

"Now we can see how they handle my traps – this should be good."

He ignored the confused and skeptical look on Brint's – and, for some reason, ALANNA's – faces and turned his attention to the first section of the tunnel, which held his pit trap. It was always good for at least one death when he was attacked by groups of creatures, and he expected that it would live up to its reputation once again. He smiled inwardly as Glert took the lead about a dozen steps in front of the Elemental Caster. The floor started to tilt, and Milton started laughing inwardly as the startled Augmenter slid down the declining platform.

His laughter died without even having had a chance of being vocalized, when he watched Glert activate his strength ability and perform some sort of super-jump. With a quick squat of his legs, the Physical Augmenter pushed against the dropping floor with such strength that he was launched forward and slightly upward. He just barely cleared the pit and landed safely on the other side, rolling with his momentum.

The force of the jump had dropped the floor so fast and powerfully that instead of rebounding upwards, the front two-thirds of the platform broke off, dropping into the pit and destroying most of the stone spikes.

"Ok, I wasn't expecting that."

Mirve was still on the other side of the pit, but since the floor on either side had a foot of safe space – which he had left so that his Combat Units would have an easier time departing the dungeon – he simply walked across the pathway. He did progress carefully, testing each step to ensure that it wouldn't collapse underneath him.

With the first trap a dud, Milton was starting to have doubts that his other traps would be effective, especially now that the two invaders were sure to be looking for them. Unfortunately, his doubts were confirmed as they approached the slicing blade trap. Since it wasn't a surprise, they had plenty of time to consider how to disable the blades, effectively rendering the trap useless.

The solution was simple when you had access to magic – raise a column of stone into the path of the blades to slow them down. When Mirve had done this, it also had the added effect of breaking a few of the strong, yet thin blades upon impact with the column. He didn't even have to work hard at finding stone – the walls and floors provided more than enough material to work with. The only thing that encouraged Milton was that after he had raised the column, the caster seemed tired and needed to swallow another Power Potion to recover afterwards.

His wooden stake trap actually fared worse, since the sheet across the tunnel was obvious if you were looking for something out of the ordinary. The solution again was simple – Glert threw an empty Power Potion vial at the sheet with enough force that it triggered the trap, forcing the stakes through the holes in the wall and crisscrossing the corridor with a wooden barricade. After ensuring that there were no more surprises in store for them, the Augmenter whipped out his sword and destroyed the stakes with powerful blows, turning Milton's' previously very-effective trap into kindling.

He had created multiple copies of each trap throughout the rest of his dungeon, which worked well against persistent hostile creatures but only seemed to annoy the two Proctans. They used the same methods of destroying his traps whenever they came across them, with the only change being the pit trap. Mirve started following close behind Glert, periodically using his ability to search the ground a short distance ahead, locating where there was a void in the dirt below. They then preceded to walk around the trap, bypassing any danger. The constant use of power, however, meant that both men had to periodically use another Power Potion to refill their abilities – the consumption of which was starting to make them look a little haggard.

Brint was looking more and more like he was having some sort of mental breakdown as he continued to watch two of men who had killed his friend easily defeat or bypass his traps. One minute he appeared anxious and fidgety, while the next he had his fists clenched so tightly in anger that he worried that he would accidentally harm himself.

"Don't worry, Brint – I'm not done yet. Watch this."

When they had traveled about 90% of the way through the tunnels, Milton decided that it was time to use his last-ditch defensive trap that he had prepared years ago for just this reason. *Well, not this **exact** reason, but this certainly does qualify.* Mirve hesitated when he used his ability on the stretch of hallway containing his trap.

"Hold up – I'm sensing a large void underneath us. It's different from those damn pits, too," Mirve said, while grabbing onto Glert's arm to prevent him from walking any further.

"How far does it extend?"

"I'm not sure – at least 30 feet, which is the extent of my sensing ability. As you know, my Air affinity is much stronger than my Earth. I'm not sure what this is, so it's your call."

Milton, ALANNA, and Brint all anxiously watched as Glert stopped to think for almost a full minute, before stating, "We've come this far – I say we chance it. I'm not going back to the company without some answers, and this place is so unusual that I believe we could sell the information about this place to the Guardian Guild for a nice payday. But I also don't want to die – so keep your damn ability working, and we'll both be fine."

Glert began walking slowly across the floor, practically shuffling his feet and cautiously tapping the stone ahead of him with his foot. When they were nearly halfway across the 40-foot stretch of tunnel that contained the trap, Glert started to relax a bit when nothing happened, until Mirve startled him by saying, "I think it ends—"

He didn't get to finish what he was about to say because at that moment Milton had his sacrificial drone stationed below remove the keystone holding the bridge aloft. Immediately it began to collapse upon itself from the middle, pulling down the two startled intruders into a giant hole leading to the underground river. They were enveloped in the falling debris, pieces of the hallway crashing together on the way down and demolishing anything caught in between them – including his now-destroyed drone. Milton could faintly hear the clacking of the tunnel pieces colliding as they ricocheted against each other, followed by multiple splashes as all the dirt and stone chunks impacted the water.

Everyone in the Core Room was silent for a couple of moments after they heard the splashing far below. It was a bit anti-climactic, but when you needed to do a job, sometimes it doesn't matter how simple the solution is – *as long as it works, who cares if it isn't flashy?*

"See, I told you I would take care of—"

Suspended in the middle of the hole, and softly floating upwards on a rotating disk of air, the two battered-looking Proctans were floating on their backs, alive and for the most part whole. Each of them sported some nasty cuts that were still bleeding and Mirve appeared to be missing his left foot – most likely it had been sheared off by some super-sharp falling debris. The two disks of air softly deposited them on the Core Room side of the tunnel, where they both lay there with moans of pain.

Milton missed an opportunity to attack as he was shocked at the cockroach-like ability of these two to survive everything he threw at them. Before he could even consider sending some of the badgers

373

he kept as guards near his core, Glert had fished out of his bag what appeared to be his last remaining health potion and downed it in one gulp, and within moments his wounds had been magically healed.

Mirve started digging into his bag as well, just as he started to scream as the shock of his foots' amputation wore off. Glert walked over and finished searching the caster's bag as well, muttering obscenities as he cut his fingers multiple times on broken glass vials. In the end, Milton saw him extract a singular intact vial – a Power Potion. Through his screams of pain, Mirve watched Glert find it and immediately put his hands out in a "gimme" motion, pleading with the Augmenter to give him the potion.

With disgust etched all over his face, Glert told the still-bleeding caster, "You're of no use to me now. Giving this to you would be a waste – and I'm anything but wasteful. But I **can** be merciful." He had a grim smile on his face as he withdrew his dagger from the sheath on his belt and bent toward the now-silent Mirve. Milton could see some stray wisps of wind try to blow the Augmenter back, but the Elemental Caster must have been tapped out because the last thing he heard before he turned his attention away was a hoarse, "Waitwaitwaitwait NOOOOOO—".

ALANNA summed up the whole situation with a very pertinent, "Holy FUCK!"

New Short-term Goal: *Emergency Measures - Update*

374

Your territory has been invaded by three unknown Proctans. Defend yourself by any means necessary to ensure your survival.

- *Determine what these strangers want – To kill Brint, discover source of Power Potion – Complete!*
- *Kill or otherwise disable the Proctans if they are determined to be a threat – 2/3 killed*
- *Stop them from reaching your Core*

Difficulty of Goal: Hard (Updated)

Timeframe: Soon (Updated)

Rewards: +5 to Insight/Luck and a 5% increase to defense of all Combat Units.

Chapter 40 – See! I told you...

Milton returned his attention back to the invaders – **invader** – and witnessed Glert bent over and wiping the blood off his dagger on the already-bloodstained robes of his latest victim. Raising himself back up, he continued down the tunnel without even a backward glance at his erstwhile companion. The next 50 feet were built in a curve, so that by the time the Augmenter could see the Core Room he was practically on top of it.

Brint was sitting along a ledge near the back of the room, but he was still visible enough that recognition was almost instant.

"I'M GOING TO FUCKING KILL YOU!", they both shouted at each other simultaneously. ALANNA snickered, and Milton would have thought it was funny if it wasn't for the fact that if the murdering Augmenter managed to kill Brint he was probably next. Removing the giant sword from his back, Glert started running toward the room with the blade pointing behind him, as if he was preparing to swing it forward.

Brint's face was contorted in a rictus of hate as he jumped down from the ledge he had been sitting on, splashing through the water as he strove toward the object of his hatred. The three badgers that he had as guards were already alert, but now their control had been taken over by the near-insane mentality of his Proctan friend. It should have been impossible considering the amount of power he had to expend to control them all but being in close proximity to the source of the power helped immensely. Milton was about to wrestle back control of them, but he was interrupted by trying to time his next move properly.

His drones activated his gate trap precisely on time, where the encroaching hostile Proctan was in no position to avoid the multi-ton block of stone that came crashing down. At least, that's what he thought before some uncanny sense alerted Glert to the danger approaching from above, causing him to drop his heavy sword behind him as he activated his speed augmentation and raced ahead of the stone that crashed down, clipping his foot and making him stumble forward to land with a splash in Milton's filter water.

Seeing him now without his main weapon, Brint and his Clawed Badger guards arrived at the entrance before he could recover from his near-death experience. Only his augmented speed allowed him to avoid all but a small scratch on his leg from the lead badger, but even the graze of one of their claws was enough to cause his leather armor to part and blood to leak out of some shallow wounds.

Hoping to take advantage somehow (which to Milton seemed insane since he had no weapon), Brint launched himself at the back of the stumbling Physical Augmenter. He wrapped his hands around Glert's neck, perhaps hoping to choke him to death, but the Augmenter wasn't fazed in the least. Switching tactics, he instead beefed up his strength using his ability, bent over, and launched Brint across the room, impacting a wall and landing with a splash next to one of the drones that had cut one of the gate trap ropes.

In his efforts to remove the other Proctan from his back, the badgers had been able to close on Glert and attack. However, since they were no longer being directly controlled by Brint, they were blind and only able to sense where he was through the sounds of splashing. Barely moving away in time, Glert stumbled backwards and fully fell into the water for the first time. Climbing back to his feet, he finally got the chance to pull out his dagger and paused as he tasted some of the water that had gotten into his mouth.

"Holy shit! This whole room is full of Power! I feel invincible now!" He flexed his muscles as if he was trying to show off at a body-building competition, laughing hysterically all the while. And that was the moment Milton shot him with his self-defensive cold laser.

Without the natural defense of a body covered in scales, hard skin, or ablative armor, the cold laser did what it was supposed to do – cover the intended victim in a block of ice. Milton took over the control of his badgers, using his **Combat Communication** skill to direct all three of them at once. They moved in to attack and slice up the frozen Proctansicle but were momentarily pushed back as something unexpected happened.

Using his outrageous speed, the Physical Augmenter moved so fast while encased in the ice that it had practically vibrated, violently shaking until it reached the critical point where it had no choice but to be expelled outward with extreme force. Shards of ice flew out in all directions, many of them pinging harmlessly against his outer shell but a couple impacted his Clawed Badgers, causing two of them minor damage. Unluckily, the third took a large shard to one of its eyes, embedding itself so far up the eye socket that it pierced its brain, instantly killing it.

Milton sent his other two badgers back in to attack, hoping that they would be able to get to the Augmenter before he was prepared to defend himself. That hope was in vain, however, as Glert recovered quickly and used his speed augmentation to run circles around the slow badgers, stabbing them multiple times within a matter of a couple of seconds. When they lay dead at his feet, he turned back to Brint, intending to finish the job he came here for.

Ever since Glert had survived his fail-safe trap, Milton had been hard at work. Knowing that he didn't have a lot of time, but now with a plethora of Processing Power/Intelligence to control quite a few units due to battle losses incurred earlier, he started production of the cheapest, quickest, and – in his opinion – deadliest Combat Unit that he could think of.

With his back end pointing away from the entrance, he was therefore able to assemble a small army, pooping out units every half-second while they hid behind his massive bulk. Brint, in his rage and focus on Glert the whole time, hadn't seen what Milton had been doing – but ALANNA had. She genuinely smiled at him, knowing that what he was doing was the hardest thing that he had ever done, but knowing he did it not only to save himself, but to save a friend.

At almost 200-strong, a veritable swarm of Blood-thirsty Squirrels flowed around both sides of his shell, making very little noise as they swam toward the distracted Augmenter. Glert was taking his time, walking slowly toward Brint while the one-time farmer was slowly getting to his feet after being thrown against the wall. He was unaware of any danger until he felt something touch the back of his lower leg, where it attached itself and started to climb up his back. He reached back with his free hand, snatched the squirrel by its neck, and brought it out in front of him so he could see it.

"What the hell is—OW!" The squirrel, not liking being picked up, had turned its head and bit down on Glert's hand, drawing a small amount of blood with its surprisingly sharp teeth. The Augmenter quickly used his super-strength to squeeze the small animal, breaking its neck and practically decapitating it. He threw it away to the side and took one more step toward Brint – but he didn't get any farther. The momentarily distraction and sacrifice of the initial squirrel was enough time for the legion of furry agents of death to reach him.

While most climbed up both of his legs – front and back – about a dozen dove down under the water and started chewing through the tough leather of his boots, using their nearly razor-sharp teeth to slice it into pieces. Using his enhanced speed this time, Glert immediately started pulling each squirrel off his upper body and flung them away, where – if it wasn't damaged too much – it immediately swam back to attack again. Within seconds, the Augmenter was covered in Milton's furry army, until a few were able to make it to his face where they were able to get a quick bite in before being snatched and thrown away.

Milton hadn't stopped creating them either – for every squirrel that was crushed or thrown savagely against a wall, two more were on their way. It was only when he realized that he was in trouble that he tried to run away from them, but by that time the squirrel divers had reached his feet, where they quickly started biting and ripping apart tendons and his Achilles. He apparently was so distracted by the other, closer squirrels that the pain didn't reach his brain before he took his first step.

Falling to his knees, no longer able to support himself with his feet being shredded, he was now even closer to the circling squirrel army. They took full advantage of this fact, latching onto his shirt and with a single bound were at his throat and face. Covered in small bite marks and dripping blood into the water, Glert's face became enraged.

Somehow using both of his abilities at the same time, his hands were a blur as they snatched a squirrel head and crushed it, dropping it before grabbing another. He was making progress as a steady stream of corpses started filling up the area around him, and Milton was starting to worry that his army wouldn't be enough. That was until his squirrel divers had switched tactics and begun attacking the one place any man would protect above all else – even his face.

The first indication that his squirrels had hit pay dirt was when the Augmenter screamed in a high-pitched startled yelp, followed by a frantic yanking of squirrels from of his crotch, where he then flung them away with crushed skulls. Milton kept the attack on his family jewels going, causing Glert to have to defend it with one hand while attempting to protect his face with the other. This insistence to protect his manhood was his downfall as he was swarmed in two places, until finally his head was so covered in fur he looked like some sort of demented werewolf.

Blood now ran freely from his face and neck, and even when he attempted to salvage the situation by abandoning his nether regions it was too late. One lucky bite had fully opened the artery in his neck, which he couldn't reach to stop the blood from gushing out in mass quantities. A last-ditch effort on his part consisted of smashing the squirrels – and consequently, his face – with devastating blows, causing more harm to himself than he probably intended. As the blows started coming slower and with less strength, Milton watched as the Physical Augmenter finally fell forward, his dying body creating a great splash and flinging random squirrels off into the water.

He wanted to make sure he didn't make the mistake of both villains and heroes in the movies he used to watch – always triple-check to ensure your opponent is dead. He doubted Glert could feign his own death – especially with the amount of blood now floating around the pool – but it never hurts to make sure. After another minute of his squirrel army tearing up the remains of the Physical Augmenter, he called them off.

"See! I *told* you they were Blood-thirsty Squirrels."

Chapter 41 – Mutations

Congratulations! Your Combat Units have defeated Proctan Male, Designation: Physical Augmenter, Name: Glert! You gain 10000 experience!

Continue to defeat your enemies to level up!

Current Combat Level: 12

Experience: 105260/133500

Congratulations!

You have upgraded the skill: *Survivor (Level 3)*

Bonus at current skill level: 15% increase in defense of Combat Units

---

New Short-term Goal: *Emergency Measures* – *Complete!*

Your territory has been invaded by three unknown Proctans. Defend yourself by any means necessary to ensure your survival.

- *Determine what these strangers want – To kill Brint, discover source of Power Potion – Complete!*
- *Kill or otherwise disable the Proctans if they are determined to be a threat – 3/3 killed Complete!*
- *Stop them from reaching your Core – Complete!*

Difficulty of Goal: Hard

Timeframe: Soon

> **Rewards:** +5 to Insight/Luck and a 5% increase to defense of all Combat Units
>
> **Bonus Reward:** For using an unconventional swarm tactic using primarily non-combat-oriented Combat Units, your rewards are doubled: +5 -> +10 Insight/Luck and 5% -> 10% increase to defense
>
> **Additional Bonus:** For surviving your first Sentient Lifeform incursion, you receive 20,000 experience

Milton was pleased at being able to take out the invaders, and yet disgusted at himself for how out-of-practice he was fighting against smarter, more powerful opponents. Looking back at the battle, he realized that instead of succeeding with the use of superior tactics, he had gotten lucky more than anything else. It was only the last part of the fight that he improvised, using a basic Zerg[36] tactic more than anything. The last century of fighting simple – and even some not-so-simple – creatures had dulled the edge he used to employ against difficult foes.

When he had first arrived on this planet, the difficulty in staying alive from day to day had pushed him to employ his Combat Units in unusual, but effective, ways. Even the traps that he had designed were a result of scrambling to find a way to defend himself from stronger, more numerous creatures. But lately, with his increased level, new facilities, and what he thought were unstoppable killing machines in his BBQs – everything had been too easy. Well, not **easy** – but he wasn't pushing himself to create new

---

[36] A very large group of units that rely on overwhelming numbers instead of technique or strategy.

and unique traps, Combat Units, or even expanding his dungeon. In the end, he had grown complacent.

Even with the discovery that people were on this planet, he failed to consider that they had something he had little defense against – **magic**. Milton vowed that he would do all he could to learn more about magic in this world – and how to defend against it. He had years and years of experience to draw from the videogames he had played, but he needed to know the rules and how it worked **here**. Even ignoring the fact that **he** had somehow inadvertently caused the magical ability to appear in the Proctans, the mere presence of people with unusual powers should have made him investigate it further than he had.

But rather than beat himself up about it anymore than he already had, he turned his attention back to Brint. His Proctan friend had busted a couple of ribs with the impact against the stone and Milton had immediately sent him to heal up in the Bioconversion Laboratory. He had to have his drones make a temporary tunnel to the side of the corridor that had collapsed into the underground river, but they were so adept at the job that they were done in less than 20 minutes. Once he was done, they all met again in the Core Room to discuss what they would do next.

"If I'm reading the situation correctly, we have a limited amount of time before this Cordpower Company sends someone – or even a group – to check up on their missing team. If they send someone

even a little more powerful than these three, I don't think we would survive as we are right now. Suggestions?"

"Let's take the fight to them. The death of these three was just the start – I won't be happy until all of them are dead. I won't let them get away with what they did," Brint spluttered, the anger in his voice not in the least lessened by all of the recent deaths.

Milton was worried that Brint's' desire for revenge would eventually wholly consume him, until he couldn't think clearly or rationally. *Just look at the last time that happened – he led those three right to my door. The next time I may not be so lucky.*

"I understand your desire for total annihilation, but I doubt you could get close enough to hurt any of them right now, let alone kill them. If you can think of a way to do what you want without getting yourself – or more importantly, me – killed, I'm listening. Otherwise, we need to think of another strategy."

ALANNA communicated directly to Milton's "mind", seemingly hesitant to speak in front of Brint, "What about the sweet-ass idea you had before we were attacked? It might potentially kill two – or perhaps, three – birds with one stone. One: you bring this Whisp 'back-to-life', hopefully curbing Brint's excessive hatred and burning need to kill something. Two: from what Brint has said, Whisp was an 'Inventor', with the ability to increase her intelligence exponentially – which could help with developing a sound defensive

386

strategy that won't fucking kill us all. Three: you might learn more about this 'magic' stuff from the experiment – and from Whisp herself."

She had a point – the more help they had the better. He was worried at first that she would freak out and want to leave immediately; however, he figured that once she knew that it probably was a bad idea to go back to where there were bad people looking for her, she would decide to stay. All of this, of course, depended on what Brint had to say. He wanted to respect his wishes and didn't want to do anything to hurt him, even if doing so would help Milton.

Brint didn't have anything to contribute other than a barely audible mumbled tirade against evil businessmen, too-powerful and corrupt companies, and wanting to bathe in pools of their blood. Milton figured it was time to broach the subject.

"Brint, I need to ask you something. If there was a remote chance that you could have your friend back, would you want that to happen? I can't guarantee that she would remember everything about her life, she may not even remember you. Would you still want her back if that was the case?"

Brint had stopped mumbling when Milton mentioned getting his friend back. When he finished asking the last question, the now-attentive Proctan didn't even hesitate before saying, "Absolutely. I would give my life for her, so if that is what it takes I'm prepared to do just that. Even if she doesn't remember me, she deserves to live – and I don't. It was because of me that she died in the first place, so whatever I can do to bring her back – up to and including paying with my life – I will do."

Well...there's that. I guess that's all the permission I need. Milton wasted no time after getting the go ahead, sending two of his drones to respectively carry Whisp's' body back from the Bio Lab to his Core Room. Once she was there, they laid her on one of the ledges, to keep her body dry out of respect.

"I suggest you look away. You really, really, really don't want to see this next part."

Since her body was a little too big to fit easily fit into his Molecular Converter, he needed his drones to reduce her size – i.e. chop her up. Brint refused to look away, stating that he had to watch so that he would be the first person she saw when she woke up. Milton tried to explain that it wasn't exactly going to work that way, but the stubborn Proctan refused to budge on his stance. Mentally shrugging, he started his drones on their grisly work.

"STOP!!! WHAT ARE YOU DOING? YOU TRICKED ME – I THOUGHT YOU SAID YOU WERE GOING TO BRING HER BACK!" Brint ran over to his shell and started banging on it, demanding that he stop what his drones were doing. Milton could feel him trying to order the drones to stop with his ability, but they were being directly controlled by the much stronger Station Core, so it was like an infant trying to wrestle with a gorilla – highly ineffective.

When the body was cut into three chunks, his drones took the pieces to the front of his shell and placed them in his Molecular Converter one at a time. Brint didn't stop hitting him, but fortunately he didn't have a lot of innate strength and was banging on one the strongest parts of his outer shell, so there was no damage whatsoever. The deed done, the now-crying Proctan collapsed in the water next to Milton, his head in his hands and his shoulders shaking with silent sobs.

"I told you to look away – that's never pleasant to watch. Ok, now I'm going to start—"

New Discovery!

After analyzing the DNA of one of the citizens of this planet, you have discovered that your Reactor Core leakage has caused a mutation in their genes. These mutations vary, leading them to have a multitude of different inherent abilities previously unheard of before you crash-landed here. Place additional samples inside your Molecular Converter to unlock different types of gene-mutated abilities.

New option for your Biological Recombinator: Gene Mutation

Whoa! Does that mean what I think it means? Milton concentrated on his Recombinator and looked under the Gene Mutation option.[37] He was right! Now he had access to a gene mutation for special abilities! However, there was only one choice on the list – Intelligence Boost +1. It was an ability that, when activated, boosted the Combat Units' Intelligence rating by +10 for five minutes and used 20 "power". He assumed that "power" was the equivalent to mana or MP in this instance.

"ALANNA – take a look at this!" He communicated directly with her, and when he shared the information she immediately caught on to the possibilities unlocked with the discovery. "But, I didn't think my Combat Units had any stats – what good would an Intelligence Boost do?"

Shaking her head with a long-suffering sigh, ALANNA said, "What makes you think they don't have any stats? Did you even try to look at them?"

"Of course, I—," he started, then stopped when he realized he had never done any such thing. He began to concentrate on one of his still-living BBQs but was interrupted by the now-vocalized sobbing and sporadic wailing of Brint. Ashamed at letting himself get

---

[37]

Gene Mutation		
Type	**Effect**	**Power Usage**
Intelligence Boost +1	Intelligence +10 for 300 seconds	20
Provides a boost to a Combat Units' Intelligence stat for a limited amount of time.		

distracted by the new discovery, he immediately pushed everything other than helping his friend to the back of his mind.

"Sorry, Brint – let's get this going now. In about an...hour or so, we should hopefully see some results."

The sobbing Proctan was still ignoring him – which Milton couldn't blame him for. He concentrated on his Combat Unit list and found what he was looking for – Proctan, Female. Instead of just selecting it for creation, he concentrated on the option and the exact DNA that was converted just a couple of minutes ago, attempting to merge the two things together.

Warning!

Making an exact DNA match without a Neurological Control Unit may have unforeseen consequences. Results may be unpredictable.

Confirm selection? Y/N

He selected Yes and only realized afterward that he should have tested this on something small first – but it was too late, the process had already begun. Just like most things, all he had to do now was wait and hope that everything turned out well.

Because if they didn't, he was pretty sure Brint would never forgive him.

Epilogue – Rebirth

Warmth. Safety. Contentment. She couldn't open her eyes, but that didn't really bother her because she felt safe and secure in this warm cocoon of squishiness. Not knowing where she found herself wasn't a concern either since she had no **need** to know. All she wanted was to spend forever in this place – without cares, worries, or pain.

She remembered pain, but she didn't know why she remembered it. And then suddenly she did – images started to flood her consciousness, memories of her childhood, memories of the first time utilizing her special ability, memories of creating inventions, memories of her good friend Brint, and finally, hazy memories of three men bursting through the door to her home. *NO! I don't want any of this! Take them away – I just want to stay here forever, ignorant of everything I was! Especially what that fucker did to me!*

Of course, her wishes had no say in the matter. Before she was ready, a cold feeling seeped into her bones, an icy frigidness that started with her feet and gradually sent waves of frozen unpleasantness up her entire body. The instant it reached her head, she felt a tug on her feet followed by a brief moment of weightlessness. Landing on something hard yet soft on her side, the impact forced her to open her mouth and breathe for what felt like the first time. Unfortunately, she was under some type of liquid at the time and inhaled a lung-full of it.

She put her hands out in front of her in a panic and felt something hard under her left hand. She pushed away from it, hoping to get out of the liquid before she suffocated. As she broke through to the surface, the cold air of the...wherever she was...immediately caused goosebumps to form on her exposed skin. Coughing up the inhaled liquid, she stayed in a sitting position for a while before she was confident she had gotten rid of most – if not all – of it. She opened her eyes for the first time with some effort, a gummy substance causing them to want to stay closed.

Looking around, she noticed that there was a large funnel-like sheet of metal above her, water dripping down a now-closed hole on the bottom giving evidence of where she just came from. Closer around her, she found she was sitting in a rapidly-receding pool of water and she could see the water being sucked up by a series of surrounding tubes. Suddenly, a feeling of warmth began to infuse her body; the heat started with her head and moved down to her feet in a glorious defeat of icy chillness. When she was fully thawed and almost to the point where the heat was becoming uncomfortable, the radiant warmth shut-off.

Standing up on shaky legs, she moved to the edge of the pool and climbed over the edge, observing all that she could of the rest of the room. Stone walls – with joins so fine that she couldn't even see them – surrounded a large rectangular room with high ceilings. She looked behind her at where she emerged and caught her breath – *that thing is huge! I wonder what it does?* A large metal cylinder sat on sturdy legs, with a metal walkway circling around the circumference leading to the top. She was intrigued and wanted to investigate, but the cold that started to steadily creep back into her bones and joints made finding clothing her top priority.

The faint sound of voices from outside a nearby door made her jump back into the pool and crouch beneath the edge. From what she could tell from the tones, it sounded like a man and a woman speaking together and getting closer to her location. She couldn't understand any words yet, but it sounded like the woman was trying to calm down the irate man with a patient yet firm tone. It was only when they sounded like they were right outside the door that she recognized the voice. She stood up, hoping that she was correct.

"ALANNA, I don't know where you are taking me, but if this is some sort of joke then it's a cruel one. I saw what happened – as much as I regret watching, I know there is no coming back from what The Milton did to her body. Now, stop this farce and let's get back to—" he stopped, jaw on the floor and eyes open so wide she thought they were going to pop out. Standing next to him was a very tiny, strange-looking woman about a foot-and-a-half tall wearing a skin-tight purple outfit of some type. On her heels was a small purple animal with six legs and a pink tongue hanging out of its mouth.

"Brint! Where the fuck am I, who the fuck is that, and why the fuck am I naked?"

Whisp couldn't help but see that the woman standing next to him looked amused when she said, "Aww, shit – I think I'm going to like her!"

End of Book 1

Final Stats

Core Status			
Name:	Milton Frederick	Type:	Station Core Prototype 3-B
Combat Level:	12	Experience:	125260/133500
Reactor Type:	Zero-point Energy	Reactor Output:	17%
Current Statistics/Attributes			
Reactor Power/Strength:	17	Processing Power/Intelligence:	40
Structural Integrity/Constitution:	16	Ingenuity/Wisdom:	42
Processing Speed/Agility:	37	Communication/Charisma:	50
Insight/Luck:	35	Sensor Interpretation/Perception	26

Skill List			
Name	Level	Name	Level
Sensor Control	2	Rudimentary Defensive Trap Design	3
Kamikaze	3	Basic Mechanical Engineering	3
Sensor Enhancement	1	Basic Technological Engineering	1
Drone Manipulation	3	Basic Construction	2
Formation Fighting	3	Primitive Defensive Weaponry	1
Cooperation	4	Tactical Mapping	1
Overdrive	1	Survivor	3
Combat Communication	3		

Available Resources	
Resource Type	# of Units
Basic Earth	205045
Basic Gravel	14038
Basic Metal	96734
Pure Water	50271
Organic Material	60452
Biological Mass	23050

Combat Unit Status	Processing Power: 40	Total Controllable Bio Units: 16000
Name	# of Units	Bio Units Used
Blood-thirsty Squirrel (Scout)	126	630
Lollipop Snake (Stealth Fighter)	12	120
Jackalope (Speed Striker)	7	30
Scaly Pygmy Wolves (Group Attacker)	12	720
Greywiener (Speed Striker)	1	100
Fluffy (Speed Striker)	1	110
Clawed Badger (Melee Fighter)	2	600
Big Bad Quizard	1	3000
		Total Bio Units Used: 5310

Author's Note

Thanks for reading The Station Core!

I implore you to consider leaving a review – I love 4 and 5-star ones!
Reviews make it more likely that others will pick up a good book and read it!

If you enjoy dungeon core, dungeon corps, dungeon master, dungeon
lord, dungeonlit or any other type of dungeon-themed stories and content, check
out the Dungeon Corps Facebook group where you can find all sorts of dungeon
content.

If you would like to learn more about the GameLit genre, please join the
GameLit Society facebook group.

LitRPG is a growing subgenre of GameLit – if you are fond of LitRPG,
Fantasy, Space Opera, and the Cyberpunk styles of books, please join the LitRPG
Books Facebook group.

For another great Facebook group, visit LitRPG Rebels as well.

To learn more about LitRPG, talk to authors including myself, and just
have an awesome time, please join the LitRPG Group.

If you would like to contact me with any questions, comments, or
suggestions for future books you would like to see, you can reach me at
jonathanbrooksauthor@gmail.com

Visit my Patreon page at
https://www.patreon.com/jonathanbrooksauthor and become a patron for as little
as $2 a month! As a patron, you have access to my current works of progress,
which I update with (unedited) chapters every Friday. So, if you can't wait to find
out what happens next in one of my series, this is the place for you!

I will try to keep my blog updated on any new developments which you
can find on my Author Page on Amazon.

To sign up for my mailing list, please visit: http://eepurl.com/dl0bK5

Books by Jonathan Brooks

Glendaria Awakens Trilogy

Dungeon Player

Dungeon Crisis

Dungeon Guild

Glendaria Awakens Trilogy Compilation w/bonus material

Uniworld Online Trilogy

The Song Maiden

The Song Mistress

The Song Matron

Station Cores Series

The Station Core

The Quizard Mountains

The Guardian Guild

The Kingdom Rises

Spirit Cores Series

Core of Fear

Dungeon World Series

Dungeon World

Dungeon World 2 (Coming soon)

Made in the USA
Las Vegas, NV
01 July 2022